Also by Andrew M. Greeley
From Tom Doherty Associates

THE BISHOP
AND THE MISSING
L TRAIN

A BLACKIE RYAN STORY

ANDREW M. GREELEY

A TOM DOHERTY ASSOCIATES BOOK
NEW YORK

This is a work of fiction. All the characters and events portrayed in this book are either products of the author's imagination or are used fictitiously.

THE BISHOP AND THE MISSING L TRAIN

Copyright © 2000 by Andrew M. Greeley Enterprises, Ltd.

A Forge Book
Published by Tom Doherty Associates, LLC
175 Fifth Avenue
New York, NY 10010

www.tor.com

Forge® is a registered trademark of Tom Doherty Associates, LLC.

ISBN: 0-812-57596-2
Library of Congress Card Catalog Number: 00-026413

First edition: July 2000
First mass market edition: July 2001

Printed in the United States of America

0 9 8 7 6 5 4 3 2 1

For Roisin, Kyle, Colum, Conor . . .

Several years ago, some folks in the Big Apple actually stole a subway train and hid it for a month. Things like that happen in New York City. In Chicago, for reasons I will not divulge lest it present a challenge to evildoers, one could not steal or hide an L train. Hence the mechanics of the theft of a train on the Brown Line described in this story are fantasy and not science fiction.

Since, as the inimitable Cindy Hurley observes, Rudy Giuliani is not mayor of Chicago, and neither is Ken Starr, it is most unlikely that Chicago police in the real world would behave like some of them do in this story.

Bishop Ryan has asked me to assure the readers that all the characters in the story are also fantastical.

Notre Dame's women's soccer team has had a very distinguished history. They are always very good and very exciting. However, the account of their season in this story and especially the battle royal with Stanford is fictional. Also imaginary are the parishes of Forty Holy Martyrs and St. Regis.

Blackie

1

"One of our L trains is missing!"

Sean Cronin, Cardinal priest of the Holy Roman Church and, by the grace of God and abused patience of the Apostolic See, Archbishop of Chicago, swept into my study with his usual vigor. Since he was not wearing his crimson robes but a gleaming white and flawlessly ironed collarless shirt with diamond-studded cufflinks, it would not be appropriate to describe him as a crimson supersonic jet. Perhaps a new and shiny diesel locomotive.

"Tragic," I said, pretending not to look up from the Dell 300mx computer on which I was constructing the master schedule for the next month in the Cathedral parish.

"And Bishop Quill was on the L train!!"

He threw himself into a chair that I had just cleared so as to pile more computer output on it.

"Indeed!" I said, looking up with considerable interest. "With any good fortune we will find neither the L train nor Bishop Quill."

Out of respect for his status among the missing, I did not refer to our lost bishop by his time-honored nickname, imposed by his unimaginative seminary classmates—Idiot.

"You South Side Irish are innocent of charity," he replied. "You have any tea around?"

Normally he would have appeared at night in my study and commandeered a large portion of my precious Jamesons Twelve Year Special Reserve or Bushmill's Green Label before he assigned me another cleanup task. Auxiliary bishops play a role in the Catholic Church not unlike that of the admirable Harvey Keitel in *Pulp Fiction*: they sweep up messes. However, it was morning, a sunny early autumn morning to be precise. Banned from coffee by his foster sister Nora Cronin, he was reduced to pleading for tea to fill his oral needs.

Before I could wave at my ever present teapot, he spotted it, stretched his tall, lean frame to the table on which it rested (surrounded by the galleys of my most recent book, *There Is No Millennium*), and poured himself a large mug of Irish Breakfast tea.

"Great!" he exclaimed with a sigh of pleasure. The pleasures of being a cardinal these days are, alas, few and simple.

I waited to hear the story of the disappearance of the L train and its distinguished passenger. He continued to sip his tea, a tall, handsome man just turned seventy, with carefully groomed white hair, the face of an Irish poet, the political skills of a veteran ward committeeman, and the hooded, glowing eyes of a revolutionary gunman.

"So what was Idiot doing on an L train?" I asked, realizing that I was missing one of the lines in our routinized scenario.

"Your brother auxiliary bishop," he said with radiant

irony as he played with the massive ruby ring on his right hand, "was mingling with the poor on the way home from his weekly day of ministry in the barrio. Preparation doubtless for the day when he succeeds me." Milord Cronin laughed bitterly.

"He will never be able to learn Spanish that does not cause laughter among those who know the language."

"That, Blackwood, is irrelevant to the present story. . . . His limousine driver was to pick him up at the Kimball Avenue terminal of the Ravenswood Line and drive him back to his parish in Forest Hills."

"Brown Line," I said in the interest of accuracy.

"What?" he exploded, a nervous panther looking for something to spring upon.

"The Ravenswood Line is now known as the Brown Line."

"The Ravenswood Line is the Ravenswood Line, Blackwood," he insisted with the sense of shared infallibility that only a cardinal can muster and that rarely these days.

"Arguably."

"So the train never arrived." He extended his tea mug in my direction and, docile priest that I am, I refilled it. No milk. The valiant Nora had forbidden milk as part of her virtuous campaign to keep the Cardinal alive. "And Bishop Quill never arrived either."

"Remarkable."

"The chauffeur became concerned and called the CTA, which, as one might expect, assured him that the train had arrived at Kimball and Lawrence on time—that's a Korean neighborhood now, isn't it, Blackwood?"

"An everything neighborhood—Koreans, Palestinians, Pakistanis, some Japanese, and a few recalcitrant and elderly Orthodox Jews who will not leave the vast apartment buildings they built so long ago."

"Safe?"

"Much safer than many others I could mention, some of them not distant from this very room."

"Who would want to abduct Gus Quill?"

"I could provide a list of hundreds of names, with yours and mine on the top."

"Precisely. . . . Anyway, the chauffeur then called the Chicago Police Department and apparently reached your good friend John Culhane, who called me about midnight. They have determined the L in fact never arrived at the terminal. Rather it has disappeared into thin air and, Commander Culhane assured me an hour ago, so has the Most Reverend Augustus O'Sullivan Quill."

Deo gratias, I almost said. Instead I took a firm stand for right reason and common sense.

"L trains do not disappear," I insisted. "Neither, alas, do auxiliary bishops, though sometimes they are treated as if they do not exist. . . ."

Milord Cronin waved away my self-pity.

"The CTA is searching frantically for their missing train. The police are searching frantically for the missing bishop. He was the only one on the train at the last stop. The driver has disappeared too. The media have the story already. I hear there are cameras at the terminal and up in Forest Hills—"

My phone rang. The Loyola student who monitors our lines until the Megan show up after school asked whether the Cardinal was in my room.

"Who wants to talk to him?"

"Mary Jane McGurn from Channel Six."

"I will talk to her," I said, as though it were my rectory.

"Hi, Blackie. What's happened to my good friend Idiot Quill?"

"Mary Jane," I whispered to the Cardinal, my hand over the phone.

Although Ms. McGurn was Sean Cronin's favorite media person—he having a weakness for pretty and intelligent women (what healthy male does not?)—he shook his head. "I'm not available for comment, am I?"

"You're in prayer for the repose of his soul?"

Milord winced.

"What was that question again, Mary Jane?"

"Our mutual friend, Bishop Quill, has apparently disappeared. Do you or Cardinal Sean have any comment?"

"Only for the deepest of deep background, Mary Jane: like bad pennies, auxiliary bishops always return."

Milord Cardinal favored me with a wry smile.

"Is the Cardinal available?"

"I think not."

No one in the media had much regard for Augustus O'Sullivan Quill. Mary Jane held a special grudge since the day he told her on camera that she should be home taking care of her children.

"The crews are descending on the Cathedral rectory at this moment. I'll be there in five minutes. We're going to want a statement about the disappearance of Bishop Quill."

"You may quote the Cardinal as saying that we are confident that Bishop Quill will be found soon."

Milord Cronin tilted his head slightly in approval of my statement.

"Nothing more?"

"Nothing more."

"Off the record?"

"We are praying for him."

"Yeah," she snorted, "so am I!"

I gently restored the phone to its base.

"We cannot permit this, Blackwood!"

"Indeed."

"Auxiliary bishops do not slip into the fourth dimension, not in this archdiocese."

"Patently."

"Especially they do not disappear on L trains that also disappear, right?"

"Right!"

"You yourself have said that we will be the prime suspects, have you not? Don't we have powerful reasons for wanting to get rid of him?"

"Arguably," I sighed. "However, as you well know, in the best traditions of the Sacred College we would have dispatched Idiot with poison."

Actually neither the State's Attorney nor the media would dare suggest that the two of us could easily do without our junior auxiliary.

"This is not a laughing matter, Blackwood," he said sternly.

"Indeed."

"The Nuncio and the Vatican will be all over us. They do not like to lose bishops."

"Even auxiliaries?"

"We have to find Gus before the day is over." He put his tea mug on the rug and rose from the chair.

"Ah?"

He strode to the door of my study, a man on a mission.

"That means you have to find him."

I knew that was coming.

"Indeed."

He paused at the door for the final words.

"Find Gus. Today. See to it, Blackwood."

He disappeared, not in a cloud of dust, since we do

not tolerate that in the Cathedral rectory, but trailing an invisible cloud of satisfaction.

I sighed loudly, saved the file, and turned off the computer. Time for the sweeper to get to work.

Tommy

2

I'm a professional gambler. I earn a decent living from this behavior each morning of the week. Then I return to my apartment in the John Hancock Center, do my daily workout, swim in the pool, and eat a modest and healthy lunch. Next I turn to the second section of my day. I turn on my big-screen television and surf the sports channels in Chicago, of which there are five. On any given day one can find almost all the forms of athletic competition that human ingenuity has devised—from hurling, which is a slightly organized version of the Irish tradition of the faction fight, to grown men riding tiny cars fit only for children in mud flats. I do not care what the competition is, no real sports freak does. I choose sides as soon as I have selected the afternoon's entertainment and make imaginary bets, as we professional gamblers always do.

When the contests are over, I make myself an adequate and tasty supper and begin to read. What do I read? Anything and everything. History, biography, popular science, mystery, fantasy, literature, classics, best-sellers—whatever looks interesting. There's a Borders bookstore across the street from my apartment. Every week or two, I amble over there on an impulse-buying expedition and collect a dozen or so books. Just now I am reading *Finnegans Wake*. With a translation. I retire early because one needs to be well rested when one enters my casino in the morning. A casino otherwise known as the Eurodollar pit in the Chicago Mercantile Exchange, the place where the word "derivative" was born. I have been very successful there, more successful than I let anyone know, so that there is no reason to want to punish my success. I don't know why I'm a good gambler in such a complex, not to say convoluted, environment. I always got A's in math in school. My mind, however shallow, is agile. I am alleged to be a good judge of people and their motives. I am not greedy. Bears win, bulls win, pigs lose. I usually follow my instincts and they're usually correct. When they begin to be consistently wrong, then I'll find something else to do. Or retire early and watch TV in the mornings too.

I avoid the bar scene on Division Street only a few blocks away from where I live. The predatory beasts who prowl there, of whatever gender, frighten and repel me. My sisters say that I am a recluse. I concede that this is partially true. I do occasionally go out socially. Thus I had dinner last week with my good friend Peter Murphy and his mountain person (as she calls herself) bride Cindasue. I am impressed with their happiness. I reflected that it would indeed be pleasant to take someone like Cindasue to bed with me every night.

My sisters and my stepmother (completely in league with them when it comes to my case) contend that I am on my way to becoming a typical Irish bachelor.

Perhaps they are right. I do not reject the genetically driven obligation of our species to assume the role of spouse and parent. I realize that sometime that obligation will overcome my reluctance. I will meet someone at a wedding or at the opera or perhaps even at the Exchange who will quite overwhelm me. She will, of course, have preselected me. We will think we are in love and perhaps we will be. We will marry. What happens then will be problematic. Marriage is a far greater risk than anything we face in the Eurodollar pit.

My family says that I don't like women and I don't trust them. That is not true. I like my stepmother very much, which is almost against the rules. I also trust women—up to the point where their agenda and my agenda are incompatible. They tend to talk these days about negotiating the differences, which means that you lose. I recognize the validity of both agendas for which our species is programmed. I would in principle be ready to sacrifice most of my agenda for the pleasure of having a woman in bed with me routinely. But I digress. . . . That's not the reason why I don't trust women. There are other reasons which I do not intend to write down at this time. Maybe I read too much.

In any event, my present difficulties began one rainy autumn afternoon when after lunch I curled up with a pot of Irish Afternoon tea and began to surf the sports channels. One game promised a contest between Notre Dame and Southern California. I didn't think it could be a football game at midweek. While I had received a better education at Georgetown than I would have received in the shadow of the Golden Dome, I had no fundamental prejudices against their athletic teams (unlike Domers, who rejoice whenever we Hoyas lose).

It was a soccer match, indeed a woman's soccer match on a cold and wet field somewhere in the shadow of the Touchdown Jesus, who seemed to be the only one watching the game. Soccer is not one of my favorite sports. When they had the World Cup here a couple of years ago I did not attend a single match. (Why go to any athletic contest when you can watch it on a large-screen television in a cozy apartment with a pot of Irish Afternoon tea next to you?) Despite the worldwide enthusiasm for the sport, in my personal hierarchy it ranks only above hockey and yacht racing for being marginally better than watching grass grow.

I was about to surf elsewhere when I found myself fascinated by the intensity of the play. The woman warriors, in a cold rain and before an empty stadium, were playing with a dedication and abandon that I had rarely observed. There was none of the macho ego, the phony cool that marks so many male athletics. These young women held nothing back. They were so fiercely competitive that they would have put even Michael Jordan to shame. Young lionesses, I thought, remembering a TV program about the frolicking and hunting lionesses in the Serengeti who wrestled with one another and charged after prey while big old Simba watched with an occasional sleepy yawn.

Fascinating. Surely there was some evolutionary advantage for the species in producing mothers of this sort.

Two things were soon apparent. Notre Dame, already leading 2–0, was pounding a game USC into the mud. And the principal lioness was a young woman named Christy Logan. Wet from the rain, her blue-and-gold Irish uniform covered with mud, her blond hair in a ponytail, this Christy Logan person, chewing gum fiercely, was nonetheless one of the most beautiful women I had ever seen.

Head lioness. Perhaps the kind that would growl even at Simba.

I realized that she was very dangerous and that the

best thing I could do was to turn to some other program. It would be most unwise to fall in love with a lioness in a TV soccer match. However, I reasoned, it was most unlikely that I would ever meet her—pardon the expression—in the flesh.

The camera focused on her often, capturing the many moods of her mobile face—anger, amusement, sympathy, determination. Especially determination. She also laughed a lot, especially at her own mistakes. It developed that Christy had been a consensus All-American during her junior year and would surely be one again this year as well as a member of the United States Olympic soccer team.

Fearsome!

The announcer said that she was from Chicago, Illinois. A warning that the odds had gone down substantially on my never meeting her in the unquestionably lovely flesh. I knew I should turn off the program and warm up my tea.

However, I must confess that I was no longer interested in the match but only in Christy Logan as she urged on her pride of lionesses, raced down the field, booted another goal by the hapless and helpless Trojan goalie, and picked up from the mud the various unfortunate Lady Trojans (as they are called by the announcer in violation of the norms of political correctness) who had fallen in combat.

The announcer, incidentally, never called the home team the Lady Irish or even worse the Lady Fighting Irish. Heaven forfend!

I admit that I engaged in the male's age-old propensity to undress mentally an attractive woman—shapely if sinewy and muddy legs, narrow, narrow waist, neatly shaped rear end, and exquisite breasts that even the soccer sweatshirt could not hide. And a sharply etched face that seemed to demand careful and respectful caresses, the kind of bones that my stepmother would say would guarantee durable beauty. Queen Maeve leading her warriors into battle.

My fantasies ran out of control. I imagined her in the shower after the match was over.

Too much, I told myself and firmly turned off the television. After I had boiled the water, and put new tea into the pot, I returned to the TV with the firm intention of cruising immediately to another channel. When the screen came up, a picture of a fiercely grinning Christy Logan filled it. Maeve had won another battle. Despite the mud on her face, she was unbearably beautiful. The match was over. The Irish had won again, on their way, the announcer said, to a possible national championship. The picture faded to a commercial. I turned sadly to a wrestling match.

She was in the shower now, I realized. Then I forbade myself to revel in that image. It would nonetheless haunt me through the rest of the day and the night and into the beginning of the session at the Exchange. Even Christy Logan could not distract me from the demands of Eurodollars, which had the advantage over Christy that they did not exist in the real world.

Given the law of six degrees of separation, I told myself as I walked home from the Exchange, it ought not to be difficult to find someone whom I knew who knew her. One of my sisters went to Notre Dame. She might know her. Or I could drive down to the Dome and sit in the rain and watch her play.

I knew I would do neither of these things. I didn't need a female lioness no matter how gorgeous.

That Sunday at the family dinner out in Oak Park, which I usually attend, the women members left me alone, more or less. They spoke rather in fury about the asshole bishop, as they put it, who had come to Chicago. We had lots of reasons for not liking him. I felt rage stirring inside me. Not typical or appropriate behavior.

"I happened to catch your soccer team on the tube the other day," I said cautiously. I instantly regretted it because I did not want to learn anything more about Christy Logan.

"Aren't they totally cool?" Amy gushed. "We're number one!"

"So the announcer said."

"Did you notice my friend Christy Logan? She's All-American!"

"Is she the little kid with black hair?"

"No way! She's like the totally gorgeous blonde that's the team captain!"

"Blonde . . . ," I said thoughtfully. Six degrees of separation had just fallen to two.

"She's Dr. Logan's daughter, isn't she?" Beth asked, trying, as Irishwomen and Irish politicians do, to locate everyone's origins and genealogy.

"She's like a great kid, really! I mean, you know, she's very smart and very funny and very, very sweet."

"A lesbian, I suppose. . . ."

Total outrage all around the table.

Even Beth, my stepmother, who often takes my side, was shocked.

"Tommy, that's a terrible thing to say. Women athletes are no more likely to be lesbian than men athletes are to be gay. And there's nothing wrong with it if they are."

"She certainly isn't a lesbian!" Amy insisted hotly.

"I think Tommy is trying to make up his mind whether he wants an introduction, Amy."

All too accurate.

"He'd want her to be a lesbian," Amy insisted. "Then she wouldn't be any threat to him."

Again all too accurate.

To change the subject somewhat, I insisted that soccer was too rough a game for women to play. I didn't believe it for a moment. The lionesses could take care of themselves. However, my claim stirred up another firestorm of controversy.

"You're not serious, Tommy. Sometimes, however, it's hard to tell when you're serious and when you're not."

How had everyone in this crowd figured me out so well?

Returning to my apartment in the evening, I marveled at how my family had re-created itself. Beth had made common cause with my three sisters in the program of taking care of Dad. It had worked very well. My father had been disastrously unlucky in his first marriage and very fortunate in his second. Luck of the draw? He really had no way of knowing either time, especially the second, since he'd been so traumatized the first time around. Much safer in the Eurodollar pit. Nor had the damn Catholic Church been any help at all. In fact, it had made matters worse. How could it believe that he and Beth were living in sin, when she had so clearly healed him and remade him and had time to love the rest of us?

If God would guarantee me a wife like Beth, I'd marry that person tomorrow. No guarantees.

My fantasies of Christy Logan in the shower returned, to be replaced by fantasies of Beth in the shower. Are erotic images of your stepmother incestuous? I didn't think so, but they weren't a good idea. I picked up *Finnegans Wake,* with which I had been struggling all week. No twelve books this week.

Someday I would have to tell Beth what a wonderful job she had done. The sisters, as much as they loved her, probably had not thought to say thank you.

I put Jimmy Joyce aside for a moment and went to

my desk. I would write one draft and send it to her personally, not post it on the family e-mail site.

Dear Beth,

Thanks again for the family dinner this afternoon and for protecting me from the schemes of Amy and Lisa and Marie. I also want to thank you for something that I suspect none of us have thanked you for yet. You have healed my father and made him a whole man again. You have healed our family and made it a family again. Moreover you have worked these miracles with grace and style. I don't know quite how you managed these wonders against all odds. But we'll be forever grateful to you. Even though we don't quite know how to say it— and I have to retreat to mail to even try to say it—we'll always love you.

Tommy

I read the letter over once. Just the right note. She would show it to Dad and the sisters and there would be hugging and crying and Beth would say, "See, didn't I tell you that Tommy was a sweetheart!"

Then I went back to Jimmy Joyce.

Having done my good deed for the year, I concluded that Christy Logan was no longer even a remote option. If she were a friend of Amy's, she would be ex officio, a coconspirator. I did not want to find myself surrounded on all sides without an escape hatch. No more fantasies and no more women's soccer on television.

Beth called me two days later and, in the midst of much weeping, thanked me and praised me as the nicest young man. My three sisters then called, independently perhaps, to say much the same thing.

"You don't miss much, son," my father said, changing the message somewhat.

"That's why I'm a successful trader."

The week was tough. No time for fantasies. I lost a lot of money on the first three days, broke even on Thursday, and won everything back and a lot more on Friday. I loved every minute of it. We professional gamblers do.

There were no women's soccer games on the sports channels. I admit I looked for them.

My priest, the one who had wrestled me back into the Church, had often argued that I was a prisoner of my illusions, which were created by my troubles with my real mother, for whose problems I had assumed too much responsibility. He had urged me to work out these illusions with a therapist. I admitted that he was probably right and that I would seek out a shrink someday to work out my anger and my fear. But not quite yet. Someday, he had warned me, God would clobber me and force me into shedding my illusions. Fair enough, I had said. I didn't believe, however, that God gave enough of a damn about me to try anything special.

This illusion was about to be proven spectacularly false.

After picking through the poor Friday afternoon fare on the sports channels, I decided I would yield to my only serious indulgence. I rode down in the elevator, walked by the Water Tower plaza, crossed the Magnificent Mile, passed Borders, and entered that den of iniquity known as the Ghirardelli chocolate store and ordered a chocolate malted milk, a sinful concoction for which they are notorious.

I put *Finnegans Wake* and the translation on a table and sat down to wait for my order number to be called. I noticed a young woman with blond hair and a baseball cap sitting next to me. As is required, her hair was in a ponytail emerging from the back of the hat. Pretty,

I thought. Then I looked again. She was wearing a blue-and-gold Notre Dame jacket with SOCCER on the back (not WOMEN'S SOCCER, be it noted). My head began to whirl. This was either a dream or an epiphany of sorts. Cautiously and without seeming to stare, I searched for the embroidered name which ought to have been on the left breast of the jacket. Her shoulder blocked my view. I waited for her to shift, or to turn a page in the book. No luck. Then a number was called. She put a bookmark in place and carefully closed her book—which was by Annie Dillard—and rose up to collect her treat, which was the same as mine.

The embroidery read *Christy, Captain.*

I closed my eyes, hoping that the world would stop spinning. It didn't. I opened my eyes, just as she returned to the table. Even in jeans, sweatshirt, and running shoes, she was an impressive apparition, bigger than I had expected, but still perfect. The spinning accelerated.

I staggered over to the phone and made a call.

"Cathedral."

"Hi, Megan, it's Tommy."

"Hi, Tommy, how's your love life!"

They all knew who I was. I'd been there often enough while I was wrestling with the Holy Roman Church.

"Disastrous, Megan, until you agree to marry me!"

"You're too young, Tommy. Want to speak to the Bishop?"

"If he's in."

"For you he's always in, Tommy."

The little witch was ten years younger than me. Maybe she was right, however; maybe compared to her I was still a juvenile.

"Father Ryan."

"Tommy, Father."

"Ah."

"Do you think God picks on some people?"

"Like yourself?"

"Yes, like me."

"I'm sure She does. One may safely assume that She doesn't like your attitude."

"Well, last week I happened to catch a Notre Dame soccer game on ESPN. Their captain is a fierce but gorgeous young woman—"

"One Christy Logan, All-American."

"That's right. Well, I'm kind of impressed by her, if you know what I mean."

"I think I can guess."

"But I feel safe because I'll never meet her, right?"

"So God has arranged it that you have met her."

"I'm at Ghirardelli's and have ordered a malted milk."

"Highly virtuous behavior."

"And she's sitting at the table next to me!"

"Remarkable!"

"She's even more impressive than on television."

"Astonishing."

"Do you think God has done this to me?"

"Beyond a shadow of a doubt."

"So I have to talk to her?"

"Certainly God leaves us free even when He pulls one of these spectacular dirty tricks and then respects our right to decline. Both God and I, however, are betting that you will indeed talk to the exceptional Christy."

"Yeah," I said. "I don't want to upset God."

"Wise young man."

I picked up my order and sat down next to "Christy, Captain" and took a deep breath. She glanced at me and then returned to her cautious consumption of the malt and serious consumption of Ms. Dillard.

I'm not exactly Leonardo DiCaprio, but my siblings insist that most young women consider me "cute." That word has so many meanings in the womanly lexicon that I don't quite know how it applies to me. Nonetheless, I was discouraged by her brisk dismissal of my presence.

"Aren't you violating your training regimen, Ms. Logan?" I said brightly.

She glared at me, a kind of twisted frown that said, How did this worm crawl into Ghirardelli's?

"That's one of the worst come-ons I've ever heard," she snarled.

"I'm not trying to pick you up, Ms. Logan," I said, smiling as best I could. "I don't pick up young lionesses."

"That's a little better." The frown slipped away, but she was still not happy with me. "Original, anyway."

"I happened to see you and your colleagues bury the so-called Lady Trojans in the mud last week—"

"You were down there?" she asked in amazement.

"No, I watched on TV."

"Then there were three of you, counting my mother and father."

"I was impressed, as anyone would be, by your team, and I noted with satisfaction that you were not the Lady Irish but simply and definitively the Irish."

She smiled. Ghirardelli's, the Water Tower, Loyola, Borders, Ralph Lauren, the new Hyatt, and everything else around evaporated.

"The problem was"—her smile turned into an impish grin—"were we the Lady Fighting Irish or the Fighting Lady Irish? So we decided that we were simply the Irish and that was that. Fighting is unnecessary."

I gulped. I was no longer an insect.

"And for the hapless Lady Trojans, useless."

She smiled again.

"We're number one and we will be at the end of the season."

"And win at the Olympics."

"Absolutely.... How come you're reading two books at the same time?"

"I read one with the left eye and one with the right eye."

"Silly." She grabbed both my books. One doesn't resist a curious lioness. "*Finnegans Wake.* That's a great book! The title is a three-way pun you know. Does it mean that the Finnegans all wake up? Or does it mean that it is a wake for a man named Finnegan? Or is it a call for the Finnegan clan to wake up and go forth in battle. The lack of punctuation suggests the first, but he probably meant all three, you know?"

God had made me read that book and bring it over to Ghirardelli's, no doubt about it.

Before I could answer, she continued, "Do you know what the story means?"

"I'm trying to figure it out...."

"WELL, I think it's about old age and dying. Jim and Nora are getting older. He wonders what it would have been like if they had stayed in Ireland and bought a hotel. Their physical love is ignited again and he realizes that life is stronger than death. It's really about resurrection and Easter and the river of love that never stops running."

She paused expectantly, waiting for my reaction.

Where had this young lioness come from?

"I hope you're right. If you are, it is a very beautiful book."

"Well, I've been wrong, once or twice.... What do you do? Are you still in school?"

"I'm a professional gambler," I said.

"Options or Merc?"

"Merc."

"You survive?"

"So far."

"Just barely?"

"A little better than that."

"You must do pretty well if you can spend time watching Notre Dame soccer in the afternoon."

"I channel surf the sports channels when I come home from the Merc."

"Cool. . . . And in the evening?"

Objection, your honor.

"Read. I don't like the bar scene."

"Neither do I," she agreed. "You finished your malt already."

I had indeed.

"Fascinated by your lecture on *Finnegan*."

She laughed, a warm, amused, faintly self-deprecating laugh.

"I talk a lot—I'll get you another one. I need a refill too. Don't look so shocked. I'll run it off on Monday. We virgins need something sweet every once in a while."

In her absence I tried to regain my aplomb. She was quite overwhelming. Perhaps God had a sense of humor.

She returned with a malt in either hand, two nourishing breasts, I thought, and then warned myself that if I permitted myself to slip into fantasies, I would never survive the rest of our conversation.

"In fact," she said, placing our drinks on the table and sitting down, "when I hear about all the problems my friends have with sex, I think chocolate is much safer. You can always run it off."

"Right," I said.

"Now"—back to business again—"what's this about lionesses?"

I tried to line up my argument.

"I noticed how intense the players were on both teams, especially yours. Most male athletes try to be macho cool about everything. Men soccer stars seem to celebrate themselves. Running around the pitch when they score a goal. You guys were into the game completely. Everything about you was involved. You didn't care what the audience thought."

"Such as it was."

"Reminded me of M.J."

"Maybe that's also the difference between the way men and women love."

That stopped me cold.

"Anyway, what about the lionesses?"

"I thought of a TV program I had seen about—excuse the expression—lady lions. Whether they were nursing their cubs or playing with the cubs or pretending to fight with one another or chasing game, they were sleek and lovely and graceful and implacably involved. While big old Simba watches and chews bones and yawns."

She nodded. "I've been to the Serengeti."

And I've only watched it on television. "Poor metaphor, maybe."

Her quick smile again. I held on to the table.

"Nice metaphor. . . . So you think I'm like a lady lion?"

"Uh, up to a point. You're not about to club me with a massive paw."

"Don't count on it."

"I'll be careful," I said sincerely.

"Nothing in this conversation has caused you to think any differently?"

"You mean that you're not like a lioness? No."

"What's your name, anyway?"

"Tommy."

"That's very nice, Tommy. You are kind of weird but definitely nice."

"Thank you, Ms. Simba."

"Where do you live?" Still collecting the facts.

"Around the corner, in the John Hancock Center."

"Really, my parents' apartment is in Water Tower! We're neighbors!"

"You're the girl next door!"

She pondered that and grinned.

"No, you're the boy next door."

"Fair enough."

"I'm in for the weekend. Get away from the books and team and relax. . . . Are you going to invite me to dinner tomorrow night?"

This young lioness actually seemed to like me. Be careful, Tommy! She and God are in conspiracy.

"Can't," I said.

"Oh?"

"Nope, if I'd picked you up, I would have invited you to dinner, but since I didn't pick you up, I can't. If I'd known—"

She waved the phony problem away. "So I'll ask you. Tommy, can I take you to dinner tomorrow night?"

"You certainly can, Christy."

"We'll eat at my father's club in the Ritz-Carlton. Neighborhood dinner."

"Grand."

"You know where the entrance to the apartments is?"

"Sure."

"Six-thirty?"

"Fine."

We both slurped up the last drops of our second malts.

"I have to go home. My folks are having a party."

"I'll walk you home."

"That's not necessary. It's only half a block. . . . But this is a weird afternoon. So why not."

So, oblivious to the rest of the world, I escorted her to the stoplight and then held her arm as we crossed the street.

She glared at me and then smiled. I was getting used to the process: first the twisted scowl and then the radiant smile.

"You are the weirdest boy I've ever met, Tommy." She shook hands with me at the door to the lobby of the apartments, some of the most expensive floor space in Chicago. "But you are sweet. See you tomorrow night at six-thirty."

"I'll be here. . . . Does this club serve really nice food?"

"What does a man know about nice food?"

"I'm a cook."

"Far out!"

Blackie

3

Following Milord Cronin's injunction to see to the re-
discovery of the bishop and the L train, I boarded the
State Street subway at the Cathedral corner and rode
down to the Loop, where, after an exhausting climb
from the subway to the L, I found a Ravenswood Line
train waiting for me. I did not like the story of a missing
L train with a missing bishop on it. It hinted of monumental evil, something huge, twisted, and depraved.
No useful purpose would be served by pondering it
before I arrived at the Lawrence Avenue terminal,
which would doubtless be swarming with cops, busy
about much useless work. The solution did not lie at
Lawrence and Kimball.

I thought of Thomas Flynn and his newfound morning star. I would have liked to be able to claim credit
for the happy juxtaposition of the two of them in their
moment of great grace in Ghirardelli's, a shining sacramental temple for perhaps a half hour. Alas for my
ego, a higher power than I had pulled off that very slick

trick, for which She was to be congratulated. Tommy was still free to hide in his dark world of angry illusions. However, unless my judgment in such matters is completely wrong (which it never is), the radiance of that aforementioned morning star would soon drive out the darkness.

I sighed to myself. Tommy Flynn did not know how lucky he was. I then turned to enjoy the remarkable ride to Lawrence and Kimball. The Ravenswood L (a.k.a. The Brown Line) goes nowhere. Nonetheless it provides a fascinating jaunt through Chicago. Lawrence and Kimball is in the heart of the city, even if it wasn't ninety years ago when the line was built. (The original charter of the "Northwestern Elevated Railway" proposed a line to run to the Cook–Lake County line.) The ride to Lawrence and Kimball, however, is not merely a journey to nowhere, it is also a journey through places where no one goes.

Having loaded passengers at the Merchandise Mart, the train turns abruptly a couple of times, as if to throw off those who might be trying to follow it, and then slides along the thin borderland that separates the Gold Coast from the slums. To the right are the pastel high-rise luxury apartments near the lake, to the left the grim red brick buildings of the Cabrini Green projects. Only the Brown Line and greensward separate the two districts, whose history is steeped in mythology and sociology. Contrary to what one might expect from Chicago School sociology, the Gold Coast is encroaching on the slum. One wonders if in the future the Brown Line might be renamed the Gold Line.

Then the train eases its way across North Avenue, by St. Michael's Church, and into what was once a German and Swedish neighborhood and is now West Lincoln Park (also called by some DePaul, after the university that abuts the L track). In this thoroughly

rehabilitated old neighborhood, the L engages in some
of its unique tricks. It slips through bathroom windows,
sneaks down hallways, creeps out through second-floor
doorways, and roars off with a furious rumble that no
one seems to notice.

There are those who claim that the Ravenswood
does no such thing, save perhaps late at night. However, those who know the neighborhood disagree, as
do those who, new in the neighborhood, still hear the
noise when the train thunders by and shakes windows
and light fixtures before it slips in and then slips out
again. One should be careful in leaving one's bed for
the bathroom late at night because one never knows
when one will encounter an L train exploding down
the hallway. Or perhaps it is only a ghost train from
yesteryear; there is no record of anyone ever being run
over on a late-night trip to the bathroom. Moreover,
no one has ever found any trace of third rails on a
hallway floor the next morning. Ghost trains or not,
living next to the Ravenswood is like living on a per-
petually active earthquake fault.

At Fullerton, the Red Line emerges from the ground
as it rushes on its long trip from Ninety-fifth Street on
the south to Howard Street on the north. The Ravenswood does not particularly like such cosmopolitan company. Just north of Belmont it turns left and heads out
into the land of the ethnics—leaving the Red Line (and
the Purple Line, about which the less said the better
since it goes to Evanston, the Prohibition Suburb) to
go their appointed ways—which include Addison and
the disgrace of Wrigley Field. As it jogs west and then
north and then west again before its final turn north,
the Ravenswood becomes absolutely unique. When the
trees are in foliage, a rider who is not quite sure where
he is might suspect that he has been whisked away to
a strange and mysterious foreign land and is now riding

on the top of a vast rain forest. The trees, many of them a hundred years old, crowd in on both sides and arch over the narrow tracks. Occasionally, the rider catches a glimpse through the thick leaves of picturesque homes below in dark shade, which seem like almost magic dwellings on a protected enchanted island.

Sometimes there are clearings and one sees wooden two-flats, usually with siding of one sort or another, sometimes two on one lot, as was the custom in Chicago until 1940. (The first house was built on the front of the lot and then moved to the back to make room for the second house.) Usually, however, the back house has been torn down and replaced by a garage that was ample for the cars of the 1930s but is rarely large enough today. Occasionally a line of yuppie town houses appears and is swallowed up again in ethnic homes. Then gradually the brick two- and three-flats appear with their Tinkertoy back porches and stairways. The lawns in the backyards are carefully trimmed and lined with neat beds of flowers. Sometimes inflatable pools replace the lawns. Patio furniture, umbrellas, and grills line the yards. Now and then the furniture is on the porches, even on the small third-floor porches. Before one has time to marvel at the back porch, backyard lifestyle that has emerged at the edge of the alley, the forest closes in again. Then suddenly one crosses the North Branch of the Chicago River, lined by thick greenery on either side and looking like a jungle stream. A single motor launch rests at a small dock beneath the tracks. Mr. Kurtz, are you there?

Finally, as if exhausted, the train sinks to ground level, sneaks down side streets and back alleys, and then, after one last turn north, slows to a halt at Kimball and Lawrence, Albany Park, once a Jewish neighborhood and now Chicago's Little Korea.

The passengers—students, office workers, some commodity traders who boarded at LaSalle and Van Buren—slip off the train, some of them saying good-bye to the friendly Hispanic American who is the train's "operator." An observer wonders if they appreciate the wondrous ride through a Chicago where nobody goes.

Despite the fortunes of transit magnates whom Theodore Dreiser made immortal, public transit in Chicago has always been a financial swamp. The federal government has spent hundreds of billions of dollars in subsidy of the automobile and thus surrounded the cities with ugly suburbs. Public transit, however, which would have held the cities together, struggles along with poor service and little money, mostly because poor and nonwhite people ride it. The L train to nowhere should indeed have been extended to the county line. We would not then need the hopeless, concrete nightmares of expressways that have to be repaired every couple of years.

When I arrived at the Kimball terminal, scores of Chicago cops were milling around on the tracks, on the platform, and in the terminal itself, not doing much, trying unsuccessfully to stay out of each other's way, and making life difficult for harmless and ordinary riders of the Brown Line. Since I was my usual unobtrusive self, I walked through them and came upon Commander John Culhane.

"Blackie," he sighed, "I figured you'd show up."

"L trains," I said firmly, "do not disappear."

"It wasn't a train," John, a trim man with rimless glasses, salt-and-pepper hair, and intense blue eyes informed me. "Only a single car on the last run of the day."

"In Chicago, John, as you well know, an L train is an L train even if it's only a one-car train."

He grinned, and for a moment the tension lifted from his open Irish face, "That's a gotcha, Bishop! . . . Three passengers left the train at the previous stop. We've found them. They each tell us that there was only one person left in the train, a priest with purple around his Roman collar and purple socks. . . . Did he really wear purple socks?"

"I'm afraid so. Arguably purple underwear too."

"There was no one else on the train except the driver."

"Who is where?"

"Nowhere that we can find. His name is Hector Gomez, married to Maria Carmela Gomez and father of three, an utterly respectable Latino family man. He did not come home from work last night. He lives only a few blocks away, so he usually walks home after the last run. As you can imagine, Maria Carmela is frantic."

"And the L train?"

"CTA hasn't found it yet. They claim that they will before the day is over. Unlike New York, where someone hid a subway train for a month, there's only a few places to hide an L here."

"Ah?"

"A cut-up in the Skokie Swift route, an unused connection between the subway and the L on the Near South side, and a couple of other places."

"And the Bishop?"

"Last seen sleeping over his breviary at the previous stop, which is only three blocks away."

"Someone could have turned the train around and taken it elsewhere?"

"At that time of night, sure. You throw a switch and the car heads back towards the Loop or wherever anyone wants to take it."

"So someone, or more likely some group of ones, could stop the train at one of the crossing streets, seize the driver and the Bishop, change a switch somewhere in the area, and ride off in the moonlight."

"I know it's impossible, Blackie, but since it has been done, it can be done."

"*Ab esse ad posse valet illatio,* as we used to say in the mother tongue."

"Absolutely—whatever that means."

"Such an accomplishment would require considerable resources, imagination, and ingenuity," I observed.

"So we assume. Since those are a given, we must find a motive. Who would want to kidnap Bishop Quill?"

"And in such a spectacular fashion?"

Again I had the feeling that we were in combat with very great evil, almost diabolic. One could presumably hire thugs—very skilled thugs who were familiar with Rapid Transit trains—to carry out the kidnapping of the train and the bishop. There was notable risk in such a daring venture, but there were more than enough men in Chicago who were willing to take such risks, if the pay was adequate. Nor would they be likely to brag about their accomplishment. However, there had to be a mastermind who had the money to pay the thugs and indeed to conceive the whole plan.

"It's possible," John suggested, "that the target was not the Bishop, but the train. Some environmentalist crackpot who doesn't like the noise of L trains at night."

"Part of the Chicago air. Those who live near the tracks do not even hear them."

"Someone new in the neighborhood?"

"And with the money and the nerve to carry out this project?" I said with a sigh. "There may be one such. If there is, surely your agents will discover him soon."

"So it looks more like the Bishop was the target, doesn't it Blackie?"

"Arguably."

"What kind of a guy was he? Did anyone have reason to dislike him?"

Although I was a bishop and I was breaking the rules, I knew I had better tell the truth from the very beginning.

"As the adolescents would say, there are tons of people who dislike him, though I cannot see that any of them have sufficient motive for this, uh, venture."

For a fraction of a second, I thought I saw a picture of the explanation. As so often happens, it vanished before I could recognize it.

"He was a cruel man?"

"Cruel and self-deceptive, a bit of a borderline personality, I fear. His cruelty was perhaps not intentional, though it seems not unlikely that he enjoyed it. He had persuaded himself, in these matters, that he was following the will of God—as discovered in church during prayer—and/or the will of the Holy Father."

"For example?"

I told him the Megan story.

"Sounds like a real creep. Sean made him put the posters back up?"

"Rather, he dispatched him to Forest Hills, where he wore out his welcome on arrival by dismissing the parish staff, terminating the sports program, and wandering through the school warning of mortal sin."

"We still have that in the Church, do we?"

"On occasion."

"So they would hate him up there?"

"Oh, yes."

"We have a lot of work to do," he said grimly. "Who else?"

"You might put Milord Cronin and his elusive éminence grise at the head of the list. He has caused us no little embarrassment."

Culhane threw back his head and laughed loudly.

"Sure, you and Sean put together this plot to stop the embarrassment and didn't realize that it would

cause more embarrassment. You're clever enough to
think up something like this, Blackie, but you're far too
clever to try it. . . . Who else?"

"I learned that his brother Peter has been substantially embarrassed in his brokerage activities by the
Bishop, whose nickname, by the way, has been, since
time immemorial, Idiot."

"We'll have to talk to the brother anyway."

"Moreover he was in contact with a certain prominent religious movement for money to build his own
TV station, a matter about which he has spoken
openly. The good bishop always assumed that those
who listened to him without making a commitment
agreed with him. They found him embarrassing and
will find his disappearance even more embarrassing."

"A lot of embarrassments, huh, Blackie?"

"Indeed."

"Mike find out about all of them for you?"

He was referring to my cousin Michael Patrick Vin-
cent Casey (in our family called Mike the Cop, as if to
distinguish him from another Mike in the family,
though there is no other Mike). A former commissioner
of police and a world-famous expert on police procedure, Mike, in his spare time (when not painting), pre-
sides over an organization with the harmless name of
Reliable Security, in which many cops of all genders
and races moonlight. In addition, he is a charter member of the North Wabash Avenue Irregulars, a group
of folk who occasionally compensate for my limited in-
sights and mobility.

"Who else?"

"You put him on the Bishop?"

I sighed in loud protest at the injustice of it all.

"I asked him to, ah, keep his eyes and ears open and
me informed. I expected trouble from our friend Idiot
but not this kind of trouble."

"Anyone else?"

"Bishop Quill was a member of the Sacred Roman Rota, the Church's appellate court, before he was transferred to Chicago, very likely to get rid of him. He made it his practice to reverse all annulment judgments that came before him, a practice not likely to endear him to the people who were involved in the cases."

"You'll have to explain that to me."

Someone shouted, "Hey, boss, we've found the driver!"

"Alive?"

"Yeah, but drugged."

"Excuse me, Blackie, I'll be back."

I opened my cell phone and punched number 5, which I remembered to be the Cardinal's private number. In fact, it was the number of my sister Eileen Ryan Kane, the federal judge. I left a message on the answering machine.

I pondered the problem, remembered that the Cardinal Archbishop of Chicago used to enjoy Illinois 1 as his license plate, and pushed 1.

"Cronin."

"Blackie."

"What's going on?"

"The train is lost, the bishop is lost, the driver who was lost is now found, alas in a drugged condition. Apparently the train was hijacked just before it came to the terminal here at Kimball and Lawrence. The Bishop and the driver—"

"Motorman, you mean."

"No, they don't have those anymore since they decided they did not need conductors. The motorman is now called the driver because he is responsible for the whole train. He looks out the window to make sure that everyone is on before he closes the doors."

"Saves money at risk to the passengers."

"The sorry truth is that rapid transit, no matter how convenient, especially for working people, has always lost money. The government subsidizes automobiles by building roads, but it refuses to subsidize rapid transit. But what do I know. . . . In any event, the Bishop and the driver were the only ones on the train. Now the driver has been found."

"Gus is dead?"

I pondered that.

"Arguably, but I think not. If you were trying to punish Gus, would you not rather keep him alive so he could witness the ruination of his career?"

"I wouldn't think that way."

"Someone might, however, someone mad enough to come up with this scheme."

"We have problems, then, whether he is alive or dead?"

"Alas, it would seem so."

"Well, I hope he is alive. I don't like to see anyone dead."

A sentiment that did him credit.

"I will report back."

I strolled over to the counter at the entrance of the terminal and purchased two Hershey's Cookies 'n' Creme candy bars and one Diet Coke. The smiling young Korean American woman behind the counter told me she was a student at Northwestern Medical School and she attended Sunday Mass at the Cathedral. She alleged that she loved my stories and asked for my blessing, which I willingly gave.

A medical student who worked part-time at an L station refreshment counter. As I always said of these nonwhite immigrants who have swarmed into our city and our country, it is a shame that they lack the good, old-fashioned American work ethic.

John Culhane rejoined me.

"We've taken him over to Augustana Hospital. He's mostly unconscious. Won't be much use to us for a while. Probably won't remember anything."

"Where was he found?"

"In an alley a mile or so down the line, behind a trash can."

"So . . . if I were the CTA and if I were looking for a lost one-car L train, I would look on one of the side tracks at the Lake Street Yards out at Desplaines Avenue in River Forest, just across Harlem Avenue from Oak Park. Quiet, peaceful place. And the Brown Line goes around the Loop and fits nicely into the Green Line, as we now call the venerable Lake Street L. It would be a nice touch for the kind of mastermind with whom we're dealing."

John looked at me for a moment, his eyes narrow. Then he waved a sergeant over to us.

"Roy, have one of our guys sneak out to River Forest and see if the missing car is on one of the side tracks out there. You got the number of the car?"

"Yes, sir."

"If it is, call me and we'll tell the CTA where they can find their car."

Then he turned back to me.

"You think the Bishop will be in the car?"

"Perhaps. I hope so. But I think it is unlikely. Our mastermind would not make things so easy for us. . . . Incidentally, John, you did me an injustice a few minutes ago when you said I was capable of elaborating a master plot. Arguably that is true. But you implied it would be a plot like this gross and rather clumsy one. I would be far more devious and subtle. I would not permit my vanity to betray me."

"Point taken," he said. "This guy will give himself away because he's so pleased with himself."

In a way that prophecy would prove to be true, but not in the sense that John had intended.

4

The Gus Quill problem had blighted the end of summer a couple of months before. The Lord Cardinal had come into my room quietly, almost timidly. He didn't even raid my liquor cabinet.

"We have a new auxiliary bishop," he said as he sank into my easy chair, which I had vacated temporarily in search of a recent report on the finances of the Cathedral parish.

"We do not need one. We already have four."

"Five," he said mildly.

"Four," I argued, counting on my fingers. "Pete, Jaime, Tony, and Steve. That's enough."

"You didn't count yourself. You never count yourself."

That was true. I take it to be exceedingly improbable that I am a bishop.

"Who is this new sweeper?"

"Gus Quill," he whispered.

"Idiot Quill!" I shouted in dismay.

"That's a cruel nickname, Blackwood." He shook his head in disapproval.

"I didn't make it up," I said in self-defense. "He is an admirable man in many ways, hardworking, pious, sincere, kind according to his lights, which are pretty dim, and delusional."

"Delusional?"

"I went to the seminary with him, if you remember. He lives in a world of his own fantasy, favored by the mighty and the powerful."

"I suppose he even thought that he would become a

judge in the Sacred Roman Rota and then come home
as a bishop."

I sighed loudly. Milord Cronin had a point.

"You should not have agreed to take him," I protested.

"I told them that I didn't need him and didn't want
him. They said I had to take him because no one else
wanted him. I continued to say I didn't want him. They
continued to say that of course I would take him."

Cardinal Sean Cronin's greatest weakness is a soft
heart. In most men, that is to say, those that don't have
to deal with the Vatican dicasteries, that would be an
unalloyed virtue.

"Why are they so eager to get him out of Rome?"

Milord Cronin leaned back in his chair as I freed the
chair in front of my computer from a stack of floppy
disks.

"They wouldn't say. Or, rather, they talked as if I
understood why. The Romans work that way."

"Presumably the Signatura overturned too many of
his Rota decisions."

"I wouldn't be surprised. He must finally have become an embarrassment."

Most marriage annulments are granted locally, with
an appeal to a review court in a nearby diocese routinely made and routinely granted. Then if one party
wants to appeal to Rome the case goes to the Sacred
Roman Rota. This happens rarely because normally
both parties are happy to be free to marry again,
though sometimes one party is furious at the Church
for granting the other that freedom. Occasionally,
someone appeals to Rome because they are angry both
at their former spouse and at the Church. Some of the
judges on the Rota love to take apart the local decision
and reverse the annulment. Then the party that has had
the annulment revoked can appeal yet again to the Ap-

ostolic Signatura, the Church's sort-of Supreme Court where yet another reversal is possible. Idiot Quill had an unblemished record of voting to reverse every annulment that came before him. The judges in the Signatura, no fans of the American annulment machine, had often reversed Quill's reversal. I make no case for the annulment machine, which is an attempt to deal with a pastoral problem that has turned into a juggernaut. If the Pope would permit divorced and remarried Catholics to receive the sacraments, the demand for annulments would virtually disappear. In the absence of such change, fervently pushed by German bishops, many priests simply give that permission on their own.

I sighed loudly. "So now he'll be an embarrassment to us."

"More than you can imagine. He's telling people that the Pope himself is sending him here as my successor to clean up the mess in Chicago!"

"What!" I rose from the chair in righteous anger not at all like me.

"Cool it, Blackwood," Milord Cronin said. "He's not a coadjutor with right to succession, much less an apostolic administrator. I don't doubt that some of the Vatican bureaucrats hinted at that just to get rid of him. I checked to make sure. My contacts over there thought it was hilariously funny. They assured me that Saddam Hussein had an equal chance to replace me."

I sat down, still, to my shame be it said, furious.

"What makes him think that he's destined to replace you?"

Sean Cronin, thanks to the stern injunctions of the Lady Nora, was in better health than he had been for years. Moreover, he was the picture of physical fitness and could easily pass for fifty-five instead of seventy. The odds were excellent that he would survive till his seventy-fifth birthday and then some. The Vatican doesn't send in successors that long before a change.

"The Pope ordained him a bishop and was very nice to him."

"The Pope ordained fifty bishops a couple of weeks ago and was very nice to all of them. That's the way he does it."

Sean Cronin raised a hand, "Cool it, Blackwood. You yourself said that Gus lives in a fantastical world. Somehow a lot of his delusions have come true because he believes them so fervently. This is just one more. . . . He came home a couple of days ago and told some of his friends and relatives up on the North Shore that he would be more or less in charge. His appointment will be announced tomorrow at seven. He's called a press conference at the Chancery at ten-thirty."

"Without asking you?" I rose again in fury.

"I said COOL IT! We can't let this man upset us or we'll blow it. I'll be there with all the other auxiliaries and take over the press conference. You'll take the calls from the media between now and then."

I cooled it, indeed instantly.

"On the record, I will take the stand that he is nothing more than the junior auxiliary bishop among five—"

"Damn it, Blackwood, six!"

I paused to consider that.

"Someone else is coming?"

"No, I'm merely hoping that for once you'll remember that you're a bishop. Maybe even dress like one for a change."

I sat down again. Idiot Quill could do a great deal of harm by undercutting the Cardinal's leadership and perhaps creating factions among the clergy. I ignored his unfair comment about my clerical dress. I often wore my bishop suit and would have worn it more if I could have found my pectoral cross and episcopal ring.

"Off the record, I will point out that Bishop Augustus Quill had the second-lowest grades in our class, has often been the victim of delusions, and was in fact bounced from Rome because he had been an embarrassment."

Cardinal Cronin leaned his chin on tented fingers. "That's pretty strong stuff, Blackwood."

"I won't say it that way."

My private phone rang. Doubtless Mary Jane McGurn.

"Father Ryan."

"Mary Jane."

I flipped on the switch for the speaker phone.

"Ah!"

"Blackie, what the hell is going on over there! There's a rumor that someone named Idiot Quill has been sent to Chicago to replace Sean. It's supposed to be announced by the Nuncio tomorrow morning at seven. Is it true?"

The Cardinal winced.

"You can say, Mary Jane, that a spokesman for Cardinal Sean Cronin denied these rumors categorically. Bishop Quill will merely be the junior auxiliary bishop. He will have no more powers than any of the others. The Cardinal, of course, welcomes his appointment. He feels that he needs all the help he can get."

The Cardinal, pleased at my skills in mediaspeak, beamed happily.

"Are you sure, Blackie?"

"Absolutely."

"The guy apparently thinks he's going to clean up the mess in Chicago."

"The Cardinal's spokesman said that there is no mess in Chicago."

"This guy is not, what do you call it, some kind of coadjutor?"

"Certainly not."

"Even you outrank him?"

Sean Cronin grinned fiendishly.

"Though not for attribution, you say that even Bishop John Blackwood Ryan will have more seniority."

"O.K. . . . Now, why do they call him Idiot?"

The Cardinal grimaced. It would not help matters for the people to know that a new bishop had such a nickname.

"On the deepest of background, his seminary classmates called him that because they thought the name fit."

"Wow! You guys are going to have fun with him! . . . You think he's crazy?"

I hesitated. We would be asked that often, almost always off the record.

"Bishop Augustus Quill is a dedicated, devout, sincere, and industrious man. The Holy Father must think that his many long years of work for the Sacred Rota have earned him the right to be a bishop. Now I go into background. He is perfectly sane but sometimes he misreads reality."

The Cardinal nodded approvingly.

"Delusional?"

"Your word."

"They got rid of him in Rome and dumped him on you and Cardinal Sean?"

"Arguably that is the case. That comment also is deep background."

"O.K. Great. I have my story for the ten o'clock news." She hung up.

Milord shook his head in mock dismay. "I'm glad you're on my side, Blackwood."

"Oh, yes."

"Where did she get the nickname?" he asked with a frown.

"Doubtless from a fellow priest, not encumbered by loyalty."

I fielded several more calls before the ten o'clock newscasts.

I also placed one—to my illustrious sibling Dr. Mary Kathleen Ryan Murphy.

"Watch Channel Six if you can. Both of you. Then call me. O.K.?"

"O.K."

Mary Jane began with Augustus O'Sullivan Quill in front of a very expensive house in Forest Hills.

M.J.: Bishop Quill, what will your role be in the Archdiocese of Chicago?

(The Bishop is a large man, not so much fat as fleshy. His round face frequently lapses into a genial smile that does not always fit the words he is speaking. His forehead is high and is often creased with lines of surprise. He is wearing French cuffs— part of the uniform—a black clerical vest, an elaborate jeweled pectoral cross, and a sapphire ring that makes Sean Cronin's ruby seem small. He laughs intermittently, especially before he answers a question. It is a superior giggle that a pastor might use when asked a silly question by a second-grader.)

A.Q.: I really can't answer that quite yet. I must wait for Our Holy Father to announce it tomorrow morning at seven.

M.J.: It is safe to say, however, that you will be working in Chicago and with Cardinal Cronin?

A.Q.: I will not deny that.

M.J.: When the Cardinal retires in five years, will you replace him?

A.Q.: Oh my, that's a premature question. I am completely at the disposal of the Holy Father. I will do whatever he asks of me. For the moment I am merely eager to integrate my work with that of Cardinal Cronin.

M.J.: You've been away from Chicago for many years, Bishop. What qualifies you to become involved in the governance of the Archdiocese?

A.Q.: Prayer most of all. I spend an hour every morning on my knees in front of the Blessed Sacrament in fervent prayer. I like to think that during that hour I learn from God what he wants me to do that day. I also rely very much on my loyalty to the Most Holy Father, who is the vicar of Christ here on earth. With God and the Most Holy Father on my side, I don't see how I can fail. The Pope has been very good to me. When he ordained me a bishop in Rome—personally and with his own hands—he told me that I would do great things for the Church back in America. I am content to leave the future to God and to the Most Holy Father.

M.J. *(Eager to cut off this flow of piety)*: Isn't it true that you reversed every annulment case on which you were a judge in Rome?

A.Q.: The collapse of the family is the greatest single threat to American society. The family is the basic unit of society. Too-easy divorce and the promiscuous use of contraceptives are destroying the country. The Church must resist these tendencies with all its power and challenge the faithful to do the same.

M.J.: You disapprove of annulments?

A.Q.: Except in rare cases.

M.J.: You will work with the matrimonial court in the Archdiocese?

A.Q.: I assume so. All my experience and qualifications are in that field.

M.J.: And you will clean up the mess there?

A.Q.: I will do whatever I can.

M.J.: Is it not true that if indeed you are appointed

auxiliary bishop tomorrow you will be the most junior of them?

A.Q.: Ah, I don't believe that term has any canonical validity.

M.J.: Why is your nickname Idiot?

A.Q. *(Blandly)*: I don't believe I've ever heard that name.

M.J. *(To camera)*: This was the first interview with Bishop Augustus O'Sullivan Quill, rumored to be a replacement for Chicago's Sean Cardinal Cronin. If this is true, Chicago's two and a half million Catholics are in for some major changes. A spokesman for Cardinal Sean Cronin denied these rumors categorically. Channel Six was told that the Cardinal, of course, welcomes Bishop Quill's appointment. He feels that he needs all the help he can get. Nevertheless, Bishop Quill will merely be the junior auxiliary bishop. He will have no more powers than any of the others. Bishop Quill has called a press conference at the Chancery office tomorrow at ten-thirty. This is Mary Jane McGurn in Forest Hills.

ANCHOR: Mary Jane, does it look like Cardinal Cronin will lose some of his powers in the Archdiocese?

M.J.: He won't give them up without a fight.

Milord Cronin beamed happily at Mary Jane's last comment. His smile was quickly replaced by the worried frown that had taken possession of his face throughout the interview. I noted that someone else in the Archdiocese had also briefed her.

"He touched all the bases, Blackwood. Humility, prayer, Holy Father, experience in Rome, protecting family life—"

"*Most* Holy Father a couple of times."

"The faithful will rally to those themes."

"What faithful! He's thirty years too late with that approach."

"You think so? Well, maybe ..."

"Those who will rally to him are those that don't like you anyway."

"Judging by my mail that will be a lot of them."

"How many times have I argued," I said with some asperity, "that crank mail is not representative?"

"I know. . . . Still, he'll be trouble."

"Oh, yes," I agreed.

The phone rang.

"Bishop Ryan."

It was my aforementioned sibling. "Hi, Punk. Hey, you and Sean have yourselves one big, fat, oily problem on your hands. . . . Is Sean there? Turn on the speaker phone! Hi, Sean."

"Hi, Mary Kathleen," the Cardinal said with a broad smile, a smile reserved for beautiful women.

"My Jungian consort is here too."

"Hi, Dr. Murphy," he said with a grin.

"Hi, Cardinal."

My sibling Mary Kathleen Ryan Murphy and her husband Joe are both psychiatrists, she a heterodox Freudian, he an eclectic Jungian. Ever since she had seduced him (not too strong a word, I believe) during a psychiatric clerkship at Little Company of Mary Hospital, the pretense, shared by all, was that she was the better clinician of the two. Everyone, including Mary Kate, knew that the pretense wasn't true.

"How are all the kids and grandkids?"

"Flourishing. Chantal's oldest is a senior in high school. Petey's wife Cindasue is expecting her first. Didn't waste any time. I think your new bishop might like that."

"Diagnosis?" I said impatiently.

"Pretty easy. Borderline personality. Unusual type.

Not very bright. Passive-aggressive. Little sexual energy. Delusional. Manipulative. Probably learned from his mother to control his father that way. Becomes the poor, innocent, sincere child to get what he wants. Then turns officious with subordinates. Will have to be slapped down hard, but even then won't get it."

"He'll mess up everything he touches," the other Dr. Murphy warned, "all in the name of God and the Holy Father—"

"Most Holy Father," I corrected him.

"PUNK," Mary Kate interjected, "stop interrupting!"

"Punk" is the mostly affectionate diminutive my siblings use for me. And their children—as in "Uncle Punk"!

"It's a well-structured complex, Cardinal. Impermeable, I'd say. He's built it over time to protect a fragile ego. Take it away and he's nothing."

I had suspected a diagnosis of that sort. There would be trouble right here in Athens on the Lake, Richard M. Daley, Mayor.

"What do we do?" the Cardinal asked weakly.

"Hit him with reality," my sibling replied. "Slap him down every time he misbehaves."

"Do not yield an inch," her husband agreed. "Ever."

"Sounds grim. . . . No cure? No treatment?"

"Only if some extraneous event shatters the system. Then he'll probably go into a sustained psychotic interlude."

"What," I demanded, "might we do to generate such an extraneous event?"

Silence from my sibling and sibling-in-law.

"Maybe," Mary Kate said carefully, "catch him making love to a mother superior on the altar during Mass."

Jenny

5

The man stares at me. His spirit comes out of his body and embraces me, caresses me, undresses me, plays with me. I should be offended, perhaps, but I am not. There is no cruelty in his gaze. It is always respectful. I am afraid of it, but I enjoy it. My mind and body go limp. I cannot think. I cannot concentrate on my work. It must stop.

If I were to target a man, it would be someone like him—attractive, gentle, intelligent. And wealthy. I do not want a man. I have not targeted him. I have done nothing to win his attention. I am precise and prim when we are at meetings and he is inspecting my work. If anything, I am shy and tongue-tied.

My friends tell me that I should remarry. They say that the reason I have put so much energy and effort into reshaping my body is that I want a man. They say men drool over me. I don't want that. I wanted to rebuild my self-respect after the divorce and the annulment fights. I've had enough of men. I want to avoid them for the rest of my life.

Yet, the first time I saw this man, who is the president of our firm, my knees became weak. I had thought that my sexual feelings had been forever extinguished. I guess I was wrong. I would like to sleep with him just to see what he is like. That's the first time I have admitted that to myself. I do not want to become involved with him or anyone else. Why did God make us with sexual feelings that continue long after we are capable of bearing children? Why did he make us so that we would be lonely when we lie in bed by ourselves? I do not want to need a man. But without one I will be lonely. I must make up my mind to be lonely.

He is still staring at me. He pretends to be working, but his eyes never leave me. Once more his spirit slips away from his body and comes to me. He covers me with his kisses. I melt.

I must stop that.

I ask one of my colleagues if I have ever seemed to hit on the boss.

She says of course not, I'm as prim as a fundamentalist teenage virgin. I should hit on him, she says. He lost his wife two years ago. He is lonely. Look at the sadness in his eyes. He's a wonderful man. You're gorgeous and the kind of woman he'd fall for. I'm not that kind of woman, I say. She replies, I mean the kind of woman who could make him happy. Just send up a signal and he'll come running.

I'm accused of doing just that, I tell her. By Donnie? Yes. She's a bitch. She thinks she owns him. She figures that she's indispensable to the firm and she ought to be indispensable to him too. He is barely aware of her existence.

She wants to get rid of me. I need the job. She'll never be able to do that. He likes you too much even from a distance to do that. You're too good at what you do.

Why must I have this sense of someone's spirit coming out to me? It's much more seductive than the first clumsy caresses. When did my husband lose interest in me? I wonder.

I am at a large dinner party in Forest Hills. I do not want to go, but the woman who invited me insists that I must get out of my house. There are several men who tried to "hit" on me, all but one of them married. I dismiss them with practiced ease. Bishop Quill is at the party. I ignore him as much as possible because I hate him so. In person he is a fat, soupy worm.

They put him next to me at the table. How could they? Have they forgotten what he did to me? He pays little attention to me. I don't think he likes women very much, especially a woman with a touch of décolletage.

"I'm surprised you don't remember my name, Bishop," I say. I know I have crossed the line and I'm going to explode.

"How would I know you?" he asks.

"You tried to ruin my life."

He looks puzzled.

"You reversed my annulment even though my husband had already married his mistress. You gave an adulterer power over my marriage."

"I do not remember the case, madam," he says coolly.

"My husband hated me. He wasn't interested in protecting the marriage bond. He wanted to punish me. That's why he appealed the annulment decision. You went along with him. I hate you. I wish you were dead."

"Although I do not recall the case, your husband had the right to appeal. You, of course, had the right to appeal." He went back to shoving tiny bits of meat into his mouth. Everyone in the room is quiet.

"I did appeal," I shout, "and they reversed you."

"That does happen," he says calmly, wiping his greasy mouth with a napkin.

I'm screaming now. "They tore your decision to shreds!" I run from the table sobbing.

The hostess comes after me. She apologizes. "I didn't know he was the one. He is a bit of a drip, isn't he?"

I apologize too. I hadn't wanted an annulment. Father Dribben said I should. It seemed so easy until Ben appealed. Then it dragged on. One more way for Ben to punish me. Father Dribben finally got the reversal reversed, I explain to her. And now he's taken poor Father Dribben's place.

I drive back down to my apartment, furious at myself. I dream about him at night—I mean my boss. We are making love. He is so sweet and kind. And so passionate. Then Bishop Quill is on top of me. I scream with terror and wake up. I am aroused and cannot go back to sleep.

My shrink listens to my story. Why are you so hard on yourself? she asks again. He is a vile little man and you told him so. You never did that to Ben. You're getting better. I'm sure everyone in the room was on your side. You wanted the annulment, she tells me. You wanted to marry again in your church. Someone better. Father Dribben knew that.

You of course understood the dream? No, I didn't, I insist. Yes, you do. All right, I do. He stands for a new life and the Bishop stands for my old life. They both want me. Brilliant, she says. You could do my job, better perhaps than I do it. I don't want to marry again. I'm just lonely, so lonely. I begin to cry. The shrink is pleased. You are, Jenny, a healthy woman with thirty perhaps forty years of life ahead of you. Of course you want a man. You are not fated to make the same mistake again. You deceive yourself when you say that you wanted to recapture your beauty merely for your self-respect. You also deceive yourself when you say you come here to straighten out your emotions, which, in fact, are healthy. Your anger and your fears are both appropriate. You are here to be sure you don't make a mistake in your quest for another man. I do not mind that. You are very wise to have a counselor in this difficult but exciting time. I am not a teenager, I tell her. I went through this once and I won't go through it again. It is time, she says.

I work hard at the office and catch up on my work. He's not here. I am not distracted. Then he comes in. There is a look of terrible pain in his eyes. I am shattered. I want to wipe the pain out of his eyes and make them glow with joy. Now it seems that my spirit goes out to him. That has never happened before. It has always been that I perceive the man thinking about me. Even Ben, before the children came. Before he thought that they and I were an obstacle to the Nobel Prize he was destined to win.

Now I envelop him without even looking at him. I run my fingers through his curly hair. I cover his beautiful face with my kisses. I unbutton my blouse and lay his head against my breasts. He sighs deeply, content with me, for a moment healed with pain. My body is aroused again, ready for lovemaking. I drive the thoughts away. This is absurd. I glance towards his office. He is looking out the window towards the lake, a faint smile on his face. I force myself to go back to work. Perhaps I should look for a new job. I say that once to my therapist. She says there will be another man there. She asks why I will not let myself be brave enough to send this man a signal. My colleague says the same thing. I must send a signal. I won't send a signal.

He calls me into his office to discuss the revisions I've made on my design. I can feel Donnie's eyes like knives in my back. He stands up, as he always does for a woman, and tells me that my dress is pretty, as he always does. We discuss the design. He complements me on it. Tells me I have a rare talent and that I am getting better every time. This one is just about perfect. I don't think he tells everyone that. I blush and thank him for the compliment. It's not a compliment, he says, flushing slightly. Well, it is that too. But it's the truth. Suddenly the erotic vibrations in the room are strong. My body betrays me and begins to prepare for intercourse. This is absurd. We successfully pretend that we are professionals, that there is nothing between us except my graphic. We finish quickly. I accept his suggestions. He's the boss. Besides, they're good suggestions. I promise him that I'll have the changes by tomorrow morning. My body feels so heavy that I can hardly walk out of the office.

Donnie strides over to my desk. What were you doing in there? she demands. He asked me to discuss my design. Let me see it she says, pulling it out of my hand. This is shit, she tells me. It's no good. We'll never use it. I think it's rather good, I reply. She tears it. I think it's terrible and I'm the one who makes the decisions around here, she states.

Fortunately the graphic is still in my computer and I can remember the changes he suggested. I see over her shoulder that he is watching us from the office. He winces when she tears the proof into little pieces and throws it in the wastebasket. You're not very good, she tells me. I don't think you have much of a future here. You ought to find yourself a new job before we get rid of you. I don't say anything.

You're trying to seduce him, aren't you? she sneers at me. I am not, I reply calmly, and think to myself, Not yet anyway. I warn you, she says, I'm not going to let you get away with that. You try one more of your fancy moves and I'll fire you myself. Now get to work on this graph I want. It's simple enough and I don't want anything fancy. I say yes, ma'am. She storms away.

I put her algorithm aside and call up my design. Perhaps because I'm so angry I find myself on a run. It flows. I incorporate his suggestions and build on them in a way I know he'll like. I glance towards his office. Donnie is in there. She is very angry. If he is, he does not show it, self-contained as always. Did he call her in after she tore up my work, or did she charge into the office to tell him she was going to fire me? Donnie has been with the firm for a long time. Everyone says that even if she is so obnoxious, she is indispensable. Has she told him it's her or me? Perhaps. I'll know soon enough. She storms out of the office, her face bright red, but she does not come in my direction. Maybe I've won. I finish my revisions. I could bring the final version into him now, but that will make more trouble. I'll put it on his desk when I arrive in the morning. No, I won't do that. She might see it and destroy. I'll give it to him myself.

You must give up your illusions, my shrink tells me. What illusions? I ask her. Your illusions that you are a failure as a woman. You believed the verbal abuse from Ben. You got him through graduate school. You typed his dissertation. You kept his house neat. You raised his children. He was so inferior as a man that he had to blame you for everything that went wrong in his career, especially the loss of the Nobel Prize. What if he is right? I ask her. What if I never was any good in bed? Do you think he was right? No, I say. I

think he was wrong about everything. Do you think
you were good in bed until he lost interest? I hesitate.
Of course. Then why do you hide behind your illusions of inadequacy? I don't know. Yes you do. I know
what she wants me to say. I don't want to say it, even
if it is true. It is too dangerous, Jenny? she demands.
Hiding is safe. If I am an adequate woman I'll have to
take risks. She sighs with relief. Can you seduce this
man if you want to? Yes. Will he marry you? Yes. Will
you be happy together? Happier than most. Then what
are you waiting for? I'm afraid.

I knock lightly on the doorjamb of his office. He
glances away from his computer. His eyes light up.
Jenny! he says. I blush. I must put an end to his ogling
me in the office. He shouldn't be looking at me the way
he does even now. I am not a heifer to be evaluated
by a cattle buyer. I have the revised design, I say. Let's
see it. He stands up courteously as he always does. As
I join him at his desk, he takes in every inch of me,
stripping away my clothes with his eyes. This has to
stop. I am not a slave on the auction block. He turns
his eyes to my design. Sit down, please, Jenny. I do,
anxious that he won't like it. You've built on my suggestions, I see. He frowns. I don't like it when my em-
ployees improve on my recommendations. He's
grinning. I relax. No, sir, I say. He sits down. So do I.
How much are we paying you? I tell him. Not nearly
enough, he says, making a note. When people in the
trade find out who did this, they'll swarm all over you.
Thank you, sir, I say meekly, an innocent peasant virgin in the presence of her feudal lord. It's perfect as it
is, he says. We'll put it into production at once. Give
this to Donnie on the way out and tell her I said to put
it in the process.

There's one more thing, sir. He raises an eyebrow.
I charge ahead. I'm not a naked slave matron on the

auction block, but you stare at me like I am. He gulps and turns red. My face is very warm. I don't mean to offend you, Jenny, he stumbles, or to harass you. I'm very sorry. I don't feel either offended or harassed, sir, I say smoothly. In fact, I feel flattered. However, people in the office might misunderstand. They might indeed, he replies, his smile returning. I shall do my best to be more discreet. Thank you, sir, I say rising to flee. Jenny, he says as I reach the door. Yes, sir? You must not be shocked that men stare at you. You are a startlingly attractive woman. So long as they do it discreetly, I say with a smile and a toss of my head.

Donnie glares at me when I give her the design and the disk on which it resides. He says to put it in the process. She looks at the design and turns up her nose in disgust. Back at my desk. I sigh with relief. Everything is settled. There'll be no more troubling stares in the office. Thank God, I had the courage to be blunt about it. Blunt but not bitchy. At the end of the day he tries to enter the elevator just as the door closes. I hold it open for him. Thank you, Jenny. You're welcome, I say meekly. Would you feel sexually harassed, Jenny, he blurts out, if I invited you to dinner tomorrow night. He was supposed to say that, but not so soon. I don't think I ought to, I begin. Then the crazy woman inside me takes over. That would be very nice, I say. That night Bishop Quill rapes me. In my dreams.

I show the shrink my graphic of "Jenny on the Auction Block." Very interesting, she says. Not quite pornographic. You have covered yourself modestly but inadequately. I see that you are now able to accept your physical beauty. That is considerable progress. You will give this to the man? Oh, no, I say blushing, not at all. At least not now. I wonder who the slave will really be? she muses.

Blackie

6

"It's ten-fifteen," the Lord Cardinal said nervously. "We have to get over there before he does."

I was searching for my pectoral cross, a silver form of the Brigid cross that my cousin Catherine Curran had designed. I had already found the plain gold band that she had also produced.

"You are the Cardinal Archbishop," I reminded him. "It would be most unseemly if you rushed over there just to head him off at the pass."

"We should tell the staff not to let him start."

"I have already suggested that strategy to them. It will be a good test of whether he can manipulate your staff to violate a direct order from you."

"From you."

"I told them I was speaking in your name."

I found the cross and stuffed it into the pocket of my Chicago Bulls jacket, a memorial to a happier year.

The Cardinal did not approve of my informal dress, though he understood the reason for it. But long ago he had sworn the most solemn oath that he would pay no attention to what manner of dress a priest might affect.

"What do you think they will do?"

"Like accomplished bureaucrats, they will stall him."

My prediction turned out to be correct.

Milord Cronin, unlike most princes of the Church, values punctuality. Even if he knows everyone is going to be late to some function, he arrives on time. And then glares at his watch as others straggle in. This time, I explained to him, he must arrive fifteen minutes late to convey the impression that he had other and better things to do besides attending this press conference, which in fact he had not called.

The Chancery auditorium was filled with the media, cameras and microphones at the ready. Chancery office clergy were milling around uneasily. The four auxiliary bishops, looking like pallbearers, waited grimly.

Augustus O'Sullivan Quill was near the podium, waiting for an opportunity to seize the mike. He was dressed in full robes, a cassock with purple buttons and purple trim, purple zucchetto, a purple cummerbund, and purple socks inside shoes with silver clasps.

"Sean, Blackie," Kas Piowar rushed to greet us. "Where have you been? We had to pull the mike away from this guy. What the hell is going on?"

"Oh you of little faith," Sean Cronin said, now in his happy Irish gallowglass mode, his blue eyes flashing dangerously. He strode briskly up to the podium. The other bishops rallied behind him, like commissars supporting a marshal of the Soviet Union. The Cardinal grasped Gus Quill's hand in a warm greeting and bathed him in his very best smile—as he eased him away from the mike.

I melted into invisibility.

I must gloss this assertion. I am the most unimpres-

sive of humans. You'd hardly notice me if you got on
an elevator on which I was riding. I'm not really invisible, exactly, merely not worth noticing. I am the little
man who wasn't there. But when I seriously make up
my mind to blend into the environment, I really am
not there. It is a very useful quality.

I realized that at some point I would have to put on
my Brigid cross, lest Catherine Curran be offended
should she see me on television without it.

Naturally, the Cardinal and I had decided what he
would say.

"It's good to see all my friends from the media
again," he began genially. "We haven't had one of
these solemn high press conferences in a long time.
This is the first one we've ever staged for the appointment of an auxiliary bishop. We should have done it
for all the other five," he gestured at the pallbearers
behind him. "They're key men in the Archdiocese;
without them nothing much would happen. I am
deeply grateful for their hardworking collaboration.
Gentlemen, thank you!"

He turned and bowed to the four of them—black,
Italian, Latino, and Polish. They smiled. The old man
was still in charge!

"I want to welcome to their ranks today our newest
and thus most junior auxiliary, Bishop Augustus
O'Sullivan Quill. Bishop Quill has at last come home
to Chicago from Rome. Gus, welcome home."

Applause from the clergy!

"He has returned to us after a long career at the
Sacred Roman Rota, one of the Vatican law courts.
Although we have a number of highly trained canonists
in our diocese, including Monsignor Ted Coffey, who
I see out there among you, one can never have too
many good lawyers in the Church."

There was just enough irony in the Cardinal's patently false comment about lawyers to draw a titter from the crowd, just what we wanted and no more.

"I have often told the Pope that I need all the help I can get. I'm grateful for adding Bishop Quill to my staff of helpers. He was, by the way, ordained last month by the Pope himself, along with fifty or, Gus, was it a hundred other bishops?"

He paused to give Gus a chance to answer.

"Fifty-six, Your Eminence," he replied in a squeaky voice.

"Right, fifty-six. I bet that when the Pope saw him in line he said to himself, that man Cronin needs a junior auxiliary. Why don't I send him Gus Quill! So, Gus, welcome aboard. It's good to have you with us."

He had, on the whole, done well enough, I thought.

Gus Quill edged towards the mike.

"Are there any questions?" The Cardinal asked the representatives of the media.

"Cardinal, you said five auxiliaries, but there are only four up there. Is someone ill?"

My cover was about to be blown.

"Bishop Ryan is around here somewhere," he said with a wave of his hand. "As often is the case, he is in one of his invisible moods."

I barely had time to pull the Brigid cross out of my jacket and put it on. The light from the Channel Six camera, after wandering a bit, picked me out, creating a partial veil from the reflection of my Coke-bottle glasses (which were reserved for public occasions because I wear contact lenses at my siblings' insistence). I smiled weakly, which is also part of the persona.

"Cardinal, is it true that Bishop Quill has been sent here by the Pope to take over some of your powers?" a reporter asked.

"I'm not sure what my powers are worth any more, but the answer is no."

Dismissive grin. Nicely done.

"Has he been secretly appointed your successor?"

"I'm in good health and have five more years before retirement. No decisions will be made about a successor till then. But to be direct, because of the rumors that always arise, I inquired of the Secretariat of State in the Vatican and the answer was a flat no."

Gus Quill was sweating profusely.

The questions went on for a few more minutes. Milord handled them all nicely. Then Mary Anne McGurn intruded again.

"Bishop Ryan, do you consider Bishop Quill a rival for succession?"

Obnoxious young woman!

I chose to ignore the question.

"Bishop Ryan . . . ?" the Cardinal said, indicating I was to answer.

I remained stoic. There was no escape but I wished to register my conviction that the question was frivolous.

"Blackie . . . ?" The Cardinal shouted, as if to wake me up.

I ambled disconsolately to the podium and intruded myself between Gus and the Cardinal.

"Would you repeat the question, Ms. McGurn?"

"Do you consider Bishop Quill a rival to be the next cardinal?"

I blinked my eyes in bemusement, glanced at Sean Cronin, and then at Gus Quill, from whose face the sweat was now pouring more profusely.

"I think, Ms. McGurn, that my chances of becoming archbishop of Chicago are excellent, about the same, in fact, as those of Jerry Krause, the general manager of the late and much lamented Chicago Bulls!"

Laughter and applause. I remained at the podium,

eyes still blinking rapidly, to fend Gus away from the mike.

"Arguably less so," said the Cardinal, stirring up more laughter and applause.

"On that happy note," he continued, "I think we can adjourn this conference and Gus and his senior colleagues and I can go to my office and discuss his responsibilities in the Archdiocese."

The media people packed their bags and began to drift out. The Cardinal threw his arm around Gus and led the way, the other bishops closing in like jailers. I hung around to test the waters.

"Good answer, Blackie," Mary Jane informed me.

"Young woman, you are incorrigible."

"You guys really shut him down."

"For the moment."

"Our kind has a good slant on him. He'll have a hell of a time changing that."

"I shouldn't wonder."

Ted Coffey, who, like Gus Quill, had been my classmate in the seminary, was less optimistic.

"You guys did a great job, Blackie," he said, shaking hands with me. He was a tall, handsome black Irishman, with a square face and deep blue eyes, one of the most successful and popular pastors in the city. "Shut him down completely."

I sighed my patented West of Ireland sigh, which often sounds like the onslaught of a serious asthma attack. "We headed him off at the pass."

"This time. He'll be back. He's always back. He never lets up. I worked with him at the Tribunal and studied with him in Rome. It's a wonder he got the degree, he's so dumb. But he keeps plugging away with his phony piety and his worship of the Pope. You guys are going to have to slap him down hard every time he makes one of his moves, and he'll be making them all the time."

"Arguably."

"No arguably about it, Blackie. He's poison. Very dangerous."

Remembering the comments of Mary Kate and Joe from the night before, I sighed again. "Doubtless you're right."

A quarter of an hour later, the Cardinal and Gus appeared at the elevator door, surrounded by the gaggle of auxiliaries. The Cardinal conducted Gus to the waiting limo, which was indeed bigger than the Cardinal's own Lincoln Town Car, and waved him off. The others went their separate ways.

"Neatly done, Blackwood," young Kas Piowar said to me.

"Perhaps."

The Cardinal waved me outside.

"Well?" he asked as we began the walk down Superior Street towards the Cathedral.

I sighed yet again. "The general feeling is that the first round is ours, but that we will have to keep fighting, perhaps indefinitely. . . . What happened upstairs?"

"He doesn't listen, Blackwood. Or maybe he can't listen. He doesn't hear what we say. We talked about a lot of things he might do, all harmless. He simply said he wanted to serve in the Archdiocese in an important way. The conversation went over his head. He wants an important job and assumes he'll get it."

"Will he?"

"No way."

"Ah."

"He speaks of assuming responsibility for the Hispanic work, right in front of Ricardo, who is our Hispanic vicar and is doing a fine job in most difficult circumstances."

"Certainly. Does he speak the language?"

"Not much. Ricky came at him with a rapid flow of Spanish and Gus stared at him blankly. Then Ricky insulted him and Gus didn't understand a word. Ricky just rolled his eyes. Gus said he was still mastering the language."

"You're not going to let him near the Latino population just to get rid of him?"

"I'll get rid of him some way, but not that way."

"Hopefully. I'm sure he is where he is in the Church because a lot of other people up and down the line got rid of him."

"He's not a bad guy, actually," Sean Cronin continued, "sincere and diffident and pious. But he simply does not hear what you say to him."

"Or won't hear."

"All right, he won't hear or can't hear or whatever. Still, I think he means well."

"His meaning well and a dollar and a half will get you a ride on our mutual friend Rich Daley's subway."

In retrospect, that was a prophetic phrase.

"You're very harsh on him, Blackwood."

"You remember what my sib and sib-in-law told us last night?"

"I'm not likely to forget it."

"I have reason to believe that the secret of his success is that people shove him off to the margins to get rid of him and then he comes right back at them from another route."

"I suppose so."

"I have but one fear," I said.

"And what is that, Blackwood?"

"Your good-hearted generosity."

He was quiet for a minute.

"Nora says that's my tragic flaw."

"I defer to her superior experience."

He paused again.

"I think I can count on your South Side realism."

"Oh, yes."

Inside the Cathedral rectory he said, "There's one small thing. Gus will stay with us here for a while. Until we sort out what he's going to do."

"His idea?"

"I guess so," Sean Cronin said weakly.

"First mistake."

"I should have asked you first."

"No one has to ask me anything first," I insisted.

"I still should have. Two weeks?" he asked meekly.

"Not one day, not one second more, or you'll have to get a new Cathedral pastor."

"No fear of that."

I wasn't so sure.

7

At first Gus Quill was not a problem in our house. He was polite and affable, quiet at the dinner table but friendly, an amused audience to the banter between myself and other members of the staff, even if he did show up in a purple-buttoned cassock. He congratulated me on the excellent food, the fine conversation, and the warm spirit of the house.

"John, no one who knew you in the seminary would be at all surprised by your pastoral skills."

He even accompanied me on my hospital visits and took notes of what I said and what I did, because, as he said, he had almost no experience with this kind of ministry.

I should have been suspicious when he called me

"John." No one calls me that, save for passive-aggressive nuns and fascistic RCIA (Rite of Christian Initiations for Adults) directors. As is patent, I am either "Blackie" (or occasionally "Blackwood") or, in the family, "Punk." My late father, Ned Ryan, called me Johnny, as in "We are the only sane ones in the family, Johnny. White sheep caught among the black sheep." Such an observation is arguably accurate.

Then one day Gus Quill decided that he had been named to replace me as rector of the Cathedral.

"John," he said one morning, halfway through the second week of his stay, "I just want you to know that I am in no hurry to take possession of this suite of rooms."

He took in with interest the mess of my room and the objets d'art on the walls—the three Johns of my childhood (pope, president, and quarterback of the hated Baltimore Colts); a print of a very bossy medieval Madonna, who was alleged to look like my mother, Catherine Collins Ryan; and Lisa Raffery, a maid of all work in a Prairie Avenue mansion a hundred years ago, whose diary had once protected me from a disastrous mistake. I had just returned from a session with the second-graders, one of the great joys of the week. I felt that the world was much like second grade, a crazy but rather benign place.

"Ah!" I said in some surprise.

"Whenever you have time to vacate it will be fine. I am content to stay in the guest room as long as it is necessary, though it's somewhat small and less than convenient."

For mostly genetic reasons, I am rarely at a loss for words. This was one of those rare times.

"By the way, John," he said in a man-to-man tone, "isn't that picture a little risqué for a bishop's study?"

He gestured at a painting my cousin Catherine Cur-

ran had given me. Like all her nudes, it was utterly
chaste. In fact, it was a painting of the famous actress
Lisa Malone, who had gone to grammar school with
Catherine and me.

"I think it's quite chaste," I replied, "though perhaps,
on occasion, distracting."

"Well, I would disagree. I'm sure Jesus wouldn't like
it."

A thousand retorts formed on my lips, but I held
them back.

"Perhaps."

"Anyway, I want to wish you all the best in your
new assignment, whatever that may be."

He shook hands with me and departed with the confident air of a man who had just taken over.

I was so astonished that I didn't feel angry. It was
most unlikely that Sean Cronin would send me out into
the fabled world that existed beyond the boundaries of
the Cathedral parish. At the minimum, he would never
be able to steal my Irish whiskey and tell me to see to
it, nor to seek my advice on how to deal with the media
vultures.

It was also arguably the case that I would be better
off somewhere else. One gets into a rut when one has
been in the same place too long. Idiot Quill would be
welcome to it. And the Cardinal to the chaos that
would follow.

I was hardly the indispensable man, was I?

I realized that these largely self-serving reflections
were probably unnecessary. I could pick up the phone,
call the Chancery, where Milord Cronin was working
this morning, and ask him what the new assignment
was, thus unleashing the whirlwind.

That, however, would be inappropriate. I would bide
my time and see what happened. I therefore departed
the rectory for my pastoral rounds—the hospital, the

dead, the dying, the sick, the troubled, the sad, the bereaved.

It was midafternoon when I returned to North Wabash. Despite considerable searching, I couldn't find the key, a not untypical occurrence, so I pushed the doorbell. No one came. I glanced at my watch. It was time for the Megan to be there. They were under strict orders to answer doorbells promptly. I had assured them that in years past many people had left the church in a rage because no one answered the doorbell.

I pushed the bell again. Still no response.

Thereupon I engaged in behavior that is politely called leaning on the doorbell. Megan O'Connor answered. Though her face was dark with anger, I knew that there was trouble because she was not supposed to be on duty. Megan Flores, the Mexican-American member of the team, was supposed to be our porter person.

"Bishop Blackie," she screamed, "we want to talk to you!"

I had a pretty good idea what the trouble was.

In their headquarters, I found Megan Flores in tears, Megan Kim solemn, and Megan Jefferson, like her Irish-American counterpart, ready to eat nails.

"Ah?"

"That terrible man made Megan Flower take down the cute posters she made!"

"He did?"

"Then he tore them up!"

"He didn't!"

Four torn posters were shoved in my face. Megan Flores, a.k.a. Flower, an ingenious graphic designer, had posted warnings that this was a NO SMOKING RECTORY, a NO FIREARMS RECTORY, a NO NUCLEAR RECTORY, and a NO DRINKING RECTORY.

I had always assumed that the last rule did not apply to the upper floors.

The posters caused laughter in all but the most reactionary visitors. Milord Cronin loved them, in part because he loved the vivacity and charm of my carefully chosen porter persons.

"Who is this iconoclast?" I demanded.

"Bishop Quill," they replied as one, each of them now crying.

"He came back from the church where he was praying for an hour," Megan Jefferson continued, "and said that God had told him those posters were not fitting. . . . What does he mean by fitting? Like a dress doesn't fit?"

"Arguably he means appropriate."

"Would God really tell him that?"

"I think that very unlikely. . . . I must report this defacement to the Cardinal," I said. "Bishop Quill is not my guest."

"And," Megan Jefferson said, "he told us God told him that we can't work here anymore after the end of the week!"

"We'll organize pickets," Megan O'Connor warned me. "We'll shut this place down, just like my great-grandfather did in the Great Depression!"

"I'll march with you! In the meantime, Megan Flores, you might begin to redo the posters."

The tears vanished.

"Even weirder than the last time!"

"Much weirder!"

Having thus reassured the troops, I ascended on our cranky and creaky elevator to the top floor of the rectory, where the Cardinal lived. I rarely bothered him up there, save on the house phone. A man is entitled to his privacy.

Conversation and laugher flowed out of the open

door of the room. The Lady Nora, no doubt.

A long time ago she and her foster brother/brother-in-law had been lovers, for a very brief interlude, I suspected. Now they were good friends, a relationship of love that certainly was sexual but also chaste. Also none of my business, save that the Cardinal had once told me about it.

"Blackie," she said, "come in and have a cup of tea."

Even in her late sixties Nora Cronin's smile could melt all the ice on Lake Michigan in the middle of winter.

"I'd love to, but I fear that the natives are restless tonight."

"Which natives?" The Cardinal raised an eyebrow.

"The Megan are in open revolt."

"We can't have that!"

"It would appear that Bishop Augustus O'Sullivan Quill tore up Megan Flower's posters and informed her that the services of the whole Megan would not be required after the end of this week. He apparently came to these conclusions after an hour of prayer in church."

"What!"

"It would appear from other indications, which have come to my attention, that he believes that he has been appointed rector of the Cathedral, a task to which he is quite welcome."

"Shite!" He rose from his chair, spilling some of his tea. His face was locked in a grim frown—Phil Jackson finally driven to outrage by stupid refs.

"Sean," the Lady Nora murmured softly as she moved to sop up the spilled tea, "that man simply has to go. I don't like the way he looks at me when he sees me in the elevator."

"One or the other of us has to," I added, "before tomorrow night at the close of business."

The Cardinal sighed, imitating rather nicely my own West of Ireland sigh.

"Blackwood, sit down and drink a cup of tea with Nora. She will tell you that she wouldn't let me fire you even if I wanted to. She has the crazy idea that you're a good influence on me."

"Arguably," I agreed.

"Now I'll go down and apologize to the Megan."

"By your leave," I said to Nora Cronin, "I'll retrieve a tiny amount of Irish whiskey from my study. Milord will need it on his return."

"Bring some for me too, Blackie. We can all celebrate the departure of that terrible man. I'll brew a fresh pot of tea."

As sure as the sun would rise in the morning and as Rich Daley was mayor of Chicago, Gus Quill would have his marching orders within the hour.

However, we had not heard the last of him. At all, at all, as the Irish say.

Tommy

8

I drifted back to the Hancock Center in a happy daze. We had covered a lot of preliminary material in forty-five minutes—material that normally would have required many dates with a woman who wasn't a young lioness. So far I was a man approved. "Weird" was not necessarily a negative word in the vocabulary of my generation. "Sweet" was definitely positive. I was definitely worth getting to know better.

And my reactions?

Who was I to resist the will of God?

Then I realized that God was playing with good odds. Christy Logan and I lived in the same neighborhood and went to the same church. We would have encountered each other anyway. Most likely. Bishop Blackie knew that too. Admittedly God had chosen a cool site for the drama to be worked out. I was a victim of a conspiracy. Not, however, at this point, an unhappy victim.

I spent the rest of the evening replaying our conversation. I had performed ably, like I normally did in the Eurodollar pit. She had found me not unacceptable. We were a long, long way from courtship. Yet it was legitimate to ask the question of whether, on the basis of what had happened in Ghirardelli's, I would, tentatively and speculatively, find Christy Logan an acceptable companion for the rest of our lives.

I remembered her enthusiastic lecture on *Finnegans Wake*. I could, I told myself, do worse.

Properly dressed in a dark gray suit and a Georgetown tie, I entered the lobby of the Water Tower apartments the following afternoon at 6:25. "Miss Logan, please," I told the doorman.

He smiled with infinite politeness. "I believe Miss Christina Logan is the only one home at present. Who should I say is calling?"

"Tommy."

He picked up a phone and pressed a button.

"Miss Logan, there is a very presentable young man named Tommy for you in the lobby. . . . Yes, Miss Logan, I'll tell him. She says, sir, that you are a few minutes early, but she'll be right down."

Promptly at 6:30—making the point that she was not uncontrollably eager?—Christy Logan appeared at an elevator door.

I gulped. "I was expecting a lioness and I encounter a goddess."

A shy goddess at that in a simple black shift with a touch of gold trim, black nylons, a pearl necklace, hair that was combed out and fell to her shoulders, a hint of make-up. I took both her hands in mine and drank her in.

"Tommy! You're embarrassing me!" she said, as a line of crimson spread down her face and over her neck.

"I'm sorry," I said quickly, letting go of her hands.

"I didn't say that you should stop embarrassing me!"

My fearsome young lioness actually wanted me to approve her appearance. Some men must have made fun of her height and her strength. Tasteless jerks. A woman could be svelte without being skinny.

I linked my arm with hers. "For a soccer All-American you sure dress up stunning."

"Thank you." She beamed. "Let's walk around the block before we ride up to the Carlton Club. . . . Are you really a Hoya?"

"Can't you tell from my superior intelligence and cultivation?"

"I've never been out with a Georgetown boy before." She was giggling.

"Then you're in for a real treat." I giggled back.

"I mean, I saw that Georgetown tie and if it wasn't that I'd disappoint Mom and Dad, I would have turned around and went back into the elevator."

"Hey, it was hard for me even to talk to a Notre Dame woman."

"Pick her up."

"She invited me out and I didn't say no. I was picked up. You must have known I went to Georgetown, my manners were so superior."

"Well, at least you're not a slob."

She clung to my arm and huddled close to me. I was acutely aware of her intense, womanly warmth and her paralyzing scent. Careful, Tommy, or you'll lose it.

"You didn't invite me to come upstairs to meet your parents. Afraid they might not approve?"

"Afraid they *would* approve. . . . Such a nice Irish-Catholic boy!"

"Compared to whom?"

"Compared to no one. I don't bring many boys around. Too many geeks out there."

"Maybe I'm a geek!"

"Maybe, but I don't think so. A little weird maybe . . ."

"But sweet."

"Moderately so." She squeezed my arm. "Hey, what's your name?"

"Tommy."

"Your *last* name. Even if I had brought you up to meet my parents, how could I introduce you? Hey, Mom and Dad, this is Tommy. I picked him up at Ghirardelli's. He's kind of cute, isn't he?"

"Moderately cute."

"A little less than that maybe, but we'll stop right here until you tell me your last name."

"Flynn. . . . I'm Amy's brother."

"Omigod! Why didn't I see that before! You have her black hair and white skin and neat teeth and twinkle in your eye and sculpted face! I must be blind! You are *really* Amy's brother!"

She touched my face as she made the comparison with Amy. Her fingers burned.

"Amy's my sister. And do me a favor—"

"I won't tell her that I picked you up in Ghirardelli's. Where we are now, we don't need that."

"Bought me with a second chocolate malt. . . . And where are we now?"

"Other than riding up to the ninth floor of the Ritz-Carlton, I haven't the slightest idea. We're not nowhere, but we're not much into somewhere either."

We laughed together.

"Do you go to church?" she asked, still clinging to my arm as we walked across the lobby towards the Carlton Club.

"Of course I go to church."

"Really?"

"Every Sunday. Sometimes more often. I was away for a while, but Bishop Blackie wrestled me back in."

"You know Bishop Blackie! Isn't he cute?"

"The Megan are cuter."

"Aren't they adorable kids! You must be an active parishioner to know them."

"Not really."

As we walked to our table in the Carlton Club, every eye turned to take in my companion. She didn't seem to notice. The black shift, I saw, was made of clingy material that emphasized, subtly and discreetly, every curve in her wondrous body; it was an ostensibly modest garment that wasn't modest at all. In the presence of this warm, exciting, apparently fragile young woman, my temporarily captive lioness, my obsessive shower room fantasies seemed inappropriate and irrelevant.

You have to treasure your temporarily captive lionesses.

As we studied our menus—having both ordered Evian water on the rocks—I said, "Christy Logan, young lioness, you'll have to forgive me if I gawk at you. You're a resplendent woman, breathtaking, overwhelming, paralyzing!"

She put down her menu and looked like she was about to cry.

"There's a lot of me, I'm afraid."

"And every inch of you is beautiful."

How had I suddenly become skillful at complimenting women? What was happening to me? I should not trust this one. She was too beautiful, too smart, too dangerous. Maybe I was the one trapped in the lion's den.

"Definitely sweet." She hid behind the menu. "Still weird. But definitely sweet."

"Moderately so."

"Maybe a little bit better than that."

"What happens after you graduate? More soccer?"

"Well I HAVE to go to the Olympics, but I'm not planning on a career as a soccer player. Maybe I'll retire as a lioness. . . . Grad school, naturally."

"In what?"

"Medical school, of course. Sports medicine."

"Where?"

"Northwestern. Where else?"

"You'll do your residency in Chicago too?"

"I'm a Chicagoan, Tommy Flynn, why should I want to go anywhere else? Have you read Alice McDermott's novels? And Anna Quindlen's?"

I admitted that I had.

"I think they're totally cool, but they're not Irish like we are."

"Totally cool"—she was still a child, Amy's age. Five, six years were a generation these days. I was robbing a cradle.

So we entered into a long discussion about whether you could tell where Irish novelists were from by how they wrote. I argued that she knew where Anna Quindlen and Alice McDermott were from because their stories were set in the New York area. She said she knew where they were from because they didn't have the same sense of parish community that we had. She also insisted that she'd known that Anne Rice was from New Orleans because her writing was so weird.

"Weird like I'm weird?"

"Totally different. Did you know she has returned to the Church? About time. Her images are all Catholic even when they're perverted."

"I see."

"You knew she was Irish?"

"I'm afraid not."

"Don't you ever look at copyrights, Tommy Flynn? It says Anne O'Brien Rice. Anyway, I'm glad she's back. Like Bishop Blackie says, "Once a Catholic always a Catholic."

"Bishop Blackie is weird," I remarked.

"Of course he is. Wonderfully weird."

"I'm not wonderfully weird, however?"

"Well"—she paused to consider the issue—"not yet, but you might be."

"If I work at it!"

"Right . . . and, Tommy Flynn?"

"Yes, Christy Logan?"

"You are gawking at me an awful lot."

"I'm sorry."

"I don't mind. I just thought I'd tell you."

"Everyone in the dining room is gawking at you."

"Do I look that odd?"

"You do not look odd, you've never looked odd, you never will look odd, do you understand that?"

"Yes, sir, lion trainer!"

"You look beautiful. That's why they are gawking."

"Really?"

"Yes, really!"

"I had my chocolate fix yesterday."

A half-mad notion entered my head. I tried to fight it off.

"I have a confession to make, Christy Logan."

"Oh?" Her faced twisted into a frown. "You're married?"

"No way."

"You're engaged?"

"Absolutely not."

"You're deeply in love . . . with someone else?"

"No way."

She paused, the frown easing.

"You're gay?"

"No, ma'am."

"Then, what?"

"Well, after watching you trample over the Lady Trojans and leave the field covered with mud and sweat and rain, I had a vivid and, I confess, delightful fantasy about you in the shower cleaning off all the muck."

"Really!" she brightened. "How wonderful! . . . Did you like me?"

"How could I not like you?"

"What's wrong with that?" she grinned. "People have fantasies, that's part of being human. I don't think anyone has had a fantasy like that about me before."

"I doubt that."

"Well, they haven't told me, anyway. When I'm in the shower from now on, I'll imagine you admiring me."

"Don't you think I was exploiting you?"

"Don't be silly, Tommy Flynn, you'd never exploit me. You were just admiring me, which I think is great!"

"Admiring you naked."

"Covered with suds and stuff. Men imagine women naked. That's why there are still humans around. I don't mind that, so long as they respect me.'

"Sometimes they don't."

"I know that, but you do, so that's all that matters. . . . And after you'd seen me cavort around the soccer field like a demon."

"Lioness."

"And you still imagined that lioness without any clothes on!"

I wasn't getting anywhere.

"Would you be outraged if someone else imagined you naked?"

"Depends on who the someone else was." She shrugged at what she thought was a silly question. "Don't expect access to the real thing."

"I don't."

"At least not anytime soon."

I left that alone.

"I kind of want to know what you like about me—in your fantasy, I mean. Maybe I shouldn't ask."

"Everything!" I said as she signed the bill.

"Well, Tommy Flynn, would you like to take a walk around Streeterville with me?"

"It's probably a little chilly. You might need a sweater."

"I brought one down to the lobby earlier this afternoon, just in case I wanted to walk after dinner."

"I must have passed another test."

"I figured you would."

"Thank you very much for dinner."

"You're welcome. Daddy will pay for it, of course, and think himself lucky that his soccer star daughter has a date with a nice young man. I won't tell him you have neat fantasies about me."

"Don't," I begged her.

As we walked across the lobby towards the elevator she said, "I never asked a boy on a date before, except for high school proms. I never took one to dinner. It's kind of neat."

"Only a weird boy would accept such an invitation."

"Kind of weird?"

"Kind of."

"Moderately weird?"

"Wonderfully weird."

In the lobby I fitted the sweater around her shoulders. She glanced up at me with an appraising look. The young lioness was falling for me. Moreover, I didn't seem to mind. This was a very dangerous situation. If I let this crazy relationship go on much longer, I might have to spend the rest of my life in a lioness's den.

Perhaps she was having second thoughts herself. We

hardly knew each other. Two hasty crushes. I would foul the relationship up if it went on much longer. She was a vulnerable young woman, at least when it came to men. Maybe I should end it after our walk.

Not a chance.

"I don't like to be pushy, Tommy Flynn."

"Sweetly pushy."

She laughed. Somehow we had taken each other's hand as we walked up the Magnificent Mile towards Oak Street. Why did my captive lioness have to be so fragile?

"ANYWAY, I have to drive back to the Dome tomorrow before it gets dark. Could we meet over at the Cathedral tomorrow for Mass?"

"No way!"

"Why not?"

"Because I'll pick you up in your apartment lobby at twenty to ten."

"Great!" she squeezed my hand. "Then my mom and dad, who go to an earlier Mass, usually do brunch in the dining room at the Carlton. It's supposed to be the best brunch in Chicago."

"I have been there and it is. . . . Are you inviting me?"

We turned down Oak Street, the dark, silent lake on one side, and the Gold Coast of East Lake Shore Drive on the other.

"Well, if you don't think I'm pushing too hard."

"You're willing to let your parents get a look at me?"

"If you promise to behave."

"I'll try."

It would be easy to please her parents. I'm charming and respectable with adults. I mean real adults, not superannuated teenagers like myself. They'd have no idea how screwed up I was. They'd like me on sight.

"Then"—she drew a deep breath—"I have to exercise

to rid myself of those Ghirardelli chocolate calories. We might swim in my pool."

My lioness in a swimsuit!

"I have a pool in my building too."

"Mine's nicer."

"It is that."

"Then you'll swim with me?"

"I'd love to."

"I mean *really* swim, not just fool around in the water."

"I *really* swim every day, Christy Logan."

"You sure I'm not pushing you too hard?"

"I feel charmed, not pushed."

Gosh, I was slick. Digging a big hole in the ground for myself too.

She squeezed my hand in gratitude.

"Tommy Flynn . . ."

"Yes, Christy Logan?"

"May I ask you a very personal question?"

"Sure."

"You may not like it. . . ."

"I may not, but I like the one who will ask it."

She took a deep breath.

"Why is there so much pain in you?"

Now who was naked?

"Pain?"

"In your pretty blue eyes, great sadness. Not all the time. Not even a lot of the time. But sometimes, especially when you look at me. Has someone broken your heart?"

"You really believe in taking a man's clothes off on a first date, don't you?"

"I didn't know it was a date. Maybe on a date I wouldn't have asked the question. I'm sorry. Please forgive me."

I put my arm around her shoulder.

"Nothing to forgive, Christy. You are, in addition to being smart and gorgeous and a soccer All-American, a remarkably sensitive and perceptive young woman."

"You don't have to tell me, Tommy."

"I want to. I've never told anyone but Bishop Blackie. It would be good to tell it to a sympathetic woman."

She put her arm around my shoulder, which was easy enough because, with her one-inch heels, she matched my five feet eleven inches.

"A woman did break my heart, Christy. It wasn't a girlfriend. It was my mother."

"Your *mother*? Beth?"

"Beth is our stepmother."

"She did seem kind of young. . . . Amy always calls her Mom."

"The girls all do. . . . I can remember back to when I was the only child around the house. My real mother was so young and so pretty and so loving. She must have adored me then. She sang to me and hugged me and laughed with me. Then when the girls came along, she changed. She wouldn't take care of us. Dad had to bring in a full-time nanny. She must have been lazy all her life. Indulged by her parents. Always a passive-aggressive person. She'd punish you by doing nothing. She'd go out to movies in the afternoon with her friends and to bars afterwards. She drank a lot and hit the girls, especially poor Amy."

"Amy seems fine now."

"She is, but it took a lot of therapy. My sisters turned out to be survivors. . . . Did Amy ever mention me to you?"

"Sure."

"What did she say?"

"She said that you were cute and rich and could be

nice when you tried to, but that you were a recluse and were afraid of women."

"And you think now . . . ?"

"You don't act like a recluse or someone who is afraid of women."

"Don't be so sure. . . . Anyway, my mother would move away from the house for long periods of time to our house down at the Dunes, then to an apartment in Oak Brook. Sometimes she'd summon one of the girls, never me because she hated me so much by then, to wherever she was. The kids hated it. She'd hit them and make them cry and then send them home, saying they were spoiled brats."

"Your father picked up the bill for all of this?"

"He still loved her. He didn't know what to do. There were times when she was wonderful again, but they didn't last very long. Then when I was a senior at St. Ignatius, she summoned us all out to a restaurant in Oak Brook. There was another woman there. Mom told us that she had discovered she was a lesbian and this other woman was the love of her life and she wanted to share this good news with all of us!"

"Was she really?"

"I don't think so. She's back with a man now. . . . Amy vomited on the spot and then rushed off to the washroom. Lisa sobbed. Marie, the one most like me, sat and stared at her, just as I did. Finally I drove them home. Monsignor Coffey said that Dad should get a divorce and an annulment. Mom made the divorce proceedings as difficult as possible. I went off to college. All the girls went into therapy. The annulment went through without any trouble. Dad had been dating Beth. I think they were sleeping together. I sure hope so. They were about to be married when we learned that Mom was challenging the annulment. Some Franciscan named Father Innocent out in the suburbs helps

people to do that. Monsignor Coffey, our pastor out in
Oak Park, said to hell with it and married them any-
how. Then the annulment was reversed by that asshole
new bishop. Someone ought to kill him. . . ."

"Tommy!"

"I usually keep the anger bottled up, Christy. I said
that in back of the Cathedral last week."

"People heard you!"

"Sure, I didn't give a damn."

"Maybe you need a therapist, Tommy Flynn."

"I am seeing someone," I said, by which I meant that
I would start seeing someone the first thing Monday
morning.

"So you left the Church and Bishop Blackie wrestled
you back?"

"It was really wrestling. I'm a lot happier now. He
says that I have to rid myself of the illusion that I am
a failure as a man because I am responsible for what
happened to my mother."

"He's right, of course."

"As Cardinal Sean says, 'Blackie is occasionally in
error but never in doubt.' "

"So you kind of half-like a woman, then you confuse
her with your mother, and you get angry at her and
screw up. So you tend to stay away from them."

"That's what Blackie says. It fits. I'm sure he's right."

"You don't seem afraid of me."

"You're different, Christy Logan. I don't want to
mess up with you."

She was silent.

"I don't know whether there's anything really between us, Tommy. A pleasant weekend, forgotten by
next weekend. However, if you think I would ever let
you get away with doing that to me, you don't know
what we young lionesses are like when we're really angry. Understand?"

"Yes, ma'am."

I was exhausted. I wanted to weep.

"You work this out with your shrink and don't ever try it on me. Understand?"

"Yes, ma'am."

"Even if tomorrow is the last day of our little romance, understand?"

"Yes, ma'am."

We were walking south on Lake Shore Drive.

"And tomorrow won't be the last day either. I won't let it be. Understand that?"

Instead of crying, I laughed. "I didn't expect you'd let it be."

Then we both laughed.

We stopped on the Drive and she pulled my head over to her breasts and let it rest there for a moment.

So we both wept.

"It was wonderful to be able to tell all of that to a woman," I said when she released me. "Thanks for listening. Sorry I had to dump it on you."

"You know damn well, Tommy Flynn, lion trainer, that your story binds us together. I think you're a hero. Silly Amy doesn't know that you're the one who held the family together. Someday I'm going to tell her."

"I didn't say that I held the family together."

"You did, though. I bet you were the one who eased Beth into the house."

"Maybe."

She was supposed to think I was a mess. Instead, she thought I was a hero. The lioness was trapping the lion tamer with sympathetic affection. I didn't mind.

We walked back along Pearson Street by that ugly museum of contemporary art that looks like a bunker that launches rockets and into the park, across from the Water Tower apartments. Christy led me into the park,

which in daylight hours is flooded with rug rats and
pretty young mothers.

"I always thought this would be a good place for
kissing. There's no privacy over in the lobby. You're
the first boy I've dragged in here. And since I paid the
bill ... well, my daddy will ... I get to say whether
there will be any kissing, right?"

"Right!"

"I'm thinking about it."

She brushed her lips against mine, cautiously, affec-
tionately, generously.

"Nice," I murmured.

Then I put my hands on her solid rear end and drew
her against me. I kissed her, not passionately, exactly,
but still with some force.

"Very nice," she sighed. "Do it again?"

"You paid the bill."

I did it again, escalating a bit.

"Very, very nice."

"Thank you, ma'am."

"Take me home now, Tommy."

"It's just across the street."

"Really?"

I led her across the street, smiled at the doorman,
and watched as she entered the elevator. She turned
towards me and waved and smiled as the elevator door
closed.

The smile carried me all the way back to my apartment.

She's staying in Chicago, I thought. No reason why
we could not be married after she graduates. The
Olympics could be our honeymoon. I'll work on cleaning up my act with a shrink. Christy would never let
me get away with old shit.

If she still wants me.

In the cold light of Sunday morning that all seemed

absurd. Let her find her own way to Mass, I told myself, and rolled over in bed after the alarm. Then I popped out of bed. I'd have to find a corsage for her. The florist at the Drake, open doubtless for men like me, sold me a corsage of roses for a very high price. Worth it, I thought, at twice the price.

I arrived at the lobby of Water Tower apartments at eighteen minutes to ten. My lioness, robed in a mauve autumn dress with a short skirt, was tapping her foot impatiently. She looked at her watch as I charged in. Then she saw the flower box and melted.

"Tommy, you're so sweet. I won't say you shouldn't have because that's rude. Thank you very much."

And she kissed me, right in front of the doorman.

I helped her pin the roses on the dress, my hand brushing mostly without intent against her breast.

"How did you know what color I'd be wearing?" She kissed me again.

"I may have dirty thoughts about you all through the Eucharist, Christy Logan."

"For the last time, if you have thoughts about me, they are not, I repeat not, dirty. Now is that settled?"

"Yes, ma'am."

I took her arm in mine and we walked over to the Cathedral. Bishop Blackie stood at the back of the church, vested for Mass.

"It's consoling to see two young parishioners coming into Mass together," he murmured, blinking through his thick glasses.

"See what he got me, Bishop Blackie, a corsage, real roses!"

For a moment she was a teen again, showing off to her favorite priest.

"I have always said that Tommy is a young man of impeccable taste, which today he proves in two ways."

She yelped happily. I felt my face grow warm.

"I'm going to phone that number tomorrow morning," I whispered to him. "I'll tell her you sent me."

"In the present set of circumstances, that phone call is mandatory."

I'm sure he changed the story for his sermon so it would be aimed at us. At me.

"Once upon a time there was this boy," he began, "a senior in college, who had a total crush on a young woman who was a junior. She was totally gorgeous and very smart and also very nice, like I mean she never got drunk, you know? She was so pretty and so popular and so cool that our hero couldn't believe that she even noticed his existence. A lot of his friends would go, 'That chick really is crazy about you,' but he thought they were just making fun of him. And some of her friends were like, 'She'd really enjoy going out with you.' But our hero, who was a very shy boy (all boys are shy even if they don't act that way, but he was very, very shy) thought that they were making fun of him too. His family had made a lot of fun of him when he was growing up, you see. Well, the young woman, whose name was Fiona, sat next to him in American Lit class and talked to him before and after class (about American Lit naturally) and stopped to talk to him when she met him on campus (about American Lit or about the women's basketball team on which she played), and about all he could do was reply with animal noises like he was a freshman in high school. You see, he thought she was like making fun of him too!

"Well, she kind of hung around his family at graduation and they thought she was totally cool. His mother was like, 'That young woman is in love with you and you're a total retard (that's the way people talked when his mother was in college) if you let her get away.' He thought his mother was making fun of him too. So he's like, 'She doesn't care about me at all.'

And his mother goes, 'There's no one so blind as he who will not see.' My story has to end here, alas. Except I must tell you that Fiona represents God."

My lioness nudged me with one of her sharp elbows.

I was distracted through much of the Eucharist by the outline of her gorgeous breasts against her dress. She says they're not dirty thoughts, I explained to God.

"Great sermon, Bishop Blackie," she said enthusiastically as we left the Cathedral. "We both really liked it."

If I permitted this relationship to continue much longer, I would never escape from the woman.

Her parents were lovely people, both handsome cardiologists in their early sixties, the woman an older version of Christina. Their other children were already married. These gentle folk clearly adored their All-American daughter. I understood why she was who she is. She had grown up in a climate of powerful and generous love. I envied her.

"Isn't this corsage lovely! I've never had a corsage for Mass before!"

Her parents smiled happily. I was clearly an acceptable date for their tomboy daughter.

"That was lovely of you, Thomas," Mrs. Dr. Logan said. Christy would look like her in forty years. I know when to go long on a future. Christy was a good future.

"Well," I said with my most charming smile, as we sat at a table and they brought us some champagne, "She paid for dinner last night, so I had to do something. I mean, she did pick me up and invite me out for dinner!"

"Tommy!" She blushed. "That's not true!"

"Let me tell you the story, Drs. Logan"—I turned on my most charming Irish political smile—"and I'll let you be the judges."

After we had collected our food from the array of

tables—and I chose enough for lunch and supper—I told the story. But not before Christy Logan complained about my selections.

"Nothing but waffles and bacon, Tommy Flynn? That's not healthy!"

"I'll make up for it all week long. Now, as to the true story about what happened at the Ghirardelli chocolate shop on Friday last. . . ."

I told a true story, though not the whole truth, starting from my coming upon the Domer soccer team on TV. I left out my prurient fantasies after the game, my call to Bishop Blackie, and Christy's crack about virgins' need for something sweet. However, I told the story with enough comic elaboration to keep the Logans, all three of them, laughing till the end.

"They love you," she whispered to me after brunch. "You pick up your swimsuit and I'll meet you in the club. It's right down that staircase."

"Yes, ma'am."

I grabbed my suit, which I had left at the desk of the Hancock Center, and rode back to the lobby floor of the Ritz, eager to see my young lioness in one or the other form of advanced undress.

She was back to jeans and sweatshirt when she met me at the door of the club.

"Promise you won't laugh at me?" she begged.

"Why would I do that?"

"I think I might have gone too far with my swimsuit."

"I doubt it."

"Mom and Dad thought you were wonderful. They said I showed excellent taste in the young men I pick up."

"No doubt about it."

I arrived in the empty pool area first and climbed into the spa. Christy emerged from the women's locker room a few minutes later, wrapped protectively in a towel.

"Promise you won't laugh?"

"I've already promised."

"Promise again?"

"I promise again."

She tossed aside the towel and jumped into the spa, as if to hide in its whirling waters.

"I'm gawking again, Christy, not laughing."

She snorted suspiciously and favored me with her warning frown.

Her modest two-piece swimsuit was not quite a bikini, but it did reveal a lot of my All-American soccer star, more than enough to deprive me temporarily of my power of speech.

She hunched her shoulders and cowered.

"I look ridiculous," she muttered darkly.

"You look like exactly what you are—a sumptuous young lioness, elegant, graceful, and so beautiful that I can hardly talk."

She looked up suspiciously, "I'm getting tired of that lioness metaphor."

I touched her belly with delicate fingers. Solid rock. She stiffened but didn't pull away from me.

"Young woman, listen to me."

"Yes, sir."

"Some idiot, probably a guy you wouldn't sleep with, caught you in a vulnerable moment and made fun of your height and strength, compared you, maybe, to those women who pump iron, and shattered your confidence in your loveliness."

"How do you know that?" she growled.

I moved my fingers along her belly. "Isn't it true?"

"Yes," she growled again.

"Two growls from Ms. Simba, better than a roar!"

She laughed and relaxed.

"I guess I still do like that metaphor."

"That miserable bastard lied. Now look into my eyes and see in their awe that he lied."

She carefully considered my eyes. "Pretty blue eyes . . . hungry eyes . . . and, oh, yes, Tommy Flynn, adoring eyes!"

Then tears and her head on my shoulder. "You seem to like Ms. Simba's belly, Mr. Lion Tamer."

"Solid muscle."

She eased away. "Always will be. . . . Now, let's swim. We didn't come here to lollygag around in a whirlpool."

She moved to climb out of the spa. I took her hand and gently pulled her back in.

"There's no rush, Christy. I'm entitled to more gawking time."

She slipped back into the waters and continued to cling to my hand. We sat in silence, enjoying the warmth and each other's nearness. I did not want ever to leave the spa, so completely had I sunk into the swamp in the last forty-eight hours. This extraordinary young woman had captivated, enthralled, enchanted me. I was in love with her, already more involved with her than I had ever been before with a woman. I shouldn't be here holding her hand. Yet I was and I didn't want to let go. It would all disappear in the cold gray light of Monday morning. For the moment, I was in permanent paradise.

"Isn't my mom gorgeous?" she said suddenly. "I mean, for someone who is kind of old."

The blarney took command.

"Your mom is not kind of old," I insisted. "She is at the zenith of her life. Treat her with more respect."

"You're so sweet, Tommy," she sighed.

"Moreover, since you are a clone of your mother, a

wise trader would go long on you as a commodity future."

She glared at me as she tried to figure it out. Then she got it.

"I'm not a commodity, Tommy Flynn," she retorted in mock anger. She pulled away from my grip and jumped gracefully into the pool. "Come on, I'll race you."

"No way."

Our swim, as she had promised, was hard work. Naturally, she swam an aggressive crawl that wore me out in five minutes. I didn't try to keep up with her. I'd never be able to keep up with her anyway.

Our lovely autumn day had turned to rain when I escorted her to her car in the bowels of Water Tower Place. We were quiet and thoughtful, she back in her uniform of jeans and sweatshirt and running shoes and "Captain Christy" jacket. Her hair back in its ponytail, she looked like a sixteen-year-old, though a very pretty sixteen-year-old.

"My e-mail address is easy to remember," she said with a giggle. "It's *Christy@soccer.ndu.edu*."

"Not Captain Christy?"

"I thought about just "Captain," but I decided that would be arrogant. . . . What's yours?"

She opened the door of her aging Taurus and slung her shoulder bag into the back seat. I held the car door for her.

"*Gaylord123@aol.com,* as in Gaylord Ravenal, riverboat gambler. . . . Don't I get a good-bye kiss?"

She jumped out of the car, hugged me furiously, and kissed me long and hard. I had no choice but to respond.

"I love you, Tommy Flynn," she said as she jumped back into the car and turned over the ignition. She waved, backed the car out, and sped off, leaving me to hold up my hand in a dubious farewell. Such easy conquests are your young lionesses.

Or maybe so easily do they trap hunters.

Anyway, it had been a breathlessly romantic weekend. It was all over and that was that. But it had been fun, great fun.

I wandered disconsolately back to my apartment and turned on the TV. A golf tournament in the Sunbelt. I turned it off and picked up *Finnegans Wake*. I threw it aside. Someone had told me how it ended. I surveyed the rest of my books. A Laurie King mystery would have to do. Before I started it, however, I called Bishop Blackie and asked him for the phone number of the therapist I was supposed to see. He insisted that I mention his name. She owed him a favor.

In Chicago even psychiatrists owe favors.

Blackie

9

ANCHOR: A month ago, Bishop Augustus O'Sullivan Quill came to Chicago amid rumors that he was slated to replace Sean Cardinal Cronin. These rumors were promptly denied by the Chicago Chancery, although Bishop Quill has never denied them. Shortly after Bishop Quill's arrival, Cardinal Cronin dispatched him to Forty Holy Martyrs rectory in Forest Hills, about as far from the Chicago Chancery as one could go and still remain in the Archdiocese of Chicago. Channel Six has learned that not all is well in that parish. Our Mary Jane McGurn reports from Forest Hills.

(Ms. McGurn appears in front of a white stone gothic church.)
M.J.: That's right, Terri. If Bishop Quill should become Archbishop of Chicago, Catholics will not be happy campers if the reaction to him up here in Forest Hills is any indication. Bishop Quill succeeded Father Matt Dribben, who retired at the age of seventy. He promptly fired most of the parish staff—the director of religious education, the director of liturgy, two deacons,

and the principal of Forty Holy Martyrs school.

(A smartly dressed and groomed matron appears on screen. The subtitle tells us that she is Ms. Loretta Heany, a former member of the Forty Holy Martyrs parish council.)

L.H.: He didn't consult with us about these dismissals. We met with him and asked why he had fired men and women who had done such fine work. He said he had prayed over the problem and concluded that they were not sufficiently loyal to the Holy Father and that it was his duty as a bishop to see that only those loyal to the Holy Father worked in our parish. We pointed out that several of these people had long-term contracts. He replied that he did not feel bound by the contracts his predecessor had entered into. We protested his arbitrary behavior and he dismissed us too. The next day he also fired the school board and the finance committee.

M.J.: What are the parishioners doing about this?

L.H.: They're attending Mass at other parishes. We have learned that the collection last Sunday was down eight thousand dollars.

M.J.: We also talked to the chairman of the parish athletic program. *(High-powered businessman on screen, John Creaghan by name.)*

M.J.: What happened to the athletic program, Mr. Creaghan?

J.C.: The Bishop phoned me one night to say that he was terminating the sports program, of which we are very proud of around here. He said that the Holy Father wanted us to help the poor and he could not approve of parish funds being spent on sports. I told him that the money was contributed privately at a dinner dance for the program. He said that didn't matter, it was still parish money. He also said he didn't approve of sports for young women.

M.J.: What will you do?

J.C.: We've scheduled another dinner dance. We'll go ahead without him. He probably won't let us use the gym. I like the Cardinal a lot. But he didn't consult with us before he sent Quill up here. If he doesn't take him back, this parish church will be empty in another month or two.

M.J.: Dissatisfaction is not limited to adults. We interviewed two students at Forty Holy Martyrs School. Their faces are obscured to protect them from reprisal. (*Two adorable sixth-graders. Names not given.*)

BOY: He comes around the school and tells us how much the Pope loves him. He's a creep!

GIRL: We young women have the right to a sports program of our own. I think he's disgusting!

M.J.: We asked the Chicago Chancery for a comment on the situation up here in Forest Hills. We were told that Cardinal Cronin has ordered Bishop Quill to rehire the staff members who were fired and to restore the athletic program. There's no sign of that happening up here, however.

ANCHOR: Were you able to talk to Bishop Quill himself, Mary Jane?

M.J. (*Who has been saving this up*): We tried to, Terri. (*Screen shows Bishop—in full robes—scurrying out of church and trying to get to the rectory. M.J. interrupts him with her mike.*)

M.J.: Bishop, do you have any comments on the unrest in Forty Holy Martyrs parish?

B.Q.: You should be home taking care of your children, young woman. (*Brushes mike away*)

M.J.: That about says it all. . . . This is Mary Jane McGurn reporting from Forty Holy Martyrs rectory in Forest Hills.

Mercifully I turned off the TV, after fumbling with the wrong buttons for a few moments. Sean Cardinal

Cronin was slumped in my easy chair, his face buried in his hands.

I sighed loudly.

"All right, Blackwood, you said I should have sent him as chaplain to an old people's home. You were right."

"What happens if he refuses your orders?"

"Then I will remove him as pastor."

"There will be a canonical process over that. It will take time."

"I know, Blackwood, I know. However, I can appoint an administrator to the parish."

"The Vatican won't like the public scandal in a trial."

"I think you're wrong there. They'll agree that the guy is a public embarrassment."

"Perhaps."

He knew more about the Vatican than I did and was usually very canny in dealing with them. A tape of the broadcast would doubtless go to the Nunciature and to the Secretariat of State.

He sat up and removed his hands from his face.

"Even his brother can't stand him."

"Peter Quill? Unless I am mistaken, he is on your finance committee."

"You know damn well he is, Blackwood. . . . He says to me, 'Idiot is still an idiot and will never change.' He thinks I should get him the hell out of there."

"My—"

The phone rang. It was Ted Coffey, Gus's old colleague at the Tribunal. I gently touched the button on the speaker phone.

"I told you, Blackwood, that the guy was vicious. He's sick. Sean has to get him out of there."

"Ah!"

"He's never had much authority before. He tried to get himself appointed officialis here and that didn't work. So he went to Rome, where they called him Alpine Augustus at the Villa Stritch, where the American bureaucrats live. He tried for years to become chief of the Rota and they kept fending him off. I saw him around the Tribunal. He was oily with his superiors and his colleagues and terrorized the secretarial staff. He's a Nazi."

"Arguably."

"He belongs in the nuthouse."

"That's a point of view. You should write one of your stories about him."

"No one would believe it."

Having made his case, Ted hung up.

"Ted is a little strong, isn't he, Blackwood? The mess up in Forty Holy Martyrs doesn't affect him or his parish."

"So I observed."

"I didn't know he wrote stories, but then what do I know?"

"Fantasy stories for small fantasy magazines. Under the name of Burke T. Burke. He started writing, he says, to escape the horror of burying a teenager every week or two when he was in Hispanic work."

"You've read his stories?"

"Glanced at them. Unquestionably literate and intelligent. Too mannered for my taste, but then I don't particularly like fantasy. The real world is more than fantastical enough."

"We're going to have to do something about Gus."

"Oh, yes."

For weal or woe, someone else did something about him first.

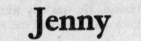

Jenny

10

We eat at the new Chevarin's. He is polite and attentive. We waste little time before we become serious. The loneliness is terrible, he says. I agree and add, The embarrassment of becoming a teenager again wars with the loneliness. So much fear, he says. Fear of death. He smiles sadly. We didn't have that when we were teens. Is there any way, I say, to contend with loneliness besides sex? For some people, maybe. Then he adds, By the way, Jenny, the image of you as a naked slave matron on the auction block is utterly charming. My face becomes very warm. A chauvinist image, I say. *Playboy.* He sighs, not really. Someone to be rescued. I have to hold back my tears. Incorrigibly romantic, I say. That's me, he laughs. What will you do with the slave matron when you rescue her? Take her home, he replies promptly. And then? Love her and protect her for the rest of my life. I tell myself I wouldn't mind being taken home and loved and protected. You'd screw her long before you get her home. Only if she wanted me to and only tenderly. I snort skeptically. We're flirting. Dangerously. We turn quickly to lighter matters.

He touches my lips with his at the entrance of my apartment building. If this is the beginning of a courtship, it will be a long and leisurely one. I like that. I do not remember my dreams, but they are about him, sweet and reassuring dreams, just as he is a sweet and reassuring man. I wake up happy for the first time in a long time.

The man pursues me relentlessly. He is skillful and confident. He knows how to attract and arouse a woman. He senses my terror, which amuses him. Therefore, he will not take me. I will have to surrender myself. That seems to amuse him too. Everything about me amuses him. Yet I see the pain of memory in his eyes. He thinks he can slake the agony of loss with me. I am a replacement, an amusing, distracting replacement. I will never be more than that. My therapist is angry at me for framing the situation in that way. Why can't you be content with what is? she asks. Does he not ease the memories of your husband and your hatred for that terrible bishop whose life you threatened and on whom you still fixate? I can't help my dreams. She sighs. You can help the illusions you recall in your dreams. They are so real, I protest.

He sends me gifts almost every day. Flowers, candy, jewelry, shameless and expensive lingerie, which I eagerly put on. He writes me slightly erotic sonnets that tear at my heart. He briefly caresses my thigh in the darkness of the opera, which is probably my fault for wearing a skirt with a long slit. He touches my breasts, a touch that, despite the layers of clothes that protect me, sends an electric shock through my body. He does all the things a man would do who wants to seduce a woman so that he owns her, body and soul. Despite his delicacy and restraint, he is still an aroused animal who, when he does own me, will consume me with hungry fury. Sometimes I want to be consumed with such hungry fury. I know that when he is inside of me, he will be thinking of his wife. I will be little more than an obscene picture. My shrink says I should either end the relationship or surrender. I hate that bishop even more than I hate my husband. He is a gross, vulgar, evil man.

We meet each other's children. I am nervous. Children, even grown children, resent stepparents. Mine, however, promptly adore him. Mom, are you sleeping with him? my daughter asks. That's a terrible question to ask your mother. Yeah, but are you? Not yet, I say, my face hot. Well, don't let him get away. You're entitled to a lover like him. He certainly worships you. He can't take his eyes off you. His eyes won't leave my clothes on, I protest. So what's wrong with that, Mom?

The next day, his children are less obvious. They are polite and friendly but, I am afraid, sizing me up skeptically. Don't worry, one of his daughters whispers to me, we like you a lot. We're just dazed by how lovely you are. My face is hot again. Thank you, I say, close to tears. We're on your side, she adds. He'll be very good to you. She's close to tears too. Later, her brother says as we're leaving, we already love you, Jenny.

And you think you're not worth loving, Dr. Murphy says. I'm only a substitute for his wife. His children want to have a substitute for his wife to make him happy. His wife is dead, Jenny; you're not competing with her. Every minute I'm with him, I say, I feel she's haunting us. Sometimes, Jenny, despite your intelligence, you're a damn fool.

He takes me to his church, the Cathedral. There is a cute, funny little bishop greeting people as they go in. I think he may be Dr. Murphy's brother. I almost say something about the other bishop. I know he doesn't like him either. He preaches. He quotes from a book by Annie Dillard.

God is no more blinding people with glaucoma, or testing them with diabetes, or purifying them with spinal pain, or choreographing the seeding of tumor cells through lymph nodes, or fiddling chromosomes than he is jimmying floodwaters or pitching tornadoes at towns. God is no more cogitating which among us he plans to place here as bird-headed dwarfs or elephant men—or to kill by AIDS, kidney failure, heart disease, childhood leukemia, or sudden infant death syndrome—than he is pitching lightning bolts at pedestrians, triggering rock slides, or setting fires. The very least likely thing for which God might be responsible are what insurers call acts of God. . . .

God, he says, suffers when we suffer. Jesus reveals to us the suffering of God. He is always nailed to the cross. God is always suffering. For some reason these words sear my soul. I begin to weep, then to sob. The man puts his arm around me, not understanding yet understanding. At times like this, he really is like God for me. Now, he even suffers with me.

At brunch afterwards, he caresses my thigh. I almost invite him back to my apartment, but I don't. Like Dr. Murphy says, I am a damn fool.

Ramon and Luis

11

"The man is quite mad," Luis says.

"Dangerously mad," Ramon agrees.

"Is there any reason to think he has been promised he will succeed Cronin?"

"Our people in Rome, who would know, say that there are absolutely no grounds for that belief."

"Yet he has come much farther than his intelligence or ability warrants."

"So have many others."

"That is true."

"Nonetheless, it seems very unlikely. We must be cautious with him."

"We will not, however, provide the money for the television station he wants?"

"That is a quite absurd proposal. Yet he is very serious about it."

"I fear he took our reserve as agreement. His kind often does."

"That is true."

"It would seriously embarrass us."

"That is also true."

"We must distance ourselves from him."

"That may prove very difficult."

"One understands how Cronin must feel."

They both laugh wryly.

"It would be most useful if he could be discredited."

"Yes, it would."

"However, we must not appear to be involved."

Jenny

12

The pursuit must end. I am aroused all the time. We both must find release, if only for the sake of our sanity. I say to him at supper, I have a naked matron back at my apartment that I might raffle off tonight. He gulps, surprised and pleased. Maybe frightened too. Frightened? I ask him. His face colors. Naked matrons, he says, are glorious prizes, but they are also a serious challenge. They tend to surrender pretty quickly, I say. At the apartment I show him the painting I have developed from my graphic. I didn't know you painted, Jenny, he says. This is wonderful. So is she. You see yourself very clearly. We face each other, both of us frightened. He opens the first button on my blouse. I cringe with sweet terror. His fingers go to the second button.

Later, I am exhausted and content in his arms. He has been very good, overwhelming me with his savage hunger. Ben was never savage, only mean. Perhaps I like savage men, who are not mean. He does not fall asleep. He continues to kiss and caress me. I feel like I am some kind of spoiled goddess. Naked matrons are a lot of fun, he says with a laugh as he tickles me. I think I'll keep this one. She amuses me. She didn't have much choice, I reply as I squirm.

Then his mood changes. He rolls over and pins me to the bed so I can't move. You belong to me now, woman, he says sternly. You're mine. I'll never let you go. That doesn't leave me much freedom, I say. All the freedom in the world to run away, he says. And I have all the freedom to chase you. Then he reaches over to his jacket pocket and removes a box. In it is a huge emerald ring. We usually brand our slave matrons before we take them away. This is your brand. He puts it on the ring finger of my left hand, a claim staked out. Then he takes me again. Spectacularly.

I wear the ring on a chain around my neck, between my boobs. My psychiatrist doesn't see it. You look very happy this morning, she says. I'm ecstatic. Will it last? I don't know. Probably not. And the man? Right now, he's like a god to me. Is it mostly up to you whether this lasts? That's not fair. I'm not talking fair. Yes, it's mostly up to me. Then I tell her he gave me a ring, an emerald. You're not wearing it? Around my neck. Does he consider it an engagement ring? More like a wedding ring. Ah, he plans to marry you? He's always planned that. I'd rather be his mistress than his second wife. Time, she says impatiently.

He knocks at the door to my apartment. I am wearing a terry-cloth robe. I have put a larger one on the table near the door. As soon as he enters, I begin to undress him, as though it were a businesslike procedure that I had done many times. He frowns, his modesty offended. Turnabout is fair play, I tell him. He smiles and relaxes. He has such a beautiful body, lean, hard, strong. You'll do till I find someone better, I say as I toss him the robe and lead him towards the bathroom. I can hardly believe I'm doing this. However, it is too late to stop.

I take off his robe and point to the shower. Reluctantly and awkwardly he enters. He doesn't like this. However, he's going along with me. He changes his mind when I join him and we lather and bathe and tickle and tease one another. We laugh and giggle and play. He now is enjoying the game enormously. I've never been in a shower with a woman, he says. It won't be the last time, I promise him. I hope not, he gasps, it beats taking one by yourself. Cheap erotic entertainment, I reply. Better than a porno flick and with a live actress. He moans with pleasure. I'm dizzy. He takes me into his arms in preparation for intercourse. I lightly push him away. Not yet, I say. Not till I'm ready and in the way I want. He bites his lip and nods his head. I hope this establishes, I say, that sometimes I will be the one in control of sexual matters—as well as others. Anytime you want, he gasps.

Later, I dry him off and take him to bed. We make love my way. He screams with pleasure and then falls asleep, utterly exhausted. I am greatly pleased with myself. Tonight I am the boss. He is my dear, beautiful slave. I dream of Bishop Quill being in the shower with me.

Proudly I tell Dr. Murphy about the interlude, without the details, the next day. So you think there was rich symbolism in taking sexual control away from him, she says skeptically. You think this signifies a change in the distribution of power in the relationship. Maybe, I say. He knows I'm more than just a receptacle. He did not know that before? she asks. I suppose he did. Now he knows it vividly. She nods and waits for me to say more, damn her. I never had the nerve to act like that before. For an amateur I think I was pretty good. Did he? His mind was blown. He'll never forget it. . . . The times I tried it with Ben, he slapped me. Slapped you! You never told me that he slapped you. Whenever he was impatient with me. Not hard; enough to hurt, not enough to leave a mark. We must ask later why you never told me. Now I want to know whether you have some confidence in your own sexual powers. I shrug. Enough to know I will do that again whenever I want to.

You ignore the most important part of the interlude, don't you? What's that? You know, tell me. No, I don't. Come on, Jenny, you know better than to play these games with me. I surprised him. No woman ever loved him that way before. Not even his sorely missed wife? Apparently not. Does it not occur to you that, for all her wonderful traits, she might not have been very good in bed? I wouldn't dare think that. The hell you wouldn't. Furthermore, does it not occur to you that your sexual skills, however recently acquired, might outshine hers? I have no way of knowing that. Is it just possible that you might be an utterly different sexual experience for him, one that he has only dreamed of and which surprises and overwhelms him? I hadn't thought that, maybe you're right. Maybe I can make him forget his wife. It would be wrong to forget her, she insists, a betrayal. My point is that he can value you for what you are without forgetting her. Do you know how many men his age in life yearn for a partner like you? So therapy has made me a pretty good whore. You're an asshole, Jenny, she says, and it's time.

She's right. If I admit it to her, there will be no running away. In the office, he sees me and rolls his eyes. We are very discreet there. However, everyone knows. They are silently cheering for us.

* * *

Another time, after Sunday brunch at his apartment, he is inside of me, just beginning to thrust. He pauses. You are astonishingly transparent, Jenny, he tells me. You have no defenses anymore. I can slip into the beautiful crystal waters of your soul just as easily as I slip into your body. Hardly a time for poetry, I think. You can slip into my body easily, I reply, because you have made me soaking wet with all the things you've done to me. I could spend the rest of our lives plumbing the depths of your astonishing mystery and only begin to know you. Still, the exploration will be pure joy.

This is all very lovely, I think. Maybe what's happened to me in the last few years have made me totally vulnerable. Maybe I've lost, or am losing, all my defenses. Why, however, does he pick this time when I'm already squirming with need to talk about it? I say to him, and while you're exploring these mysterious depths you can fuck me whenever you want. I use words like "fuck" and "screw," which I have never used before, and which he never uses because it shocks him. I enjoy that too. For the love of God, I cry, time-out's over! Let us get on with the game! Indeed, he says, as he begins to thrust again, for the love of God. I tell myself later, as I nap in his arms, that I guess I can put up with the poetry.

He tells me that I am losing my defenses, I tell Dr. Murphy. That I have become transparent. Do you think that's true, Jenny? I don't know. Maybe. Is it harder to hide? Physically, I can't hide at all. Emotionally . . . I don't know. Would you like it if most of your defenses vanished, at least with him, so that you became almost totally vulnerable in his presence? I'd be terrified. You know that's the price you will have to pay if you continue with him? I understand that, I say.

In fact, I'd never quite understood it that way before. So? I don't know.

He drives me to a small home he owns on a lake to see the autumn leaves. It is a secluded spot in the woods, on the shore of a smooth, silver lake. Perfect for an assignation, I say. Is that what this is? he asks. Just a nice domestic weekend with some fucking thrown in for amusement.

We are very domestic. He lights a fire. I prepare the meals. I fear her presence in the house, but there are no traces of her. We walk in the woods and sing together. There is no strain between us. One weekend is not a true test. I am not surprised that we are compatible. That's not the problem.

I sketch a little. He tells me I'm astonishingly good and that I should do it more often. I know that. I've known it for years. Then I do him a little sketch of me peeling off his clothes. He is disconcerted but he loves it. I tell him that I may do a whole series on him as a lover. I can hardly wait, he says.

We attend Mass at a small local parish on Saturday afternoon. He drives the car with one hand and explores my thigh under my miniskirt with the other. I don't stop him. He reaches my most tender region and stops. I gasp. He laughs and continues. I am tumescent when we leave the car for Mass. Bastard, I tell him. He laughs. You'll have to wait till after supper. I'm not going to ruin my beef Stroganoff, just because you can't keep your hands to yourself. He laughs again. I do too.

The sermon is terrible. However, I pretend to listen intently. Since turnabout is fair play, I torment him on the way back to the cabin. The Stroganoff can keep. After dinner we sit on the porch and watch the sun set behind the pines and the lake turn black. We sip the port I had brought along. What are your imperfections, Jenny? You're the one who slips into the mystery of my soul. How do you see them? I have lots of imperfections, I tell him. The worst one is fear. You are afraid now? Yes. Of what? That I don't deserve the happiness I feel and that it will slip away. Odd, he says, I feel the same way.

The next morning we are like comfortable married people. We eat our breakfast—Belgian waffles with sausage and a fruit cocktail—in our robes and sip tea and read the papers as we watch the Sunday morning television. He calls me Maureen once and does not notice. I would never call him Ben. I let it go. The second time, I challenge him. I'm Jenny, I say firmly. Dear Lord, he says, shocked and embarrassed, I'm terribly, terribly sorry. I'm furious. I want to go home now. She is here after all, haunting me. Astonishing words come out of my mouth. No problem. I understand. It's all right. He holds my hand tightly. Thank you, he says. Don't worry about it, I say. I won't get angry when it happens. It's perfectly natural. I've turned on the spa, he says. It will warm up in a hurry. How warm is it outside? I ask. It will be in the seventies by noon. Have you ever made love outside? I ask him. No, he says. Neither have I, I admit. I suppose we will have to try it. This will show him that I am not angry, that I don't mind a competition that I am certain to win. He needs a little healing. Why not? He agrees. So we try it.

Late in the day, he became impatient with me when we were preparing to drive back to Chicago. Jenny, leave that stuff. We should be on the road. I cowered. Don't be angry at me, I begged. I'm sorry. His eyes were wide in surprise. I'm not going to hit you, Jenny. I'm sorry I was impatient. Your instinct to clean everything up was probably right. I stood in front of the sink, my head bowed. Here, let me help put things away.

He wasn't much good at it, but I let him help.

Ben hit you, Jenny. Slapped me, enough to hurt, not enough to leave a mark. He was pretty good at it. How often? He stood transfixed, a platter in one hand, the other on a cabinet door. Hundreds of times, I suppose. Not much at all at the beginning. A lot later on, when he said it was my fault he lost the Nobel. You didn't use it in the divorce? Finally, we did. My daughter, who had seen him do it, threatened to testify. He and his lawyer backed off. I'll never hit you, Jenny. Never. I know that. I'm sorry I made a fuss.

You didn't get angry at him when he called you by his wife's name, Dr. Murphy says in some surprise. No. Well, yes. I was very angry, but I didn't want to hurt him, so I kept my loud, shanty Irish mouth shut. So now you will never be able to humiliate him again when he slips. I guess not. You are improving, Jenny. You realize that your competition model is not very useful. I don't know, Dr. Murphy. Can you imagine a woman with a man like that and a hidden place like that who never once screwed him, excuse me, made love to him outdoors? Do you think he would have asked her, Jenny? It should not be up to the man to ask, I insist, astonished at myself.

He and I are sitting on the couch in his apartment, partially undressed, cuddling together like two companionable married people, relaxed and content. My boobs are bare, my bra hanging on my arms. He likes me that way. I don't know why men like boobs so much. However, they do, and that's their privilege. He begins to talk about himself. I am amazed. His parents were immigrants. He lived in poverty as a child, worked his way through high school and college and graduate school. He's proud of what he's done, but not sure that it wasn't mostly luck. He worries about the company, though it's in good shape. He has enough money to retire tomorrow and wonders what he would do then.

He and his wife married young, high school sweethearts. She was pretty and vivacious, though her health had been poor even as a child. Her spirit was wonderful, but her poor body couldn't keep up with her. As the children came along, she experienced one health problem after another. Gradually, she became an invalid, brave, uncomplaining, and exhausted. He had become a caregiver, when he was not at the office. That was all right, he loved her. She was sad because she had become a burden. It wasn't a burden, but it was still difficult. She told him often during her final days that he should remarry quickly. He refused even to think of it. He had fallen out of the habit of sexual love and felt he could do without it. He dated only occasionally, afraid of that world at his age. After two years, however, the loneliness tore at him. It was all right during the day. At night here, in the apartment, it seemed like hell. Then they had hired me, as he saw it, a poised, intelligent, sexually appealing woman. He wanted me, all of me. He was frightened of the agonies of the pursuit until I gave him a sign that it would be all right. Even then he was terrified of a misstep—that he would, in his hunger and awkwardness, not respect me.

We are both weeping. I thought you were a skilled, polished seducer, I tell him. Your instincts were flawless. He is surprised. He says that he's probably a bad risk. I laugh and tell him that he's the best that's likely to come along. I draw him close and caress his face. He sighs contentedly. I tell myself that neither of us is what the other thought. That's all right. I now love him much more than I had before. I offer him a boob. He licks the nipple gently till it is ready. Then he draws on it with his lips. Fire rushes through me. He needs a wife and a mother and a mistress. What man doesn't? When we make love later, it is gentle and sweet, the best yet.

He is not the man you thought he was, Dr. Murphy tells me. He's better, I reply. More complicated, more problematic, more fragile, she says. More human, I say. Not the challenging sexual conquest you expected? Still that, and now a challenging human being. You can deal with that? Certainly, I tell her. I want to. I know I can. Why so much more confident? Because he gave himself to me last night. Then I add, besides, I told my husband, my ex-husband, to fuck off yesterday. What! He borrows money from me. Calls me and demands a couple of thousand dollars or he will try to reopen the divorce settlement. I know he won't be successful if he tries that. However, I want to avoid the hassle. Yesterday he was quite rude. You're sleeping with a rich man. You can afford to help. After all it's your fault that I didn't win the prize. You owe it to me. He is completely convinced that it is my fault because I distracted him from his work. It's none of your business whom I'm sleeping with, I tell him. How many times have you been unfaithful to your trophy wife? He warns me about going back to court. I tell him never to ask me for money again. He tells me that I will regret my refusal. Then I tell him to fuck off. I don't feel guilty either.

I put my head in my hands. The man and I are two flawed and wounded people, Dr. Murphy. Not as badly flawed and wounded as others, but still far from what we might have been and should be now. Still we can carve out some happiness together in whatever time we have left. I have no doubt of that anymore. You're be-

coming a dangerous woman, Jenny, she tells me. You
like yourself that way. Now it's time.

I see him at the office and am sexually aroused. Tumescent all the time. I encounter him in a corridor. Free
at lunchtime? I ask him. Yes, he says. Want to grab a
bite to eat? No. No? Is the apartment the firm keeps
for guests free? Yes, it is. Good, I'll see you there at
noon. Oh, yes, Dr. Murphy, I've become a very dangerous woman.

Peter

13

"I had lunch with my brother at the club today, Grace. It was a hellish experience. As soon as we walked in the place became as quiet as a funeral home. Some of my best friends turned their backs on me. Two women got up and walked out. Sure, I tried to point these things out to him. But you know Idiot. He only sees the things he wants to see.

" 'Do you realize what you are doing to me and my family?' I said to him when we were seated. 'We don't dare show our faces in public. They blame us for you.'

"He tucked his napkin into his Roman collar and dug into his salad. You know the way he eats, systematic, dogged, disgusting.

" 'I don't understand what you are talking about, Peter.'

" 'All the things you've done at the parish—firing those people, dismissing the parish council, closing down the sports program. People hate you and they hate me because I'm your brother.'

" 'I'm doing only what the Holy Father wants me to do,' he said calmly. 'I became convinced that those men and women were not teaching sound Catholic doctrine and morality. If I am to be true to my mission as a bishop, I must dismiss them.'

" 'And insulting that young reporter on camera... Now you'll have the media against you all the time.'

"He kept munching away at his salad like a self-satisfied little rabbit.

" 'Someone needed to speak the truth to her. The Holy Father tells us that mothers of young children should not work unless they absolutely have to.'

" 'My wife Grace works, Peter.'

"The main course arrived. He began to cut the beef into tiny bite-size pieces like he always does.

" 'But she opened her store only after the children were raised. The Holy Father does not object to that.'

" 'Don't you have any thoughts of your own? Does the Pope do all your thinking for you?'

" 'The Pope is the Vicar of Christ. He tells us what Christ wants us to think.'

" 'Are you going to follow Cronin's orders about restoring jobs to those people you fired?'

" 'I will have to pray over it, Peter. It would not be wise at this time to risk an open fight with him, even though I believe he is close to heresy.'

" 'For the love of heaven, don't say that on television!'

" 'I do not intend to say anything on television. The media are the enemies of the Church. I plan, with the help of the Legion of Corpus Christi, to open my own television station here to preach true Catholic doctrine to all the faithful.'

" 'Those creeps.'

" 'They are loyal to the Most Holy Father.'

"I was so disgusted by the way he ate the meat that I couldn't touch my own food.

" 'When are you going to launch your TV station?'

" 'In God's own good time.'

" 'Are you really going to be the next archbishop of Chicago, Idiot?'

" 'I have been given reason to believe that, Peter. Yes, I have.'

" 'When?'

" 'Whenever the Most Holy Father directs me to assume control.'

"He's shrewd, Grace, not nearly as dumb as he sometimes sounds. He realizes now that he can't afford to get into an open fight with Cronin, who has plenty of friends in Rome. . . .

"Do I think the Pope really sent him to Chicago to straighten out the mess? I'm not sure. He sincerely believes it, no doubt about it. But you know how he is, he misreads what people say to fit his own fantasies. I kind of doubt it. Cronin doesn't seem worried. He chatted with me at the last finance committee meeting when some of the other guys wouldn't look me in the eye. . . .

"Sure I talked to Idiot about your shop. Over dessert—well, his dessert. He slogged down a huge helping of chocolate ice cream, smeared his napkin.

"I said to him, 'Idiot, do you know what this is doing to my business? I lost five big accounts in the last two days. One man said to me that he wanted no part of a relative of yours.'

" 'That is unjust,' he said calmly.

" 'No one comes into Grace's shop anymore. She has the reputation of selling the finest dresses in Forest Hills. Now her clients are going to the mall instead.'

" 'That, too, is unjust,' he says, wiping chocolate off his mouth, 'and I regret your difficulties. But I must follow God's will and do what I have been sent to Chicago to do. This is only the first phase. When people see that this is how the Most Holy Father wants a bishop in Chicago to act, they will respond with enthusiastic faith.'

" 'And we may be broke.'

" 'Surely, Peter, you exaggerate,' he said. . . .

"Will he obey Cronin? I think he will. Sean is one tough son of a bitch when he has to be. Just like his old man. If I had to bet, I'd bet on Sean. But Idiot is tough in his own sloppy, goofy way too. . . .

"What do you mean, Grace? Well, yes, I agree with you, it would be helpful if we could find some way to take the wind out of his sails."

Tommy

14

The first sessions with the therapist, a handsome woman in her early sixties with probing gray eyes, were hellish.

"Why will you not admit that you have incestuous feelings about your stepmother?"

"I have admitted it, Dr. Ward. She's a knockout. I admire her. She's been wonderful for the family. I don't feel guilty for finding her sexually attractive."

"And she finds you sexually attractive?"

"I don't know. She likes me. I've been an ally. I think she finds me amusing."

"An ally? You did not resent her when she replaced your mother?"

"Resent her? I urged Dad to marry her. He needed a wife, the kids needed a mother."

"You did not resent her replacing your mother?"

I considered that.

"Not much to tell you the truth. My sisters did at first. I was happy that Mom was out of our hair."

"Once, however, you loved your mother very much."

"When I was a little boy and she sang and laughed and told me stories."

"When did you start to hate her?"

"It's hard to say. Probably when she started to hit my sisters."

"Hit them?"

"Mostly when she was drunk and they were unruly, as little kids are. They were too much for her."

"She had no help?"

"Dad hired a full-time nanny to do all the work. Still Mom could not stand them. That's when she moved out on us."

"So you have a very strong love-hate fixation on your mother?"

"Not much of anything anymore. I feel sorry for her. I don't think of her much. You're right, memories of love from early childhood, then anger afterwards."

I noticed that my hands were clenched and that my shirt was wet. I was fortunate that these sessions were after my morning at the Exchange, not before.

"Then you transferred these feelings to your step-mother?"

"And maybe to every other woman too?"

"You go too fast."

"I suppose I do. . . . You could say I love Beth. She's brought peace to the family. My sisters are making it into adulthood all right. I remember the first time I met her. . . ."

"And your reaction?"

"I was surprised that Dad had found such an attractive woman."

"You wanted her for yourself?"

I laughed.

"I don't deny it. . . . To be more specific, I hoped I

could find someone like her—good-looking, smart, tough."

"And her reaction to you?"

"She was frightened, of course. She saw me as a potential enemy."

"And you reacted?"

"You wouldn't believe it, but even at sixteen I could be a charming, genial Irishman. I turned on all my charm. I think she began to see me as an ally."

"I can believe it. Here was a mother figure you could desire safely."

"Hey, I'm not denying it. She decided that I was a potential ally. Which I was. Most of what she did with the girls, she did on her own. They identify with her totally. She asked me occasionally for suggestions and I made some on my own. It was a kind of professional relationship."

"You never felt any resentment towards her?"

I paused to examine my reactions.

"I went off to Georgetown when they were married. I suppose that if I had lived at home, something might have gone wrong. I'm not sure. I never had time to feel that she was getting too close and then push her away."

"Which is how you deal with other women?"

"That's my record so far."

"You do not live at home?"

"No. I felt it was better to stay out of their way. I wanted to feel I was independent, I guess."

"And the alluring presence of your stepmother would have been disturbing?"

Did Beth disturb me? You bet your life she did. Why hadn't I perceived that before?

"I didn't think of that then, but you're right. Neither of them needed me, except as an advisor on the telephone."

"You resented that?"

"I didn't think so then. Maybe I did. I just wanted to get out of the house."

"And this soccer person, is she like Beth?"

An obvious question. Had I fallen in love, if I had fallen in love, with a replica of my stepmother?

"Let me think about that. Neither of them is passive-aggressive like my mother. Both are strong women. Christy . . . she's a lioness. I wouldn't call Beth a lioness."

"What would you call her?"

"I'm not sure. . . . My point is that she's not as . . ."

"As what?"

"As fearsome as Christy."

"Fearsome? You fear the soccer girl?"

"Soccer woman."

"Of course." Dr. Ward permitted herself a small smile.

"No, I admire her courage and her strength and her determination."

"Domineering?"

"Doesn't need to be."

"Aha, that is very important. However, we are out of time."

I walked back to my apartment, feeling worn and discouraged. On the one hand, I hadn't learned anything I didn't already know. On the other hand, it all seemed new and vivid and deeply troubling. My thought at the end, that Christy didn't need to be domineering, was brand new. Like the shrink, I thought that was very important.

In the apartment I ate two cartons of yogurt, hardly a balanced lunch, and compensated for that by sinking my teeth into an apple.

I turned on my Dell Latitude LT and checked my e-mail.

The top message was from a certain *Christy@soccer. ndu.edu.* About time she wrote. Why should I take the first step, right?

> Hi Tommy,
>
> I'm so embarrassed. It's been hard to write this e-mail because I'm ashamed of my behavior over the weekend. You were very tolerant of me and I have to apologize to you. I have the biggest crush I've ever had in all my life on you. I threw myself at you like a silly fourteen-year-old. I was shameless. I don't know what happened. Maybe it was the mixture of laughter and pain in your pretty blue eyes. Anyway, I'm sorry I was such a geek. I don't blame you for not writing to me. You don't have to answer this letter.
> Christy Anne Logan☹

I turned off the computer. She was as flaky as the rest of them. Stupid kid with no sense at all. I was free of her. It would be easy. Just take her advice and not reply. I wouldn't even have to go back to my shrink.

I threw myself in my recliner chair and turned on the televison. ESPN.

God intervened again. We were back on the muddy pitch in South Bend. The Fighting Irish were taking on the Lady Huskies, a deadly serious foe and a serious competitor for the national championship. They had not one but two potential All-Americans.

Why do you do these things to me, God?

You don't have to watch her, asshole, God replied.

I know.

Naturally, I did watch her.

At the end of the game, er, match, I was drained. I remained in my recliner, exhausted, collapsed, wiped

out. Not so beat, however, that I didn't permit myself
a brief visit to her shower room. She was counting on
me being there, wasn't she?

I called up her letter from the "Old Mail" file and
fashioned a reply.

Dear Christy Anne Logan,

God played another one of her tricks on me this afternoon. I came home after a heavy session with my
shrink, feeling rotten and disgusted with myself and the
world. I turned on the TV, which happened to be on
ESPN, where it usually is. I found I was back on the
same swamp that you Domers call a soccer pitch and
that the Irish were fighting the dreaded Lady Huskies.

Well, there was one big difference between the
match and the one last week against the Lady Trojans—
besides the fact that the Lady Huskies are a dangerous
rival. The difference for me was that I was no longer a
mildly interested spectator, indulging in spectator sport.
The beautiful blond lioness rushing down the field was
now a woman I knew. She was, you should excuse the
expression, which is not intended to be possessive, my
Christy.

Why, I wondered, does this lovely young woman,
with whom I'm thoroughly besotted, play such a rough
game? Why does she have to roll over in the mud like
she's a two-year-old? Why does she lie there in the mud
after one particularly obnoxious Lady Husky knocks her
down like she's unconscious? Why do even the Lady
Huskies seem concerned about her? Do they think she
is indispensable for their Olympic trip? Will she ever get
up? Then she bounds up with a crazy grin, wipes the
mud off her face with her shirtsleeve, and keeps on playing. On the bench, the coach of the Fighting Irish looks
worried, but she knows better than to pull Captain
Christy Anne off the pitch unless a stretcher is needed.

I perceive that my Christy Anne is the strongest, fiercest, most determined woman on the pitch. I realize that I had better act right with her all the time, or I'll be clubbed like an unruly cub. I'll never dare to act like fat, old, lazy Simba.

The Lady Huskies are game, but they don't quite have it. They keep the score tied at 1—1 until the last five minutes of the second period. Then my fearsome lioness streaks among them and, with a mighty boot from her gorgeous leg, puts the Fighting Irish ahead. I note that she is limping. What's happened? Why doesn't the coach take her out? Probably because it would be worth her life if she tried!

Then to sew things up, she sets up one of her wings (is that the right word?) for a final score. Fighting Irish 3, Lady Huskies 1. Naturally! Even then the coach doesn't pull her out. When the ref blows her whistle, the defeated Huskies swarm around her to embrace her. They know who the champ is. Then she limps towards the locker room, chatting merrily with her teammates. I am reluctant to violate her privacy by joining her in the shower. I know, however, she will be disappointed if I'm not there. So I enter, respectfully, of course, and watch her wipe off all the mud, an awful lot of mud, if I may say so.

Now as for your confession of a crush? Tell me about it! I've never been so smitten in all my life! We'll just have to see how it works out and not run because it's all kind of scary.

Anyway, I'm sorry for not writing before today. Congratulations on your mighty victory. And take care of that ankle.

Love,
Tommy☺

Well, that was that. We were into the second phase of our love affair. Exploration, I suppose one could call

it. "Getting to know you." Here was where I usually
goofed up. If I survived through that . . .

My fantasy of her naked body in the shower was
now so intense and so sweet that sometime we'd have
to consider—ugly word—commitment. We were too
young. She was too young, and as Megan at the Cathedral said, I was certainly too young.

After supper I turned on the Dell again. As I expected, there was another e-mail.

Tommy, Tommy, dearest Tommy,

    I'm sitting here in front of my screen sobbing my
heart out. My ankle really hurts and I'm on codeine and
Empirin or something like that and am totally flaked out.
I'm feeling real sorry for myself, so I try my e-mail,
though I know you wouldn't answer and there was your
wonderful and funny and loving letter.

    Yes, we'll just have to see how it works out. I prom-
ise I'll never lose my nerve again.

    I'm too filled up with emotion to say anything else.

All my love,

Christy

Peter

15

"Have you heard the TV, Grace? . . . I know the store is open. This is important. The Idiot has disappeared. Perhaps we are rid of him. On an L train. After his Spanish lesson. He rides it part of the way back to Forest Hills and then his driver brings him back to the rectory. . . . Sure it's an affectation. And last night he wasn't on the usual train. They say that the train has disappeared too. . . .

"I know L trains don't disappear, Grace, though you've never been on one, so how would you know? . . . Yes, he's not at the rectory and he's not at the parish where they've been trying to teach him Spanish. . . .

"Of course the police know about it. It's on television. Maybe they won't find him. . . .

"I know it's one more disgrace for us, but after it's over they'll forget about him. . . .

"Yes, I hope so too.

"I have to go, Grace. The police are here to question me."

Luis and Ramon

16

"So matters arrange themselves well at last."

"I wonder if that is so."

"Why is that?"

"The fool had publicly aligned himself with our work. We may be blamed for his disappearance."

"That is possible."

"He may also reappear. We have no idea what condition he will be in or whom he might blame."

"With all the lies that are told about us, we may be suspected."

"What should we do."

"We must inform our superiors, of course."

"Naturally."

"We must also see whether any of our contacts in the police force can tell us anything."

"If he is dead, it is a great scandal, though possibly a relief for us."

"And if he is alive, his career will be finished. It will be very difficult for the fools who sent him here."

"Our friends in Rome will make that point."

Blackie

17

My candy bar in one hand and my Diet Coke in the
other, I drifted out of the terminal and into Albany
Park. The streets were lined with vast apartment buildings, with twenty or thirty apartments around large
courtyards. When they were built, before the Great Depression, they would have been considered moderately
luxurious, their face brick colorful, their windows large,
their rooms spacious. They appeared at the end of the
L line because they were only a half-hour from the
Loop and what was still in the countryside in those
days. Jews, with a long tradition of apartment-house
living behind them in Europe, had moved into the
neighborhood after the First War—or to put it better,
perhaps, after the first phase of the thirty-year war from
1914 to 1945. They left behind much less attractive
immigrant neighborhoods in Rogers Park and Douglas
Park. Synagogues, temples, community stores, and delicatessens sprang up on the main streets, especially on
Lawrence Avenue. One could walk the streets of Al-

bany Park in those days (I am told) and think one was in Brooklyn or Queens instead of Chicago.

Then, with changing times in the late forties and fifties, many of the Jewish residents made the pilgrimage, like other Americans, to the suburbs and their single-family homes, especially to Skokie. Some Jews remained in Albany Park, especially in newer single-family homes at the north end of the neighborhood. After them came families of almost every nation under heaven—Japanese, Indians, Pakistanis, Palestinians, Filipinos, Thais, Laotians, Vietnamese, Afghans, and especially Koreans. Most of these groups had strong family cultures and a work ethic that made white Americans look lazy. While there were troubles among teenagers and some gangs, the family ties were strong and Lawrence Avenue, while run down, was more cosmopolitan than it had ever been. Albany Park was the American melting pot of the 1990s.

I noted that a Jewish delicatessen on the corner of Lawrence and Kimball promised deluxe pastrami sandwiches, which meant pastrami with coleslaw in the sandwich. I resolved that I would stop there on the way back. I wandered down a couple of alleys off streets near Kimball. Three-story back porches had seen better days, perhaps, and the backyards were gravel instead of lawn, but the alleys were neat and orderly.

Did I know what I was looking for? Certainly. I was looking for Idiot Quill, who I was now convinced was not dead but, like the unfortunate motorman, uh, driver, lying somewhere in an alley, waiting to be found. Not necessarily in an alley close to the L terminal, but perhaps.

Why was I convinced? It would take me a long time to figure that out. An unconscionably long time, I might add.

I was about to give up my perhaps quixotic quest in

an alley behind apartment buildings in the fifty-one-hundred block of North Central Park. I noticed at the far end of the alley an irregular object against an old garage, one that, like most of the others, was far too small for contemporary cars, save the VW. The object looked like a roll of old tarpaulin, something that should not exist in this spotlessly clean alley.

I bent over the tarp and pulled it back. Indeed, it was Augustus O'Sullivan "Idiot" Quill in his shorts, which to my surprise were not purple. He was warm and there was a pulse in this throat—alive and moderately well and a problem for all kinds of folk, myself included.

Patently he had overdosed on some kind of narcotic—or more likely had been overdosed. I sighed, searched in my various pockets for my phone, feared that I had lost it back at the terminal, then discovered that some malicious leprechaun had hidden it in the pocket of my obsolete Bulls jacket.

I was lucky enough to punch Mike the Cop's number the first try.

"Reilly Gallery, Annie Reilly."

"Truly," I said.

"Yes, of course, who else . . . Is that you, Blackie? I have a huge collection of oatmeal-raisin cookies for you when you get a chance, and apple-cinnamon tea to go along with them."

"I can resist anything but temptation, especially by such delights, as you well know."

"You're on the Bishop Quill case? You want to speak to Mike?"

"Alas for my fading gallantry, yes."

"Blackie . . . Find anything?"

"Oh, yes. In point of fact, I found the pastor of Forty Holy Martyrs Church in Forest Hills."

"I figured you would. Alive?"

"It would seem so. . . . My problem is that I have no direct link to the ingenious John Culhane. Perhaps you could seek him out and tell him he can find two bishops, one as conscious as he usually is, which may not be very conscious, and the other OD'd on, if I am not mistaken, some variety of heroin."

"And where can he find these prelates?"

"In an alley behind the fifty-one-hundred block on North Central Park."

"I'll call him. Be careful, Blackie."

I then pushed the "1" button.

"Cronin."

"Blackie . . . We have one live but badly drugged bishop. I have summoned the Chicago Police Department. Doubtless they will transport him to Augustana Hospital."

For a moment, no sound at the other end. Milord Cronin was doubtless sizing up the appropriate reactions of calls to Rome and the Nunciature.

"Where did you find him?"

"In an alley . . ."

"In an alley?"

"Precisely. In fact, in an alley behind the fifty-one-hundred block of North Central Park."

"Any other details I should know?"

"He was clad only in his shorts, which, you will be relieved to hear, are not purple. I am no expert in such matters, but I would venture that someone has injected him with a massive dose of heroin."

"Heroin?"

"Heroin."

"You found him yourself?"

"Naturally."

"I won't ask how."

"Don't. Trade secret."

Called a hunch.

"All right, Blackwood, I'll make the calls. Someone should be around the proper congregation in Rome. . . . Go over to Augustana with him and see that they treat him right."

"No."

That stopped Milord Cronin cold. Almost never did he hear that word from me.

"NO?"

"Am I the Cardinal Archbishop of Chicago? Is Idiot Quill my auxiliary? Will the Chicago media wonder where the Ordinary of the Chicago Archdiocese is when all they see is the easily missed auxiliary?"

He laughed, his most unrestrained laugh.

"Easily missed and very dangerous . . . Where should I pick you up?"

"At the Kimball and Lawrence terminal."

"See you soon."

A blue-and-white squad car, blue light whirling frantically, turned down the alley, followed by a police ambulance with an even more frantic light. I knelt next to my brother bishop to say a prayer for him and to give him conditional absolution before he faced the hospital and the end of his career.

18

You knew that this guy would hide the L train in the last place the CTA would look for it?" John Culhane asked me as he drove me back to the terminal and my rendezvous with Milord Cronin.

"Moreover, since the Brown Line goes around the Loop, it would easily have access to the Green Line, as the Lake Street L is now called, much to the delight of the West Side Irish."

"Why the hell would he go to all that trouble?"

"Doubtless for the same reason computer hackers create viruses. It pleases his ego to outsmart everyone and in a spectacular way. He is arrogant. He intends to flummox all of us."

"He won't get away with it."

"Arguably."

"And when you learned that he had dumped the driver in an alley near the terminal, you figured he would dump the bishop in the area too. So you went out and found him just as I had figured that out."

"You had many other things on your mind."

John Culhane grunted. "The driver is in and out of consciousness," he continued. "He has no recollection of what happened. The medics say he may never remember, unless he lets us hypnotize him."

"Even then you will learn little," I pointed out. "A car across the tracks. Several masked men force their way into the train. A couple of them hold him and another injects him. He loses consciousness. Perhaps the men are Hispanics."

"A drug gang moonlighting and paid enough not to brag about what they did?"

"The man is a monster," I sighed. "He is, however, vain. Therefore, he is likely to take a chance that will undo him."

"Tell me more about this annulment stuff. I don't understand it at all."

I sigh my loudest sigh. "Few do. We have failed to explain what the sacraments are and hence the faithful don't understand what it means when we talk about marriage as a sacrament."

"An outward sign instituted by Christ to give grace," he recited the Baltimore catechism answer.

"Not inaccurate, but hopelessly inadequate. A sacrament is designed to reveal something about God, and in that revelation grace, God's love, is communicated. Thus, the Eucharist reveals the God who gives us food and drink and Jesus to sustain our faith. In marriage, the union between man and woman, pace Saint Paul, discloses that God loves us with a passion that exceeds, but is not totally unlike, the passion between man and woman."

"Why have I never heard this before?"

"Because we've been too stupid to put it that way. In any event, it is patent that a certain amount of maturity is required for a marital union to reflect the implacability of God's love. Church law has recognized for some time that there are impediments to the reception of the sacrament, such as physical incapacity, meaning inability to consummate the marriage, and the intention to exclude a permanent union or childbearing. In the 1960s, the American hierarchy, concerned about the pastoral problems of divorced and remarried Catholics, persuaded Rome to expand these impediments to include psychic incapacity, which has come to mean the lack at the time of marriage of sufficient emotional maturity to form a union which reflects that which exists between God and his people."

"At that age who is mature?"

"Arguably. My own conviction is that such maturity is reached only when the couple surmount some critical situation. At that point, divorce becomes unthinkable."

"So almost any divorce could justify an annulment? Catholic divorce?"

"De facto, that would seem to be the case, though piously our matrimonial tribunals would deny it. Thus we have a solution to the pastoral problem of divorced and remarried Catholics, but one that causes some scandal because perhaps nine out of ten annulments in the world are granted in America and because the arguments I have just detailed are too subtle for many, especially those who do not want to understand them."

"So there's some kind of hearing?"

"And then a pro forma review. Given the pain and the anger and the trauma that accompany divorce, an ecclesiastical annulment often aggravates the tensions between husband and wife. Thus they have one more situation in which to hurt each other. However, when it is over they are free to try again, or at least to start receiving the sacraments again."

We had parked by the Kimball and Lawrence terminal. Cops were still swarming around.

"Wouldn't it be easier simply to let them receive the sacraments?"

"Oh, yes. Then the annulment courts would have to close down. . . . The German bishops proposed this to Rome on the grounds that God wants everyone around the banquet table and were promptly slapped down. In this country, many priests do that in the rectory office."

"Including you?"

I was not about to go on the record on that one.

"There is another loophole, called the 'internal forum' solution. If a person who wishes to remarry for one reason or another is unable to obtain an annulment, she or he may still argue that there was never a real sacramental marriage. When that argument is presented to a priest, he may say that if such be the case, then that person has the right in the natural law to contract a new marriage and continue to receive the sacraments. This is called "internal forum," which means that it is a private, almost secret, decision, valid but not publicly ratified by the Church."

"A lot of priests do this sort of thing?"

"Actually the priest has no authority, he is merely a consultant. The person makes a decision in conscience and in theory could do so without a priest. The Vatican would like to have the priest act as a kind of judge, imposing conditions and perhaps arguing against the act of conscience. But it is a long way from Rome to most rectories."

"I see."

I doubted that he did. However, bright man that he was, he would be able to explain it to others.

"The parish priest's concern is with the spiritual welfare of his people. He can be quite creative in getting around those rules which he finds impede that welfare. Sometimes this attitude leads to abuse, sometimes not."

"Where does Bishop Quill fit into the picture?"

"Normally both the husband and wife are delighted to have some sort of closure to their failed marriage. However, a few are unable to comprehend the enormous change in the Church's attitude towards divorce that is latent in annulments. Some feel that the Church is taking away their marriage. Some argue that their children are made illegitimate—though the annulment degree legitimates them if that is the real worry. Some say, I know I had a real marriage—though the argument is that it was real but not sacramental. Finally, some are so angry at their sometime spouse that they want to prolong the agony to punish the spouse and perhaps the replacement spouse. There is a retired Franciscan named Father Innocent—really—in the western suburbs who directs such aggrieved parties in the appeal procedures. So they choose to appeal the decision to Rome, to the Sacred Roman Rota, on which Bishop Quill served with notoriety, if not with distinction."

"Oh?"

"He reversed with gusto, if not convincing arguments, every case that crossed his desk. One can imagine how the other party and possible substitute spouse reacted to that. They had thought it was all over and they are back to ground zero. Some just walk out on the Church, arguably not without reason."

"No appeal?"

"There's always the possibility of an appeal to the Apostolic Signatura, which is the church's Supreme Court, or to another tumulus of the Rota, if anyone wants to bother. In fact, I understand that on every appeal Bishop Quill was reversed, which is perhaps why he was sent to Chicago."

"What a mess . . . Why is the Church in the legal business anyway?"

"For a long time it was the only legal force in Europe. For a couple of centuries all the popes were canon lawyers. We remain in it from force of habit. The Greeks are much more tidy about these matters. Decisions about remarriage are made in the local parish."

"The implications here are that someone whom Bishop Quill hurt by his decisions might have set up this plot to discredit him."

"That might be the case. In truth, however, it is an extraordinarily baroque form of revenge."

"We should find out who in Chicago suffered from his reversals?"

"That would be one way of proceeding. I cannot promise that the results of such a quest would be successful. It is one thing to hate a man and to want revenge and quite another to elaborate such a twisted mechanism for discrediting him."

"Maybe the guy is a computer hacker."

"Or woman."

"How could a woman think up something like this?"

"How could a human think up something like this?"

At that point a sergeant approached the Commander's unmarked car with some more news. Having ascertained it was not relevant, I disembarked from it and proceeded across Kimball Avenue to the delicatessen, where I purchased two deluxe pastrami sandwiches and two iced teas. I had just returned with these treasures in hand when the Cardinal's black Lincoln Town Car pulled up.

"What do you have there, Blackwood?"

"Lunch, two deluxe pastrami sandwiches of the sort that one can find only in the few remaining authentic Jewish delicatessens in this city. Enjoy, it's good for you."

"No chicken soup? Hey, this is good. Don't tell Nora that I'm eating it."

"The protein is also good for you."

We had just finished this gourmet meal when the driver pulled into the emergency entrance of Augustana Hospital. The media folk were placed to prevent our entrance. Milord Cronin, with his ruby ring and his emerald pectoral cross, waved aside their questions and slipped through them. Invisible as always, I ambled along in his crimson wake, though the only cardinalatial sign he wore was a red thread around the gap that revealed his Roman collar. It was enough.

"You stay here, Blackwood," he said to me in the lobby, "and sniff around."

It was an accurate, if unflattering, description of my work.

19

M.J.: Cardinal Cronin, what is Bishop Quill's present condition?

S.C.: He's intermittently conscious. He recognized me. He, ah, kissed my ring.

OTHER JOURNALIST: What happened to him, Cardinal?

S.C.: Someone injected a very large dose of heroin into his veins, almost enough to kill him.

M.J.: Will that have a permanent effect on him?

S.C.: We hardly think so. In the short term, he is likely to be disoriented and confused.

O.J.: Has he taken heroin long, Cardinal?

S.C. *(Controlling impatience)*: Anyone who knows Bishop Quill knows that he does not use drugs. He hardly even drinks. This event is part of an attempt to discredit him. We do not propose to let that happen.

M.J.: Why would someone want to discredit him, Cardinal? Might it be because of the unrest in his parish?

S.C.: I hardly think so, Mary Jane. It's much too violent an assault to be the result of a parish feud.

O.J.: Have you informed the Pope?

S.C.: I was in touch with the Nunciature and the Congregation of Bishops this morning. It's too late in the evening to call them again. I'll report tomorrow.

O.J.: Will the Vatican remove him because of this incident?

S.C.: That would be most unfair.

O.J.: How soon will he return to his parish, Cardinal?

S.C.: The doctors say it may take some weeks. I called Father Matt Dribben, the retired pastor of Forty Holy Martyrs, and asked him to become temporary administrator.

M.J.: How did all this happen? I mean the L train and the bishop and everything?

S.C. *(Thin smile)*: I think I'll leave that to the police, Mary Jane.

M.J.: What sort of man would create such a plot, Cardinal?

S.C.: Person, Mary Jane.

M.J. *(Embarrassed)*: Yes, Cardinal.

S.C.: The same kind of person who makes computer viruses.

O.J.: Will you remain here with the Bishop?

S.C.: Of course. Thank you all very much.

20

"How did I do?" the Cardinal asked me in the lobby of the hospital.

"I could not have done better myself."

"I must really be getting sneaky, huh?"

"Arguably."

"Did they believe me?"

"Up to a point. The possibility that a bishop of the Holy Roman Catholic Church is a drug addict is too good a story for them to give up completely."

"Do they believe that the Vatican will not dump him?"

"We Americans," I observed, "have the innocent notion that a person is innocent till proven guilty. From their years of wisdom with human depravity, not excluding some of their own, the Curia Romana believe that an accused man is guilty till proven innocent and he really can't prove himself innocent."

"You're right, Blackwood. He's burnt flesh. . . . Look I'm going to stay here for awhile. I'll have my driver take you back to the Cathedral, where you can man the fort."

"I can easily ride back on the Brown Line."

"As the Megan would say, NO WAY. I don't want to lose two bishops in the same day."

Back at the Cathedral, Megan Jefferson yelled at me as soon as I came in the door, "Is that you, Bishop Blackie?"

"No, it's the prophet Elijah," I murmured.

"There's this funny man who can't really talk English on the phone. He says he's the Pope and wants Cardinal Sean!"

"I'll take it." I walked into the office the Megan had appropriated for themselves and took the phone from her hand. I will not attempt to replicate the Nuncio's broken English.

"Bishop John B. Ryan," I said curtly.

Only when speaking to representatives of the Holy See do I so identify myself.

"Where is the Cardinal?" he demanded.

"He's at the hospital with Bishop Quill."

"What have you done to this poor man? Why have you killed him?"

"To whom am I speaking?"

"I am the Nuncio!"

"Ah, good afternoon, Your Excellency. This is Bishop John Blackwood Ryan. As I said, His Eminence is at the hospital with Bishop Quill."

"This is terrible, what you have done to him. A bishop murdered in Al Capone's city. There will be serious repercussions in the Holy See."

"Actually, Your Excellency, it is Michael Jordan's city. And if you would do me the honor of listening to me, you would realize that Bishop Quill is not dead. He is in the hospital and, at the risk of repeating myself for the third time, His Eminence is with him."

"He is not dead?"

"No, Your Excellency."

Intelligence is hardly required to be a successful papal diplomat.

"What happened to him?"

Now the fun starts.

"He was kidnapped. Someone injected him with a near lethal dose of heroin. He is presently recovering."

The cry of horror at the other end of the line could not have been louder if I had told him that Gus Quill had been found making love with a mother superior on the high altar of the Cathedral during solemn Mass.

"You must keep it out of the media!"

"I'm sure that Your Excellency is sophisticated enough to realize that nothing is kept out of the media in this country."

"Why does Cronin do these things? They will be unhappy in the Vatican with him."

"I assure Your Excellency that the Cardinal had nothing to do with it."

"You must find out who did this terrible thing!"

"The Chicago police are currently investigating."

"The police!" he wailed again. "The police must be kept out of it. Speak to the authorities!"

"The authorities in our city, Your Excellency, as you surely realize, are mostly Catholic. They will therefore avoid any hint of covering up for the Church."

As time would tell, that was not a fully adequate statement of what would happen.

"I want Cronin to call me at once."

"I will relay that message to His Eminence."

"They will be very angry with him in Rome."

"As is his custom, Excellency, he will quiver with fear at the prospect."

"Is that man real?" Megan Jefferson, who had been listening wide-eyed, asked.

"No, Megan, he is not real."

It might be thought that this exchange proves beyond all doubt that I'm innocent of ecclesiastical ambitions. Alas, it does not. I was talking bishop-speak to him and he had not the slightest notion that I was pulling his leg. It did not matter, however, because, as I had explained to Megan Jefferson, he was not real. No way.

I retired to my quarters to ponder the events of the day. I still had to make my visits to the hospital, but they could wait till I heard from the Cardinal. I had no intention of phoning him to tell him that the Nuncio had demanded that he call to report his reasons for introducing heroin into the bloodstream of Augustus O'Sullivan Quill.

The issue, I told myself, as I turned on my e-mail, was not who might have wanted to make trouble for Bishop Quill. There were legions of people who did not like him, including most of the parishioners of Forty Holy Martyrs. But among these myriad suspects, who would want to put out a contract on him? Even if we had a list of those who hated him that much, who among those might have had the resources and the imagination to put out the contract? Perhaps, when the police assembled such a list, a name would appear that made sense. I thought that, however, to be unlikely. Our friend was clever enough to not be on one of those lists. The police would search diligently. There would be media stories with veiled hints—in Chicago, very veiled—that the Church was covering up again with the help of the authorities. It could get messy.

Our friend was very vain, however. He would want to show off his cleverness. Then, perhaps, we would have him.

It could take a long time.

My personal line rang.

"Punk? Your sister."

"Eileen? I did not leave a message when I mistakenly called your number this morning."

"No, Mary Kate!"

"Ah, the famous Mary Kathleen Ryan Murphy!"

"You're baiting me, Punk!"

"Would I do that?"

"Yes, you would, and I'm one of the few who catch it. You and Sean have a real load of shit on your hands now!"

"That thought has not escaped me."

"He's going to come apart at the seams, really go psychotic. What will Rome do?"

"Try to put him in a monastery somewhere?"

"He hasn't done anything wrong!"

"The Vatican will assume that if a bishop's bloodstream is filled with heroin, he wanted it there."

"He may never recover, you understand that?"

"I had not thought it would be that bad."

"It might not, but it easily could be. You and Sean should get him out of Augustana—a good place, but not for him—and get him into a private room at St. Joseph's. Get him a first-rate psychiatrist, I can make referrals if you want, and round-the-clock psychiatric nurses. And keep a close eye on him."

"Of what gender should these respected colleagues be?"

"Women, of course. His problem was clearly with his mother."

She gave me three names, all presumably Catholic.

"Mind you, Punk, you may have to warehouse him for the rest of his life. His ego simply cannot stand this kind of trauma."

"He will not be the first Chicago bishop to whom this has happened."

"If you don't slow down, the same thing will happen to you."

"Is that the clinician talking or a concerned sib?"

"Punk, you're no good, you never have been! Tell Sean to give me a ring."

No reason that the Cardinal should take my word for it. I sighed.

I did not ask her what the symptoms of my imminent psychic collapse might be. She would doubtless describe behavior in which I had engaged since childhood, behavior that led the women in the family to conclude, not unreasonably, that I was a changeling.

The phone rang again. It was the Cardinal.

"Blackie! What the hell have you been doing on the phone? I've been trying to get you!"

"Talking to my sib, who proffers psychiatric advice free of charge."

"Good, I'll have to talk to her. I'm on the way back. We have a gosh-awful mess on our hands. I'll be there in about ten minutes. Don't go away."

"I had not planned to. . . . The Nuncio was on the phone . . ."

"To hell with him!"

That was, I felt sure, not his considered opinion. However, even when he considered it, Milord Cronin was not likely to change his mind.

Again the phone rang.

"Blackie, Nora."

"Indeed."

"How's Sean taking it?"

That's what a lover always wants to know.

"Wonderfully well! He's at his manic best!"

" 'See to it, Blackwood,' you mean."

"Oh, yes."

"None of that weltschmerz stuff he does sometimes?"

"Not yet."

"You'll let me know?"

"Bank on it."

How many Irish Catholic matrons in Chicago, I wondered, knew what weltschmerz was?

Milord Cronin, on rare occasion, becomes weary of life and dubious about his efforts through his life. That happens to men in their early seventies, I have been led to believe. But then, at what age after twenty-five does it not happen?

He thereupon strode into my room, roman collar pulled out of his clerical shirt—none of these vests that other bishops affect for Sean Cronin—and hovered over me like a caged black leopard with his forelegs against the bars of his cage.

"He's geeked out, Blackwood. Totally. Out of his mind."

Thus had the Megan jargon influenced him.

"Predictably."

"Hysterical! Shouts prayers! Begs the Pope to help him! The good Swedish people at Augustana don't know what to do with him. . . . What did Mary Kate say?"

"She recommended that we move him to St. Joseph's, put him in a private psychiatric room, and assign a first-rate woman shrink, excluding herself, by the way, to take care of him. She thought it possible that he might not recover. Incidentally, she predicted the psychotic symptoms you described."

"I'll phone her."

Naturally. Two celebrities do not trust a mere sweeper bishop to be an adequate intermediary.

"She gave me this list of names."

He glanced at the list as he sank into my easy chair, which I had thoughtfully cleared in anticipation of his arrival.

"All Catholics, I see."

"Arguably."

"Why women?"

"She remarked something about the problem being his mother."

He nodded as he put the list in the breast pocket of his jacket.

I prepared him a libation of the very best Bushmill's

Green Label single malt Irish whiskey. Normally, he steals it himself. Today, however, had been a very bad day.

" 'Tis yourself that has the heavy hand! . . . Don't tell Nora!"

"My lips are sealed."

"Sometimes I think you work for her instead of me."

"Which would display excellent taste on my part."

He sipped the Bushmill's, of which it can be said, without any fear or hesitation, that it surely does clear the sinuses.

"Good stuff. . . . What do we do now, Blackwood?"

"We continue our existing posture. Bishop Quill was mugged by person or persons unknown. We have full confidence in the ability of the CPD to resolve the matter satisfactorily. It is absurd to think that Bishop Quill was a heroin addict or ever used narcotics of any kind. He is recovering from the incident, but it has been a brutal blow to his, ah, health. . . . No, that won't do. Let us say, to his organism."

He inclined his head in agreement and continued to sip his whiskey in slow and thoughtful quantities. "That makes sense. We will not tell them that Bishop Ryan is continuing his own inquiries."

"What does *he* know about such matters? I should think it would be wise to wait till the waters settle down. This one will take time."

He inclined his head again. "Any hunches?"

"Someone monstrously clever. Vain, unbearably vain. That will finally do him in, I believe."

"Gus is finished, you know, even if he recovers."

"It would seem so. However, he was probably finished anyway when they shipped him out to us. I would imagine those behind such a deployment will scurry for cover."

"He had his illusions. Now they have become delusions, perhaps permanent."

"Solves a lot of our problems. Admittedly it creates some new ones, but they will pass. As you doubtless recall, one of your predecessors spent thirty years or so in an asylum, quietly passing his time in prayer and good works."

"Bishop Duggan . . . and everyone soon forgot about him."

"We all have illusions. We cannot survive without them."

"Like your delusion that you are my éminence grise?"

"Arguably. The path of wisdom is to discern which are harmless and which are deadly. Usually the latter are ones that involve a lower estimation of oneself than is appropriate. In this matter, I believe that both Bishop Gus and his tormentor have the same problem."

"Gus's delusion is that he's going to be archbishop of Chicago!"

"He needed that delusion to escape from the truth that he was perfectly capable, upon ordination, of being a kindly parish priest—a truth that still survives in his quixotic attempts to identify with the Hispanic poor. He ran to escape mediocrity, failing to realize that what he was escaping wasn't mediocrity at all but his low estimate of himself."

"Sounds like you picked that up from the good Mary Kathleen."

"It is but common sense."

"And his enemy?"

"A person of monumental illusions, which he has doubtless reinforced this day."

He drained his glass with a single swallow, a blasphemy that made me cringe. Then he jumped up, took my list of possible therapists from his pocket, and said,

"I'll call Mary Kate now. She's at home?"

"Indeed."

"Meantime, you start thinking about who the enemy is. See to it, Blackwood!"

Invigorated by the water of life, he ventured forth like the USS *Langley*, a ship with which I am familiar, moving at flank speed.

An image of the enemy flickered in my preconscious, danced for a moment, and then slipped away.

He would be back. Or she.

Tommy

21

"The soccer person really said that to you?" the shrink says when I tell her about the fantasy bit—mostly to get her reaction.

"Yes, ma'am."

"She has had a lot of experience with men?"

"I don't think so. She says she's a virgin."

"Where would she get such an attitude?"

"She reads a lot."

"Such as?"

"She explained *Finnegans Wake* to me the other day."

"And she plays soccer? Like Mia and Brandi and that bunch?"

"Yes, ma'am. . . . Do you think she needs to see a psychiatrist?"

The doctor snorted. "That one? About that, you should not worry. . . . Now, tell me about your father."

So she didn't think Christy was weird. Well, she wasn't.

"He's a great man, Doctor. A brilliant lawyer, witty, charming, generous, kind. Everyone loves him."

"Yet he could not keep your mother in line?"

"He did everything he could. He let her have her freedom. He found a nanny for the kids. He paid her bills. He asked for a divorce only after the lesbian thing, and then only because Monsignor Coffey—that's our pastor out in Oak Park—told him it was time. He couldn't have done anything more."

"I see . . . But never once did he tell her to stop this foolishness and see a therapist or he would end the marriage?"

"Oh, no. Dad could never do anything that cruel."

"Would it have been cruel, especially in the early days?"

"Terribly cruel."

"What would your mother have done if he had delivered that ultimatum?"

"I don't know."

"Was there a chance she might have done what he demanded?"

"I suppose so."

"Then was it not cruel for him to have remained silent?"

"I don't see why!" I said hotly.

"Was it not the only chance the poor woman had?"

"Dad could never have done that! He loved her too much!"

"Or perhaps not enough."

"I don't get it, Doctor. He was wonderful to her."

"Was he? Did he not in fact subsidize her neuroses, whatever they were?"

"You don't know my father!" I said furiously.

"You are right, Thomas, I do not know him. But I do know that in intimate relationships one must sometimes be firm with the partner. Not to be firm is unfair and cruel. To withhold firmness is not a sign of love, but of a failure of love."

"But . . ."

"Those who love are firm all the time, every day. It usually is easy and routine, though sometimes it has to be more forceful. Without it love is impossible. Do you not understand this?"

My stomach tightened.

"Yeah. I guess . . . but I love my father!"

"Of course you do, Tommy. One can love another very much and yet harbor resentments against that person. I suggest that all through those years when your mother misbehaved, you were deeply angry at him for not intervening on your behalf and that of your sisters to make her stop. You resented the fact that he did not make her return to the lovely woman who sang songs to you when you were a child?"

"I can't remember ever feeling that way!"

A great, yawning hole opened up under me.

"It does not follow that you did not feel that way—and in your unconscious you still do. How could it have been otherwise?"

"There was nothing he could have done!"

"That you say now. You couldn't have known that then."

"You mean I have to work all that out with Dad now?"

"Did I say that, Thomas?"

"No."

"Does your father ever argue with your stepmother?"

"With Beth? . . . I don't know. I don't think so."

"Probably he doesn't have to. Every intimate couple has to draw limits."

"Beth would be a lot easier. . . . Maybe they do it in lawyer talk."

"Probably they do. Your mother was a serious problem. She would frighten many men. I do not blame your father. I merely suggest to you that his reaction was not adequate. You were furious with him because, among other things, you had to protect your sisters when he did not."

"O.K., but if you're right, what's the point of that now?"

"I suggest, Thomas, that your problems with women are not the result of your resentment towards your mother but of your resentment towards your father."

"That's silly!"

"Hear me out. In your early relationship with a young woman, you are charming and she becomes fond of you. Then she does something that strikes you as irresponsible. You both underreact and overreact. Thus you confuse the young woman and drive her away. You don't complain about something that bothers you, habitual tardiness, for example, and then you lose your temper."

Ouch.

"That's a pretty fair description," I admitted.

"The problem is that you have no good model for how to draw the line when a line must be drawn, gently, lovingly, but firmly without putting the relationship in jeopardy."

"Oh."

"With the soccer person, that may not be a problem. It is altogether possible that she would simply refuse to let you put the relationship in jeopardy. Nonetheless, it might not be a risk you want to take."

"I certainly wouldn't, but how do I learn at this stage of life?"

"You watch how others do it. When there is a problem, however mild, with the soccer woman, you deal with it immediately, waiting for the proper moment, of course, instead of putting it off."

"I don't want to hurt her feelings. . . . Damn, I sound like your description of my father!"

"It is time, Thomas. Think about our conversation."

In the harsh grayness of a Chicago autumn, I looked

around, not sure where I was or what I should do next. My emotions were in a jumble, like the pit on a witching day. I could not figure out what emotion to concentrate on. No, there was one that was paramount. My psychiatrist thought that my lioness was a remarkable young woman. Of course she was. Worth going through all this hell for?

Silly question.

I walked home briskly, determined to think through what we had said to one another instead of watching television.

First I sent an e-mail to *Christy@soccer.ndu.edu*.

Christy my love,
    Another bad session with the shrink. I think I'm digging pretty deep and learning a lot about myself. But that's not your problem. What I wanted to say is that on the basis of what I say about you, she thinks you're remarkable. I knew that all along, but it's nice to have a very wise woman confirm it. I suppose you won't like me talking to her about you. If you do mind, I'm sorry.
All my love,
Tommy

A reply came back while I was changing my clothes to go down to the exercise room.

Dearest Tommy,
    Sometimes for a sweet, wonderful boy, you have the strangest ideas. Why would I object to you talking to your shrink about me? I'd be offended if you didn't tell her about me. If I'm important to you, why would you not talk about me?
    What does she like about me?
    I wish you were here, or I was there, so I could kiss you.
Christy☹☺

I thought I'd better reply right away.

Captain Christy,
  She is impressed with your reaction to my shower-room fantasies.
Confused,
Tommy

I had hardly finished when she fired back.

Tommy,
  WELL, I don't know what's so unusual. I'm, after all, a healthy young woman, with all the hormones that come with that. But if it makes her like me, I'm impressed. One thing, however, in some locker rooms, there are other girls in the shower with me. You are NOT, I repeat ABSOLUTELY not, to have fantasies about any of them. Is that clear?
Jealous lioness☹

I threw back my head and laughed. Vintage Christy.

Dear Lioness,
  I wouldn't dare. Besides, unlike Simba, I'm monogamous. Finally, those other young women couldn't possibly compare with you.
  I'm going to my workout now.
Love,
Simba (human variety)☺

22

"Let us return to your stepmother," my shrink said, confusing me once again by changing the subject at the beginning of a session. "Do you have fantasies about her like you do about the soccer woman?"

"You mean about playing with her boobs in the shower?"

She shrugged, as though that were an acceptable male description of fantasies.

"Not as vivid or as sustained."

"But naked?"

"Yes, I guess so."

"Would she be as pleased as your friend at Notre Dame?"

"I would hardly think so. I could never ask her."

"Why would she not be pleased?"

"She's married, to begin with, and she's my stepmother."

"But you don't call her Mom, do you?"

"No."

"Your sisters do?"

"Sure."

"She would like it?"

"I think she'd be very pleased."

"But you don't?"

"Well, we're both adults, equals, kind of."

"In fact, you are not. She is married to your father. You cannot be her equal."

"I suppose that's right."

"So by not calling her Mom, at least on occasion,

you preserve the illusion that she is, in some remote sense, sexually available to you."

"You have a dirty mind, Dr. Ward," I said with my most charming Irish grin.

"We all do, Thomas."

"So if I call her Mom, the incest taboo will eliminate my fantasies about her boobs?"

"Minimize and contain them," she said evenly. "After all, you are not an archangel."

"Christy says that if we didn't have fantasies there wouldn't be any humans left."

"She is quite right. Now, I want to ask you a question about Christy."

"Shoot."

"Do you intend to marry her?"

"It's early days, as the Brits say."

"Granted."

"I don't want to answer that question."

"Yet you will."

"Doctor, I am here struggling with this stuff because I don't want to foul up with her."

"It is time."

A couple of Rubicons challenged me the following weekend.

Beth phoned me while I was reading.

"Tommy, it's Amy's birthday this coming week. I thought we'd have one of our little family parties for her on Sunday. Do you think you would be free to come?"

Such a timid question. Was Beth afraid of me? Hadn't I been an ally?

"Great idea, Beth. Sure, I'll be there. What time?"

"Say, noon. She'll have to drive back to the Dome."

University of Chicago graduate. We had socialized her to the proper word.

"Sure, it'll be fun."

"It will be good to have you."

"Beth . . . don't hang up. Would it be all right if I brought a girl, uh, I mean, a young woman?"

"A WHAT?" She was genuinely shocked.

"Er, a young woman?"

"A DATE?"

"I don't know if you could call her that. I think you will all like her."

"I'm sure we will. We'll be looking forward to meeting her."

Smooth, counselor.

As soon as we ended that conversation, I phoned a certain number at Notre Dame.

"Christy?"

"I thought this was an e-mail romance. They're more sexy."

Impossible young woman.

"Your friend Amy has a birthday next week."

"I know THAT," she said impatiently.

I had interrupted serious study.

"They're having a party for her."

"I know THAT too. A private family party."

"I have permission to bring a date."

"Where are you going to find a date?"

The young lioness was making fun of me.

"I tried three or four and they said they were busy. I thought you might want to join us."

"Oh, Tommy, I'd love to. . . . Amy will just about freak out. How formal is it?"

"Clean jeans, nice blouse."

"Got it. I won't tell her a word. We'll have a ball. . . . Will your parents like me? I mean as your friend and not just as Amy's classmate."

"They'll about geek out."

"Tommy, I keep saying it, but it's true. You're the sweetest boy in all the world. Don't forget to buy her a present."

Sweetest boys in all the world need to be reminded to act right.

"Why don't you buy for me a totally sexy gown and robe!"

"Great! She'll really geek out."

"Why am I nervous?" she asked me as we pulled up to our house on Oak Park Avenue. "What a wonderfully funny old house!"

"You're nervous because you're now not Amy's classmate, but my, er, date."

"Girlfriend."

"Woman friend."

"Friend."

"All RIGHT."

We got out of the car and walked up the creaky old steps. She held my hand. Nothing like making things explicit.

Amy threw open the door.

"Christy, you are totally NOT his date!"

"Friend," I said.

Amy threw her arms around Christy, then around me, and then around Christy again. She thinks she's going to be a bridesmaid and godmother, I thought.

"How long have you been dating?" She screeched.

"I wouldn't call it dating," Christy said thoughtfully. "How long would you say, my love?"

The "my love" was part of the act.

"It seems like forever," I said.

Amy screamed and hugged us both again.

She certainly approved of the relationship.

Inside the house. Time for introductions.

"Mom," I said to Beth, "I think you've met Christina Anne before, though in perhaps a different context. Christy, this is my father, Thomas Patrick Flynn, always called Thomas to distinguish him from his son. Dad, this is Christina Anne Logan, All-American soccer player from your alma mater."

Dad rose to the occasion, as I knew he would.

"Christy, I've read a lot about you and heard even more from my daughter. I'm delighted to meet you . . . and astonished that you are in the company of my son. Astonished and delighted."

"He's a soccer fan," Christy said, her eyes gleaming wickedly.

Already she had made common cause.

"Why didn't you tell me, Christy?" Amy, still hysterical, demanded.

"Had to protect my reputation."

Then I saw the tears in Mom's eyes. If I had known it would mean that much to her, I would have used the word long ago. Tommy Flynn, you're a jerk.

There was much hugging and kissing.

"Thank you, Tommy," Mom whispered as she kissed me.

"Long overdue," I replied, close to tears myself.

Thus a whole class of minor fantasies slipped out of my life. My shrink had been right.

It was a festive afternoon. Amy was "totally geeked out" by my present.

"Even if you picked it out, Christy, I never expected him to buy me anything like this."

"He really has very good taste," my love insisted, "for a man."

We had to break up early because both the Domers had to return to school. It was agreed that Amy would ride down with us and then back to Notre Dame with

Christy. After some discussion, I was permitted to sit in the front seat with Christy. No heavy kissing at the door of the Hancock Center.

Why the hell not?

So, I kissed her quite passionately before I climbed out. She responded in kind. I'm sure Amy's eyes bulged.

"Love you, dear," I said.

"Love you too," Christy gasped. "Write me a nice e-mail, would you?"

Amy would be certain that the two of us were in love.

Well, weren't we?

So I sent her an e-mail.

Dear young lioness,

You certainly did embarrass me in front of my sister in the car with that wild lioness kiss. I felt very awkward. Amy is probably convinced that we'll marry right after you graduate. It was a very nice kiss, by the way, but you caught me completely off guard.

I know now that you're back there under the shadow of the Golden Dome, you'll settle down and concentrate on your school work.

Love,

Tommy

The next morning, there was a reply waiting for me.

Tommy, you geek! If you think I'm going to play the game you play with your poor sisters, you're even weirder than I think you are. I agree that it was a nice kiss. Makes me shiver to think about it.

Love,

Christy Anne

We saw each other several times in the next few weeks. She would drive into town at the end of the day for a movie or a concert or an opera, always dressed smartly, as though she were an accomplished, professional woman instead of an adolescent hoyden.

"What time is this opera over? I have to drive back to the Dome."

"Eleven-thirty. And you won't drive back to the Dome."

"Whadayamean?" She twisted her face into her patented frown.

The hoyden, cum lioness, reappeared.

"I mean, it's better if you stay at your parents' house."

"I don't want to stay there. They don't know I'm in town. What will they say?"

"You'll tell them you were at the opera with Tommy, and they'll be pleased. You can even tell them that Tommy made you stay at home."

"No. I can do what I want!"

"Not on my time."

"Whadayamean, your time?"

"I invited you to drive in for the opera. You're my responsibility. I don't want you driving home in the small hours of the morning without any sleep."

"I've done it before!"

"Regardless."

"You sound just like my parents."

"That's because I'm so old."

She thought about it and then reluctantly agreed.

"Well, at least you didn't threaten never to take me out again."

"No, but you have to stay at their house every time you come in for a date."

"You think you can run my life?"

Was I doing this right, I wondered.

"I wouldn't dream of that, Christy. I'm just trying to protect my sleep."

The frown disappeared and was replaced by her radiant smile.

"You're weird, Tommy, but I still love you. . . . Thank you for being concerned about me. You're right."

It was that easy. No evidence of any improvement in my skills. She was capable of docility on certain occasions, that was all.

We would kiss after such dates and engage in mild caresses. Nothing serious. I insisted to myself that this was still a remote courtship. Nothing would be serious for a long time.

I watched the games on TV. Notre Dame was sweeping through the season. However, in the ratings they were number two or three behind Stanford. The Cardinal, I was informed, were very good and very stuck-up and played very dirty.

My heart was in my throat during every game. My lioness never let up, not even when the team was a couple of goals ahead.

Blackie

23

That the Church of the Forty Holy Martyrs in Forest
Hills would be a late Renaissance baroque edifice was
most appropriate, it had always seemed to me. Not that
the suburb itself looked like a Renaissance town. Far
from it; if anything, the community looked like someone had designed the homes to be eighteenth-century
Tudor, not so large as the Tudor castles in Britain and
Ireland, but far warmer (or cooler, in the summer), better lit, and with infinitely more convenient conven-
iences. It was far and away the wealthiest parish in the
city, a fact of which its members were fully aware and
very proud. That Matt Dribben, Canaryville Irish,
should be pastor there seemed at first to be one of Sean
Cronin's little jokes, though his name was on the per-
sonnel board's list, which went to the Cardinal. The
good burghers of Forest Hills were skeptical about the
appointment. How could a man who had worked
among African Americans (some of the parishioners
said "blacks," or even "Negroes," since being politically

correct was hardly on their agenda) most of his priestly life possibly understand their spiritual needs? They reckoned without Matt's South Side Irish political instincts and his utter innocence of every kind of ideology.

The rectory, in which I sat eating lunch with Matt, was utterly inappropriate for such a parish—an old farmhouse that had stood for more than a century on the land the Archdiocese had bought long ago for a parish in Forest Hills. A succession of pastors had remodeled it, but they resolutely refused to demolish it, despite the claim of many of the parishioners that it was an eyesore that had a negative impact on property values.

"So, are you here, Blackie, to investigate the harm that poor Gus did to his parish, or to look for suspects?"

Matt had just celebrated his seventieth birthday and retired as pastor. He was tall and skinny, with a few thin strands of hair plastered neatly on the top of his head. His brown eyes were pleasant and very shrewd and his grin charming, till you realized how shrewd he really was.

"Are they not the same question?"

He clapped his hands enthusiastically.

"No wonder Sean made you a bishop! You learn quickly!"

"Ah, no, Matthew. I was born with that knowledge!"

He applauded again.

"Well, if you want to know how important a pastor is to a parish, I can answer that for you. It takes him years to accomplish any good, and then his successor can destroy it overnight. Your good friend Gus Quill wiped this place out overnight. I could hardly believe the devastation. The poor man had no sense of people at all."

Which was one good way to describe a borderline personality.

"Usually reliable sources, however, tell me that peace and tranquillity have returned."

"Yeah," he sighed, "just when I was looking forward to some peace and an improved golf game in retirement." His eyes narrowed. "Sean is not thinking of sending you up here, is he?"

"Not very likely, Matthew, since he knows full well I would retire the next day."

"You're welcome to it, you know."

"You will be here as an administrator indefinitely, Matthew. Perhaps, when you are satisfied that Gus's mess has been swept away, he would accept a plea for retirement. However, I would not count on that."

"It is kind of good to get back here. I hoped the new pastor would let me stay in the rectory. I didn't think I'd be responsible for the place."

After a three-month postretirement vacation, Matt Dribben was delighted to be home again.

"You have succeeded in restoring tranquillity to the people of God in Forty Holy Martyrs?"

"Tranquillity is not something they are very good at. They'll complain about poor Gus for years. Still, the worst is over, except for the staff. They're a harder nut to crack."

"Indeed."

"Dessert . . . maybe a dish of chocolate ice cream?"

My bad habits had traveled before me.

"Only a small dish."

Matt grinned, infinitely pleased with himself.

"You never put on any weight do you, just like me?"

"I am forever doomed to be pudgy. . . . Now tell me, Matthew . . . which of your parish staff is most likely to have connived a plot against Augustus O'Sullivan Quill?"

"Aha! Now we get down to cases! I figured you'd ask that question!"

"Indeed."

"I don't have to tell you, Blackie, that since Rome won't ordain women or married men, we have a priest shortage. So we fill up the vacancies with laypeople and an occasional permanent deacon. Good staff are hard to come by, even if you pay them well. Who wants to be a second-rate priest!"

In fact, I paid the Megan three times the going rate for baby-sitters and counted myself lucky. I was reasonably satisfied with my lay staff too, and paid them accordingly. However, no one was more important than the ones who answered the rectory doorbell.

"So, you make do with what you can get . . . former priests, former nuns, folks that like to hang around church, those who want in on the church power action. Some are good at what they do, others not so good. Some are kind and gracious, others are bossy, still others are neurotic. The pastor has to warn and cajole, encourage and restrain, particularly those who want to deny sacraments at every turn of the corner. Especially he must realize that he is dealing with fragile egos. On the whole, my crowd is pretty good, though it will be a while before they recover from poor Gus. He kind of stood for everything they hate and fear in the Church."

"I understand," I said with my most sympathetic sigh.

"Take Orlando Carlin, for example. He has a Ph.D. from Harvard in education. He was a Jesuit with an eye for the ladies. One of his pretty students twenty years ago was Sister Joel Reed. Enough said. He could do much better, so could she. However, they never got over being a priest and nun, even if they were keeping house. So they're here, waiting for the Church to change its mind on them. She's become a kind of an angry ideologue and he's, well, he's still got an eye for the ladies."

"Here in the parish?"

"I don't think so. I warned him once. He still flirts a little. . . . My point is that she's a fine director of religion education and RCIA and he's a brilliant adult educator. Could they have connived to poison poor Gus with heroin? Sure, they could have. They're both angry enough and smart enough. Did they? I kind of doubt it."

"Why?"

"They're too full of themselves to bother with revenge. But what do I know? Judge for yourself."

"Hmm . . ."

"Then there's poor Herman Crawford, our organist and music director. Good music doesn't come cheap anymore. Herman is neurotic as all hell. Requires constant reassurance. Wants to sing 'Palestrina' every Sunday. Afraid no one likes him. Actually does a damn good job. Probably gay, not active as far as I know. I figure that's none of my business as long as he doesn't take up with a kid from the parish, which the poor guy would never do."

And it used to be fun to be a pastor!

"I can see why Joel Reed and Orlando Carlin would have a grudge against Gus Quill, but why your presumably gay music director?"

"Someone whispered into Gus's ear that Herman was gay after the choir Mass on Sunday. Gus went up to the choir loft and fired him on the spot in front of the choir. Said that he wanted no perverts working in his parish. Poor Herman has been brooding ever since. There's a lot of rage in the man."

"Gus didn't even bother to spend an hour in prayer before he did it?"

"Huh? Oh yeah, I see what you mean. They tell me that was his standard line whenever he dismissed someone. He would not reconsider the decision because he had prayed for an hour over it before he decided. That was the line when he fired the whole parish council in one fell swoop."

"Ah?"

"Do you have a parish council?"

"Doesn't everyone?"

"Do they try to tell you how to run the parish?"

"Not twice."

"A lot of people around here, who have nothing much else to do, like to meddle. My father wasn't a precinct captain for nothing. I kid them along and it works out. They come up with a lot of good ideas. . . . Anyway, I've set you up for an interview with Larry Henning, the chairman of the parish council. As long as he thinks he's my right-hand man, he does a fine job with them. Gus said he couldn't be his right-hand man anymore. Broke the poor guy's heart."

"He is your right-hand man, Matthew?"

"Course not. I have a dozen or so around the parish who think that. Maybe two or three really are, including Crystal Lane, our youth minister, who is a saint."

"I don't get to see her?"

"She's not on the list of people. Believe me, Blackie, she likes teenagers, she's gotta be a saint."

I like teenagers too, and I'm not a saint, but that didn't prove anything.

"Ms. Reed and Dr. Harmon will be in their offices now. They insist on seeing you together. Incidentally, she's not 'Joel' anymore but 'Joe,' with an *e* on Joe."

"Indeed."

None of the interviews were especially pleasant or informative, not that I had expected them to be.

"The first thing we want to know, John," Ms. Reed

charged in, "is whether that fucking bastard will be back here."

Arguably she had once been a pretty young nun. Now she was an older woman whose face and soul had been twisted with free-floating rage. I knew her kind well. While I did not like them, I sympathized with their plight.

"He is recovering slowly," I temporized. "It will be a long time, if ever, before he is ready for arduous ministry."

"Typical bishop shit. I want a straight answer."

Her husband, still handsome with iron gray hair and shifty eyes, smiled tolerantly.

"That was a straight answer," I replied.

"I say that whoever kidnapped him did the goddamn Church a big favor. I wish I had thought of it."

"Indeed."

"What my wife means," Orlando Carlin drawled, still very much a New England Jesuit, "is that many of us work here at considerable financial sacrifice because we still have the dream of a Church renewed according to the spirit of the Second Vatican Council. We don't think it was right for the Cardinal to send a man like Idiot Quill up here."

The point was well taken. What could I say?

"The Cardinal was taken aback by his actions. As you know, he ordered Bishop Quill to rehire everyone he had fired."

"He should have apologized to us," Joe snarled at me.

"I think his reassignment of Father Dribben was an act of good faith and good will to everyone in the parish."

"Old Matthew is all right," Orlando conceded. "Perhaps a bit too clever by half, but basically a good heart."

"Now, you really want to know whether we had any part in kidnapping him and shooting him full of heroin, don't you?" his wife barked at me.

"My goals are more modest. I'm trying to learn if anyone has any ideas who might have committed the crime."

"Crime! I'd say it was an act of heroic virtue! We didn't do it. We're both sorry we didn't think of something like that. If we knew who did, we wouldn't tell you."

Poor woman. The trauma of change in the Church had ruined her life.

"The thing is, Blackie—I may call you that, may I not?"

"Everyone does."

"The point is that on occasion revolutionary political action is not inappropriate. Poor Idiot pushed his community in the direction of valid revolutionary action. I can tell you without violating any confidences that there was considerable discussion about what course of action we as the oppressed should take. I can also assure you that no one shed any tears over his fate. . . . Is he really a vegetable?"

Ah, the clichés of the 1960s! How nostalgic.

"He is suffering from an acute psychotic interlude," I said. "The doctors hope for a recovery."

"You understand that we must be silent about what conversations our colleagues may have had with us. This was an oppressed community, as I'm sure you realize. We were entitled to seek liberation."

Forest Hills victimized by oppression, indeed. Not to put too fine an edge on the matter, this was bullshit, playacting revolution. Yet it was possible that there had been some kind of conspiracy in the parish.

I approached Herman Crawford with delicacy. Since Milord Cronin's brother, Cardinal Prince Josef Ratzinger, described gay people as "fundamentally disordered" there has been no other way.

"Father Dribben," I told him, "reports that you have a great love of Giovanni Pierluigi."

His soft gray eyes lit up, "No one has ever written religious music like the maestro of 'Palestrina,'" he said. "Not even Byrd or Lassus. You have a polyphonic Mass at the Cathedral, don't you, Bishop?"

"We have a folk choir, a Gregorian scola cantorum, a polyphonic choir, a Celtic choir, and several children's choirs. It seems reasonable to assume that such is the obligation of a cathedral."

Herman, in a tiny office next to the choir loft, surrounded by piles of musical scores, was a trim, nice-looking young man with rimless spectacles and a high forehead.

"Do you think God hates me because he made me gay, Bishop?"

"I think God loves us all, as a parent loves a child. He doesn't hate anyone."

"Is it God's will that I'm gay; is it part of His plan?"

"God works with everything that happens and draws us to Herself by Her own ways. In that sense, surely it is God's will. However, it is not God's will that we suffer for what we are. When we do suffer, God suffers with us."

He sighed sadly. "I try my best, Bishop. I do what I can."

"I'm sure you do."

"Bishop Quill said that I was objectively evil. In front of the whole choir. He is the one who is objectively evil, isn't he, Bishop Ryan?"

"It was a terribly un-Christian thing to say."

"If I had a gun or knife, I would have killed him. He deserved to die."

"Ah?"

"I don't know whether I mean that. I was beside myself with rage. I couldn't speak. I rushed out of the choir loft screaming."

"And the choir?"

"Oh, they came after me. What else could they do?" No homophobes in that choir.

"So there are many people here in the parish who are not unhappy at Bishop Quill's sickness?"

"Everyone is happy about it, except some old fuddy-duddy reactionaries and Crystal, of course, but she's a saint."

"I have heard of the young woman. Did not the bishop fire her?"

"He didn't notice her. She's sweet and pretty and kind of tiny and no one notices her at first. He banned all teenagers. However, he didn't realize that he had a youth minister. Even if he fired her, she still wouldn't hate him. Like I say, Crystal is a saint."

Or perhaps, the only forgiving Christian in the parish.

"Was there discussion of getting rid of Bishop Quill?"

"Sure there was. Everyone wanted to get rid of him. I'm glad he's gone crazy. If you ask me, he was always crazy. I hope they keep him in the loony bin for the rest of his life. I hate him."

"Do you think that anyone in the parish might have been involved in his kidnapping?"

"I don't know and I don't care," he shouted hysterically. "He got what he deserved!"

The atmosphere of hatred for Gus Quill in the parish was intense and dangerous. Still. I must tread carefully.

"I can understand the feelings."

"I didn't do anything to him, Bishop. I didn't. I couldn't. I wouldn't want to hurt anyone."

"I would not think so," I reassured him.

"This is a wonderful parish. I don't ever want to leave here. Is he coming back?"

"I don't think you have to worry about having to leave here."

"Thank you, Bishop, thank you very much. I didn't have anything to do with what happened. I really didn't."

I gently disengaged from this tormented man. We had done terrible things to him. As Matt Dribben had said, Gus didn't know people. Rather, more clinically, other people barely existed for him.

As I waited in the rectory office for the arrival of Larry Henning, the chairman of the parish council, I reviewed the bidding. Parish staff often confuse how they feel with how the parish feels. That there was a poisonous attitude towards Bishop Quill on the staff was beyond question. In the rest of the parish, there was doubtless general dislike, but hardly a will to get rid of him. Not so soon anyway. Yet there were certainly groups of parishioners, especially those who most closely identified with the parish, who shared the staff's nearly irrational hatred. It would take more resources than I had to investigate the whole parish.

Much to my surprise, I found my cell phone in the pocket of my now sadly obsolete Bulls jacket. Even more to my surprise, I pushed the right button the first time.

"Reliable Security, Casey speaking."

"Indeed!"

"Blackie! What mischief are you up to now?"

"I am exploring the community of the People of God in Forest Hills, also known as Forty Holy Martyrs parish. I think there is need of a much more intensive investigation."

"You want us to poke around? Reliably?"

"And discreetly. There may have been an organized

conspiracy up here. I am skeptical of the hints I hear, but we cannot exclude them. In a community with this much talent and this much money, there are surely individuals who could be our mastermind."

"No doubt about that. . . . Any ideas about where to start?"

"The usual spots, commuter stations, beauty salons, barber-shops, the places where people talk."

"We'll have a go at it, Blackie. No promises."

"I expect none."

Lawrence T. Henning, as he introduced himself, was a cautious and careful man, from his expensive navy blue Italian suit to his carefully groomed widow's peak hair. He carried, not too lightly, the aura of a major corporation executive, which he surely was not. His dark eyes were expressionless, and not once in our conversation did he smile. In an earlier era in the Church, he would have been the all-powerful head usher, truly the pastor's right-hand man. Now he was a figurehead who took himself very, very seriously.

"I'm happy to meet you, Bishop Ryan," he said with a firm handshake. "There have been bad times here. In all candor, the parish needs healing."

"Father Dribben seems to be doing his best."

"Father is a wonderful priest. The former pastor left a lot of wreckage behind."

"So I understand . . . and not a little anger?"

"That is to be expected. A parish is not quite like an accounting firm. The ties are fragile. They can be destroyed very quickly, more quickly than I would have expected. It will require a long time to restore them."

"Like Humpty Dumpty?"

"I beg your pardon?"

"All the king's men couldn't put him back together again."

"In all candor, I doubt that the parish will ever be

restored to its previous condition. Father and I are trying our best."

"I'm sure you are. . . . Is it true that Bishop Quill swept out the whole parish council at his first meeting with them?"

"In the first five minutes."

"How did it happen?"

"We meet regularly on the first and third Mondays of each month. The Bishop came into the conference room in his full robes. He informed us that he had just come from church, where he had prayed for a solid hour about the meeting. Ms. Mary O'Hanlon—her husband is O'Hanlon Industries, I'm sure you know—asked whether the contracts with the parish staff would be honored. He told her that such a question was no one's business but his own. Then Joseph Toliver, the commodity trader who I'm sure you've heard of, said that since the parish was liable for a suit, it was indeed our business. Then the Bishop stood up and ordered us out of the rectory. I tried to reason with him. He told us that we had no canonical powers and no right to meet except at his request. He warned us to leave or he would call the police. We left."

"And went not gently into that good night?"

"I beg pardon?"

"You all were quite angry and so you raged against the failing of the light?"

"What could you expect, Bishop? Many of us have put enormous time and energy into the parish. It is an important part of our lives, of our very identities. As the kids say, 'Martyrs! The biggest and the best!' "

Would, I wondered, the forty holy martyrs, had they ever existed, have approved this class-based cry? I rather doubted it.

"Down in the city there are rumors that the kidnapping of the Bishop, and the injection of heroin into his bloodstream, were somehow devised up here."

"How could there not be such rumors? Personally, I don't credit them. We are not that kind of people. On the other hand, one can never be sure. The Chicago police, I am told, discount such a possibility. Nonetheless, I certainly feel safe in saying that there were few regrets up here at the Bishop's misfortune. Moreover, there was great joy when Father Dribben returned. People said that the Cardinal had redeemed himself."

"I'm sure he will be delighted with that vote of confidence. . . . And your own personal feelings?"

"Personal? I don't think they matter. However, since you ask and in all candor, I was not disappointed to learn what happened to him. He had it coming."

The man paused, as if trying to control himself within his image of the corporate executive.

"In all candor, Bishop," he continued, his thin lips tight, "if I had learned of a conspiracy to destroy him without killing him, I would have joined it."

"I see."

"However"—he relaxed, having recaptured the mask that went with his role—"there was no such conspiracy that I know of. That is not to say that there might not have been one. If there were, it was carried out with the utmost secrecy."

"It was," I sighed, "a very professional operation, the sort I would expect from this community."

"Exactly."

When he left, I sneaked into the kitchen to make myself a cup of tea and perhaps exorcise the headache that these worthy Christians had produced. A small, waiflike girl child appeared.

"Father Matt said you'd like some tea before you left, Bishop. I'll make it for you. I might even find some cookies for you."

"Wondrous. . . . You would be Crystal?"

She giggled. "How did you know that? Oh, well, everyone seems to know who I am."

The young woman's smile was arguably the most radiant currently to be found on the planet. In an earlier age, she would have been a novice in a religious order. Now she was a youth minister who looked younger than most of her charges.

We sat at a booth in the kitchen to drink our tea and eat our cookies.

"I hope you don't think me forward, Bishop Ryan." She grinned at me over the rim of her teacup. "Father Matt said I could talk to you."

"Father Matt is patently the boss."

She giggled again, then tried to become serious.

"I'm going back to school next autumn to study for my doctorate in psychology at Loyola."

Saint Thérèse went to the Carmel in Lisieux. This counterpart a century later would go to Loyola for a doctorate in psychology. Thus God plans the lives of bewitching young women for every era.

"Admirable."

"My contract here will be over and I really couldn't commute downtown, so Father Matt said that I should talk to you about—"

"You're hired," I said.

"Oh, Bishop!" She jumped up and clapped her hands. "I'm so happy. I promise you that I will do a good job."

"Somewhere here I have a card," I said searching through my pockets. Naturally, I didn't have a card.

"I know where the Cathedral is, Bishop."

Who didn't?

So it was arranged that she would stop by the Cathedral and we would talk about her employment. I assured her that the fact of such employment was a

settled matter. How else do you deal with a saint when
you find one?

"Tell me about Bishop Quill," I said.

Her face clouded.

"Poor, dear man, there was so much good in him,
Bishop Blackie. No matter how hard he tried, he just
couldn't get the good out."

So quickly I had become Bishop Blackie. She would,
upon arrival, make common cause with the Megan
against me.

"Why do you think that was?"

"I suppose his poor mother isolated him from everyone else." She shrugged. "The goodness is still there. I
could see it sometimes in his eyes."

It was a diagnosis that my far more sophisticated
sibling could but endorse.

"You're not angry at him?"

"Why should I be angry at him? . . . Will he recover?"

"Perhaps. The doctors are very cautious."

"I will keep praying for him."

Matt walked to the car with me.

"A fifty-five black Thunderbird. Appropriate. . . . So
you talked to Crystal and hired her on the spot?"

"What more could one do?"

He laughed.

"She's no fool, Blackie."

"I noticed that."

I also noticed that she was the only one in the whole
parish who had some sympathy for Gus Quill.

"You're planning to visit those gombeen men down
the street, from the Legion of Corpus Christi?"

"Arguably."

"Today?"

"I must return to my hospital calls at the Cathedral. Later in the week."

"Giving the illusion of not being in a rush."

"Perhaps."

"They're a sneaky bunch. Watch out for them."

Tommy

24

Finally, it was time for the national championship—the Irish against the Lady Cardinal at the Florida State pitch in Tallahassee. What would the Irish do on a pitch that wasn't mud-soaked?

"Will you beat them?" I asked Christy on the phone.

"That's a silly question, certainly we'll beat them."

"That's what I like from my young lionesses—fierce confidence."

"They're very good, Tommy. Very stuck-up, but very good."

She had learned the sports lingo. Before a big game, you are both very confident and very respectful of the tough opponent.

I decided that I would fly to Tallahassee to see the match. Why not? I would not, however, warn her beforehand. She didn't need to know that I was in the stands for the first time.

The Florida panhandle at that time of the year was like a South Sea Islands paradise compared to the City of Chicago, Richard M. Daley, Mayor. The temperature on the field at game time, the media predicted, would be in the middle nineties.

The local papers were filled with news of the game. Even the *New York Times* had a moderately long story. It was all Stanford. Multicultural team, great talent, maybe the best women's college soccer team ever. Gifted players, a musician, an actress, and an artist. Young African-American coach. Number one all season. Undefeated. Their adversary? Plucky young women from a school more famous for its men's football team. All-American captain Christy Logan was probably no match for the faster All-Americans on Stanford's team.

Well, we would see.

There has been little love lost between Notre Dame and Leland Stanford Jr. Memorial University since the notorious incident at Stanford when their band ridiculed Catholicism at half-time. The University, a model of political correctness in all other matters, argued that the band was an independent organization and the University was not responsible for what it did. The argument, need I say, cut no ice either at South Bend or among the Irish alumni, real and imagined, around the country.

As a Hoya I was strictly neutral. I didn't like either of them.

The sun shone brightly over Tallahasse that afternoon, a bad sign, I thought, for the Irish, who were mudders. The small stadium around the pitch was almost filled. I saw the Drs. Logan at a distance, but did not want to bother them.

The warm-ups struck me as ominous. The Lady Cardinal, in bright red uniforms, seemed bored and sullen, as if they felt it was a disgrace that they had to play against a patently inferior team. They also looked mean, very mean. That judgment, however, was from a prejudiced perspective. Christy's young women in dark blue and white with gold trim acted like the playful pride of lionesses they were. Christy had them smiling and laughing. Certainly not intimidated, but perhaps too loose.

For the first part of the first half, under the searing sun, the Cardinal ran all over the Irish. They were indeed lightning fast and very physical. One of them knocked my young heroine on her butt several times. The officials had apparently decided that they were going to let the young women play soccer and not interfere with the game.

Stanford scored early on an easy goal when the Irish defense collapsed. They swaggered around like they were South American male soccer players. It was all over.

However, Christy, shouting orders, warnings, and encouragement, rallied the pride, which settled down to a grueling defensive game. They held the Cardinal to nothing more than a few ineffectual shots at the goal. Finally, as the half wound down to this last minute, the chief lioness broke through, raced towards the goal, faked a shot that drew the Cardinal goalie (one of their All-Americans) in her direction, and then rifled the ball across the pitch to a wing, who easily drove it in.

It was 1–1 at half-time. A wise gambler, quite apart from his loyalties, would have gone long on the Irish, despite the fact that the Irish walked off the field sweating profusely and the Cardinal seemed unperturbed by heat. The bay area was much warmer than late autumn Chicago, I realized. The Cardinal had the weather on their side.

Stanford came out in the second half with renewed

fury, fast, brutally rough, and grimly determined. This time, however, Notre Dame was ready for them. They withstood the onslaught. My Christy was all over the pitch, stealing the ball from their allegedly faster and better All-American strikers. The crowd, which had been pro-Cardinal at the beginning, was now on the Irish side. Someone struck up the notorious (to a Hoya like me) victory song. I sang it, God help me, at the top of my voice.

> *Rally sons of Notre Dame,*
> *Sing her glory, and sound her fame*
> *Raise her Gold and Blue,*
> *And cheer with voices true,*
> *Rah! Rah! for Notre Dame.*

> *We will fight in every game*
> *Strong of heart and true to her name.*
> *We will ne'er forget her*
> *And we'll cheer her ever,*
> *Loyal to Notre Dame.*

> *Cheer, cheer for Old Notre Dame*
> *Wake up the echoes cheering her name,*
> *Send the volley cheer on high,*
> *Shake down the thunder from the sky,*
> *What tho the odds be great or small*
> *Old Notre Dame will win over all,*
> *While her daughters are marching*
> *Onward to Victory.*

Christy shook her fist and grinned at the crowd.

"You from Notre Dame?" a young woman with a thick southern accent next to me asked.

"Nope," I said. "One of them is a friend of mine."

"The big blond?"

"As a matter of fact, yes."

"No doubt who the best All-American out there really is."

It turned out she was on the Florida State University team. She also admitted that the chief lioness was totally beautiful.

"I hadn't noticed."

The match ebbed and flowed up and down the pitch. Near misses for both sides. Superb defensive play. I still would have gone long on the Irish, though they were clearly exhausted. Christy loved last-minute victories, didn't she?

Then, with only three of the forty-five minutes left, one of Stanford's All-American strikers broke free and dribbled down the pitch. The Notre Dame defense was momentarily disorganized. The Cardinals bench shouted, "Sonia! Sonia!" There was no one between her and the goal.

Then, almost out of nowhere raced the top lioness. As she had done all afternoon, she deftly booted the ball away from Sonia without hitting her. Then she charged back up the pitch through both disorganized and exhausted teams, Sonia in hot pursuit.

Christy broke free from the swirling masses of red and dark blue jerseys and dashed towards the goal. She was going to drive all the way in so the goalie wouldn't have a chance to block the shot.

Then Sonia caught up. She stuck out her foot and tripped Christy before she could kick the goal. The crowd gasped as Christy landed face down on the turf. There was dead silence for a moment as she struggled to her feet and shook her fist again. Loud applause from the crowd. This time I started the singing of the victory march.

The ref appeared with a red card. Sonia was banished from the game. No replacement permitted. Sonia shouted obscenities. The Stanford team rallied around her. The Stanford coach went crazy. The crowd booed. The ref was not impressed. She pointed towards the locker room and banished both Sonia and the coach.

The official ruled that there would be a penalty kick. She waved both teams away from the goal. The Cardinal screamed again. Christy limped towards the line. One on one, I thought, Christy and the goalie.

Christy faked with her shoulders, then booted the ball by the goalie, who fell on her face as she dove to stop it.

Christy jammed her finger against the sky. Notre Dame was number one! I had won my imaginary bet.

Then she waved off the coach. She was just fine. She continued to hobble, however.

The last two and a half minutes were brutal. The Cardinal abandoned all restraint and turned the match into wild melee. Restrained by Christy's stern warnings, the Irish hung back and let Stanford destroy themselves. The crowd sang the victory march over and over again, albeit only the last stanza.

I mean, who knows the other verses?

I worried about my brave lioness. She was limping badly. The match ended. The Cardinal stalked off the field without a word of congratulations. Christy collapsed on the bench, obviously in great pain. I rushed down the steps, past a startled state cop to whom I shouted, "My girl is hurt," and over to the bench. The Drs. Logan had beat me to it. The rest of the Domers stood by in frightened silence.

Tentatively, Mary Logan ran her finger down her daughter's left leg. Christy screamed.

Mary looked at her husband. "Fibula! If we're lucky, it's only a hairline."

"My leg is not broken!" Christy yelled, wincing with pain. "We have to celebrate!"

"The first thing to do is to immobilize the leg," John Logan said to the trainer. "Do you have a gurney?"

Someone had rolled one out.

"I don't need a gurney!" Christy protested. "I'm fine!"

"And call an ambulance."

"Yes, doctor. Tallahassee Memorial?"

"Of course."

"No ambulance!" Christy cried.

I interjected myself into the dialogue.

"Christy Anne," I said gently, "Please grow up for a few moments. Your parents are doctors. If they say your leg is broken, it's broken. They want to fix you up so you can go to the Olympic tryouts. Now don't make matters worse than they already are."

She glared at me. "What are you doing here?"

"Came to cheer for the Irish lionesses."

"Well, since you're here, the least you can do is to hold my hand. It hurts!"

I held her hand, my heart breaking at her pain.

Mary Logan, fitting the temporary splint in place, looked up at me and smiled.

"Thank God you're here, Tommy Flynn."

"Ouch!" Christy wailed as the splint was slipped into place. "Tommy, where are you! Tighter!"

I squeezed as tight as I could.

An ambulance rolled onto the pitch. A crowd had gathered, Notre Dame players, fans, and interested observers. A TV camera was grinding away. Christy waved as they rolled her onto the ambulance. Her parents climbed in. Somehow or the other I did too. Then, just as the door closed, Christy raised her hand and finger. NUMBER ONE.

"She played for two and a half minutes with a broken leg?" I asked John Logan.

"And kicked the winning goal. . . . Tommy, we never

had anyone like her in our family. She's a throwback!"

Apparently the ambulance driver had radioed to the hospital. A young resident was waiting for us outside the door of the emergency room.

"Real fighting Irish," he said as they rolled Christy down to ground level. "I'm John Peters. I went there too."

"John Logan, Doctor. I'm Christy's father. Mary Logan, her mother. We're also alumni."

Doctors recognize other doctors. I don't know how. Same with priests.

"Let's all sing the alma mater song," Christy suggested through gritted teeth.

"St. Mary's, in my day," Mary Logan set the record straight.

They wheeled my wounded lioness into an emergency room.

"We'll have you fixed up in a few minutes, Ms. Logan. We'll take some X rays first. . . . What is your diagnosis, Dr. Logan?"

"Call me Christy. . . . Where are you, Tommy Flynn? Why aren't you holding my hand?"

I recaptured the hand from which I had been detached when they were wheeling her into the hospital.

"If we're lucky, a hairline fracture of the lower fibula."

Very gently the doctor ran his finger along her lower leg. Christy yelled in protest.

"Right there, Christy?"

"Yes, Doctor," she said. "Make it go away. That's what doctors are for."

"We'll give you a shot and take you down to X ray. I'll call Dr. O'Halloran, our orthopedic person. She's a Domer too."

"Just so long as there's no one from Stanford!"

"What's that noise?" Dr. Peters said, startled by a roar from the lobby.

"Christy's teammates," I suggested.

"Tommy Flynn," the lion queen ordered, "go out there and tell those geeks to chill out. This is a hospital. There's sick people here."

"Yes, ma'am."

"Then come back and hold my hand."

"Yes, ma'am."

The lobby was in chaos. Two outnumbered security guards were trying to restrain a group of noisy, smelly young women in blue-and-white soccer uniforms, a couple of them waving unopened bottles of champagne. There were also some adults—coaches, trainers, hangers-on, and one tall priest.

"All right you geeks," I yelled. "Christy says you should chill out."

Instant silence. Even in absentia, she was in charge.

"First of all, she's all right. It's probably a hairline fracture of the lower fibula, which, if you have to break your leg, is the best way to do it. They're taking X rays and the orthopedic specialist is on her way. They're giving her a shot now to ease the pain—that's medication, not gin!"

Laughter.

"The resident in charge is Dr. John Peters. The orthopedic specialist is Dr. O'Halloran, first name unknown, gender female. They're both Domers. I think Christy will get the red carpet treatment she deserves and expects. . . . Now if you geeks keep quiet, I'll see if I can arrange a little celebration."

"Are you Christy's boyfriend?" a child, no taller than five-two, asked me.

"No, ma'am. I'm her lion trainer."

The security guards continued to struggle to ease the crowd out of the lobby.

I dashed down a corridor, asked a nurse where Public Relations was, and ran down another corridor. The sign on the door said LORETTA CLIFFORD, COMMUNITY RELATIONS.

I brushed by the secretary.

"Ms. Clifford, we have a situation down in the lobby. The captain of the Notre Dame soccer team is in emergency with a broken leg—"

"Did we win?"

Another one of them. Figured.

"You did. The team is in the lobby wanting to celebrate with their heroine. The security people, understandably, are trying to get rid of them. . . ."

Ms. Clifford knew her work. She picked up a phone and gave a few terse orders to Security.

"I think we can control the situation if we permit them to talk to Christy after her splint is applied and to have a few sips of champagne."

"You can deal with them for that?"

"They'll do whatever Christy says."

"Right! It's a deal."

She was on the phone again as I left the office.

Back in the lobby, there was a truce between the Domers and the cops.

"I'll be right back," I shouted. "Cool it!"

Inside, Dr. Peters and the Logans were looking at X rays.

"What's your guess, Dr. Logan?"

"Your call, Dr. Peters," Mary Logan said, peering intently at the X rays.

"Lemme see," Christy demanded. "It's my leg."

"There's a crack in the front bone of your lower leg right here, Christy. We may not have to set it."

The orthopedist arrived in T-shirt and shorts, called away perhaps from a pool side. Gorgeous. She was African American.

"You poor child, what did they do to you!"

"She like totally tripped me!"

"I saw it. . . ." She looked at the X ray. "I'm Jean O'Halloran, by the way."

"These are my parents, they're doctors too, but they're no good unless I have a heart attack. The lug is Tommy Flynn. He holds my hand, which he isn't doing right now."

I returned to my duty.

"You played on this for three minutes?"

"Two and a half."

"Did you know it was broken?"

"I'm like, now you've done it, Christy, but you totally can't quit now."

"Child, as a Domer I applaud your courage," she continued to peer intently at the negatives. "As a doctor and a parent, I think you're crazy."

"That's the kind of things lionesses do," I observed.

"Will I be able to play in the Olympics?"

"Well"—Dr. O'Halloran pondered—"maybe. If you're very, very careful and do exactly what I tell you to do and what the orthopedists in Chicago say. . . . What hospital, Dr. Logan?"

"Northwestern."

"Alf Hightower? The best."

"I'm going to medical school next year," Christy informed her. "And I'm going to specialize in sports medicine."

The painkiller was beginning to have an effect.

"Fine, but even then you don't diagnose yourself, right?"

"Yes, ma'am."

"Now we're going to put a splint and a brace on this leg, give you another shot, keep you here overnight, and let you go home to Chicago maybe on Monday. It's crutches for two weeks at least, understand?"

"Yes, ma'am."

"Dr. O'Halloran . . . ," I intruded.

"Yes, Tommy Flynn, hand-holder."

"You may not have noticed, but the lobby is filled with Domers, the team mostly. They want a brief celebration with Christy. I cut a deal with Loretta Clifford that if it was all right, one small sip of champagne for everyone and they'll go home."

"After we get the splint on. You a precinct captain or something, Tommy Flynn?"

"Not yet."

I grabbed a stack of paper cups from a supply cart that had been left unguarded. In the lobby, Loretta Clifford, standing with the security people, looked amused.

"All right, geeks!" I shouted. "Another message from herself!"

Silence.

"She says you're making too much noise. When she tells you to chill out, you should chill out, right?"

They chilled out.

"Now, here's the deal. Dr. Jean O'Halloran says that it is indeed a hairline fracture. They're putting a splint and a brace on it, giving her another shot, and keeping her in till tomorrow. She'll come out here and you can open two—count 'em, two—bottles of champagne. Everyone gets a small drink, Christy only a sip. Then you leave quietly and Christy has a long night's sleep. Got it?"

They nodded solemnly.

"You," I said to the small girl child who was a fearsome striker on the pitch, "pass around the paper cups. One to a customer. Christy has this painkiller stuff in her, so she may be a little more geeky than usual. But I'm not sure that we'll be able to tell the difference."

More laughter.

I went back to Christy's room. Dr. O'Halloran was carefully adjusting a splint.

"Hurt, child?"

"No, Jean, but Tommy Flynn should be holding my hand just the same. That's all he's good for, you know?"

They all laughed. Tommy Flynn as milady's fool.

"What do you think, Dr. Logan?"

"As Christy says"—it was Mary Logan's turn to speak for the family—"we'd only be a help if she had a heart attack or needed heart surgery. It looks fine to me."

With infinite delicacy, Dr. O'Halloran locked the brace in place.

"No messing with this child, hear?"

"Yes, ma'am."

"Now you go out there and have your little celebration. Then we'll take some more X rays and put you to bed."

"Tommy Flynn, you push this wheelchair."

"Yes, milady."

So we entered the lobby with all four medical doctors in tow. The media were there already. Two TV cameras.

The waiting Domers broke into cheers. Someone gave Christy the championship cup, which she shook triumphantly. They opened the two bottles of champagne, poured a little into every paper cup, and gave a cup to Christy. As I had ordered, it contained only a sip.

"To Christy!" the small girl child shouted.

"Christy!" They all bellowed

Then someone, surely not I, did the inevitable.

" 'Cheer, cheer for old Notre Dame'—let's have all three stanzas!"

Hoya or not, I sang along with them.

"Chill out!" the lion queen ordered.

They did.

"Dr. O'Halloran says that if I keep all the rules, my leg will be fine for the Olympics. You geeks know how good I am at keeping rules, right?"

Derisive laughter.

"So I expect you all to make sure I do, right?"

Universal agreement.

"I'm fading fast," she admitted. "I want to thank all of you for winning and for putting up with me all season long. You're the greatest! And we're number ONE!"

They had to sing the victory song again.

Two TV reporters pushed their way through the crowd.

"Christy, do you think Sonia tripped you deliberately?"

"No way," she said firmly. "In the heat of the game, we all do things that we wouldn't do normally."

"How do you feel now, Christy?"

"Happy . . . and very sleepy."

Then they left quietly. Mary Logan wheeled her back into the emergency room.

"What's your name, son?" the tall priest asked me.

"Tommy Flynn, Father."

"You a senior?"

"I was five years ago—at Georgetown!"

He shook hands with me. "Even Hoyas have souls. That was a superb performance."

"Thank you, Father."

"Are you, uh, Christy's . . ."

"Not yet."

He shook hands again.

"She'll be a fortunate young woman when you are."

Gulp.

In the emergency room, they were inspecting another

set of X-ray negatives. The lioness was pretty well tranquilized.

"Looks good," Dr. O'Halloran said. "We'll do another set tomorrow, Dr. Logan. Four sets to bring home to Dr. Hightower."

"I think my hand-holding services are no longer required," I said.

I leaned over and rested my lips against hers.

"Be good, Christy Logan, national champ."

"I will, Tommy Flynn, hand-holder." Then her voice sank to a whisper. "Would you smuggle a malted milk into this place for me?"

"Sure."

John Logan walked me to main entrance of the hospital.

"Are you staying at the FSU Marriott, Tommy?"

"Yes, sir."

"We are too. Maybe we can have supper tomorrow night when we get herself out of here."

"Sounds great."

"She is the most unusual of our children," he began tentatively.

"I can believe that."

"She has never paid the slightest attention to us. She doesn't do bad things, drugs or drink or boys, and she's always respectful."

"I don't doubt it."

"However, we have absolutely no control over her."

"I don't doubt that either."

"You tell her what to do and she goes along."

"Sometimes."

He sighed. "I don't know what your secret is, young man, but more power to you."

"Thank you, sir. I may need it."

* * *

I did smuggle the malted milk back into the hospital later. It was easy. The security folk thought I was one of their guys.

Christy's room was semidark. Wearing a hospital gown, she was lying on a bed with her leg suspended in the air. She looked like a sixteen-year-old again. Mary Logan was sitting in a chair next to the bed saying the rosary.

"Hi," I whispered. "I was told to smuggle in three malted milks, one for you, one for Christina Anne, and one for myself."

"Thank you, Tommy. She's dozed off. But I'm sure she'll wake up for you."

"I don't want to bother her."

"No bother. She'll go right back to sleep."

"How's she doing?"

"Fine. She's a strong and healthy young woman. The leg will heal quickly. She may feel twinges occasionally on cold and rainy days. They'll remind her of her great triumph. It really was great, wasn't it, Tommy Flynn?"

"The greatest!"

"Bishop Blackie called. He said that it was arguably the greatest victory in the whole history of the Fighting Irish."

That sounded like Bishop Blackie.

"Christina dear, that nice young Tommy Flynn is here with a treat."

Her eyes opened wide.

"WELL, it's about time."

We consumed our three malted milks, I kissed her good night, and slipped away.

No doubt that the Logans were on my side.

The papers the next day were filled with the story. Stanford's formal protest was the main topic. They had complained that as important a game as the national championship should not be decided by an official's mistake. Sonia was quoted as saying, "I never touched her. It was definitely a fake. We shouldn't lose because the ref was too dumb to spot a fake." Their coach insisted that it was a blatant misjudgment that "cannot be permitted to deny our young women a national championship which is rightly theirs." The Notre Dame coach had only two words to say: "Sour grapes." Unnamed experts argued that the soccer federation would most likely reject the protest since there was no precedent for such a reversal of a ref's decision. There were rumors that Sonia would be banned from soccer for a year, and thus precluded from trying out for the United States Olympic team.

Somehow it was not so newsworthy that a young woman with a broken left leg (admittedly only a hairline fracture) had won the game.

The most powerful element in the rehash, however, was a *New York Times* spread of frames from the TV tape. It showed Christy deftly stealing Sonia's dribble without touching her, skirting around the Cardinal player, and dribbling down the pitch, and next Sonia sticking out her foot, and then the actual contact, and finally Christy tumbling to the grass. There was no doubt that she had been tripped.

The *Times* headed the story: TRIP, REAL OR FAKE?

I spent the day in the FSU bookstore and reading beside the hotel pool.

Pale and subdued, Christy hobbled into the restaurant of the FSU Marriott that night on crutches. She was wearing a gray pant-suit with white trim at the neck and cuffs, and her pearl necklace and earrings. Wounded lionesses have to look chic.

I made a big fuss of helping her into her chair.

"How you doing?"

"I ache everywhere. Otherwise, I'm fine. I can't even swim for two weeks. I'll be like, totally fat."

"No more secret malted milks!"

Her eyes widened in feigned innocence.

"I'd never do that. Some weird boy might try to pick me up."

She was on her way back.

"The media were waiting for us when we came downstairs," John Logan said with a sigh. "Those Stanford people are real geeks."

"Totally," His daughter agreed. "Like, they go, what would we do if the USSF told us to give the trophy back, and I'm like, Stanford would have to come to Notre Dame to get it and bring their geeky band along with them."

"I thought you hit just the right note, dear, when they asked you whether you thought the USSF would suspend Sonia, and you said if they did, you'd write a letter asking them to change their minds."

"I didn't mention that if she showed up at the Olympics, I'd trip her back!"

"Christy!" her parents said together.

"She's only joking," I said. "Actually, what she would do is take Sonia out for a malted milk and then poison her."

She survived the trip to Chicago well enough. Dr. Hightower confirmed Dr. O'Halloran's diagnosis. I drove down to Notre Dame a couple of weekends to see her. She had recovered her high spirits and was obeying all the rules. I was a little too elderly for the campus life; however, there were a couple of good concerts and one good lecture, for which only a handful of the Domers showed up.

Geeks!

I told myself as I drove back late Sunday night—the rules I made for Christy didn't apply to me—that our relationship was unchanged. We were still good friends and still nothing more than that. It was harder each weekend to persuade myself that this was anything more than fantasy.

Blackie

25

"We are very honored that you deign to visit us, Your Excellency, however informally."

"You will, of course, have an aperitif. Some sherry, perhaps?"

One of them was Father Luis, the other was Father Ramon, trim men of medium height, sallow skin, and dark brown hair. Not twins exactly, but so similar in posture, accent, and voice that I could not tell them apart. That was, perhaps, part of their game. Their residence was an elaborate mansion two blocks down the street from Forty Holy Martyrs. They had greeted me in a drawing room that would have been worthy of Philip II.

A couple of centuries ago, they would have worked for the Inquisition. Now they were trying to subvert the whole Church so they could run it. They had lots of clout in Rome, but were not smart enough to know how to use it. Besides, the Church was now too confused to be open to subversion.

I accepted a very small glass of sherry, a beverage from which my attendant leprechaun did not deign to steal.

"We very much regret the difficulties with Bishop Quill."

"It is perhaps necessary to assert that our people had nothing to do with his appointment."

"In fact, we have learned from the highest authority that our people in Rome opposed the appointment."

"They foresaw the troubles which would occur."

"And warned others what would happen."

"Indeed."

This was nonsense. They were merely covering their tracks, as they always did.

"It is true that he came to us about a television station, which he proposed to build here in the parish to combat the godlessness in the secular capitalist media."

"It is also true that we ourselves have given some thought to such a project."

"We had not gone beyond remote planning. Naturally, we would have consulted with the Cardinal."

"Naturally," I agreed.

"Bishop Quill had certain peculiar mannerisms."

"He seemed to assume that because he had presented his plans to us, we accepted them."

"Ah?"

"We had in fact agreed to nothing."

"Nor would we ever have agreed to cooperate with him."

"He was, how should I say it, too, ah, unstable."

"We would have to raise large sums of money for such a project."

"A building, electronic equipment, staff."

"Television is every expensive, as I'm sure you know, Bishop Ryan."

"We would owe it to our supporters to retain control of the station."

"That would have been most difficult if Bishop Quill was, uh, involved."

"I take your meaning. . . . Therefore, you were not displeased to learn of the Bishop's unfortunate, ah, experience?"

I might just as well have suggested that the Pope was not Catholic.

"Quite the contrary, we deplore it."

"It is most unfortunate."

"Very bad for the Church."

"He was such a very peculiar man, was he not?"

"Yes, very peculiar."

"We trust he is recovering well?"

Why was everyone so eager to be reassured that poor Gus would not recover?

"As well as can be expected. The doctors are cautiously optimistic."

"Thanks be to God!"

"He will be able to return to the parish?"

"Perhaps, though at the present time that does not seem likely."

Their relief at such good news was all too obvious.

"Such a tragic story."

"Yes, it is."

"I am told that there is some suspicion that your friends could have been involved in his kidnapping."

Shock, dismay, outrage. Always polite, however.

"Surely not!"

"A man of your sophistication knows how many false things are said about us."

"We would never be a party to such evil."

"We know of no one who could carry out such a convoluted crime."

"Why would anyone spread such rumors about us?"

"It is defamation."

They did protest too much. On the basis of the past history of their group, they would do almost anything to further its goals. However, they would stop short of murder. But this wasn't murder, was it?

"I quite agree," I said soothingly. "I merely felt that, in conscience, I had to warn you about the rumor."

"We are most grateful for the warning."

"We will take action to counteract it."

"We will delay the television station indefinitely."

"Please assure His Eminence of our continued respect and esteem."

I promised them that I would.

I left them, quite certain that they would be buzzing as soon as I was out the door. They would be on the phone to Rome immediately. Even if most Romans had closed their offices, the office of the Legion was always open for emergency phone calls from its worldwide troops.

On the way over to Peter Quill's house, I called Mike the Cop and told him to add the Legion of Corpus Christi to his list of suspects. To save another phone call, I also instructed him to look into Peter and Grace Quill.

The Quills, well-preserved, elegant folk, both with dyed hair and various kinds of cosmetic surgeries, were not especially pleased to see me. They were polite, but distant. They offered me a preprandial drink which, in view of the drive back to the city in rush hour, I declined. They seemed relieved that no pretense of hospitality was necessary.

"We understand your interest, Bishop," Peter Quill began heavily, "and we'd like to help. You must understand that we were never very close to Augustus."

"His mother practically excluded Peter from her life when Augustus was born," Grace continued impatiently. "Some sort of Catholic fortune-teller or mystic, or something like that, promised her before Augustus was born that he would be a priest and a bishop. All the family attention and concern and money went to him."

"He did not call us when he was appointed bishop," Peter said. "We learned that from television."

"Nor did he inform us that he had been appointed pastor up here," Grace continued. "We were not, need I say, delighted."

"You were not happy to have your brother in the parish?" I said with mock surprise to Peter.

"Hardly," he replied. "There has always been something a little strange about Augustus. I don't know how to describe it. . . ."

"Creepy," Grace snapped. "He always made me feel uncomfortable."

"I don't know that I would use that word, Grace. Perhaps unusual. It's not merely that he lacked most of the human graces. Many priests are that way. Rather, he really didn't seem to care much about people."

"Except the Pope."

"When our kids were younger," Peter went on, "and he used to come around to visit, he lectured them about the Pope until they were sick of hearing about him."

"So he was an embarrassment to you?"

"Definitely!" Grace exploded. "People blamed us for whatever he did. Guilt by association. It wasn't fair."

"Whoever said the world was fair?" Her husband shook his head sadly. "Women stopped coming to Grace's dress shop, though it is the most fashionable one on Green Bay Road. My brokerage business suffered too. We weren't in terrible trouble. Still, it wasn't easy."

"So unfair!"

"How's he doing, by the way?"

Finally, an inquiry about his brother's health. Not much love lost in that relationship.

"He's suffering from a serious psychotic episode. The doctors think he will recover eventually, though they are cautious."

Peter Quill nodded. "Poor Augustus . . . I suppose his career is finished?"

"Arguably."

"That was all that ever really mattered to him, wasn't it, Peter?"

"What surprises me is that he got as far as he did. Don't they recognize psychopaths in Rome?"

"Usually too late. It is not easy to diagnose a borderline personality, much less to understand one. . . . I assume that since the return of Father Dribbin, your fellow parishioners are more sympathetic to you."

"Women are returning to my shop, Bishop. However, it's slow, very slow."

"My business is coming along too," Peter Quill added. "Not as quickly as I would like. Eventually, I am confident the nightmare will be over."

"That's what it has been, a nightmare!" Grace agreed.

"It's very awkward, Bishop Ryan," her husband went on. "He's my brother. I don't want to be disloyal to him. We never say in public what we're saying to you. Yet I was not sorry to learn what happened to him. If he had remained here much longer, he would have completely destroyed what we both had worked so long to build up."

"We even spoke of ways to get rid of him," Grace admitted. "Send him away somewhere for a long vacation, or catch him molesting little boys. We couldn't come up with anything. We were delighted that someone else got him."

"I don't ever want to see him again," her husband

said. "The very thought of him brings the nightmare back."

"Do you know who did it, Bishop?" Grace asked. "I'd like to shake his hand."

The conversation might have been an act. However, there was so much explicit hatred in it, I questioned whether it could have been faked.

As I struggled with the rush hour, I pondered in dismay how much anger and hatred there was for Augustus O'Sullivan Quill in Forest Hills. Only the good Crystal seemed immune.

I informed Megan Kim, who was the officer of the day, that a young woman named Crystal Lane might show up at the rectory. She wanted to be a youth minister, but I had my doubts. Megan nodded solemnly.

I had no doubts at all. However, I wanted to put the Megan in a situation where they would feel constrained to defend her against my doubts.

Thereupon I reported to the Cardinal, who had just returned from the Chancery office in a not untypical state of gloom.

"Let's have the bad news, Blackwood. There's no reason why you should be the only one with good news."

I therefore reported the bad news.

"I never should have sent him up there," he admitted. "He was a lot crazier than I thought he was."

"Could not the same remark be made of many of your colleagues in the hierarchy?"

"Our colleagues, Blackwood. How many times do I have to remind you that you're a bishop too?"

"I must try to repress it."

"Today, I think that is an excellent idea. If you pretend not to be a bishop, maybe everyone will forget it and you won't have to put up with the shit."

"Arguably."

"It sounds to me like the case is insolvable. Maybe that's just as well."

"No mystery is insolvable," I said firmly.

"Well, then solve it, Blackwood. See to it."

"One other thing . . . I hired away Matt's youth minister today at his recommendation because she will be studying at Loyola. Her name is Crystal."

"So? You're responsible for the parish. Just so long as I don't have to be youth minister."

"She's patently a saint."

"How do you know that?"

"She's the only one I've talked to who feels sympathy for Gus Quill."

"All right, she is a saint. That's all we need around here—a saint! Sign her up! Meanwhile, solve this mystery. . . . See to it, Blackwood!"

"You've already said that."

Jenny

26

There is a terrible noise at the door. Someone shouting "Police!" I put on a robe and slippers and, still mostly asleep, go to the door. The police are there. They shout at me. I can't understand what they're saying. Something about kidnapping Bishop Quill. Do I deny that I threatened his life? I'm too sleepy to answer. A woman cop handcuffs me, hands behind my back. She gives the cuffs a cruel twist that hurts. A lot more terrible things are going to happen to you, sister, unless you tell the truth. They drag me downstairs. There's a TV camera taking pictures as I am thrown into a patrol wagon. Don't try anything, sister, says the woman cop, shoving me, or you'll really get hurt. I tell myself it's a dream, a terrible nightmare. Somehow I know it isn't. Where are you taking me? None of your fucking business, she says. Eleventh and State, says a male cop. We're going to put you in with all the other whores.

Where's Ned when I need him? Why isn't he here to protect me from these monsters? I am very angry at him. After what seems a long ride, we pull up to a building with blue lights on it. The TV cameras are there too. Someone shouts, Jenny, why did you kidnap Bishop Quill. They shove me into the building brutally and then into an elevator. I don't know what I've done wrong. However, already I feel guilty. I'm dragged into a room with no windows. Two men and a woman, all looking smart and tough, shove me into a chair. The woman sits across from me. Another man, much younger and not so tough-looking, comes in. They tell me their names. Two captains and a lieutenant. The young man is an assistant state's attorney. They warn me that I am already liable to charges of perjury for denying to the arresting officers that I had threatened to kill Bishop Quill. Would you please take off the handcuffs, I ask. The state's attorney says he thinks the restraints are unwarranted. The woman across the table tells him to mind his own fucking business.

I want a lawyer, I say, a memory from a movie or a TV program popping into my head. Why do you want a lawyer, the woman captain snarls, if you're innocent? Come on, the state's attorney says. You haven't read her the Miranda rights. You haven't told her she can make a phone call. You keep her in restraints that are not appropriate. You expect me to go to a grand jury with this stuff? You've already lost the trial. Whose side are you on? snaps the woman. The side of the law, he says. If she confesses, the woman replies, you don't have to worry about Miranda rights. The hell I don't. The media will convict her, the woman argues. Look, says the young man, either she gets her phone call or I get out of here. All right, let her make her fucking phone call. Privately and with the cuffs off. They call the cop who had handcuffed me. She removes them with another vicious twist. What the hell are you doing, says the young man. I'm an officer of the court. I have to note these things. Shut up motherfucker.

I do get in a phone booth. The young man gives me a quarter to make the call. I call Ned. The phone rings and rings. Isn't he home? I hang up and try again. This time he answers, his voice groggy. Has he been sleeping with someone else? Yes? he says. Jenny. The police have arrested me. I'm at Eleventh and State in hand-cuffs and my nightclothes. They've been brutal. Come help me, please. I'm not having a nightmare, am I? No, I say impatiently, it's my nightmare. All right, he says. I'll be right down. I'll bring Manny Horowitz, our liti-gator. Not a word till we get there. Incidentally, what is the charge against you? I don't know. Something about kidnapping Bishop Quill. Assholes, he says. I love you.

It is nice to hear that, but why isn't he here to protect me? I will not say a word to you assholes, I tell the cops, until my lawyer is here. They throw me into what they call a holding pen. It is filled with prostitutes who make fun of my nightclothes.

Tommy

27

The first thing I heard was someone shouting that if I didn't open the door they'd break it down. I assumed it was a nightmare. Just in case it wasn't, I grabbed for a robe and stumbled to the door. I opened it. There were four cops and two Hancock Center security guards.

"Why did you threaten to kill Bishop Quill?" one of the cops shouted at me.

Then I knew it wasn't a nightmare.

"I didn't threaten to kill anyone."

"OK, motherfucker, you just committed perjury. We're taking you down to Eleventh and State and we'll beat the truth out of you, got it, asshole? Cuff him!"

The cuffs felt real enough. O.K., I tell myself, this is not a nightmare. They didn't read me my Miranda rights. Rogue cops.

"I want to make a phone call," I shouted at them as they wrestled me towards an elevator.

"Shut your motherfucking face." One of the cops

nudged me in the back with his club. "You get to make a phone call when we want you to."

At that point I remembered that my father had made tons of money on suits against cops who had done only what these guys had already done. O.K., Dad, some more business for you.

There are TV cameras in the lobby. The whole business. Convict a guy at the door of his house as you drag him out in his nightclothes, which in my case were shorts and a robe.

"Tommy, why did you try to kill Bishop Quill?" one of the dumb women journalists shouts at me.

"Get all of this down," I screamed at her. "It'll be great evidence for a suit against the Chicago Police Department. They haven't read me my Miranda rights or let me make a phone call, either."

"I'll Miranda you," said the cop with the billy club as he pushed me into the wagon.

"He hit me with that upstairs," I yelled at the reporter. "Ask the Hancock guards!"

Inside the wagon, he raised his club to hit me in the head. "Go ahead, asshole," I sneered. "You'll do time if you hit me."

I would later realize that was an absolutely stupid thing to say. I was angry, however, and testosterone had flooded my bloodstream.

Another cop grabbed his hand. "The motherfucker is right. We could be in deep shit."

"The Deputy Super said to play it tough."

"Yeah, who do you think gets fucked, us or the Deputy Super?"

Deputy Super, huh. That was interesting information.

At Eleventh and State, I beat the dumb woman reporter to the punch.

"They haven't read me my Miranda rights," I

shouted. "They won't let me make a phone call, and they have beaten me with a billy club."

They pushed me into the building in a hurry, so I didn't get a chance to score any more points.

Later, Mom would say to me, "Tommy, weren't you taking a lot of risks? Suppose he had hit you over the head?"

"Big judgment," I said.

"Scrambled brains," she said.

"Yeah," I said, realizing that I was an asshole too. However, I was not completely ashamed of myself.

"I want my lawyer," I bellowed when they got me off the elevator and dragged me down the hall.

I continued to shout and they continued to ignore me and shove me around. Finally, they pushed me into an interrogation room. Two very tough-looking cops and a young blond were waiting for me.

"Shut up, asshole," said the cop who was apparently in charge. "WE do the talking in here."

"You haven't read me my Miranda rights, you haven't let me make a phone call, you're trying to interrogate me without my lawyer present, and one of your arresting officers attacked me with a billy club. I'm not saying a thing till my lawyer is present."

"Is that true, Captain?" the blond asked.

"He's full of shit. And you stay out of this, understand?"

The young woman looked scared stiff, but she stuck to her guns. "I will not stay out of it. If you did not read him his rights, you have already lost the case."

"Fuck the case. The media has the story."

"Oh? You let him make his phone call or I will go out and tell the media that the State's Attorney is washing his hands of the case."

"Whose side are you on?"

"The side of the law, Captain."

The young woman lent me a quarter.

"Are you Tom Flynn's son?"

"Yeah. Do I look like him?"

"A little bit." She laughed to herself. "You certainly act like him."

Beth answered the phone.

"Flynn residence."

"Mom, it's Tommy. I'm at Eleventh and State, charged apparently with attempted murder and perjury. They haven't read me my rights yet, they wouldn't let me make a phone call, and a cop hit me with a club. I'm still in cuffs! We got a great case!"

"Tommy! Are you all right?"

"Having the time of my life! Let me talk to Dad."

I told Dad the same story.

"Why, Tommy? Why would they do such stupid things?"

"The Deputy Superintendent is apparently behind it. I think they want some kind of conviction in the media."

"The Superintendent is away. . . . All right, Tommy, I'm coming down there. I'll bring Cindy Hurley along to be your lawyer. Not a word to anyone till she arrives."

"Got it!"

"Tommy . . ."

"Yes, Dad."

"Don't do anything foolish. Rogue cops are dangerous cops."

That sobered me a bit.

"Not me, Dad."

Later, when my bloodstream had cleansed away the adrenaline and the testosterone, I realized how foolish I had been. Then revulsion, humiliation, and guilt overwhelmed me. I understood how the innocent people who had been convicted in the Communist show trials had come to feel guilty.

"Not a word before my lawyer arrives," I informed the assembled group in the interrogation room.

"And when will that be?" the captain sneered.

"When she comes," I replied.

"OK, smartass, we'll throw you in the holding pen with the bums and the drunks and the perverts."

"You heard that, Ms. State's Attorney?"

"I did. Captain, you shouldn't say things like that. Moreover, you shouldn't do them."

"What we do is our business."

"All right, you've been warned." She turned to me. "Who will represent you, Mr. Flynn?"

"Cindy Hurley."

She winced.

The holding pen wasn't so bad, except the men in there were so pathetic. There but for the grace of God goes Tommy Flynn. Then I thought for the first time of my young lioness. What would she think when she woke up in the morning and discovered I was in jail on a murder charge?

For the first time I felt the guilt and humiliation that would devastate me in days to come.

Hours later, still cuffed, I was dragged back to the interrogation room. Cindy Hurley swept in like the Golden Horde.

"All right, assholes," she shouted, "what the hell is going on here? Are you the state's attorney?"

"Yes, ma'am," the cute blond replied in a trembling voice.

"I note that that my client is in restraints. I note that you have observed this. I hold you responsible."

"Yes, ma'am."

"Actually, Ms. Hurley—"

"You're Tommy Flynn?"

"Yes, ma'am."

"I'm Cindy Hurley, your attorney. You won't speak till I tell you to speak. Got it?"

"Yes, ma'am."

In fact, Ms. Hurley was an attractive woman, also blond, about Mom's age.

"Now, assholes, explain to me why my client is under restraints. He is a law-abiding young man with no criminal record. There is no reason to think he is dangerous. . . . You haven't a criminal record, do you, Tommy Flynn?"

"Some parking tickets."

She bit her lip to repress a grin, something that she would do often as the interrogation went on.

"Therefore I direct and insist that my client be released from restraints. We won't even begin the discussion until that occurs. You understand, Ms. State's Attorney?"

"Yes, ma'am. I agree."

The captain looked like he would willingly kill the two women who were ruining his game.

"You're going pretty far, counselor."

"You don't know any law, Captain. Neither did the asshole that assigned you to this interrogation. You've already gone too far."

The cop who had cuffed me was summoned to uncuff me.

"Ms. Hurley—"

"Yes," she snapped.

"May I say something?"

Again she repressed the grin. "What?"

"This officer is the one who hit me in the back with his club and threatened to hit me over the head."

"Is he now? Officer, you seem to be missing your name card. I have your badge number already. Do you want to tell me your name?"

"Mason," he said with a ferocious scowl.

"Thank you, officer."

We arranged ourselves around the table, the captain across from me, the lieutenant next to him, Ms. Hurley next to me. The captain turned on the tape recorder and muttered the day and time and the names of those present.

"I want to add some things for the record," my lawyer said immediately. "My client has been dragged out of his bed in the middle of the night, put under restraints, beaten by a police officer named Mason, and brought here to the interrogation room without being read his Miranda decision rights. To my knowledge they have yet to be read. He was at first refused permission to make a phone call. I have reason to believe that all of this has been done at the connivance of the Deputy Superintendent, who at this moment is doubtless watching through the screen on the wall. All right, Captain, ask your first question. . . . Tommy, don't answer it till I tell you that you should."

"Finally," the cop growled. "Your name, sir?"

I remained silent.

"You can answer that, Tommy."

"Thomas Patrick Flynn."

"Your occupation?"

"Commodity trader."

"Is it not true, Mr. Flynn, that in front of Holy Name Cathedral on Sunday, September nineteenth, in the presence of several witnesses, you made a threat on the life of Bishop Augustus O'Sullivan Quill?"

So that's what it was about. I looked at my lawyer.

"Answer it, Tommy."

"No, sir, it is not true."

"We have witnesses—"

"My client denies having said it, Captain. Save your witnesses for the courtroom."

"Did you say anything about Bishop Quill?"

Ms. Hurley nodded.

"I believe I did."

"So you don't deny you threatened his life?"

"Captain, you need a course in logic. My client did not admit a threat. All he has admitted so far is that he said something about the Bishop. Wouldn't it be intelligent to ask him what he said?"

"All right, Mr. Flynn, what did you say?"

Christy nodded again.

"To the best of my recollection what I said was that someone ought to kill him."

"You don't consider that a threat on his life?"

"Drop it, Captain. It won't fly. My client admits an angry comment about Bishop Quill, perhaps an imprudent comment. You can never twist that into a threat no matter how hard you try. You'd better have a lot more evidence to justify tonight's events."

Somewhere, deep down, the part of me that was worried heaved a sigh of relief.

"Is it not true," the captain plunged ahead, "that you use scheduled drugs?"

Before I could deny it, Christy Hurley exploded.

"You'd better have strong evidence to back up that question, Captain. Do you? Moreover, you better be prepared to explain to me how that's relevant to the present charge."

The captain fumbled the ball. Ms. Hurley was right. He was an inexperienced interrogator. She caught my eye and I shook my head.

"Everyone knows that those traders are all on drugs. It's pertinent because Bishop Quill was poisoned with an injection of heroin."

"Let me get this straight. Because my client is a trader, and because you have proof that all traders use drugs, you have reason to believe that he injected the heroin into the Bishop's veins?"

"I want to establish that your client had access to the scheduled drug that was used in the kidnapping."

Ms. Hurley laughed contemptuously. "He and maybe a half million other people in Chicago . . . You gotta be kidding. Tommy, you may answer the man's question about the use of drugs."

"I'm not sure what a scheduled drug is, Captain. I have, however, never used illegal drugs."

"Next question," Ms. Hurley snapped.

"Where were you on the night of October second?" She nodded.

"I don't remember where I was. Probably in my apartment reading. That's what I usually do at night."

"So you have no alibi?"

Blackie

28

Somewhere, light years away, a telephone rang. Another hospital call. I was not on duty tonight, was I?

"Father Ryan," I said automatically.

"Blackie? Mike. We have a situation developing."

"Ah?"

"Eleventh and State has interjected itself into the Quill case. They've dragged two people out of bed, cuffed them in their nightclothes, alerted the media, and accused them of being involved in the kidnapping. They have no evidence except for hostile comments about the Bishop. John Culhane has already investigated them quietly and tentatively cleared them. It's a play to take credit for breaking the case without ever going to the grand jury."

"Despicable."

"Worse than that. To cover their asses, they've told the media that they have moved quickly in response to a demand for closure from the Catholic Church! It's been on TV all night."

I glanced at the clock next to my bed: 5:00 A.M.

"Which Catholic Church?"

"The Roman Catholic Church!"

"Ah, that one!"

"Has the Archdiocese put any pressure on anyone?"

"The Roman Catholic Archdiocese of Chicago?"

"Not the Greek Orthodox!"

"Certainly not! . . . Who did they arrest?"

"Thomas Flynn Jr. and Jennifer Carlson. They have implied a conspiracy between them."

Two of my parishioners! A great rage surged within me. This atrocity would not continue!

"John says they have nothing?"

"Nothing but a deputy superintendent who wants to make a name for himself while his boss is out of town."

"I see. . . . You may tell John that we will have a statement to make before the sun rises."

I thereupon ascended to the Cardinal's suite of rooms. Asleep, Sean Cronin looked remarkably peaceful. I shook him. He was reluctant to leave the peace behind. Finally he opened his eyes.

"It can't be the last judgment," he said, "because you don't look like the angel Gabriel."

Under the circumstances, that was not a bad line.

"We have a situation," I informed him.

"I assumed as much."

I told him what had happened.

"Bastards—push people around to get publicity and then blame us!"

"Indeed."

"We'll need a statement."

I recited what I had formulated on the way up the stairs.

"Yeah, that's good. Who should give it?"

"You would be overkill. I would be underkill."

"Jaime?"

"My very thought."

"See to it, Blackwood. I have an hour's sleep still coming."

Thereupon I descended to Father Keenan's quarters. He would think that a sunrise statement in front of the Cathedral would be fun.

Jenny

29

They take me back to the room without the windows. My hands are still bound behind my back. I need to go to the bathroom, but they won't let me. A little bald man with elfin eyes says, I am Emanuel Horowitz, your attorney. They won't let me go to the bathroom. He looks around at the cops. Officers, he says, we must straighten a few things out before our little conversation begins. You will release my client and permit her to go to the women's washroom, where she may wash her hands and comb her hair. Otherwise, there will be no conversation. Do I make myself clear? His voice is so calm and soft they do not seem to hear him. The fuck we will, says the woman captain. Madam, my attorney replies, I must ask you not to use such language. I am an Orthodox Jew and I find such language personally offensive. My client is clearly a lady and I'm sure she finds it offensive. Please refrain from using it. I'm a lady too, the captain says. Madam, the lawyer replies, I assure you that you are not.

Somehow, he gets his way. When I return from the washroom, my hair combed and the belt on my robe tied properly, I feel a little better—brutalized, humiliated, violated, but awake and alive. The boy who is the state's attorney even smiles at me. Now we may begin our conversation, the lawyer says.

Jamie

30

(Television scene in front of Holy Name Cathedral just before sunrise. Father Keenan is a tall, handsome, self-assured young man with blond hair and natural presence.)

J.K.: I'm Father James Keenan of the Cathedral staff. I have a statement from the Archdiocese of Chicago. *(He pauses to let the solemnity of this fact sink in and then begins to read.)*

We have learned that the Archdiocese is being blamed for the arrest of two Cathedral parishioners during the night in connection with the Bishop Quill case. It has been said that the police had to pull them out of their beds and handcuff them in the middle of the night because of pressure from the Archdiocese. We categorically reject that allegation. It is a lie. We have no complaints against the careful detective work of Area Six. We agree with Area Six that there is no substantial evidence against these two people. We are unable to understand the reasons for this carefully staged attack on their rights and on the rights of the Archdiocese. We demand that whoever is responsible for the allegation of pressure from the Archdiocese retract that allegation. *(Another pause)*

This is the end of our statement.

(The sun peeks up to survey the situation. Apparently she is pleased because she continues to rise.)

(Questions surge from the media vultures, irritable now after a long night of running around. Father Keenan smiles charmingly but shakes his head.)

QUESTION: Has Cardinal Cronin seen this statement, Jaime? *(It's the question he has been waiting for.)*

J.K.: He has approved every word.

QUESTION: Has Bishop Ryan seen it?

QUESTION: Did Bishop Ryan write it?

J.K.: Who?

QUESTION: Bishop Ryan?

J.K.: *(Wicked grin)* Who's he?

(He turns and walks back into the Cathedral. Madam Sun, now patently pleased, sheds her nightdress of clouds and rises higher in the sky.)

The Cardinal helped himself to another cup of tea.

"The young man is good, Blackwood. You've done a fine job of training him."

"He needed no training," I said, stating only the obvious. "I think we have won this one."

"Arguably."

This stealing my line was becoming a bad habit. We watched the scene at Eleventh and State as the valiant Cindy Hurley attacked the police department.

"Now we must see to the healing of those who have been savaged. It will require discretion," I remarked to the Cardinal.

"Why would the cops try such a stupid trick?"

"Mostly for the media. Do not think that they have lost. Even if they had no evidence against their two victims, even if they are forced to release them, even if they never bring them before a grand jury, the element in the police department who sponsored this caper will still look to the public like they have acted vigorously. They have created the impression that these two innocents may well have conspired to poison Gus Quill."

"Won't they sue?"

"By the time the case is settled out of court, the public will have forgotten what it is about. The Deputy Superintendent has carried the day, though he may well have overextended himself this time. I suspect that he is not very bright. We will have to await the return to the city of the real Superintendent and the comments of the Mayor."

"That Carlson woman is gorgeous, isn't she?"

"I did notice that."

"How old is she?"

"Timeless."

Tommy

31

"Captain, this is an outrage. All you have is one quote from my client that only proves he was very angry at Bishop Quill. It was not a threat. You have no other evidence. This was not a fishing expedition. It was a deliberate attempt to intimidate my client. It failed. Now either charge him formally or release him."

Ms. Hurley's anger was not feigned. She was genuinely furious. I was exhausted and now feeling violated. These bastards, we'd get the whole lot of them.

"We have other evidence, counselor."

"The hell you have. I am willing to wager that Area Six found nothing against my client."

"We have other evidence."

"Suit yourself, charge him if you dare. . . . Ms. State's Attorney?"

The cute blonde had been mesmerized by my attorney.

"Yes, ma'am?"

"I'm sorry to disturb your reflections. Have you

heard anything you might want to bring before a grand jury?"

"Against your client?"

Ms. Hurley drew her breath impatiently. "Yes, of course, against my client!"

"No, ma'am. Nothing."

"All right. Captain, I am declaring this interrogation concluded. I am advising my client to walk out of this police station unless you and the idiots who dreamed up this fraud are crazy enough to charge him."

She stood up. I stood up. The cop looked confused. My knees were shaking.

Jenny

32

My wonderful Jewish lawyer has tied the police up in
knots. The only evidence they have is the stupid comment I made at that party. I'm innocent. Why do I feel
so guilty? Someone brings a note in to the captain. He
glances at it and tells us that we may leave. We're not
finished with you yet, he warns. Nor are we finished
with you, officer, my lawyer says ominously. Outside,
Ned is waiting for me. He puts his arm around me. I
don't want anyone's arm around me. I feel soiled. I
need a long, hot bath. Alone. He doesn't get it.

A boy joins us, wearing a robe and slippers. I'm
Tommy Flynn, Ms. Carlson, he says. I'm from the Cathedral parish. They arrested me too. He is a cute little
boy. I think I remember him. I just want to say, Ms.
Carlson, that at this hour of the night or day, or whatever it is, and after all you've been through, you're the
most beautiful woman in the world. I hug him and
begin to weep.

I weep all the way back to my apartment. May I

come in? Ned asks me. No, I want to be alone. All right. He just doesn't get it. I don't want a man slobbering over me. I want to be alone with my pain and my guilt and my humiliation. Forever. I don't want to see you anymore, I tell him. I am quitting my job. Go away. Don't come back. I take off his ring and try to give it back to him. He won't take it. I throw it on the sidewalk and run up the stairs, sobbing. As I close the door, I see him bending over to pick up the ring. He still doesn't get it.

The next morning Dr. Murphy says to me that I was cruel. You took out your trauma on him. You don't get it either, I yell. I'm through with him. Is that fair? I don't care whether it is fair or not. You're not really angry at him. You're angry at yourself. I am NOT! I leave her office and promise myself that I will never return.

Tommy

33

Ms. Hurley gave them hell on television. "Rudy Giuliani is not mayor of Chicago, Rich Daley is. Ken Starr is not state's attorney, Dick Divine is. These things do not happen in the city of Chicago or the county of Cook. Mr. Horowitz and I are prepared to go into court to demand relief for our clients so that this will never happen again to anyone."

If we've won, I wondered, why do I feel like such a rotten jerk? I was dumb to say that about the Bishop, a real asshole. I made a fool out of myself with the cops. I just wanted to go home and hide for a couple of weeks. What an idiot I was.

My lawyer hugged me and told my father that it was a damn good thing for him that I had decided not to be a lawyer, because I was so much better at the game. Dad was pleased as punch. So was Mom, who also hugged me.

"Poor Tommy," she whispered.

Lawyer or not, she understood how I felt.

Like a total jerk.

I would certainly not be going down to the Exchange today. Or anytime soon. People would look at me like I was some kind of monster.

Christy? My young lioness?

I winced.

I was in no mood for her exuberance. I had barely thought of her during the night's ordeal. She was not important to me. She was still a kid. I did not want her slobbering over me. I could take care of myself. She had been a big mistake. I would have to get rid of her.

Dear Christy,
    As you've probably read in the papers or heard, I've been through a hell of a night. I have to put myself back together again. It will take time. I think we'd better break up. I'm sorry.
Tommy

She didn't reply. Either because she was very angry at me or because she understood. I didn't care. It was all over with her. It should never have started. I was free again. Thank God.

Blackie

34

"The poor guy has always been a locomotive out of control, Blackie," Ted Coffey observed. "He's run over a lot of people without noticing them. Small wonder someone wanted to destroy him."

I was sitting in the parlor of St. Regis rectory, just south of Chicago Avenue and just east of Harlem Avenue in Oak Park. The homes around this, the mother church of Oak Park, were stately old Victorian mansions, just like the rectory. North of Chicago Avenue was the Frank Lloyd Wright historic district of Prairie School homes, none of which had ever attracted me as a place to live in. Across Harlem was River Forest, once, long ago, the most prestigious of the western suburbs and even now an elegant place to live. St. Regis had spawned the other parishes in Oak Park and the newer ones in River Forest. It proudly called itself the mother church of the western suburbs. Now, in a more yuppie and racially integrated neighborhood, it boasted modernity as well as history. I had decided to pay a visit to Monsignor Theodore Coffey, J.U.D., the acknowledged leader of all Catholic and ecumenical activities in the two suburbs. Perhaps he could give me some clues that would excite the image that lay latent, deep down in the sub-basements of my brain.

"Was he morally responsible for what he did? How can I answer that question, Blackie? Is a diesel locomotive without a motorman at the controls morally responsible?"

Ted, wearing gray slacks and a maroon-and-white St. Regis sweatshirt, was lolling in his recliner, the confident and able pastor of a hectic modern parish—and one much less precious than Forty Holy Martyrs.

"Take the case of Tom Flynn and his family. Tom is a great lawyer, a descendent of a powerful Oak Park family, a solid Catholic, with perhaps slightly old-fashioned ideas about family life. He marries a pretty and lively wife—at least they say she was pretty. I wasn't here in those days. Four kids are too much for her. I don't know. Maybe she should have had no more than two. I guess Tom wanted four. She flakes out. I mean, *really* flakes out. By the time I get here, she's around the bend and over the top. Tom stubbornly, too stubbornly, tries to hold the family together. Finally she leaves them more or less permanently in her lesbian phase.

"I tell Tom he should get an annulment. He's sufficiently old-fashioned to hesitate. I really have to push him into it. He's been dating Beth for a year or two. He's enough of a hardhead that he doesn't think they'll fall in love. Naturally, they do. So we get him the annulment. No sweat. Whatever she may have seemed when they married, the poor woman has deep problems. You can imagine what all this is doing to the kids. Young Tommy, who has problems of his own, holds the family together. God knows what this does to *him*.

"Anyway, they have the marriage already scheduled and they learn that Mrs. Flynn, the first one, egged on by Father Innocent, the Franciscan out in Oak Brook who does these things, has appealed to the Rota and the annulment is annulled. The Chicago tribunal sends out the decision. It's horseshit, Blackie. Of the three judges who hear the case, two are senile and the other is Gus Quill. I'm sure we can win an appeal—which we eventually do. I tell Beth and Tom we'll go ahead with the marriage. I'll take the heat from downtown. Tom gets scruples. Beth insists. So does young Tommy. They get married and live happily ever after, until young Tommy gets arrested the other night."

"So I understand."

"Is Gus to blame? He's written an idiot decision because he doesn't give a damn about the people. Or is Tom, because he waited so long and exposed his kids to so much insanity? Or Beth, because she seduced Tom? Or Tommy, because he's worried about his kid sisters? How do I know!"

He walked over to the teapot and poured the two of us fresh cups of tea.

"The trouble with evil, even if it isn't evil for which the person is morally responsible, is that it generates more evil. Whoever put out the contract on Gus seems to be doing everyone a favor. Then they drag poor Tommy out of bed and make him the fall guy. You and Sean get him out with that statement, but the shadow still hangs over him, and he's all fouled up again. . . . His sister Amy tells me in tears that he has broken up with his girlfriend. How much can a nice young guy take? Whose fault? I don't know."

"Did downtown ever give you any trouble about Tom Flynn's remarriage?"

"Not a word. I bet they never noticed. . . . Now this woman they picked up—what a knockout she is—her husband was a preening little jerk who couldn't keep up with her in any way, especially sexually. So he beats up on her and blames her for his failure to get a Nobel Prize, which he would never get anyway. Then he runs off with a graduate student. Matt Dribbin sends her downtown for an annulment. Again, no problem. Enter Father Innocent and this little academic prick and we get another appeal and another reversal, which Gus writes. Poor Jenny goes into a tailspin, a serious one. So Matt asks me to work on a reversal. We finally get that through and she pulls out of the tailspin. She's a classy lady. So they drag her out of her apartment in her nightgown with the TV cameras rolling and she goes back into the spin. Whose fault? Gus's? Her husband's? Father Innocent's? The whole Church's? Jenny's, for not being tougher? You tell me, I don't know."

"God does, fortunately."

Even in the seminary, Ted's laugh had been infectious. It had improved with years of hard and successful priestly ministry.

"Yeah, and He's on our side. She, as you would say. I don't know why I worry about these things. I do my best out here and hope it works out. Beth and Tom were one of my success stories. Her stepdaughters really love her. They pray she gets pregnant, like she wants, so they'll have a little sister. You don't get that usually from stepdaughters."

"Might either Tommy or Ms. Carlson have participated in this conspiracy against Gus?"

"Might they have?" He frowned and twisted in his chair. "Sure, they might have. They were both angry enough, and they both are clever enough. They'd have to put out a contract or get someone to put it out. Did they? I doubt it, but you never can tell about people.

If they did, I don't blame them. I don't think anyone else would either."

"I think we have a mastermind behind this," I sighed. "I know Tommy well enough to know that he's not a mastermind. Ms. Carlson?"

"She might be. Always struck me as a deep one, but I still doubt it."

I sighed again. "So, it's almost anyone?"

"I wish I could help, Blackie." He squirmed in his chair, frustrated by his own powerlessness. "I really do."

"Tell me more about Gus. I didn't know him well in the seminary. I thought he was a creep who they shouldn't have ordained."

"Between you and me, I learned later that most of the faculty thought so too. However, he manipulated the rector like he has manipulated a lot of other people ever since. Somehow, he created the assumption that he would be ordained and the rector didn't try to fight it. That was the technique right up to being made bishop here. Thank God he'll never succeed Sean."

I grunted my assent.

"In his first assignment, a black parish—as we called it in those days—on the South Side, he persuaded the pastor, a nice old guy, without too much smarts, that the Cardinal, the old Cardinal, wanted him to work at the Chancery. He edged his way into the matrimonial court, where they say he was an absolute disaster. They made him a clerk to keep him out of trouble. . . . Is it true he tried to take the Cathedral away from you?"

"He apparently believed that he had been given the job."

"That's the technique. You're the first person I know who stood up to him."

"In fact, the Cardinal did."

"He should have stood up to the Vatican and refused

to accept him. He should never have sent him to Forty Holy Martyrs."

"It did give the Cardinal a chance to reappoint Matthew."

"Come to think of it, you're right. Does Cronin really think that way?"

"Without my help, sometimes."

That took Theodore back a moment. And contributed nicely to my image of gray eminence, which was not without its uses.

"Well, you beat him anyway."

"Go on with the story."

"This next time around I'm involved and I'm ambivalent about it even today. The Chancellor called me and told me that the Cardinal wanted to send me to Rome to study canon law. I liked my work in the barrio, loved it, as you know, and didn't want to go. I argued for three days. Finally, the Chancellor said, 'You're going,' and that's that. Just before Sean came here. He would have let me out in a minute. So, anyway, lo and behold, Gus has been telling everyone that the Cardinal wants to send him to Rome to study canon law. He says it so often and with such conviction that everyone believes him. They figure he'll goof up during the first semester over there. Then the appointments come out, and lo and behold, he goes to Rome and I'm left in the barrio. Great, I won my argument. Then the Chancellor calls and says the Cardinal doesn't want to be unfair to me. 'We're sending two to Rome this year,' and that's that."

"Amazing."

"He plays the same game in Rome, but this turns out to be a plus for me. I'm scheduled to go to the College of Noble Ecclesiastics to study for the diplomatic service. Can you imagine me spending my life with those creeps?"

"In truth, I cannot, Theodore. You would drive them crazy with your energy and disregard for rules."

"You got it, Blackie," he says with his contagious laugh. "I tell Sean Cronin that I'll leave the priesthood. He's new in the job and he doesn't know what to say. Fortunately, Gus has been scheming to get himself appointed to the Rota. He pulls it off again. Sean says he can't afford to give up two priests, so I come home to work in the matrimonial court for a while. Then I get back in the barrio part-time. Then they send me out here. An exciting life. Poor Gus sits around Rome and does nothing but write incoherent opinions, almost always minority opinions. So, I owe him."

"And the Cardinal."

"Indeed, yes. And the Cardinal."

"Indeed" was my line, but I have no patent on it as I do on "arguably."

He refilled my teacup and brought out a few shortbread cookies. In a package. One makes do with whatever one can.

"Not to put too fine an edge on things, Theodore, but we have no idea how many people he might have screwed during his life as, to change the metaphor, he roared down the railroad tracks."

"Most likely someone in Chicago, don't you think? Someone who couldn't stand to have him around as a bishop."

"Arguably."

"It strikes me as the kind of thing your friends the Legion of Corpus Christi up there in Forest Hills might try. They could see Gus manipulating their bosses in Rome to give him the TV station they want to build."

"A point I had not considered."

"Stay for lunch? We've got chocolate ice cream."

"My weaknesses are known all too well, Theodore. I must, however, return to do my hospital visits."

"Stay in touch. If I get any bright ideas, I'll call you."

I drove up to Chicago Avenue to turn on Harlem. Then I remembered the existence of Peterson's Ice Cream on Chicago, just east of Harlem on the Oak Park side of the line. My late father had often argued that it was the best ice cream emporium in the metropolitan area. He was, in this matter, as in so many others, quite correct, even taking into account his native West Side bias.

So, in honor of the old fella, I consumed a large malted milk as an early lunch. Then I drove down Harlem, under the L tracks near where the missing L train had been found, and to the Congress Expressway (as we Democrats call the Eisenhower Expressway) and returned to the Cathedral.

I reflected that I still knew nothing about the assault on Augustus O'Sullivan Quill.

35

"Ms. Carlson to see you, Bishop," Megan O'Connor informed me crisply.

"Very well."

"Bishop Blackie," the proto-Megan whispered into the phone, "she's like totally ravishing."

"If you say so, Megan."

Nevertheless, I did put on my Roman collar.

"She's in your parlor," Megan said with a significant roll of her eyes.

"Don't worry, Megan, I'll leave the door open."

"You always do that when there's a woman in there."

That was true.

"I'm sorry to disturb you, Bishop," Jenny Carlson said to me meekly. "I thought you might want to talk to me."

"I always want to talk to a parishioner," I said.

She was, through no fault of her own or conscious effort, a deeply disturbing woman. In a gray business suit with a long skirt, she seemed rather prim. However, she quietly radiated an intense sexual appeal that filled the whole office. Men would go crazy for a touch of her hand. How old was she? Somewhere between thirty-five and fifty, with no clear hints in her smooth complexion and finely carved figure as to which number would be closer to the truth. After a moment, one did not care.

"Not much of a parishioner, I'm afraid. I didn't attend Mass for a long time. I came here a few Sundays with Ned. Now that we have broken up, I've stopped attending."

"You will, however, begin again next Sunday."

"Yes, Bishop, I will."

"Ravishing" was too mild a word. How could her first husband have left her?

"Thank you for the help when I was at Eleventh and State. Mr. Horowitz, my attorney, said that it was the statement from the Church that forced the police to release us."

"We were later supported by the Mayor and the real Superintendent."

And by the subsequent quiet transfer of the Deputy to a harmless desk job.

"I want to apologize for all the trouble I've caused by my stupid comment at the party in Forest Hills. I'm afraid I lost my temper."

"Ah."

"I'm not angry at him anymore. I was then. And

again when the police released us. However, now I merely feel sorry for him."

"And forgive him?"

She paused, thought for a moment, and then said firmly, "Yes, I forgive him. Why not? I did it to myself, the way I reacted to the reversal of my annulment. That should not have mattered as much as it did to me. Anyway, it was reversed. Father Dribbin and Monsignor Coffey got it reversed."

"So I am told."

The virtuous Mary Kathleen, whom I presumed Jenny had been seeing, had done her work well with this woman.

"My anger was really at my husband. He appealed the annulment, though he had already remarried, out of pure spite."

"Ah."

"Anyway, I know you're still investigating the case. I hope you find out who kidnapped Bishop Quill. It will remove suspicion from me and from poor little Tommy Flynn."

I did not think of the legendary Tommy Flynn as either poor or little, but what did I know?

"You have very good reason for suspecting me, Bishop."

"Why would that be so?"

"You know I hated Bishop Quill. If you've seen my work at the Reilly Gallery—"

"Very interesting work," I said quickly.

It surely was. It did not fit with the demeanor of this pious matron, but it did fit all too well with the erotic aura that surrounded her. Which was she, fire or ice, or arguably both?

"You know what a twisted imagination I have. I could have cooked up that scheme or a dozen others like it."

There was no question about that.

"Perhaps," I answered, "I would prefer the word 'fantastical' to 'twisted.' However, there is some reason to doubt that you would have the ruthlessness to carry them out."

She smiled wryly. "Probably not, Bishop Ryan. However, you can't assume that, can you? . . . If you have any questions you want to ask . . ."

If this woman had told me that she had just flown across the Atlantic Ocean without the benefit of an airplane, I would not have doubted it.

"Do you speak Spanish?"

"Only a few words."

"Do you use drugs?"

"No, I don't even drink much. I'd be afraid of drugs."

What else? Quick, Blackwood, start thinking!

"When was the last time you were on an L train?"

She smiled.

"I don't think I've ever been on one."

There was a hint there, perhaps not pertaining to her. A picture of an L train in the back of my head.

So she could smile.

"We have nothing on you, Ms. Carlson—"

"Jenny, please, Bishop—"

"We have nothing on you, Jenny. No one does. Area Six, once again in firm control of the investigation, has nothing on you, though for reasons of discretion and prudence, they're not about to say that."

"And are still watching me—"

"Not systematically."

"I hope they find out who really did it. I'd like my name cleared, though somehow that doesn't seem as important as it used to be."

She stood up, ready to leave.

"You have indeed broken up with Ned?"

She shrugged listlessly. "I just don't need a man in my life now."

"That can hardly be a permanent orientation?"

"My shrink doesn't think so. I stopped seeing her after . . . after I was arrested. I had to go back to her like I had to go back to Ned's firm. I don't know what will happen."

"We will leave it, for the moment, in the hands of God, who doubtless has Her own plans for you."

God is notoriously empirical and pragmatic, as I argued in my little book about William James, in his style of telling the stories of our lives. He would not like an ending to this story that excluded Ned.

"You will be at the Eucharist next Sunday and thereafter?"

"I promise, Bishop Blackie."

I escorted her down to the Megan's lair.

"Megan, would you give Ms. Carlson a box of our collection envelopes? She has undertaken to attend the Eucharist every Sunday."

Jenny Carlson laughed happily. So she could laugh too.

"She's already in the parish," Megan insisted, "I've seen her in church."

Typical of those of her gender and ethnic group, Megan always had to argue.

"Now she is formally a member of the parish. So we make it official."

"Course, I saw her in church." Megan had pulled a registration card, but still had to have the last word. "She's the best dressed woman at Mass."

Jenny laughed again. "You're a sweetheart, darling."

"Well, the Bishop says we have to be friendly to new parishioners. You know what bishops are like."

"Oh, yes," Jenny said. "I know what bishops are like."

After Megan had registered her and given her the collection envelopes, I escorted Jenny Carlson to the door.

"I'll be looking forward to seeing you at the Eucharist, hopefully along with Ned."

Her face turned pink. "Maybe, Bishop Blackie, maybe."

"She is," I remarked to Megan, "merely a prim and proper middle-aged woman."

"So's Annette Bening."

My generation would have said Sophia Loren, not that it mattered.

Back in my room, as I flipped on my computer, I pondered the interview. If she had been involved in the assault on Gus Quill, it would have been a very clever ploy to confront me in my fortress and admit she might have been, and also to proclaim, with apparent spontaneity, her forgiveness of Gus.

And to sign up for the parish and jest with irrepressible Megan.

Or she might have been exactly what she purported to be, a lovely and lonely matron pining for lost love—lost but not irrevocably lost. I hoped that was all she was and I hoped that she would recover Ned. Yet I could not be sure. I would have to leave her to Area Six and John Culhane.

A few minutes later Milord Cronin, freshly returned from a confirmation, ambled into my room.

"Was that Jenny Carlson leaving the rectory?"

"It was. She formally joined the parish. So we registered her and gave her collection envelopes."

"Yeah? . . . You know she looks like an attractive but very prim and proper middle-aged matron."

"So," I said with a loud sigh, "does Annette Bening."

36

"*Bishop Blackie,*" *Megan Flores, a.k.a.* Megan Flower, said, "that terrible Tommy Flynn boy is down here flirting with me and disrupting my work."

"Are you bragging or complaining, Megan?"

She giggled. "He says he wants to see you."

"Then I had better come down, had I not?"

"O.K."

"Like Megan O'Connor goes," Megan Flores warned Tommy as I drifted into the office area, "you're much too young for me."

"Either too young or too old, Bishop Blackie," he said to me. "That's the story of my life."

"Arguably," I said with considerable skepticism in my voice.

In the security of my office, he collapsed.

"I'm a wreck, Bishop," he confessed. "A shambles. I know that I ought to shake off that stuff, but every night I dream someone is knocking at the door. How come people don't tell us how awful it is to be dragged away by the cops, with the TV cameras catching every move, every word, every expression?"

"It's a horror they want to forget, Tommy Flynn."

"I want to forget it too. I feel shattered. Everyone is nice—Mom and Dad, my fellow traders—they all hate the cops too. I take positions now more than I trade. My nerves are shot. I don't trust my instincts."

"You're losing money?"

"No, not really. I'm still doing all right. The fun has gone out of it."

"Perhaps it will come back."

"I suppose so. . . . When I try to read at night, my imagination replays everything that happened, all the mistakes I made, what an idiot I was."

"The conventional wisdom is that you were brilliant."

"They got it wrong. . . . I stopped going to my shrink—did I tell you I finally got one? She's very good. I made an appointment with her for the day after tomorrow. She'll say the same thing."

"Your lioness?"

"It's all over, Bishop. We broke up after the . . . incident. I have too much to straighten out. I don't need her daffiness. She's just a kid."

"Yet older than the worthy Megan who unanimously agree that you are too young for them."

"They're only kidding. . . . I sent Christy an e-mail the morning after and told her that we were breaking up. She didn't reply, which proves that she's very angry at me. That's good. I don't want to hurt her any more than I already have."

Noble words, huh?

"Or perhaps, like the skilled hunter she is, she is merely biding her time."

That stopped him. He pondered the possibility, not without some pleasure, I observed.

"No way," he finally decided, "she's not that clever."

"I have always judged her to be extremely shrewd under that, ah, daffy enthusiasm. Lionesses tend to be very shrewd."

"I don't think the metaphor goes that far."

"Well, it's your metaphor."

"I'm not here to talk about metaphors, Bishop Blackie. . . . First thing, how is poor Bishop Quill doing?"

"Right now the doctors say that he is a little better

than might be expected, sometimes even quite rational."

"Yeah, I'm glad to hear that. I felt kind of sorry for the poor guy. He's an idiot, and maybe a dangerous idiot, but no one deserves to have their personality blown away."

"Tommy Flynn, you are growing up!"

"Maybe . . . I apologize for my stupid remark about him that Sunday. I didn't mean it even then. Temporary temper."

"So you've forgiven him?"

"Why the hell not?" he said with a deep frown. "Why the hell not? I maybe had reason to be angry at Dad and at my mother—I don't mean Beth—but the Bishop was only a cog in the annulment machine. As it turned out, we didn't need him anyway. The family is happy now. My real mother is even talking about marrying the guy she's with now. Maybe she's grown up too."

Tommy Flynn's trauma had improved his human sensitivities. Or maybe only permitted them to come out into the open. Nonetheless, I suspected that, in fact, he was experiencing the delayed effects of his first love. I had little doubt that the Fighting Irish would return to fight another day.

"A happy ending."

"A human ending, like in a really good novel. Nothing's perfect, but things get a little better, like later Stephen King."

"Arguably."

"Look, I know you'll eventually solve this mystery."

At that point, he knew a lot more than I did.

"I have a reputation to uphold."

"So you have to suspect me, don't you?"

"We are assured by Area Six that there is nothing to link you to the assault on Bishop Quill other than your unwise remark on these very premises."

"Yeah, but you're smart enough to know that I might have faked that so I could throw people off the track."

I was not, in fact, that smart.

"You're capable of it, I agree."

"I'm a pretty clever guy, when you stop to think about it, Bishop Blackie. I'm not bragging. A guy has to be clever to succeed in my business. I know how to take smart risks and win. Well, I used to. I could have cooked this whole caper up, know what I mean?"

"And so you did?"

"Hell, no! I'm just saying I might have, and you should keep your eye on me if you're professional about solving this thing."

"I'm not a professional, Tommy Flynn. I see things. Try as I might, I can't see this one yet. I will, however. I doubt very much you'll be in the picture, however."

"I sure hope I won't. . . . Are there any questions you want to ask me?"

Could he and the startling Jenny have contrived this common approach? Hardly. Were they both trying to discharge residual guilt from their arrest trauma? Was I a shrink? What did I know?

This time I would not try to fake questions.

"None at all at the moment. Should there be any, I'll feel free to call you."

"Yeah, thanks . . . I'm not sure why I'm even bothering you. Like I said, I'm a mess, a total geek."

Ah, the Fighting Irish word. You came, Tommy Flynn, because you wanted to be reassured that you had not heard the last of that young woman. No way.

"Time and counseling will help, Tommy."

"I guess so. It's not like I was a prisoner of war or anything."

"A trauma in the middle of the night is a trauma in the middle of the night."

Especially if your earlier family experiences inclined you to expect the worst.

"Yeah," he said as he stood up to leave.

At the door of the porter person's room, he added, "See you around, Megan."

"Not if I see you first, señor,"

At the door, I offered him the consolation he needed. "I am prepared to take a position with you, Tommy Flynn."

"Yeah?" His eyes lit up at the prospect of a contract offer.

"I want to go long on Christina Anne Logan."

He thought about it.

"I don't gamble with princes of the Church."

37

I stared out the window on Wabash Avenue, neither the Magnificent Mile nor State Street, that great street, but a workaday Chicago street, stretching for its final leap to glamour. It never looked like much out of the window of my study, and probably never would. On a late November day when there was what the Irish would call a fine, soft rain in the air (meaning a torrential downpour), it looked like a bland wall to Dante's Purgatorio—though not D. M. Thomas's—dull, dreary, and depressing. I sighed loudly though presumably only God could hear me, and I doubted She paid much attention to my sighs.

The problem with the strange case, as Dr. Watson would have put it, of the bishop and the L Train, was not that there were no motives or an absence of people who rejoiced in the decline and fall of the Most Reverend Augustus O'Sullivan Quill, J.C.D., D.D. Quite the contrary, there were tons of people, as the Megan would have said, who rejoiced in his decline and who declared that they would cheerfully take credit for that decline. They felt that whoever had cooked up the scheme was a genius and should be richly rewarded, instead of being turned over to the Chicago Police Department and the State's Attorney for the county of Cook. All available suspects, with only two exceptions, would have cooked up the plot if they had had the opportunity. In the words of Ted Coffey, "Blackie, the guy was a frigging genius. You and Cronin owe him a debt of gratitude."

Such a marvelously forgiving folk, these Chicago Catholics. Milord Cronin and I dissented from this conventional wisdom. However much an idiot Idiot was, he had, as a creature of God, certain basic human rights. Those rights had been violated—cruelly and shamelessly. We could not accept this, no matter how many times he had violated the rights of others. Moreover, he was a priest of the Archdiocese. Milord Cronin had a duty to protect and care for his priests. As his gray eminence, I shared in some way in that responsibility.

Besides, I did not like unsolved mysteries.

Earlier in the day, after my visits to the local hospitals, I had paid court to the Reilly Gallery, to collect my dues of apple-cinnamon tea and oatmeal-raisin cookies. I had discussed the mystery with Mike the Cop and his beauteous childhood sweetheart and present wife, Annie Reilly. With the Irishwoman's determination to stand by her own kind and to repeat that loyalty as though it were the only observation on the case that really mattered, she had insisted that "Jenny Carlson wouldn't hurt a fly."

"Ah," I said, for the sake of the argument, if for no

other reason, "the valiant Jennifer is a woman of considerable depth, imagination, and passion, all of which our mastermind certainly has. Mike, you have seen some of her computer graphic art—do you consider her capable of twisted fantasies?"

"She's a wonderful woman," the good Annie interrupted as she replaced the oatmeal-raisin cookies that the leprechaun who haunts me had deftly stolen. "If she was going to kill anyone, it would have been her worthless husband!"

"I like her and I like her work." Mike did not dispute his wife, wisdom in any man, especially if he's Irish. "We will sell a lot of it here. There's mystery in her, Blackie. She has the kind of fantasy life that could come up with anything. And the kind of passion."

"She has a good man who loves her," Annie protested. "Why should she put that in jeopardy?"

"I understand," I noted, "that they have broken up."

"She's seeing your sister. No way will Mary Kate tolerate that."

It was true that my sister could be very directive when the mood and the situation suited direction—in my case all the time.

"My people could find no trace of an anti-Quill conspiracy up there," Mike reported. "A lot of hatred, a lot of complaints, and a lot of satisfaction that he's gone and Father Dribben's back. No conspiracy. That doesn't mean there wasn't one. If there was, we'll only find out by accident when someone breaks down and talks about it."

"I feared as much. . . . On the other hand, to return to those who were arrested," I continued as Annie refilled my cup with apple-cinnamon tea, "the young Tommy Flynn seems utterly transparent."

Ms. Reilly firmly believed that caffeine was not good for one, even though I argued that the medical research had shown that *real* tea was an effective preventive for heart disease and cancer. I could no more persuade her to accept that finding than I could persuade any woman that one did not catch colds from going outside without a hat.

"Tommy," Mike pointed out, "comes from a long line of Irish political fixers. His father is, among other things, your classical Irish political lawyer, as was his grandfather and his great-grandfather before him. While the present generation is honest, sternly so, the same could not be said of its predecessors."

"Ah . . . I assume Tommy became a trader to break the family tradition."

"There is not that much difference between an Irish political lawyer and an Irish commodity trader," Mike continued. "Their strength is their ability to push the envelope farther than anyone else, and cover it with charm."

"Tommy is a sweet boy," Annie turned her defense now to a male of the species. "He always is so polite and friendly when he rides down on the elevator with us."

The Reillys, like Tommy Flynn, lived in the John Hancock Center, our city's proto-skyscraper.

"That's what I mean." Mike nodded his head as if his wife had made his case for him. "He's a charmer and a fixer and an operator. Nothing wrong with that, God knows. He is not, however, as sweet as he might appear."

This was characteristic dialogue between Sean Cronin's gray eminence and the head of both the North Wabash Avenue Irregulars and Reliable Security. Mike never cleared anyone. There were those who said that he was Watson to my Holmes, or Flambeau to Father Brown. Annie, however, had often suggested that I was his Captain Hastings.

"I think that young woman he's dating is just wonderful," Annie continued. "I'm sure they'll get back together again too."

"The girl next door—"

"She defines the term 'Fighting Irish,' " Mike agreed. "The winning goal on a broken leg . . . If I had to hunt for suspects, I'd take a close look at those Corpus Christi priests up in the North Shore. They have a lot of money. He was after it for his TV station, which they thought would embarrass them. You'd never get anything on them, Blackie."

"Arguably not . . . When it is a question of their protecting their work, they are notoriously flexible in their ethics. They certainly weren't unhappy that Gus Quill is, so to speak, no longer in play. They are quite devious, but perhaps not all that smart. However, they are smart enough to know that if they should fund a TV station to compete with the good Mother Angelica, it must be theirs, not anyone else's."

"I think Cardinal Cronin would be great on TV. He should have his own program. And, Blackie, this is absolutely the last of the cookies—don't give me that leprechaun stuff either."

"There are, of course, Gus's worthy brother and sister-in-law, the pious Peter and Grace Quill, though like Fathers Ramon and Luis, as they call themselves, their ability to devise a grand plan is questionable."

"I have something on them for you, Blackie." Mike reached for a stack of papers. "They are under considerable financial pressure. Peter went bearish in the market because that was what all the clever talking heads said a wise person would do. He lost a lot of money, both his own and his clients'. Her dress store up there on Green Bay Road has been quite successful. But it hardly covers for Peter's mistakes. They would have bounced back if the Bishop hadn't alienated just about everyone up in Forest Hills."

"And now that he is incarcerated in St. Joseph's Hospital?"

"Out of sight, out of mind. Peter and Grace have benefited greatly from his kidnapping. A murder would have done them more harm, but a disappearance seems to have suited them just fine."

"All too many folks," I agreed, "seem to think that the destruction of a mind is not as serious as the destruction of a body."

"It's a crazy case, Blackie," Mike said. "I don't think I've ever run into anything quite like it."

"There are numerous folk up in Forty Holy Martyrs who do not regret the sad fate of their sometime pastor."

"Why would they connive to kidnap him? Hadn't the Cardinal ordered him to restore all the people he had fired?"

"Perhaps they didn't think the order would have any effect. Certainly Gus had not obeyed it at the time of his disappearance. I have the impression that they wanted him out of there, regardless. Whether they would have and could have organized so quickly such an elaborate scheme seems problematic."

"Then who would have?" Annie demanded as she discovered some cookies of whose existence she had perhaps hitherto been unaware.

"That is the problem," I agreed as I bit into one of the treasures. "There are lots of people who would like to have disposed of Gus Quill, but no one who clearly had the ingenuity and the resources to do so. We are back to our anonymous mastermind."

"And that could be almost anyone who had found good reason to seek revenge against Bishop Quill,"

Mike concluded. "Blackie, I think it might be insolvable."

"There is no such thing as an insolvable mystery," I said firmly.

"You were never a cop," Mike said with a laugh.

"It is curious, is it not," I went on with more determination than I felt, "that the only folks with whom I have spoken who are no longer angry at Gus, and who feel sorry for him, are the two that your sometime colleagues down on South State Street arrested?"

"Tommy Flynn is probably too besotted with the tigress next door to think of anything else," he admitted. "Jenny Carlson is another matter altogether."

"She's a good woman!" Annie insisted.

"Doubtless she is a disturbing and admirable woman," I said. "Yet she is so profoundly mysterious—"

"That man of hers will have his hands full," Mike agreed. "If he gets her back."

"You two are terrible! Just because a woman of her age is naturally erotic, you think she is a femme fatale!"

"I wouldn't dare suggest that!" Mike grinned.

"And the question is whether she wants him back!"

"Erotic appeal," I said, falling into my Solomon mode, "is a blessing limited neither by age nor by gender. . . . Yet there is something about the fair Jenny that suggests a link between passion and anger—"

"With a husband like hers, she should be angry!"

I did not say that the anger could easily be transferred to a more vulnerable target.

"I have some more information about the parish staff for you, Blackie. How did Father Dribben put up with those people!"

"Good staff are hard to come by in the contemporary Catholic parish. Good staff and emotionally balanced staff even harder to come by."

"There's nothing wrong with the Megan," Annie interjected, still defending womankind of whatever phase in the life cycle.

"Inarguably . . . the Good Matthew managed to keep his unruly team in line by a blend of patience and wit, both nearly inexhaustible."

"That nun . . . Joe Anne Reed?"

"Former nun."

"Whatever. She participated in some demonstrations in which church property was defaced. Her husband, the former priest—"

"Orlando Carlin, the director of adult education."

"He has a bit of a wandering eye."

"That does not surprise me."

"Herman Crawford, the organist—"

"Is gay. That, too, does not surprise me."

"He is currently unattached. The chairman of the finance committee is a high-powered corporate officer. Nothing on him. He doesn't need the job. On the other hand, Larry Henning, the chairman of the parish council, is from the west side of the parish. . . ."

"Which means?"

"That he is a relatively small-time staff number cruncher in a big firm. A lot of his personal status is tied up with that parish council."

"Indeed!"

"Your bishop friend was a threat to all of them. Some of the more conservative parishioners might have tattled to him. Even the threat to tattle would have been enough to put them in jeopardy."

"Which of them might have come up with such an elaborate plan?"

"Only the finance committee chair could have carried it off, but why should he bother?"

I sighed.

"My conclusions exactly."

I wandered back to the Cathedral rectory, turned on

my computer, listed the suspects, and then turned off the computer without bothering to save the file. The quick image of a solution, which had often teased me in other similar matters, had turned itself off. All I knew was what I knew the day I had found Gus Quill in the alley behind North Central Park Avenue—that an ingenious but vain mastermind was behind it.

So I sat there and watched the rain fall on Wabash Avenue and the living and the dead.

With no warning, the image machine turned on again and remained on. An L train.

The picture was quite impossible. No way it could be true. How could we ever prove it, even if it were true? Vanity! Oh, yes. There was a marvelous way the mastermind could exercise vanity, a way to leave a hint that he could point to eventually, when it was safe to do so. And then laugh at all of us.

I pondered the solution. It fit all the known facts. I hesitated to move out of my comfortable easy chair. A brief period of resting my eyes was certainly in order, was it not?

Reluctantly, I forced myself to rise. Leaving Jaime Keenan and the Megan in charge, I walked to a certain store. After considerable searching of its wares, I found the area of my interest. Within that, I at first found nothing. Then, after a more detailed search, I found exactly what I knew should be there. I purchased the item and I slowly walked back to the Cathedral. The Megan were all present in their little hutch, babbling away. The presence of only one was required. The rectory had become the functional equivalent of a mall.

"Tell Father Keenan I'm back, and I'll be with the Cardinal."

"Yes," they said hardly affording me any notice.

I rode up in the elevator and interrupted Nora and

the Cardinal in their afternoon tea, real tea. I accepted the offer of some. No cookies were in sight. I gave Sean Cronin my purchase. He and Nora inspected it. Both turned pale.

Jenny

38

Buy you lunch? I say as I lean against the door jamb of his office. Everyone is watching us, hoping . . . I do not know what they are hoping. I swore to myself I would never do this. Raw need is too much for me. I must have him again. It is Dr. Murphy's fault for forcing me to face my own passion. Tied up, he says. Supper, maybe. Fine, I reply. Where? he asks. Savarin? He smiles, as if he knows the implications. He ought not to take me back. I am emotionally unstable. He knows that. I am turning out wild and attractive designs now that everyone, even Donnie, likes. Annie Reilly is preparing an exhibition of my computer art, which reveals just how crazy I am and, even worse, how much I am preoccupied with sex. Everyone knows I'm unstable and will always be unstable. I no longer care what they think.

He is waiting for me at the restaurant, smiling faintly as I walk in right on time, trying to give the impression that I am a sophisticated woman of the world, though my legs are trembling. This is what being in love with a man is like, I realize. It means your body cries out for him the instant you see him, that you want him inside you even as you sit down next to him, casually aloof while he orders drinks. The usual? he asks. I nod. However, it is my treat. He orders a bottle of expensive red wine. I do not argue about it. He says something nice about my latest design effort. Crazy woman, I reply. Gifted woman, he responds. Gifted and crazy. He shrugs.

I forget all the possible apologies I had rehearsed. Do you have the ring with you? Yes. I hold out my left hand. May I have it back? He removes the ring from its box and slips it on to my ring finger. I dissolve into warm surrender. We should marry, Jenny. Oh, yes, I say as I weep. Soon. Then I won't be able to act like an idiot again . . . and I'll be in your bed every night. He nods solemnly. I'll like that very much. When? I take a deep breath. Before I came over here I called Bishop Blackie and asked him to pencil in a date the week before Christmas. He laughs happily.

That was audacious, Dr. Murphy says the next morning. His love wasn't in doubt, I reply. Mine was. I knew he'd take me back. You had a fine domestic evening? Wonderful.

Tommy

39

I knew I was in truly serious trouble. My rejected lioness had phoned me the night before.

"We just totally have to have lunch tomorrow," she instructed me.

"After work? One-thirty at Trader's Inn?"

"Yucky!"

"How about the Italian Village on Monroe, across from the bank?"

"I know where the Italian Village is," she said firmly.

My throat was tight and my hands were wet when I hung up. I knew that the call would come. You don't get rid of a young lioness like Christy Anne Logan without a struggle. She would want to talk it over, find out why I had broken up with her, and offer me a chance to change my mind. I dreaded such conversations. They never worked out. How could I dig in my heels and tell her stubbornly that it would never work out between us? A woman always designed such tête-à-têtes so that the man would look bad to himself and to her friends. Then she could return to her coven and tell them how awful he was.

Well, in Christy Anne's case to her pride of lionesses, all of whom would say that they knew I was no good the first time they met me.

The first time they thought I was adorable. But what did it matter?

Someone in the back of my head whispered to me that I was full of shit. The humiliation of my arrest and the continued suspicion of the police, some of whom trailed me most of the time, perhaps waiting for my first purchase of a scheduled drug so they could arrest me, had shaken the foundations of my personality, down there in all the sub-basements where the rats ran around amid the sewer water.

I was making no progress with my shrink, who now seemed to have abandoned objectivity and to be on Christy's side, along with Mom and my sisters.

"Ja," said the shrink, "once more you are not a man, once more you are afraid of the Woman. You fear that you cannot cope with her."

"Precisely," I would agree fervently.

Christy Anne strolled into the third floor of the Italian Village ten minutes late, a deliberate ploy so she could make a dramatic entrance.

Dramatic it was. She was wearing a shiny, metallic black pantsuit with a crimson sweater, thick crimson belt, crimson earrings (perhaps rubies), and crimson lipstick. She was a sophisticated woman of the world, almost thirty perhaps, with thorn-stick cane. No, she was a late adolescent, giving such an excellent imitation of a woman of the world that you had to look very closely to notice how problematic this role was for her.

"You're gawking, Tommy Flynn," she instructed me as I helped her into her chair.

"So is everyone in the room."

She snorted derisively. "You're the only one with your mouth hanging open."

These young lionesses can be tough. I was in for a long lunch.

"How's your leg doing?"

"It's healing nicely," she said with an impatient frown. "That's what Dr. Hightower says anyway. He's letting me swim at last. I totally have to exercise. Would you believe it, Tommy Flynn? I've put on four pounds!"

"It doesn't show," I said gallantly. In fact, it didn't show.

"I feel totally gross, fat, pudgy, ugly. I have to order a salad today."

"You're wearing a girdle?"

"Certainly NOT!"

"Well, then you don't look fat, pudgy, and ugly."

She snorted again, as if to say, a lot you know, Tommy Flynn.

"What's happening on the Olympic front?"

"Oh, that!"

I ordered a bottle of red wine, which, strictly speaking, she could not drink because she was not quite twenty-one. Despite her good intentions, she ordered ravioli with meat sauce.

"You're not driving?" I asked as the bottle arrived.

"I took a cab down from my parents' house." She waved away my concern. "I'm not crazy, Tommy Flynn."

"I never thought you were. . . . Now, about the Olympic tryouts."

"You keep saying 'tryouts,' Tommy Flynn. I'm like, totally, going to make the team! That's a given!"

No false humility for this child.

"O.K."

"I can start training for them again in February, so

I'll lose the weight and be fine. No problem! Doc Hightower says that occasionally on a cold, damp day, I may feel a little twinge. I tell him that it will remind me of winning the national championship."

What else would she say?

"And the Stanford girl, er, woman?"

"Sonia . . ." she sipped the wine. "Well, you do have good taste in wine anyway, Tommy Flynn. . . . Oh, Sonia's no problem. Our team wrote letters to the Soccer Federation asking them to give her another chance. So they postponed her suspension till after the Olympic tryouts. She's like on the phone to me in tears. . . ."

"She's taking Irish-Catholic charity now, is she? Will she make the team?"

Christy shrugged. "Maybe, but I don't think so."

As we talked, I realized how captivating this young woman was, even in ordinary, small-talk conversation. I was sinking deeper into trouble.

"She goes, like, can we be friends? I'm fersure. She's, like, you can trip me or something if you want to. I go, that's not the way we Irish-Catholic women do it. I'll take you out for, you know, a malt some night and poison it. It took her a moment to realize I'm joking."

"Italian women, actually."

She waved her hand, "Regardless. Anyway Jesus said we're supposed to forgive, so I'm counting on some extra favors from Him."

She accepted the offer of Parmesan cheese.

"How could He refuse?"

How could anyone refuse?

She dug into the pasta like it was going out of fashion.

"I'm starved," she said. "Two o'clock is kind of a late lunch for me."

"I'm sorry."

"No problem." She waved a fork laden with pasta.

"Now, Tommy Flynn," she said after a gulp of wine, "there's absolutely no way we're breaking up."

"Oh?"

"I'm, like, how can we break up when we're going to be married at the end of May right after I graduate?"

"What!"

"That's all settled, Tommy Flynn, so don't even argue about it."

"But—"

"My mom is, like, the woman always has to bring closure to a romance. So, I'm bringing closure. It's simple. Besides, this virginity stuff can't go on forever—I want a man in my bed with me!"

"Men," I stammered, "are crude, smelly, and don't clean up."

"Amy says you're fastidious."

"She doesn't know the meaning of the word."

"Well, actually, she goes, my brother is obsessive."

"We're too young," I said.

"*You* may be too young." She paused before bringing a forkful of pasta to her mouth. "I'm not too young at all. I'll be three weeks younger than Mom when she married Dad."

"Megan at the Cathedral says I'm too young for her and she's only sixteen."

"Well, maybe you are too young for her, but not for me."

This was outrageous. I had been backed into a corner. She couldn't do this to me.

"We hardly know one another."

She waved away that suggestion with a shrug of her strong and shapely shoulders.

"Maybe you don't know me, but that's all right, you can find out about me. I know you, however, and that's that. Besides, Mom and Dad know you too, and they, like, totally love you. My dad goes, Christina, you'll never find another young man so perfectly suited for you. And I'm, like, tell me about it, Daddy."

"Oh."

"And your family thinks it's wonderful. Your dad goes, it's time Tommy settles down."

"Settles down!"

"Well, you know what he means. . . . This stuff is really good."

She continued to destroy the ravioli.

"Besides," she went on in serene confidence, "we have to start dating again. I'll totally need some foreplay to prepare for marriage. You can't expect me to do it all on our wedding night."

I gulped and choked on my wine. The best thing I could do now was to run.

"Foreplay?" I sputtered.

"You know, mess around with my boobs and stuff."

The image of engaging in such amusements affected me like a blow to my head. I was reeling. I felt my fists clench.

"Are you all right, Tommy Flynn? I don't want you choking to death on me!"

"I'm fine!" I gasped.

When I had recovered, I fell back on my last line of defense.

"Christy, I can't even think of anything that serious with these police charges hanging over me."

"Foreplay isn't serious," she said, her eyes averted and a tint of red in her face, "it's just playing around a little."

"I mean marriage!"

"Oh, *that*! Don't be silly. Bishop Blackie will solve that. He always solves mysteries."

That her presumed intended was being shadowed by the police was a matter of no concern to her at all. Like my shrink had said.

"I don't know, Christy—"

"Besides," she said jabbing her wine glass at me, "you, like, totally know that if you marry me, you'll never regret it a single day for the rest of your life."

There could be no question about that.

However, I weakened not because she spoke the truth, but because young lionesses have such sad eyes when their hearts are about to break.

"I don't know, Christy," I said again. "I could probably make some time this afternoon."

Defeat and pain in her wondrous blue eyes, she put down the wine glass.

"For what?"

"To go shopping for a ring. Do you want to come with me so I don't make any mistakes?"

"No way!" she said with a triumphant grin. "Surprise me. I'll like whatever you like! It doesn't have to be too big!"

No way it didn't have to be big. I'd call Mom and ask her if she could spare me an hour from the law to validate my choice.

"You can, like, give it to me this evening before we have supper at Mom and Dad's."

"I can indeed."

We were both flooded with tears.

"I suppose you can give it to me at Ghirardelli's."

"Funny thing, I thought you would suggest that."

So you see how tricky God is.

Blackie

40

"Your problem, Ted," *I said* to Ted Coffey, "is not so much your vanity, though that's what did you in. Your problem is your illusions. You thought that if it hadn't been for Gus Quill, you would be in his place, the new auxiliary bishop and the putative heir to Cardinal Cronin."

"I don't know what you're talking about," he frowned at me. "You always were a little weird, Blackie."

We were sitting around the conference table in the Cardinal's office. Milord Cronin was wearing his ring and his pectoral cross, as he always did in such circumstances. Through the efforts of the worthy Jaime Keenan, I was wearing mine too.

"Arguably," I replied. "Nonetheless, as you yourself said to me, he almost blocked your study in Rome. He did interfere at the last minute with your appointment to the College of Noble Ecclesiastics. Instead of an exciting career representing the Pope around the world and dodging the daggers of your colleagues, you came back here to the matrimonial court, which, by your own admission, was unbearably dull. You were, however, a great success in working with Hispanic Catholics and became one of the most respected priests in the Archdiocese. You are a perennial member of the Council of Priests and have been its chairman twice. You have worked wonders in your parish in Oak Park, which was moribund when you arrived. You have helped countless people who have had troubles with the Church, of whom the Flynn family were but one example. That wasn't enough. You covered up your disappointment well. However, your frustrated ambitions, driven by your illusions, poisoned all of that."

"Sean, this guy is crazy!"

"My guess is that you had too much integrity to succeed in papal diplomacy and that you may have come to realize it. You were happy in your work and satisfied with the respect of your fellow priests. Yet your resentment of Gus Quill continued to fester in your soul. When he appeared in Chicago with his foolish assumption that he would be the next cardinal, you determined to finally undo him. In which determination you were quite successful. Presumably you had access to a drug gang from your service in the barrio. They may well have done the job at a clerical discount, or even free. Your plan was only marginally risky, and your young friends executed it brilliantly. Exit Gus Quill as a practicing bishop, much to the joy of all too many people."

"I'm getting out of here, Sean," he rose from his chair. "This is intolerable nonsense! I don't have to put up with it!"

"Sit down, Ted," Cardinal Cronin said firmly.

Ted Coffey sat down. Wondering, perhaps, if I knew

the whole truth, he had become anxious and uncertain, his eyes flicking back and forth rapidly.

"Your weakness," I went on implacably, "is your vanity. It was a nice touch, a signature of a sort, to tell your associates to dump the Ravenswood Line train in the yards at Desplaines Avenue, on the fringes of your parish. No one would pick up on the clue, you assumed. Nonetheless, you put it there. So you could laugh at the stupidity of the police. And at my stupidity too. If you could not be a bishop in Chicago, despite your brilliance, you would show, to your own satisfaction, that my much vaunted mystery-solving skill was, if you will excuse the expression, fictional. It took me a long, long time to see your signature on the L train, a train you could easily drive by and gloat over long before the cops or the CTA would find it."

"This guy is as crazy as Idiot is," Ted snarled at the Cardinal.

"Arguably," the Cardinal seemed to agree—and stole my line without my permission.

"Once I realized how vain you were, I wondered if you might have left us another clue. I recalled that you had once written fantasy stories under the name of a certain Burke T. Burke. I wondered if you had tried to turn one of those admittedly ingenious fantasies into reality. I visited a science fiction bookstore specializing in old magazines, over on LaSalle Street. After considerable searching, I found an issue of a magazine called *Fantasy Mystery* in which there was a story by Burke T. Burke called "Getting Rid of Gus." You even called the doctor that your protagonist wanted to eliminate Gus Quill. You described Gus with both accuracy and venom. The disappearing L train was added to the story. Perhaps there is a story somewhere else from which you lifted that component. We are searching for it."

Sean Cronin opened the crimson leather cover of his notebook and edged a photocopy of "Getting Rid of Gus" towards Ted.

There was a long silence in the office, the silence of a graveyard.

"I would have made a better bishop than him. Better than you too."

"Arguably," I said, beating the Cardinal to the line.

I felt no particular happiness in the solution of the mystery.

"You caused great worry to the driver's wife and indirectly to your sometime parishioner, Thomas Flynn Jr., whose fragile sense of self was devastated by his arrest."

"He'll be all right." Monsignor Coffey shrugged that off. "I did you guys a favor by getting rid of Idiot. He's out of your hair permanently now. You should be grateful to me."

"Perhaps," I agreed. "Yet Gus Quill had the right to the integrity of his soul, such as it was, every bit as much as you and I do. You destroyed him or tried to because of envy and vanity and illusion. Added to the malice of that act, you did it to a man who, however flawed and inadequate, was a fellow priest."

"So what! You'll never be able to prove anything. Neither will the police! You wouldn't dare turn me over to them."

Finally, the Cardinal spoke in a calm, controlled voice.

"Ted, this story of yours would enable them to make a powerful case and to certainly solve the crime."

"You'd never turn a priest over on the basis of a bit of fiction he wrote ten years ago!"

"You're saying that I should become an accessory after the fact to your crime? If I learned one thing during the years of the pedophile mess, it is that a cover-up never works. As you yourself said many times at the meetings of the Council of Priests, we must always tell the truth."

"They'd never indict me!"

"Don't be so certain," the Cardinal said grimly. "They might not get a conviction, but then again, they might. My advice is that you get a good lawyer and plea-bargain with them."

"No!" He stood up, ready now to storm out of the office. "Why did you have to bother? Why didn't you leave me alone! Is Gus that important to you!"

I leaned forward and pointed my finger at him. "Like every human being, he is important! So are the two parishioners you have exposed to public suspicion and humiliation."

"I didn't intend that to happen!"

"It happened just the same," the Cardinal said coldly as Ted prepared to leave in righteous fury. "Just a minute, Monsignor, before you leave. I'm asking you to resign as pastor of St. Regis, effective at once."

Ted whirled on us.

"I'll fight you. I'll demand a trial."

"I hardly think so. If you do not resign, I will suspend you and appoint an administrator."

"Fuck you!" Ted Coffey exited in righteous rage.

I picked up the phone and called the Reliable Security number.

"Casey."

"Blackie."

"We found the L train story. It was written six years ago, after he became pastor of the parish in Oak Park. Sure enough, they parked the train in the Desplaines Avenue Yards. Why would anyone take such a chance?"

"Driven to it by his vanity." I put my hand over the

phone to speak with the Cardinal. "Mike the Cop found Ted's L train story."

The Cardinal nodded.

"I assume he awaits your instructions."

"He does."

"Tell him to turn both of the stories over to John Culhane."

"Follow plan A," I said to Mike on the phone before hanging up.

"The arrogant bastard," Milord Cronin said through tight lips. "The arrogant, obnoxious bastard."

"In his own way," I agreed, "as self-deceived by his illusions as Gus Quill."

The Cardinal inclined his head in agreement.

"I presume the story will be leaked, Blackwood?"

"Too good not to be."

"I suppose so. Prepare some kind of statement. Innocent till proven guilty. Deplore the whole matter. Suspended until the civil authority makes further decisions. Will they indict him?"

"Oh, yes. He'll doubtless plea-bargain."

"I'll send Jaime out to Oak Park as administrator. He's from that part of the world. Do you mind?"

"It is time." I sighed heavily at my loss. Just to put it on the record.

"No one will know that you solved the mystery?"

"They will not learn it from me."

He laughed ironically and the hoods flashed back from his blazing blue eyes. "A lot of people will guess. As I have said on some previous occasions, I'm glad you're on my side."

"Arguably."

41

Some Sundays You permit matters to arrange themselves better than on other days. Thus this morning two couples, both very much in love, appeared at the rectory to make proper arrangements—and to be congratulated by the Megan—before they were ushered into the pastor's office, which had been redone to look like an aging parlor in an old-fashioned Irish house. The first couple were Jenny Carlson and her lover, who wanted to be married the week before Christmas, on the day Jenny had providently requested. The second couple were both parishioners, the boy and girl next door, even if next door was the John Hancock Center and the Water Tower apartments. I was exhorted to bless the engagement ring ("Isn't it totally excessive, Bishop Blackie!") and enter a date in late May for a wedding.

You have permitted these two matters to arrange themselves very neatly. The couples are quite different. The older couple are quiet, intense, and deeply passionate. The younger couple are exuberant, zany, and unpredictable. Yet in the most crucial matter they are both alike. Usually, when two people wander into a rectory in a romantic daze, both are focused on themselves and on the forthcoming event. With Your Grace they grow out of this. However, both couples this morning were focused on care and concern for the other. Their love models Your love for us and the way we should try to love You.

All very clever on Your part, if I may say so.

*   *   *

Then I took a taxi, driven by the ever faithful Mr. Woods, up to St. Joseph's Hospital, not trusting myself to drive in the falling snow. (Only, however, because my sibling had called and warned me "not even to think about it!")

Dressed in black trousers and white shirt, Gus Quill was sitting in a chair next to his bed, reading Graham Greene's *The Power and the Glory*. Next to him was a stack of so-called Catholic classics.

"Blackie! Good to see you again! Very generous of you to come up here in the snow and on a busy Sunday before Christmas. . . . Do you know this book? Fascinating! I had no idea it existed!"

I admitted that I did and sat down on the other chair in the room.

We discussed Greene and J. F. Powers and Edwin O'Connor and the other authors Gus was systematically working his way through.

He had not put himself completely back together again. However, he was making progress. The various shrinks who presided over him went so far as to say "remarkable progress." Oddly enough, there were few traces of the old Gus. He was putting together a new persona. Or, perhaps, discovering an old one.

Remarkable.

"So it was Ted Coffey?" he said finally.

"It would appear so, if one is to believe the papers."

"What will they do to him?"

"They are negotiating a plea bargain. The state's attorney does not want to bring a priest to trial. He'll plead guilty and be sentenced to probation. The hangup now is whether he will name his accomplices. In fact, he dare not do so, or they will doubtless kill him.

The state's attorney knows that and will back off from such a demand."

"And the Church?"

"Retire him with a full pension and ask that he leave town."

"Poor guy. I really feel sorry for him. I wasn't worth all that trouble."

"He was caught up in his illusions."

"Like I was, only mine were different. . . . Well, I think I'm getting rid of them, at least I hope so."

Mary Kathleen had predicted such a realignment might happen. She had also warned that it might be fragile.

"I suppose you solved the mystery?" he went on.

"My answer to that when asked is, What do I know about solving mysteries?"

He slapped his leg and laughed. "That's really funny, Blackwood, really funny. . . . Did you see the posters your porter persons sent up to me?"

The Megan, dubious despite my suggestions, had prepared posters for Gus's room: NUCLEAR-FREE ROOM, SMOKE-FREE ROOM, NOISE-FREE ROOM—THIS MEANS YOU, DOCTOR! and ANNOYANCE-FREE ROOM—THIS MEANS YOU, NURSE!

"They're very clever."

"Thank them for me. I'll thank them myself if I ever get out of here."

"I'm sure you will, Gus."

"One thing I want to ask you about. The desire I've always had to work with the poor—I don't think there was anything wrong with that, do you?"

"Certainly not."

"Would you think the Cardinal could find a way for me to do that when I'm feeling better?"

"I'm sure he would be delighted."

"Would you mention it to him?"

"Absolutely."

It is up to You, as all manner of things are. It is not, however, a totally improbable idea.

As I left his room, Gus Quill was fingering his rosary beads.

So what do I know?

The snow was falling heavily, but Mr. Woods was waiting for me. He drove carefully through the slush on Lake Park, picked his way along Fullerton, and then at last escaped to the relative freedom of Lake Shore Drive. The snow was falling so thickly now that one could barely make out the skyline and the green and red lights that festooned it for the season.

I asked to be let out at Chicago and Michigan.

I walked a couple of blocks down the Magnificent Mile, bright with the white lights the Mayor likes to put everywhere to celebrate the birth of Your son. I imagined hosts of angels at work above me, busy protecting cars and drivers and trying to make us human creatures realize once again that this is the time of the year when we should smile.

Then I walked back to the Cathedral to admire the Christmas decorations the Megan had created for the offices—exuberant and in good taste.

I want to pray for Gus Quill and Ted Coffey, for Jenny and her Ned, for Tommy Flynn and his lioness, for Sean and Nora Cronin, for Mike and Annie, for all my family, for peace everywhere in the world where there is trouble . . . and for anyone else I ought to be praying for. And, oh yes, for Crystal Lane too.

It is late at night now. I can neither pray nor think any longer.

Good night.

Chicago, April 18, 1999
Third Sunday after the Feast of Our Lord's
Resurrection.

"Blackwood, I need a favor." Sean Cronin, Cardinal Priest of the Holy Roman Church and by the Grace of God and heroic patience of the Apostolic See, Archbishop of Chicago, leaned casually against my door-jamb.

I was instantly wary. Cardinals don't need to ask for favors. Something was afoot, something more serious than Sherlock Holmes' "the game."

"I cannot recall that there is a marker on the table," I said cautiously.

I was appealing to the Chicago School of economics, not that made famous by all the Nobel folk over at The University but by Chicago politicians: its premise was that you can ask for a favor from someone who owes you one for a previous favor (a "marker"). I owed Milord Cronin no favors, not that it mattered.

"I want you to go to Paris," he said, ignoring my appeal to proper procedure.

"Paris, Illinois?" I asked, blinking my eyes in feigned surprise.

"Paris, France!" he said impatiently as he strode to the cabinet where I stored various liquid refreshments. "You've been there, of course."

He poured for himself a more than adequate amount of John Jameson's Twelve Year Special Reserve (now at least a quarter century old). In the reform of life imposed on him by his twice-widowed sister-in-law, Nora Cronin, he was permitted one of those a day and two cups of coffee. It was early in the afternoon for him to fill his quota.

"As you know, we Ryans travel only in cases of utmost necessity. The journey to Grand Beach, Michigan, represents the outer limit of our travels, save for an occasional venture to the Golden Dome to cheer in vain for the fighting Black Baptists."

This was surely the case. We risked going beyond that limit only for reasons of business or love, new or renewed. Neither of these issues impacted on my life.

We never, of course, drove to Milwaukee.

"You have to visit Paris, the City of Light."

"The city where they kill cardinals and bishops in front of your good friend Victor Hugo's cathedral."

"That was a long time ago," he noted, removing a stack of computer output from my easy chair and sinking wearily into it.

If he wanted me to go to Paris, then I would go to Paris. However, it was necessary that we act out the scenario.

"Nonetheless, the French do it periodically."

"I owe a lot to Nora," he said.

"Patently your health, arguably your life."

"So, I want to take her to Paris for her birthday."

"A virtuous intent."

"And I want you along to add an air of legitimacy to the trip."

Aha! So that was the nature of the game!

"My abilities as a chaperone are even more modest than my other abilities."

"All you have to do is to be around."

"Patently, I am quite unnecessary. While arguably your virtue might appear under suspicion to some among the uninformed, the virtue of your admirable sister-in-law is beyond question."

Foster sister and sister-in-law to be precise since Nora had been adopted by the Cronins as a child and later in life married her late foster brother Paul Cronin.[1]

"If an auxiliary bishop is in tow, no one will be suspicious."

An auxiliary bishop plays a role not unlike that of Harvey Keitel in the film *Pulp Fiction*: he sweeps up messes. This was a somewhat new extension of that role.

"The uninformed trust me less than you."

"Nora deserves this trip."

He was actually pleading with me, indirectly and circumspectly as befitted his role.

"This is a busy time in the parish."

All times in the parish are busy.

"One of your young guys can take care of it for a week."

In fact, any one of them could take care of it better than I could.

"Perhaps."

"Besides, Blackwood, the Cardinal Archbishop of Paris has an interesting little problem. He hasn't asked for your help, because he doesn't know about you, but he needs your help just the same."

---

[1]See *The Brother's Wife*.

"Ah?"

This was the bait, the double chocolate malted milk on the table.

"It would seem that one of his most talented young priests has disappeared from the face of the earth."

"Indeed!"

"Into thin air, so to speak." He swilled the whiskey around in its Waterford goblet. "Do you want a drink? It's your whiskey, after all."

"What sort of thin air?"

"Third-century Gallo-Roman thin air!"

"Remarkable!"

"Yeah, a famous TV priest, young, good-looking, great preacher, a little too right-wing maybe for your tastes, name of Jean-Claude Chretien."

"The Church in France seriously needs right-wing TV preachers if it is to succeed in its efforts to bring back the Bourbon monarchy. Whether such a preacher will speak to the needs of the twenty-five percent of young people in that country who are unemployed is perhaps an open question."

Milord Cronin peered at me over the rim of his drink.

"Like I always say, Blackwood, I'm glad you're on my side . . . In any event this young man has, or perhaps I should say had, some training in archaeology. He was showing a couple of TV producers through the excavations under Notre-Dame in preparation for a program about the continuity of the Church in France."

"Doubtless he intended to make clear that the original Parisi were Celts."

"Doubtless, Blackwood. Anyway, he vanished. Turned a corner and when the producers caught up with him, he wasn't there anymore."

"Fascinating!"

"Arguably," Milord Cronin agreed, stealing my favorite word.

"I would be correct if I assumed that there is only one access to these ruins?"

"Yep. And people at the cashier's desk who recognized him from his TV program swore he never left. . . . So the assumption is that he jumped into a house they had unearthed in the ruins and returned to the third century."

"Arguably where he belonged."

"I suppose that there are more rational explanations. However, no one has ever found him."

I could think of some obvious ones. However, assuming that the Paris police still worked in the tradition of C. August Dupin and Inspector Maigret, they would have thought of them too. The disappearance could be conveniently accounted for perhaps. But the motive was another matter altogether. Murder? Perhaps. Fleeing from the priesthood? Arguably. Or something more sinister and cynical? The basic principle of disappearance was easy enough. You needed a few forged credentials, some credit cards and bank accounts under a new name, a place to come to earth and stay until the police gave up and stopped looking—either because they figured you were dead or had made up your mind not to be found. If, however, you were a celebrity—like a prominent TV priest—it was much more difficult to come to ground where you would not be known. More difficult, but not impossible so long as you had a loyal team of coconspirators and lots of money.

The Church might take the position, especially if there were no ransom demands, that you were dead and that Communists or radicals had killed you. At at point the Church would quietly stop hoping that you'd turn up and begin to hope that you would not.

"So"—Sean Cardinal Cronin bounced from my easy

chair, neglecting to replace the pile of computer output which represented the parish schedule for the next six months—"when we get there and you're not busy with your chaperone duties, you can see to it, Blackwood!"

He thereupon departed my study with his best maniacal laugh, a crimson guided missile going into orbit.

On the whole, as Holmes would say, it was a matter not without some interesting points.

"Punk, you really have to go to Paris with Sean and Nora," insisted my sister, Mary Kathleen Ryan Murphy, who was on the phone almost as soon as Milord Cronin left the room. "You owe it to him."

"Ah," I said. "I am unaware of what that debt might be."

I had already committed myself, more or less, to the venture. Family scenarios however, had to be preserved.

"You should stay at the Abbey where Joe and I stayed when we went over with Red Kane and Eileen."

Eileen Ryan Kane, a judge in the Federal Appellate Court, was the number two matriarch in our family.

"The Abbey," I replied, "is in Lake Geneva, Wisconsin."

"No, I mean the one in the Saint Germain district, near the Sour Bean."

My virtuous sister is perhaps the finest woman psychiatrist in Chicago, which is to say the finest of any. However, her geography leaves something to be desired.

"St-Germain-des-Prés," I said, "across the Luxembourg Gardens from the *Sorbonne.*"

"Whatever"—she dismissed my cavils as irrelevant,— "it's an eleventh-century convent."

If it were it would be a precious museum. Seventeenth century more likely.

"I don't like convents."

"Don't be ridiculous, it's darling. Right near the Saint Surplus metro stop."

"St-Sulpice," I said.

"Whatever . . . Well, I've told Nora about it."

"Patently."

I did not tell her that *l'abbaye St-Germain* was right around the corner from the *Institut Catholique*—the Catholic presence near the Latin Quarter after theology had been forced out of the *Sorbonne*, St. Thomas Aquinas's university. That information was utterly irrelevant. Besides, what did I know?

So the matter had been settled. The family had once again made sure that I would act right, despite my proclivities not to do so. In fact, I would accompany Sean Cronin to the ends of the earth. I had no doubt that he could get to the aforementioned outer limits without my help, but he would not be able to return unless I were along for the ride.

The phone rang again. Crystal Lane, our resident mystic and youth minister, who answered phones until the Megan (four porter persons with the same name) appeared after school.

"Senator Cronin, Bishop Blackie."

"Thank you, Crystal."

"I'll pray for you while you're away on the trip."

That would not be an innovation. Crystal prayed all the time for everyone. Even she knew about the ill-advised journey. Even before I did.

"Thank you, Crystal," I said with my heavy West-of-Ireland sigh. "I'm sure I'll need the prayers."

"Blackwood, you're a dear," Nora Cronin began.

"Patently."

"Poor Sean needs time away from Chicago."

The word "poor" on the lips of an Irishwoman indicated high praise.

"Doubtless."

"And so do you."

This was simply not true. I never need to be away from Chicago. Even in the winter.

"Perhaps."

"It's very sweet of you to come. I'm sure we'll have a wonderful time. You know everything about Paris."

The Lady Nora thought I was adorable.

"It will do as a city," I admitted.

They had been lovers long ago, adulterous and sacrilegious lovers. Passions like that never really go away. I would accompany them so that they would be reassured that the passions would not escape from the currents in which they had been controlled for decades. I knew well that nothing like that could ever happen. But they didn't.

I had been to the City of Lights despite my pretense that I had not. It had a terrible, blood-soaked history. I knew too much of that history to enjoy my visit. I am not psychic like my friend and colleague Nuala Anne McGrail, but there were too many ghosts—of peasants and queens, of saints and sinners, of innocents and monsters—wandering about. However, the French, with the exception of their politicians, their intellectuals and their clergy, were nice people—just like every other people, though patently not as nice as the Irish.

Truth to tell, I liked sparring with the haughty French hierarchs I had encountered. I looked forward with considerable interest to this delightful amusement.

There was, of course, the interesting matter of the TV priest who had leaped back into the third century.

Fascinating.

"I won't go home with you!"

Annabel clutched at the sheet on her hospital bed.

She tried to tell Luis that she didn't believe he was her husband and she didn't want to go with him.

But before she could speak, he told the nurse, "My wife is becoming agitated."

"No," Annabel said, "I'm not. I—" She felt the prick of a needle and tried to object. "But—"

Luis interrupted. "Take it easy, my dear," he soothed. "You'll rest and feel better."

"I don't want to rest." She fought the mist that closed around her. She didn't want to be alone with Luis.

He looked at her, a strange and knowing smile in his silver-gray eyes. "Sleep, my dear," he said. "When you wake, I'll be right here with you."

And that, of course, was what she was afraid of.

Dear Reader,

We've got six great books for you this month, and three of them are part of miniseries you've grown to love. Dallas Schulze continues A FAMILY CIRCLE with *Addie and the Renegade*. Dallas is known to readers worldwide as an author whose mastery of emotion is unparalleled, and this book will only enhance her well-deserved reputation. For Cole Walker, love seems like an impossibility—until he's stranded with Addie Smith, and suddenly... Well, maybe I'd better let you read for yourself. In *Leader of the Pack*, Justine Davis keeps us located on TRINITY STREET WEST. You met Ryan Buckhart in *Lover Under Cover;* now meet Lacey Buckhart, the one woman—the one wife!—he's never been able to forget. Then finish off Laura Parker's ROGUES' GALLERY with *Found: One Marriage*. Amnesia, exes who still share a love they've never been able to equal anywhere else...this one has it all.

Of course, our other three books are equally special.
Nikki Benjamin's *The Lady and Alex Payton* is the follow-up to *The Wedding Venture,* and it features a kidnapped almost-bride. Barbara Faith brings you *Long-Lost Wife?* For Annabel the past is a mystery—and the appearance of a man claiming to be her husband doesn't make things any clearer, irresistible though he may be. Finally, try Beverly Bird's *The Marrying Kind*. Hero John Gunner thinks that's just the kind of man he's *not*, but meeting Tessa Hadley-Bryant proves to him just how wrong a man can be.

And be sure to come back next month for more of the best romantic reading around—here in Silhouette Intimate Moments.

Yours,

Leslie Wainger

Leslie Wainger
Senior Editor and Editorial Coordinator

Please address questions and book requests to:
Silhouette Reader Service
U.S.: 3010 Walden Ave., P.O. Box 1325, Buffalo, NY 14269
Canadian: P.O. Box 609, Fort Erie, Ont. L2A 5X3

LONG-LOST WIFE?

BARBARA FAITH

Silhouette®

INTIMATE™MOMENTS®

Published by Silhouette Books

America's Publisher of Contemporary Romance

SILHOUETTE BOOKS

ISBN 0-373-07730-0

LONG-LOST WIFE?

Books by Barbara Faith

Silhouette Intimate Moments

The Promise of Summer #16
Wind Whispers #47
Bedouin Bride #63
Awake to Splendor #101
Islands in Turquoise #124
Tomorrow Is Forever #140
Sing Me a Lovesong #146
Desert Song #173
Kiss of the Dragon #193
Asking for Trouble #208
Beyond Forever #244
Flower of the Desert #262
In a Rebel's Arms #277
Capricorn Moon #306
Danger in Paradise #332
Lord of the Desert #361
The Matador #432
Queen of Hearts #446
Cloud Man #502
Midnight Man #544
Desert Man #578
Moonlight Lady #623
Long-Lost Wife? #730

Silhouette Special Edition

Return to Summer #335
Say Hello Again #436
Heather on the Hill #533
Choices of the Heart #615
Echoes of Summer #650
Mr. Macho Meets His Match #715
This Above All #812
Scarlet Woman #975
Happy Father's Day #1033

Silhouette Desire

Lion of the Desert #670

Silhouette Shadows

A Silence of Dreams #13
Dark, Dark My Lover's Eyes #43

Silhouette Books

Silhouette Summer Sizzlers 1988
"Fiesta!"
Silhouette Summer Sizzlers 1995
"The Sheikh's Woman"

BARBARA FAITH,

a long-time contributor to Silhouette Books, passed away in October of 1995. She will be greatly missed by her husband, fellow authors, friends and all the editors who have worked with her, and by her readers. Her books captured the spirit of adventure and love that she displayed throughout her life. Barbara's warmth and energy were infectious and joyous and touched all who knew her in person and through her stories. She leaves behind a wonderful legacy.

Prologue

Bright, blinding sun. Burning her skin, parching her lips.

Thirsty. Oh God, so thirsty. Ran her tongue over dry, cracked lips. Tried to move. Hurt too much. Everything hurt. Headache. Monster headache. She reached up to touch her head and felt crusted blood.

Slept for a while. Awoke to the slap of waves against the small rubber boat.

Night closed in around her. She slept again, and in her dreams she heard the screams and saw, as through a misty darkness, the terrible scene of violence.

And wept dry tears.

Another day. The sun blistered her skin, burned through her eyes into her skull. She dreamed of iced tea, chocolate sodas with cool, minty ice cream, ice cubes tinkling in a tall glass of lemonade.

Another night. The same dream of horror. They screamed again. Who screamed again? Screamed and kept screaming.

Daylight. No sun now. Mist rolling in. Enveloping her in moist coolness. She tried to catch the mist with her tongue, but when she knew she could not, she closed her eyes and drifted on the gentle sea, drifted into that fine mist.

Chapter 1

"**M**iss? Young lady?" A hand on her shoulder. "Come on now, wake up."

The light hurt her eyes. She blinked, tried again and focused on the man bending over her. A dark-skinned man with wire-rimmed glasses. Large nose in a nice face. White coat.

"I'm Dr. Hunnicut."

"That's nice." Her eyes drifted closed.

"Stay awake," he said. "Talk to me."

"Sleepy."

"You can sleep later." He gave her shoulder a gentle nudge. "I want you to wake up now. Come on, open your eyes."

She tried to will him away, but when he wouldn't go, she opened her eyes again. "Where ... where am I?"

"In a hospital in Nassau."

"My head hurts."

"You've had a concussion and you've got a bad sunburn."

That's why her skin hurt.

"You were dehydrated when you were picked up—"

"Picked up?"

"But you're safe now, you're going to be all right." He leaned down and held a light in her right eye. "Look up," he ordered.

She did and he said, "Uh-huh," then turned the light on her left eye. When that was done, he said, "Can you tell me your name?"

"It's..." She stopped, a little bewildered, then took a deep breath and tried again. "My name is..." She looked up at the doctor, uncertain, frightened. "It's..." Sweat beaded her forehead.

"That's all right," he said. "Don't be alarmed. A lapse of memory sometimes happens with a concussion. Can you tell me where you're from or where you were going when the accident happened?"

An accident? What kind of an accident? She willed herself to stay calm. "I'm from..."

"Try to remember," the doctor prodded.

"Don't push her." A man she had never seen before stepped forward. "She's tired. Let her rest."

She looked up, grateful to him for standing up for her. He was very tall, at least as she looked up at him from the bed he seemed very tall. He had a strong, somewhat angular face, a nicer nose than the doctor and silver gray eyes.

"Your name is Annabel," he said. "Annabel Alarcon." He took her hand. "You're my wife."

"Your...your wife?" Her heart started beating hard and she felt the gray mists closing in around her again.

His hand tightened on hers. He leaned closer, holding her with his silver eyes. "Annabel Alarcon." His voice became a whisper through the tunnel of her darkness. "Annabel. Annabel . . . my wife."

No, I'm not! she thought she said. But the words were unspoken and the mist enveloped her.

Screams cut through the darkness of her mind, piercing and shrill. "My God! Oh my God, what's happening? What . . . what are you doing?"

Screams echoing in her mind before they faded into nothingness.

Oh please, oh please, oh please . . .

A bright kaleidoscope of color whirling round and round in her brain. Colors so bright they hurt her eyes; flames orange and blood red that ripped and tore upward through the sky. Up and up before they fell back on top of her. The sky was falling . . . falling.

She screamed . . .

"Annabel. Annabel, my dear, you're dreaming. Wake up."

"Oh, God," she moaned. "They were screaming."

He put his arms around her and, lifting her close, whispered, "Who was screaming, Annabel? Tell me. Tell me about your dream."

"No," she whispered. "I can't."

"Yes, you can. Tell me."

She shuddered and brought her hands up to cover her eyes.

He took her hands away. He smoothed her hair from her face and, when she was a little calmer, asked, "What happened on the boat, Annabel?"

"I don't know. I don't remember." She was trembling, her teeth were chattering.

"Try, Annabel. Try to remember."

"No." She pulled away from him. "Who are you?"

"My name is Luis Miguel. I'm your husband."

Luis Miguel. The name meant nothing.

He eased her back into the bed. In the dim light from a lamp at the other end of the room, she looked up at him. His face was too strong, too masculine. Very tanned. His eyebrows were dark, his nose was straight. His silver gray eyes, Spanish eyes, she thought, seemed to be hiding secrets she could not understand. His mouth... The breath caught in her throat. His mouth was both sensuous and cruel, as cruel as pictures she had seen of the ascetics who had ruled over the Spanish Inquisition.

"Luis Miguel Alarcon," he said. "Your husband."

"What... what kind of a name is Alarcon?"

"Spanish."

Spanish eyes. She wondered how she'd known.

"My family came from the north of Spain, near Burgos."

She shivered and he said, "Are you cold? Do you want a blanket? Shall I turn down the air-conditioning?"

"No." She gripped the edge of the sheet. "No, I'm all right."

"You've been through a terrible ordeal."

"Have I?" She shook her head. "But I don't remember. Tell me... please tell me what happened."

He pulled a chair closer to the bed. "You were picked up by a fishing boat and flown to the hospital here in Nassau. You had been found drifting in a rubber raft thirty miles east of Eleuthera." He took her hand. "I chartered a plane and flew in two days ago."

"But if I didn't know who I was, how did you... why did you think it was me?"

"You went to Miami ten days ago to do some shopping. The night before you were to fly back, you called to say you were going to return on a friend's boat. I didn't want you to. We argued, but you insisted. That was five days ago."

"I don't understand. I flew to Miami from where?"

"We'll talk about that later."

"But what happened?"

"All anyone knows is that there was an explosion at sea and that you were the only survivor."

"An explosion?" She touched her head, trying to remember. And when she could, she asked, "Where do you live?"

"Not me, Annabel. We. We live on San Sebastián."

"San...?" She shook her head. "I've never heard of it."

"It's a small island in the Bahamas, north of the Caicos. It's our private island." He tightened his hand around hers. "I'll take you there as soon as the doctor says you're able to travel."

She couldn't do that, couldn't go anywhere with this man, this stranger. Frightened now, she said, "I don't know you. I don't want to go with you."

"Annabel—"

"I'm not Annabel. I'm..." She struggled up, frantic now, searching for a name. Searching...

He rang for the nurse. She hurried in and he said, "My wife is upset. Can you give her something to help her sleep?"

"Of course."

She reached for Annabel's arm. "No!" Annabel said, and tried to pull away. "No, please."

"Now hush, dear." The nurse gripped her arm, quickly swabbed a spot and inserted the needle. "You'll rest now," she said when she released Annabel.

"I don't want to rest," Annabel protested. "I want to get out of here. I want to go back to..." Oh, God. Back to where? She saw him exchange a look with the nurse, raise an eyebrow and shake his head.

She felt herself slipping away and fought to keep her eyes open. "No," she whispered as the darkness closed in.

The next morning a nurse with cocoa brown skin came into her room with a copy of the *Miami Herald*. She handed the newspaper to Annabel, announced that her name was Rebecca and, after she had taken Annabel's blood pressure and temperature, said, "It's a pure miracle, being picked up the way you were. The coast guard found some debris from a boat so they think you were on it and that there was an explosion of some kind."

She handed Annabel the newspaper. "It's a couple of days old," she said, "but I thought you'd like to catch up on what happened. The story's on page three."

There was a picture of a woman being carried from the fishing boat onto the pier at Nassau. And a headline that read Mystery Woman Connected to Explosion at Sea.

She stared at the photograph. "May I..." She swallowed hard. "May I have a mirror?"

"There isn't one. I mean, the only one is the mirror over the washstand in the bathroom."

"Please," Annabel said.

"All right. I have one in my purse. I'll bring it."

The nurse hurried out of the room, and when she returned she handed Annabel a small mirror.

She stared at the face in the mirror, a face she had no recollection of ever having seen before. Tangled blond hair. A brush of bangs over the wide forehead. A bump with stitches near her hairline. A long red scratch on her cheek and a bruise near her temple. And frightened blue eyes that looked almost too big for her face. The face of a stranger.

She handed the mirror back. "I don't know her," she whispered.

The nurse stared at her, startled, chagrined. With a shake of her head she said, "But you will. Soon as you feel better you'll remember everything, Annabel."

Annabel. She looked at the face in the mirror. Did she look like an Annabel? And what, after all, did an Annabel look like?

With hands that trembled, she picked up the newspaper and began to read. The story that followed told about the remnants of a boat, thought to be a pleasure craft, that had been found off the coast of Eleuthera. The coast guard had no idea as to its origin, the registry or the names of the owners. The only clue was a windbreaker jacket with the name Z. Flynn emblazoned on the chest that had been found floating with the wreckage.

Flynn, the story read, was from Pompano Beach, Florida. He had been a captain for hire as well as a deep-sea diver.

The story went on to recap her rescue and her transfer to Nassau. She had been wearing shorts and a shirt when she'd been picked up. She had no identification. The only thing that had been found was a gold doubloon in the pocket of her shorts.

Annabel reread that part. A gold doubloon? Doubloons were...what? Old Spanish coins? They had to do with pirates and the Spanish Main. What was one doing in the pocket of her shorts? And where was the coin now?

"Where are my clothes?" she asked the nurse. "It says in the paper that I was wearing shorts and a shirt when I was brought in."

"Your husband threw them away."

"And the..." Annabel indicated the story she had just read. "And the gold doubloon?" she asked.

"I'm sure he must have it." Rebecca grinned down at Annabel. "A gold doubloon to add to what he already has."

"He's rich?"

Rebecca looked surprised, then she smiled gently and said, "I forgot. You don't remember, do you?"

Annabel shook her head. "Not him, not anything." She hesitated, then, motioning the nurse closer, whispered, "I really don't believe he's my husband."

"Not your husband? Of course he is, dear."

"How can you be sure?"

"I saw your marriage license."

"You saw..." Annabel raised herself to a sitting position.

"You were unconscious the first day after you were brought in. Mr. Alarcon came the second day. When he said he was your husband, the doctor asked to see some proof, and Mr. Alarcon showed him your marriage license and an old passport.''

So it was true. This man, this stranger, was her husband. She looked at the nurse and slowly shook her head. "I don't remember him," she said. "I don't remember anything about him."

"Would it help if I told you what I know?"

"Yes. Yes, please."

"It isn't much, only what I've heard from the doctor and the other nurses. Apparently your husband is something of a recluse. Stays right there on his island when he's not off somewhere sailing. He has a home in Madrid, too, and he goes there once or twice a year. He inherited a fortune and he's made a fortune.''

"Doing what?" Annabel asked, curious to know more about this man who said he was her husband.

"He's a real adventurer," she said. "Just like those old-time pirates. Only he's a modern-day pirate."

A modern-day pirate. The thought frightened her even more than he did.

That afternoon, two men from the coast guard, along with a man from the FBI, came to the hospital to speak to her. Luis Miguel was in the room when they arrived. He offered the chair to the FBI agent, then moved to the foot of Annabel's bed and stood looking down at her.

One of the men from the coast guard called her Mrs. Alarcon. The FBI agent, who said his name was Charles Buchanan, took a tape recorder out of his pocket.

"I understand from your husband that you're having difficulty remembering things."

"Yes."

"But surely you remember something." He waited, and when Annabel said nothing, he asked, "Do you remember anything about the boat you were on?"

She shook her head.

"You were with other people. Who were they? Where had you come from?"

"I . . . I don't know."

"She called me from Miami to say that she was leaving from there with friends," Luis Miguel said.

"What friends?" The agent turned back to Annabel. "What were their names?"

"I'm sorry." She shook her head. "I don't remember."

"Do you know their names, Mr. Alarcon?"

"No, I'm afraid not."

Buchanan frowned. "What about Flynn? Have you ever heard the name Zachary Flynn before, Mrs. Alarcon?"

"No."

"Mr. Alarcon?"

"Yes, I knew him. He worked for me for a short time."

"When was that?"

"Several years ago."

"You have no idea who he might have been working for at the time of the accident?"

"No, I don't."

One of the men from the coast guard stepped forward, a young man with an earnest face and nice brown eyes. "We're pretty sure there were other people aboard," he said, "in addition to you and Mr. Flynn. We picked up pieces of clothing, both men's and women's, but there was nothing we could find to identify the boat. You're the only one who can help us, ma'am. Can't you try to remember? Surely there must be something—''

"That's enough," Luis said, stopping him. "My wife has been through a terrible ordeal. She's had a concussion and she suffers from headaches. This is a difficult time for her, gentlemen, so if you don't mind, perhaps we could leave this until she's feeling better."

Buchanan frowned. He hesitated, looked from Luis to Annabel and asked, "What are your plans, Mr. Alarcon? I understand from the doctor that your wife will be released from the hospital the day after tomorrow. What will you do then? Do you plan on staying in Nassau for a while?"

Luis shook his head. "I've had my boat brought here to Nassau. My wife and I will sail back to San Sebastián as soon as she's released."

"San Sebastián?" Annabel clutched at the white spread that covered the bed. Her throat tightened and her mind screamed, No! No, I can't!

Luis saw her panic and moved quickly to her side.

She tried to say, "Listen, I don't—" Tried to tell these men that she didn't want to be on a boat again, that she didn't know the man who said he was her husband and she didn't want to go with him.

But before she could say anything, he cut in and said, "I'm sorry, gentlemen, but I'll have to ask you to leave. All of these questions have upset my wife."

He reached for the buzzer beside the bed and rang for the nurse. Rebecca hurried in. "My wife is becoming agitated," he said. "She needs to rest."

"No," Annabel protested, "I'm not. I—"

"Hush, dear," he said, cutting her off again.

The nurse took her arm. Annabel felt the prick of the needle against her skin. "Gentlemen," Luis said, "please."

The member of the coast guard with the nice brown eyes looked upset. Buchanan said, "We'll be back when you're feeling better, Mrs. Alarcon."

"But I'm not . . ." she tried to say. "I—"

Once again Luis interrupted. "Take it easy, my dear," he soothed. "You mustn't get excited. You'll have a little rest and then you'll feel better."

"I don't want to rest." She fought the mist that threatened to close in around her. She wanted to tell the young man with the nice brown eyes not to go away, but he had already turned and with the other men had left the room. Left her alone with Luis Miguel Alarcon.

He looked down at her, a strange and knowing smile in his silver gray eyes. "Sleep now, my dear," he said. "When you wake up I'll be right here with you."

And that, of course, was what she was afraid of.

Chapter 2

The dream, again the dream. Flashes of orange red fire. A man, mouth agape, screaming, screaming... And the woman? What woman? Facedown on the deck, blond hair matted with blood, unmoving.

She tried to scream a warning but her voice came out in a mewling whisper of sound. "Run...run..."

"Annabel." Someone shook her. Someone said, "Wake up. You're dreaming. Wake up!"

She opened her eyes and in the shadowed light of the room she saw him, the man who said he was her husband.

"What is it?" he asked. "What were you dreaming?"

"A woman...there was a woman. I tried to get to her, but I..." She looked at him. "Why couldn't I?" she whispered. "Why couldn't I help her?"

"You were hurt." He stroked the hair back from her face. "Who was she, Annabel?"

"I . . . I don't know."

"Try to think. Try to remember."

"I can't! Don't you understand that I can't!" She turned away and buried her head in the pillow. "I don't remember." Her voice was muffled, weeping. "I don't remember."

"You have to . . ." He stopped, bit back the words. This wasn't the way. He had to wait, be patient. Eventually she would remember. And when she did?

He stood for a moment looking down at her. Then he turned and left the room.

"I've got good news for you." Dr. Hunnicut smiled down at Annabel. "You're ready to leave the hospital."

"Leave . . . ?" Her hands clenched the white bedspread. "But I—"

"It's all arranged. Rebecca will help you dress. It's a beautiful day, good sailing weather."

She hated his cheerfulness.

"I bet you can't wait to get out of the hospital nightgown," the nurse said. "Your husband has bought you some nice new clothes."

She looked from the nurse to the doctor, who said, "You're going to be just fine, Mrs. Alarcon. I've given Mr. Alarcon a prescription for pain in case you need it, and something to help you relax."

The nurse took her arm and Annabel swung her legs over the side of the bed. For the past two days she'd been allowed to get up to take a shower and walk the halls. Though she still felt a little weak, she knew her strength was coming back. Her strength, but not her memory. God, how that frightened her.

"Come along," Rebecca said. "You mustn't keep your husband waiting."

Her husband. She looked at the nurse, then the doctor. "I don't remember him. I don't want to go with him."

"But, my dear..." Dr. Hunnicut shook his head. "I know this must be difficult for you, but give it time."

She fought back tears. "How much time?"

"It's difficult to say. You could remember everything tomorrow or..." He shook his head. "Well, actually, one can't say in a case like yours."

One can't say? And what am I supposed to do meantime? Go into the unknown with a man I've never seen before?

And what if what he said was true? What if Luis Miguel Alarcon really was her husband? What would he expect from her? That she behave like a wife? Share his bed?

The nurse took her arm. "It's almost noon," she said. "We want to be ready when he comes, don't we?"

We? With one last desperate look at the doctor, Annabel let the nurse help her into the bathroom.

She left the hospital forty-five minutes later in a wheelchair. She wore new white duck pants and a red-and-white-striped T-shirt. Shorts and shirts and swimsuits were packed in a new overnight bag.

Rebecca wheeled her out to a waiting taxi. Luis Miguel took her arm and helped her in. "Happy sailing," the nurse called out when the taxi started up.

Annabel stared straight ahead, hands clenched at her sides, fear knotting her throat. "I don't think I can get on a boat again," she said. "You told me you chartered a plane to get here. Couldn't we do that? Fly back to your island, I mean."

He reached for her hand. "You've always loved the water, Annabel. Besides, the sea air will do you good, put some color back into your cheeks. With good weather the trip will take three days, four at the most. By the time we reach San Sebastián you'll feel like a new woman. Besides..." He smiled. "The fresh air might help jog your memory."

There was a part of her that didn't want her memory jogged, that didn't want to remember what had happened that fateful day. She looked down at the hand that covered hers. Had she really lived with this man on his island? Had she loved him? She gave him a sidelong glance, saw him watching her and quickly lowered her eyes.

What had it been like, she wondered, living with him, making love with him? He seemed so forbidding, so overwhelmingly masculine he frightened her. Would he expect her to sleep with him once they reached his island?

The taxi stopped at the entrance to the wharf and the driver said, "Here we be, boss."

Luis Miguel offered his hand to Annabel and helped her out of the cab. All around were the bustle and the ripe, rich smells of the waterfront, the salty tang of the sea, of fresh fish and fruit and flowers.

Stall owners called out in a singsong calypso lilt, "Fresh fish! Come buy here, buy fresh fish. We got conch fresh from de sea, bass and shrimp and de shark. Fresh, fresh, lady and mon. Come see. Come buy."

Food stalls hawked pigeon peas and rice, green turtle pie and baked plantains. Fruit stands sold pa-

payas, mangoes, guavas and soursops. Dark-skinned children darted in and around the stalls, laughing, calling out to one another. Women with hair turbaned in red or blue bandannas wove straw baskets and wide-brimmed colorful hats. Men in undershirts and tattered jeans hefted whole hands of bananas. A skinny man with a wide, white-toothed smile strummed a guitar and sang, "Come Mr. Tallyman, tally me banana..."

Luis Miguel stopped in front of one of the stands that sold the bright-colored straw hats. "We'd better buy you a hat." He picked out a big-brimmed one and handed it to Annabel. "Try this," he said.

When she put it on, he nodded, paid the woman and, taking Annabel's arm, led her through the crush of people toward the marina and out onto the dock.

There were so many boats, deep-sea fishing boats, small pleasure crafts, motor sailers and cabin cruisers, sixty-foot yachts and small sailboats.

"Our boat is down here at the end," he said. "The *Straight On till Morning.* Do you remember?"

"Straight on?" She shook her head.

"It's from *Peter Pan.* The way to Never-Never Land, Annabel. Second star on the right, straight on till morning."

She looked at him, bewildered. "No," she said. "I don't remember."

It lay sturdy in the water. Trim and sleek, white and royal blue. Forty feet? Fifty? She stopped. "I can't do this," she said.

"Do what?" He looked at her, dark eyebrows drawn together in a frown. "What do you mean you can't do this?"

Her voice rose. "I'm not going with you." She tried to back away from him. "I won't go with you. You can't make me. I don't know you. I'm not going out on the water with you."

He hesitated, as though not sure what to do, then with a muttered oath he scooped her up in his arms. When she struggled, he swore and, tightening his arms around her, hurried down the dock toward the boat. "Samuel?" he called out. "Samuel!"

A black man wearing cutoffs and a seaman's cap came up from below. "Hey, boss man." He grinned in greeting, then the grin faded. "The lady she be sick, sir?"

"Yes, she is. Help me get her aboard, please."

"No!" Annabel cried. "I don't want to. I don't want..."

He handed her down to the other man then quickly jumped down beside her. "She's just out of the hospital," he said. "I'll take her down to the cabin. She'll be all right. Are we all gassed up? Ready to go?"

"Soon's you be giving the word."

"I'll take care of Mrs. Alarcon first. Bring me a glass of water, will you?"

He carried her, still struggling, down a few steps, past a galley and what looked like a salon and into a cabin, where he laid her on the bed. "Take it easy," he said. "Just take it easy, Annabel."

"Let me go!"

"Here be the water," Samuel said.

Luis took two pills out of the bottle in his pocket and held them out to her. "Take these," he said.

"No."

"I don't want to have to force you, Annabel."

"But you are forcing me."

"No, I'm taking care of you." He sat down on the bunk beside her. To Samuel he said, "Leave us, please." And when the other man had gone, he said, "I'm taking you home, to our island." And more gently, "You really don't have a choice. You have nowhere else to go, no memory, no money, no one except me."

"But I don't know you," she whispered.

He clasped her hands in his. "I'm not going to harm you, Annabel. I only want to help you, to take care of you." He released her and placed the two pills in the palm of her hand. "These will make you relax," he said. "Please take them."

She looked at him and knew he was right. She had no choice but to do what he said, to take the pills, to go with him.

She swallowed the pills with a sip of the water, and when he said, "Lie back now," she did. She had no memory, no money. No one except him.

He left her. She felt the gentle rock of the boat against the waves, then the sound of a motor, the cry, "Cast off!" And the man Samuel calling out, "Have a safe trip, boss man. I be coming next week with the supply boat."

The other man wasn't coming with them. She would be alone on the open sea with Luis Miguel, the man who said he was her husband. But she knew, somehow she knew that he had lied. He wasn't her husband. She wasn't even sure she'd ever seen him before.

She struggled to stay awake, to fight the pills he had made her take. But the sound of the motor and the rocking of the boat lulled her so that, in spite of herself, her eyes kept closing. In a little while, though she told herself she would not, she slept.

She awoke sometime later to the slap of waves against the hull of the boat, the metallic clink of the halyards against the mast, the creak of boards. They were moving but there was no sound of the motor.

She lay for a moment trying to figure out where she was, then sat up and brushed her hair back from her face. She looked for the head, saw a door and opened it, wondering how she knew that a bathroom on a boat was the head.

Toiletry things had been laid out on the washstand, a comb and brush, shampoo, a pale coral lipstick. She picked up the brush and forced herself to look in the mirror over the washstand. "Who are you?" she whispered, as if the mirror could give her the answer.

But the face that stared back at her was the face of a stranger.

She splashed cold water on her face and brushed her hair, and because she knew that she could not stay down here forever, she left the cabin and went up the few steps to the salon and the galley, then up onto the deck.

The sails, unfurled to catch the sea wind, were stark white against a clean blue sky. The man who said he was her husband stood at the helm, feet planted apart, facing into the wind, suntanned and fit. His body was lean, muscled, his waist narrow, his stomach flat. He looked like an athlete, not the muscle-bound, jock-type athlete, but like a long-distance runner or a man who scaled mountains just for the fun of it. He was, she supposed as she stood watching him, handsome in a rugged, totally masculine way.

He looked up and saw her watching him. "How do you feel?" he asked.

"Better."

"Are you hungry?"

She nodded.

"There's meat for hamburgers in the refrigerator, along with the makings for a salad. I'll come down in a minute and show you how to light the stove."

"I know how."

He looked at her, suspicion in his eyes. "So you do remember."

"No. I..." She looked bewildered, uncertain. "I...I don't know why I said that."

He shot her a look of disbelief but didn't say anything.

After a little while he pointed toward a small island. "I'm going to put in there and anchor in the cove for the night. We could have a swim before dinner if you'd like."

"No." She gripped a stanchion. "No, I don't want to swim."

"The exercise would be good for you."

"No." Fear pinched her face and she turned away.

Okay, he told himself. She's been through a terrifying ordeal. It's natural for her to be afraid of the water. He wondered then if he'd been heartless in insisting they sail back to San Sebastián instead of chartering a plane, as he had when he first heard about the accident at sea. But he'd wanted these three or four days alone with her to try to find out if, after all, she was faking her amnesia. He didn't think she was, but he had to be sure.

She stayed where she was, as though afraid to let go of the stanchion, until he guided the boat into the shallows of the cove. The water was calm here, a pale turquoise shadowed by the fading light of day. Palm trees lined the white sand beach, sea grape plants

clustered near the shoreline, where yellow hibiscus and
Madagascar jasmine grew. Deep purple bougainvillea
climbed up what must have been the remains of an old
fort.

Luis dropped the two anchors. "Sure you don't
want a swim?" he asked. And when Annabel shook
her head, he poised himself at the rail, arched his body
and dived into the water. He cut cleanly through the
surface and she could see him swimming there, underwater, his tanned body strangely white. When he
came up he started swimming, muscular arms reaching out, stroking hard.

She watched him for a moment or two before she
went down the four steps into the galley and took the
makings of a salad out of the refrigerator. When the
salad was made, she set the table with dishes she found
in the cupboard. She didn't start the hamburgers until she felt the boat tilt and knew that he'd come
aboard.

He walked into the galley, a towel around his neck.
Droplets of water glistened in his dark hair, and his
skin smelled of the sea. He glanced at the table, then
at the hamburgers sizzling on the fire. "I'll just have
a quick shower," he told her, and disappeared through
the cabin and into the head. Five minutes later he came
back wearing a clean pair of cutoffs and a black T-
shirt.

"Would you like a beer?" he asked.

She shook her head.

"But you like beer." He opened the refrigerator,
reached for a can and popped it open. "Try it." He
handed it to her. She took a sip, made a face and
handed it back to him.

"The burgers are ready," she said.

He glanced at the table. "Where's the mayonnaise?"

"Mayonnaise? You like mayonnaise on your burgers?"

"No, but you do."

Annabel shook her head. There were a lot of things she didn't remember, but one thing she was sure of—never, ever in her life had she put mayo on a hamburger. Cheese, mustard, onions and lots of little sliced pickles. But mayo? Uh-uh.

So it seemed he was testing her, trying to find out by little things like this whether or not she was faking. As though anybody in their right mind—if indeed she *was* in her right mind—would fake amnesia.

She slid the burgers onto the buns and slapped them down on the table. If he was aware of her anger he didn't say anything. He shoved a tape into a battery-powered radio-cassette player and the music of a slow and sensuous bolero began.

"You always liked Spanish music," Luis said.

"Did I?" She stabbed at a piece of lettuce. "I don't remember."

"But you will. Someday you'll remember everything."

"How long...?" She took a deep breath as though to prepare herself for the question. "How long were we married?"

His mouth tightened. He looked out of the porthole instead of at her. "For eight years."

"Where did we meet?"

"In New Orleans. At a Mardi Gras party."

"Is that where I lived?"

He bit into the burger, waited, then said, "No. You lived in Miami. You were from some place in Oregon."

"Where?"

"I don't remember."

"What about my parents? Is that where they live?"

"Your parents are dead."

She balled the paper napkin up in her fist. "Brothers and sisters?"

"You were an only child."

"What about...?" She tried to keep her voice level, her tone impersonal, as though she were talking about someone else. "What about friends?"

He shook his head. "I'm sorry, I don't know your friends."

Had there been no one in her life except him? No parents, no siblings? No friends? The food stuck in her throat. She felt a sense of confusion, of utter helplessness.

"I'm...I'm not hungry." She stood. "I'm going up on deck."

He started to get up, then stopped. Maybe she needed this time alone to sort things out. It would be best not to push her, to give her a little space. As much space as two people could find, sharing a boat.

He finished eating, and when he had cleared the table he put two cups of coffee into the microwave and took them up on deck. She was sitting in the bow of the boat, looking out to sea. In the last rays of the setting sun the sky was saffron yellow, and clouds, mauve-colored and heavy, hastened the encroaching darkness. A lone egret skimmed low over the water in search of a fish, and behind in the trees he could hear the call of night birds.

He loved it here in the Bahamas, loved the quiet, the sense of being so far from civilization.

The last rays of the sun reflected on Annabel's face in a rosy glow of color, and with a start he found himself thinking how pretty she was, not classically beautiful perhaps, but certainly appealing in a waif-like kind of way. She sat with her knees drawn up to her chin, staring out at the sea as though searching for an answer to all of her questions. Questions he would not answer. At least not yet.

She turned suddenly, and as if she were reading his thoughts, she asked, "Who am I really?"

He crossed the deck and, when he had handed her a coffee, sat next to her. "You're Annabel Alarcon, my wife."

"Annabel." She looked into his eyes for a moment before her gaze shifted and she stared out at the sea. "Like Annabel Lee," she said, and began to recite.

"And this was the reason that long ago
 In this kingdom by the sea,
 A wind blew out of a cloud, chilling..."

She hesitated. "She died, you know. Poe's Annabel Lee died."

"Yes, I know."

A sigh shuddered through her. "I looked in the mirror today. I don't look like an Annabel."

That made him smile. "What does an Annabel look like?"

"I don't know. Not like me, I think." A sigh shivered through her. "Are all the nights like this in the Bahamas?" she asked.

"Most of them are."

"Tell me about San Sebastián. Where is it?"

"Some forty nautical miles east of Grand Turk."

"I don't know where that is."

He took a sip of his coffee. "The Bahamian archipelago covers hundreds of barren islands and islets. Only about twenty of them are inhabited. In the seventeenth and eighteenth centuries the Bahamas offered pirates ideal bases. During the Civil War, Confederate blockade runners used the islands, and when Prohibition came, liquor was smuggled through here. Later, of course, it was drugs."

"How long have you lived in the islands?"

"Almost fifteen years now. I was raised in Spain. My family was in the import-export business and they traded goods in the Bahamas. I spent my school vacations here with my father, and when I was out on my own I decided this was where I wanted to live."

"Are you still in importing and exporting?"

"No." He waited a moment, as though deciding how much to tell her. "I'm in the salvage business."

"Salvage?"

"I hunt for sunken treasure."

"The nurse at the hospital in Nassau told me there was a gold doubloon in my pocket when I was picked up," Annabel said. "Gold doubloons came off old Spanish ships, didn't they?"

"Yes."

"Where is it?"

"I'm keeping it for you."

"How did I get it?"

"How indeed?" he said.

Annabel stared at him, chilled by the sudden coldness in his voice. For a little while she didn't say anything, nor did he. It was dark now, and still, with only the gentle slap of water against the hull and the muted cry of a night bird to break the silence. Mingled with the smell of the sea she caught the scent of the Madagascar jasmine, and suddenly, unexplicably, she felt an overwhelming sadness, a sadness that went far deeper than her inability to remember. For this was a remembered sadness, soul-deep and painful.

She stood and, gripping the rail, looked out over the water. What was it? Dear Lord, what was it? And because there were no answers, she said, "I think I'll go below."

He stood. "Of course. Do you need any help?"

"No, I . . . I'm all right." And because she had to know, she asked, "Where will you sleep?"

"In the salon."

"Oh." She took a deep breath. "Well then, good night, Mr. Alar. . ." She stopped and took a deep breath. "Good night, Luis Miguel."

"Luis," he said. "Call me Luis."

Annabel nodded. Then she turned away from the railing and left the deck.

Chapter 3

Whatever breeze there had been died during the night. The air grew still, hot and muggy. When Annabel awoke a little before seven, she took a shower, pulled on a pair of shorts and a shirt and, when she smelled coffee, went barefoot into the galley.

Luis was at the stove, clad in French-cut black bathing trunks that left very little to the imagination. "Too hot to sleep?" he asked.

"Uh...yes." As Annabel averted her eyes, she remembered reading in a nineteeth-century book of etiquette that a lady never looked below the second button of a gentleman's vest. This gentleman wasn't wearing a vest. Actually, he was all twentieth-century male, great material for a centerfold, with broad shoulders and a waistline most women would have given their teeth for. The patch of curly dark chest hair came to a vee over his flat stomach and narrowed to a thin strip that disappeared beneath the black trunks.

Maybe she didn't remember much about anything else, but she certainly knew a good-looking man when she saw one.

"We'll leave in a little while." He handed her a mug of coffee. "How about a swim before breakfast?"

"I don't think so."

"Well then..." He finished his coffee and went topside. When she felt the motion of the boat, followed by a splash, she took her coffee and went up on deck. The water looked cool and inviting, pale turquoise in the early morning.

When he saw her he circled back toward the boat. "It's great," he called to her. "Come on."

She hesitated, then with a nod said, "I'll go put a suit on."

She hurried below and grabbed one of the suits she'd found when she unpacked the suitcase. There were two bathing suits, one a white bikini, two small swatches of material that seemed barely enough to cover her. The other one, a red-and-white polka dot, was even smaller. With a muttered curse she stripped out of the shorts and blouse and put the white bikini on. It fit like a second skin. *"Ni modo!"* she mumbled. Then stopped, startled because she had no idea why she'd said it or what it meant.

She was still frowning when she went up on deck. Luis was swimming a few yards away, but when he saw her he waved and started back toward the boat. She saw now that he'd hung a ladder over the side in case she wanted to ease into the water.

She ignored the ladder and, like him, poised near the railing and dived in. For a split second, just before she hit, she wondered if she knew how to swim. But it was all right. She cut the surface of the water, went down into the cool turquoise depths, then rose and started swimming toward the island.

He watched her. She had one hell of a figure but she was too pale. For the next few days he'd put her to work out on the deck, have her polishing the brass, maybe mending a sail, something to keep her out in the sun and get the color back into her cheeks. But pale or not, she was an eyeful, a nicely wrapped package of small woman in the skimpy white bikini that he really didn't approve of.

He swam up alongside her. "Want to explore the island?"

She looked at him, treading water. "All right," she said, and together they started toward shore.

He let her get a few yards ahead of him before he went after her. She reached shallow water before he did and waded ashore. Nice bottom, he found himself thinking. Fantastic legs. And when, as though reading his thoughts, she turned to frown at him, he grinned at her. She didn't grin back.

They walked up to the sandy beach without speaking. The island looked scrubby, uninhabited, as though, Annabel thought, they were the first people to set foot here in the last two hundred years. It seemed strange and a little scary that she was here on this deserted island, miles from civilization, with this stranger who said he was her husband. And because that made her nervous she walked back to the water's edge.

The boat lay at anchor, sails down, gently moving with the waves. *Straight On till Morning.* Had she ever seen her before? Had she ever sailed her with this tall, bronzed man who stood beside her?

"Pirates plied these waters," he said. "Some say they buried their treasure on small islands just like this one."

"Jewels and silver and gold doubloons." Annabel looked up at him. "I wonder how I came to have one. A gold doubloon, I mean."

"Maybe you were looking for buried treasure." He hesitated. "Or sunken ships. Spanish galleons or pirate ships that went down centuries ago."

"The nurse in the hospital in Nassau told me you were like a modern-day pirate."

"A pirate?" He laughed. "*Sí*, maybe I am." He gazed out at the water, a strange and questing look in his eyes. "I'd have liked to have been one," he said. "One of the buccaneers who plied these same waters."

"Out to pillage and plunder?" she joked.

"With a red bandanna tied around my head, a sword in my hand and a pretty wench over my shoulder."

A wench like her. A woman as fragile and as beautiful as she was. I'd have fought a hundred men for her, he thought. I'd have taken her... you... and I'd have made you a prisoner on my ship. I'd have wooed you and won you, and one day you would have stood beside me at the wheel as my woman. My wife.

In a way he had made her his prisoner. The day he'd stood by her hospital bed and declared that she was his wife, he had in effect made her his. For better or for worse? No matter. He'd taken the step and claimed her for his own.

And what would happen when she regained her memory? he asked himself. But no, he didn't want to think about that now. He'd cross that particular bridge when he came to it. Meantime...

"We'd better get back to the boat," he said. "I'd like to make Samana Cay by dark." He glanced up at the sky. "I'm not sure I like the look of those clouds."

"A storm?" Annabel asked, feeling a nudge of fear.

"Maybe." He waded into the water. "Last one to reach the boat fixes breakfast," he called over his shoulder as he plunged into the surf.

She was a good swimmer. He had half a mind to hold back and let her win, but he didn't think she'd like that, so he beat her by two lengths. When she reached the ladder she clung to it, breathing hard, small breasts pushing against the thin white fabric of her suit, drops of water clinging to her long lashes.

"You're pretty good," he said.

"You're better."

"I'll have my bacon crisp and my eggs over easy."

She laughed—it was a good sound—and swung one foot up on the ladder. When she grasped the sides he put a hand on her bottom to steady her. She froze, then quickly pulled herself up and onto the boat.

He climbed up after her. "Let's not bother to change," he said. "We'll dry soon enough in the sun." He handed her a towel and took one for himself. "Besides, I'm hungry."

And though he had kidded her about the loser fixing breakfast, he went down to the galley with her, and while she set the table, he started frying the bacon.

"Toast or an English muffin?" he asked.

"English muffin."

They sat across from each other in the breakfast nook with the fastened-down table and chairs. He took a tape out of a rack above his head and popped it into the cassette player. When Jimmy Buffett started singing, Annabel smiled.

"That's nice," she said.

"It's one of your favorites."

"It is?" For a little while she'd almost forgotten that she'd . . . forgotten. It was pleasant sitting here across the table from Luis, listening to music, even though she was sure she'd never heard the song before.

Buffett sang nicely, but with unfamiliar words.

"It's very hard," she said. "Not remembering is very hard."

He put down the fork he had just picked up and reached for her hand. "Your memory will come back, Annabel. One of these days—"

"One of these days?" Tears stung her eyes. "I have no past," she said. "No memory of a mother and father or friends."

She looked at him so intently he almost flinched.

"I don't know where I went to school, if I went to college, if I had a career. What did I do before we were married?" She withdrew her hand. "*If* we were married."

"I wish you would trust me," he said. "I wish you could understand that I'd never do anything to hurt you."

Jimmy Buffett sang about being a pirate out of time.

A modern-day pirate like Luis. She bit into a piece of bacon. It stuck in her throat. She pushed her plate away and stood. "I'm going to change," she said.

"All right." He watched her go into the cabin and close the door.

"It's very hard," she'd said. "Not remembering is very hard." He wanted to go to her, to hold her and reassure her. But he couldn't, not yet.

He finished his breakfast, and after he had cleared the table and put the dishes in the sink, he went up on deck. And when he had hoisted the sails and they caught the wind, he eased the *Straight On* out of the cove and headed toward the open sea.

Late that afternoon the clouds rolled in. The sky grew dark and the water turned a sullen flat gray, dead calm at first so that the sails hung limp, unmoving. The *Straight On* lay becalmed, suspended somewhere between sky and sea in an eerie silence.

Luis climbed the mast and with binoculars scanned the sea in every direction. He'd figured to reach Samana Cay in another couple of hours and he needed the wind. He could use the motor, of course, but if they ran into trouble they might need the motor more than they did now. There wouldn't be a place where he could gas up until the cay.

The air was hot, steamy. Thunder rumbled in the distance, lightning snaked through the sky. Annabel paced the deck, her face pinched, eyes worried.

The storm hit with the suddenness of a tornado, with a wind that churned the waves and brought the rain in slashing torrents. The sails billowed, the boat lurched.

"Go below!" he shouted at Annabel.

"Can I help? Tell me what to do."

"All right." He motioned her forward. "Take the wheel. I've got to lower the sea anchors."

She hurried toward him. He covered her hands with his on the wheel. "Keep her steady," he said. And when he was sure she had a firm grip he ran forward, clinging to stanchions as he made his way across the deck.

The thunder was closer now, right above them, booming with great clashes of sound while lightning flashed and the rain came in blinding sheets that made it almost impossible to see.

When the waves started breaking over the deck, he made Annabel go below and closed the hatch after her to keep the cabin from flooding.

He'd been in storms before, but never in a gale like this. Before they'd left this morning he'd checked weather conditions with the weather bureau. "Some rain and wind coming in across Cuba," it had said. "Doesn't look now as if it would bother the Bahamas, not unless it changes course, but stand by for other advisories."

He'd checked every thirty minutes after that. An hour ago the report had said, "The storm is picking up and changing course, coming right across the Great Bahama Bank and heading toward the Caicos."

He'd known then that they were in trouble, but he hadn't expected it to be this bad. He tightened his hands on the wheel, his face grim, worried. The *Straight On* was a sturdy boat, but was she a match for a storm like this?

The sails billowed and snapped. The boat cut through the water, the wind at her back, fighting on, wallowing through waves that threatened her. He held her fast, eyes narrowed, trying to see through the slanting rain. Hold her steady, he told himself. Hold her steady and we'll be all right.

A blast of wind hit. The boat surged up on an eight-foot wave and hung suspended. He was surrounded by walls of churning water. He clung hard to the wheel and held his breath. "Come on," he urged. "Ride it out. You can do this. You can..." The boat crashed down the lee side, wavered there and righted.

The wind hit hard. Something snapped. He looked up in time to see the mainmast go. It swung straight toward him, the sail flapping wildly in the wind. He put up a hand to shield himself and tried to duck. The mast grazed his head, staggering him, and fell with a crash to the deck.

He swiped a hand across his face. When it came away bloody, he cursed aloud. And called himself a damn fool because he'd wanted to go by boat instead of chartering a plane to take Annabel to San Sebastián. He'd done it because he'd wanted to stir her memory, to try to force her to remember what had happened on that other boat. Never mind that stepping onto a boat again would be difficult for her, he'd thought only of his own selfish reasons for wanting her aboard. But, *Dios,* he hadn't counted on anything like this.

How frightened she must be, huddling below in the cabin, afraid the same thing would happen to her that had happened before. What had he done to her? What if the boat capsized? What if they...?

She came toward him, fighting her way through the wind and the rain. "No!" he cried. "Go back! Go back!"

"You're hurt." She reached out to him. "You're bleeding."

"It's nothing," he yelled over the cry of the wind. "You've got to go below."

She didn't even bother answering him. Instead she pulled her blouse off and, linking one arm around a stanchion, tore it with her teeth. When it ripped, she took a strip and wrapped it around his head, struggling to keep her balance.

"Get out of here! Damn it, do as you're told."

A wave washed over the deck and the boat lurched. Annabel grabbed him around the waist and hung on. The boat staggered, then righted and struggled on.

"Go back. I don't want you up here."

"Too bad," she shouted. "I'm staying."

If there had been any way he could have secured the wheel, he'd have picked her up and carried her below. But all he could do was yell at her, and obviously that wasn't doing a damn bit of good.

An hour went by, two. His shoulders ached, his head hurt. She stood next to him, hanging on to the stanchion, wind and rain whipping her hair back from her face.

Almost three hours went by before the wind began to die. The waves diminished and the rain, though it didn't stop, slowed.

"Go below and make some coffee," Luis said. "I'm going to check for damage. I'll be down as soon as I can."

This time she didn't argue.

He checked the broken mast and swore a steady stream in Spanish. It had snapped in two. He hoped they'd be able to make it into Samana Cay and wondered how far they'd been blown off course.

When he dropped the anchors fore and aft he went below. Annabel had changed from shorts and bikini top to a pair of jeans and a navy blue T-shirt. She'd pulled her hair back into a ponytail.

"Take a shower," she ordered in a no-nonsense voice.

He started to tell her he didn't need a nursemaid, but thought better of it. He took the shower, pulled on a pair of khaki shorts and went back to the galley.

"Sit down," she said, and he sat.

She made funny little muttering sounds as she washed the head wound, rubbed an antiseptic cream on it, then she fastened a patch over it.

"Thanks," he said, and stood. But when he felt a sudden wave of dizziness, he slid back down into the booth. "There's... there's brandy in the cupboard over the stove," he told her.

She got the brandy and quickly poured some into a glass and handed it to him. He downed it and felt better. "For you?" he asked.

"I don't think I like it."

"You need it." He poured a splash into his glass and passed it to her.

She took a sip and made a face. "Drink!" he said, and she did.

She'd made coffee and ham sandwiches. He ate a sandwich, felt better, and ate another one. "You were pretty good out there," he said.

"Thank you."

"Do you ever do what you're told?"

"I don't know." A smile tugged at her lips. "I don't remember."

He laughed and felt some of the tiredness ease. "I'm sorry."

She looked puzzled. "About what?"

"I shouldn't have made you come by boat. I should have chartered a plane the way you wanted me to."

She shrugged. "What do we do now? Can we still make it to Samana Cay tonight?"

"I don't think so. We've probably been blown off course by the storm. I'm going to check our position as soon as we finish eating."

"If we can't, will we be all right here?"

"Sure." If they didn't get another blow. If they weren't too far off course. If he could repair the sails.

"What about the mast?" she asked. "Can you get that fixed in Samana Cay?"

"I doubt it. But we can make minor repairs there, enough to get us to Grand Turk and on to San Sebastián."

San Sebastián. His island. Again she felt that niggle of fear of the unknown. And of him.

When they finished eating, she cleared the dishes while he checked their position.

The rain didn't let up. He put a cassette on; Ella Fitzgerald was wonderful singing the blues. Annabel poked through his books and settled into one of the easy chairs with *The Old Man and the Sea* while he went over his charts.

He liked being here with her like this, feeling the gentle roll of the boat, the slap of waves against the hull and the slow and steady beat of the rain. The quiet calm after the storm.

She looked up and saw him watching her. "Does your head hurt?" she asked. "Are you all right?"

"I'm fine."

"Maybe you should take a couple of aspirin and get some rest."

"I will as soon as I finish the charts."

She got up and went to stand beside him. "How far off course are we?"

"Not too far. We'll make Samana Cay sometime tomorrow." He looked at her. "You were very brave today."

She shrugged. "Everything happened so fast. I heard the crash. I thought you were hurt."

"And you came to help me."

"Well . . ."

He put his hands on her shoulders. Maybe it was a delayed reaction to the storm, the fear he'd felt when the boat had climbed that eight-foot wave and he'd thought they weren't going to make it. Maybe it was the sound of the rain, the warmth of the cabin, the comfort of being here with her. He murmured her name, "Annabel," and even though he had promised himself he wouldn't do this, he drew her into his arms and kissed her.

She stiffened. "No," she said against his lips. "No, please."

He couldn't let her go, couldn't stop kissing her, because the feel of her mouth under his, the softness of her in his arms were good. Oh yes, so good.

She put her hands against his chest and tried to push him away. "Stop," she whispered. "Let me go."

"You're my wife," he murmured against her lips. "You belong to me. I have the right—"

"No!" She backed away from him, and bringing her hands up to cover her face, she began to weep. "I don't remember. I don't remember."

He let her go. He was ashamed, more ashamed than he'd ever been before. She didn't deserve this. He shouldn't have tried to kiss her.

"I'm sorry," he said. "I didn't mean . . ."

Still weeping, she turned away.

"Go to bed." His voice sounded harsh. "Just…just go to bed, Annabel."

And this time she did as she was told.

Chapter 4

They made Samana Cay at a little after noon the following day. Luis put in at a sheltered cove, and when he dropped anchor, he and Annabel set to work mending the ripped sails.

It was a perfect summer's day with just the hint of an offshore breeze. Annabel, barefoot, clad in white shorts and T-shirt, wearing the straw hat Luis had bought for her in Nassau, sat cross-legged on the deck and worked diligently, trying not to look at Luis.

For a while last night she had let her guard down. In the coziness of the cabin, with the sound of the rain and the gentle rocking of the boat, she had felt a sense of ease and a relaxing of tensions she hadn't felt since the first moment she'd opened her eyes in the hospital in Nassau. She and Luis had weathered the storm together and come through unscathed. Somehow that had brought her closer to him.

It had given her a nice feeling last night to look up from her book and see him there bending over his navigation charts. She had studied his face to try to find something...some little thing about him that would jog her memory.

And, yes, she had felt a softening toward him, the beginning of a willingness to accept the fact that perhaps, after all, he had been a part of her life. But then he kissed her.

Had she felt a familiarity in his kiss? A sense of having been in his arms before? She didn't know. She didn't think so.

"You're my wife," he'd said. "You belong to me."

But did she?

He'd stopped when she asked him to, but would he the next time? If there was a next time.

When she got up this morning there had been coffee on the stove, a mango and banana on the countertop. And though she could hear him moving around on the deck, she stayed below until he brought the boat into the cove.

When at last she'd gone topside he'd said a brief "Good morning" and put her to work mending sails.

There was little conversation. After he gave her instructions on how to mend a sail, he left her to check out the boat, to make sure nothing had come loose during the buffeting they had taken.

"Everything seems to be all right," he said when he came back up on deck. "We'll be able to make it to Grand Turk by tomorrow. They'll repair the mast there."

"How long will it take?"

"With luck, a couple of days. We should be home by the end of the week."

Home. Would she recognize it? Once she saw it, would she remember?

"How about if we go ashore? It would be cooler there under the trees."

The island looked inviting, and yes, maybe it would be cooler than here on the boat, but she wasn't sure she wanted to be alone there with him.

"Look," he said, as though reading her thoughts, "about last night . . . If I offended you—"

"You did."

"I'm sorry. Maybe it was the storm, Annabel, the danger we'd been in. Maybe it was the way you looked curled up in the chair with the light on your face." He shot her a glance, then quickly looked away. "I'm sorry," he repeated. "It won't happen again."

When she didn't say anything, he said, "Look, we're going to be cooped up here on the boat for a few more days. We can't avoid each other so we might as well make the best of it. I think we ought to take the dinghy over to the island, maybe have lunch and a swim and try to relax. There's ham and cheese for sandwiches and we could take some cold beer."

"I don't like beer."

"Then we'll make lemonade. Whatever you want."

She put aside the part of the sail she'd been working on. She was hot and tired because she'd had very little sleep last night. She didn't particularly want to spend the afternoon working in the sun, but she wasn't sure she wanted to spend it on the island with him, either. But at last she nodded and said, "All right. I'll make the sandwiches."

Twenty minutes later Luis lowered the dinghy over the side. He handed Annabel an oar and together they rowed over to the island.

It was more lush than the other islands they'd seen, filled with all sorts of flowering vegetation, with red hibiscus and wild orchids, angel trumpet trees and amaryllis. The water here was a clean, clear aquamarine, the sand pure white.

When Luis spread a blanket on the sand, Annabel arranged the plates and set out the food. After they'd eaten, Luis said he was going to explore. He asked her if she wanted to come along. She said no.

It wasn't just that she didn't want to be alone with Luis any more than she had to. The fact was that she still hadn't gotten her strength back. Though her wounds had healed, the emotional trauma of not being able to remember her past had drained her. And yes, the storm had taken its toll. Now as she sat looking out at the water, her eyes started to close. She lay down, telling herself she would only rest for a little while, and went almost immediately to sleep.

She dreamed, not the frightening dream of fire and death, but rather of Luis. "You're my wife," he said in her dream. "You belong to me. I have the right..." He kissed her, warm, wet kisses all over her face. Her ears. Kisses that tickled her ears.

"Stop it!" She tried to push him away and awoke to find not Luis but a dog standing over her, licking her face. He was a scrawny black Labrador. Well, part Labrador. Heaven only knew what the other part was.

He looked down at her with big, sorrowful eyes, raised what looked like a brown patch of eyebrow and barked. She came fully awake and saw Luis grinning down at her.

"I—I thought you..." She blushed, afraid he could read her mind. "Where did he come from?"

"I have no idea. He just suddenly appeared out of the bushes, came bounding at me, barking his head off, stopped a few feet from me and wagged his tail."

"But how did he get here? On the island, I mean."

"He probably belonged to somebody who stopped to picnic and swim. Maybe he ran off to explore and they left without him. Maybe they deliberately dumped him. Looks like he's been here for a while, getting along on what fish he could catch and whatever else he could find to eat."

"Poor dog." Annabel patted the blanket. "Come on, fella. I'm sorry I scared you away." The dog came to her and she scratched its ears. "What's your name, boy?" She reached for its collar. "There's nothing on it," she told Luis. "No name or address. We'll take him with us, won't we?"

Luis nodded. "We can't leave him here."

"Poor guy, all by himself on a deserted island. Just like Robinson Crusoe." She looked up at Luis. "That's what we'll call him, okay?"

We. For the first time she'd said "we." As though they were a couple. That brought an unexpected lump to his throat. "Sure," he said, "that's fine." Then he announced, "I'm going for a swim. Want to come?"

Annabel hesitated. She felt a little groggy after her nap and the water looked inviting. Maybe it would clear away the cobwebs. "Okay," she said, and turning away from him, she stripped out of her shorts and shirt.

The top of the red-and-white polka-dot bikini, made of maybe an ounce of material, hugged her neat little breasts. He said—he *tried* to say—"*Bueno,* let's go," but the words came out with the pubescent squeak of a twelve-year-old.

Madre de Dios, this was some kind of a bathing suit, not what he'd expected when he gave one of the nurses in Nassau money and asked her to shop for him.

"Buy some toiletries for Mrs. Alarcon," he'd said. "Some shirts and shorts and a couple of swimsuits." The other things had been more or less all right. But this! The way Annabel looked in this was enough to drive a man to drink. Or into the sea. And because no drink was available, he waded out and plunged head-first into a wave.

She followed him in, caught a wave, came out the other side and started swimming. Robinson Crusoe, Rob for short, she decided, ran up and down the beach barking, probably afraid that once again he was going to be left behind.

Luis swam up beside her. "I'll get him cleaned up once we're back aboard." He looked back at the dog, looked out toward the boat, looked up at the sky, anywhere except at Annabel. But how could he not see the way the water clung to her eyelashes or the way the sun turned the skin of her shoulders to a rosy alabaster?

"Maybe we've had enough," he said.

"But we've only just come in." She turned on her back, floating, looking up at the sky. "It's so beautiful here," she said.

She was a water nymph in a polka-dot bikini, blond hair fanning out behind her, water lapping over her breasts and hips.

"Think I'll go in," he said. "Talk to the dog."

That brought a puzzled smile. She turned to look at him just as a roller moved in. It caught her unaware and tumbled her beneath the water. He made a grab for her when she forced her way to the surface, sputtering and laughing. He held her up, his arms around her waist, his body close to hers.

"I didn't see it coming." She was a little breathless, but enjoying the thrill of the breaking waves.

Another wave brought them closer. "Anna?" Luis said.

She looked at him, startled, her eyes wide, lips parted. "Anna," he said again, and kissed her.

His lips were salty. That was her first thought, how warm and salty his lips were against hers. Another wave broke over their heads, and instead of fighting it, they sank beneath the surface of the water, down into the aquamarine depths with his mouth still on hers, his arms and legs pinning her to him.

She opened her eyes and looked into his. Silver eyes. Did she kiss him back? Did her tongue touch his? Did her body yearn toward him? Was the fire that snaked through her belly real or imagined?

They broke through to the surface. She gasped for air, and before she could break away he kissed her again, kissed her and kept kissing her. He pressed his body to hers and she felt his throbbing hardness. She couldn't breathe, she couldn't think. She only knew she had to get away from him before...

She put her hands against his shoulders. "Please," she managed to say. "When you... when you kiss me like that I can't think."

"Annabel," he whispered, breathing hard. "Annabel, I—"

"Let me go," she said.

He reached to tuck a wet strand of her hair behind her ear. His hand lingered for a moment, then he let her go and started swimming, straight out, as though all of the monsters in the sea were after him.

Annabel stared after him. With a strange little smile she turned and made toward the shore, wondering why, when her feet touched bottom, her legs were trembling. When she reached the shore she collapsed onto the sand. The dog Rob came over. He sat on his haunches, head cocked to the side, as though to say, "What's the matter, lady? You look a bit done in."

"I am done in." She reached out and scratched his ears. "Done in and turned inside out." By Luis Miguel Alarcon, a man she didn't remember. But maybe her body did. Was that why she had responded to him? Because even though her conscious mind didn't remember, her body did?

That scared her. She had to keep her emotions in check, had to be careful until she knew who she was and who *he* was.

He'd called her Anna, and for the shadow of a moment the name had somehow jogged her memory. Then the moment faded and so had the memory.

Twenty minutes went by before he swam back to the beach. "Guess we'd better get back to the boat." He sluiced the water off his body and tried not to look at her. But heaven help him, he couldn't help it. She'd taken the bikini top off and put her T-shirt on. If anything she looked even sexier than before. Great legs, small nipples pushing against the cotton material.

He picked up the basket she'd packed their luncheon things in and took the blanket from her. "Come on, dog," he muttered, and headed for the dinghy.

They rowed back to the boat without speaking. She went up the ladder first and he handed the dog up to her. Rob was nervous, trying to wriggle out of his arms. But when Annabel said, "Take it easy, boy," he settled down.

Luis hefted the dinghy onto the deck and, when he'd fastened it in place, said, "You shower first. I'll clean the dog before I come down."

He didn't quite meet her eyes, nor did he make any mention of what had passed between them. But later that evening when she carried their dinner of a crabmeat salad onto the deck, he said, "I'm afraid I owe you another apology. I was out of line. When we were swimming, I mean."

She nodded, accepting his apology. He shouldn't have kissed her, but she wasn't sure that what followed had been entirely his fault.

"I prefer that it doesn't happen again," she said stiffly. Then, because it troubled her, she added, "You called me Anna."

"Did I?"

"Yes. It sounded strange. Maybe more familiar than Annabel."

He waited, and when she didn't say anything, he said, "I always called you Anna when we were in Spain."

When you were dressed in a fine Spanish gown, he thought, but did not say so. With your hair piled high on your head and held in place with a Spanish comb, you became Anna for me, regal and beautiful, everything I wanted you to be.

Spain. She had no recollection of ever having been there.

"We'll go this fall."

"This fall?"

"Hurricane season. We always leave the island that time of the year."

We. Always. She felt as if she were losing her mind. How could she have lived with this man, loved this man and not remember? She looked away from him, emotions close to the surface, tears threatening. Rob padded over. She scratched his ears and he rested his head on her lap.

The sun lowered over the sea and the sky flamed into a brilliance of flamingo red, pale apricot and, finally, to a softening of pink and mauve. They didn't speak, they only sat there, watching darkness come. And when at last the stars appeared, the night became more beautiful than any night had been before.

And because, for a reason she did not understand, she felt the threat of tears, she stood up and said, "I'm a little tired, Luis. I think I'll say good-night."

"Good night, Anna."

Anna. Again that jolt of recognition. She looked at him, trying to see his face through the darkness. And with what sounded like a sob, she turned and disappeared down the steps into the cabin.

When Rob came to lean against his knee, Luis rested a hand on the dog's head. "What have I done?" he said. "What have I done to her?"

He sat for a long time, lost in thought as he gazed out over the sea, eyes narrowed as though by his steady gaze he could look beneath the surface, down into the watery depths, down to where the sunken galleons of the past rested. There were treasures there in the graveyard of the deep, priceless jewels, fortunes in silver and gold doubloons.

He reached in his pocket and took out the gold doubloon that had been in Annabel's pocket when they'd found her, and he rubbed his thumb back and forth over it. It was smooth to his touch, and heavy.

How many more of them lay somewhere beneath the waters of this vast stretch of the Bahamas? Gold doubloons, waiting to be found.

She'd had this piece of gold, she knew where the treasure lay. If he could make her trust him, if he could unlock the secrets of her mind, then the fortune that had lain beneath the sea for almost three hundred years would be his.

Annabel was the key. He would keep her until he had unlocked the secret of her mind. And then?

He went to stand by the rail. "Annabel," he whispered into the night. "Anna."

They made Grand Turk on the following day and put in for repairs. The boat yard there was small but adequate, and Luis, wanting to be sure the mast was properly repaired, spent most of his time with the workers to oversee the work.

Because she was alone most of the time, Annabel spent her days doing absolutely nothing. She lay in a chaise on the deck, reading from the supply of books Luis had aboard. She stopped only to prepare lunch when she knew it was time for him to return, and later a light supper, which they usually had out on deck.

This was a time of recuperation for her and she took advantage of it. Each day she felt herself grow stronger. She gained a little weight and grew tanned from her hours in the sun. She swam several times a day, greater distances each time. And walked. Clad in shorts and a shirt, the straw hat from Nassau plunked down upon her sun-streaked hair, looking like a boat bum or a beachcomber, she roamed the small island, Rob at her side.

Once, away from the town on a remote stretch of beach, a man suddenly appeared from behind some brush. Bottle in his hand, he stopped in front of her and said, "Hey, whatta we got here? Whoee! Ain't you a sight for sore eyes!"

He took a step toward her, blocking her way. Rob, teeth bared, growled.

"Call yer dog off." The man waved the bottle at her. "Just tryin' to be friendly. Offerin' you a little drink is all."

"I don't want a drink." She started past him; he reached out a hand to stop her and Rob leapt.

The man went down, squealing in terror. She said, "Rob!" and the dog backed off.

As soon as they were out of sight of the man, she knelt beside Rob. "Good dog," she said, hugging him. "Good dog."

When she told Luis about it later, he said, "Thank God he was with you. But just in case, you'd better stay close to the boat. Anyway, we're leaving tomorrow. The day after that we'll be in San Sebastián."

Would she recognize the island? Would the sight of it bring back her memory?

She stood at the railing, looking out at the dark water. San Sebastián. His island in the sea. Would it be her home or her prison? A shiver ran through her and Luis said, "What is it?"

"I'm not sure. I wonder if I'll recognize it, the island, your home."

"Your home, too."

She turned and, looking into his eyes, asked, "Is it, Luis? Is it?"

He stiffened. "Of course."

"I think I'm..." The words came with difficulty, as though she were afraid to say them, to tell him how afraid she was.

He said it for her. "I understand. I know how difficult this must be for you." He rested his hands on her shoulders. "But don't be afraid. I'm here, Annabel. I'll take care of you." He kissed her forehead. "Everything will be all right once we reach San Sebastián."

But later, alone in the cabin, the fear came again. Fear of the unknown, and of him.

Chapter 5

She was in the galley frying fish for their noonday meal when Luis called down to her to come topside. When she scrambled up the stairs he said, "There, off to your right. San Sebastián."

The sun was in her eyes and for a moment she couldn't see. Then she shaded her eyes and saw it, a small island there in the middle of the sea. Tall, swaying palms lined the edge of the white sand beach. Beyond, the rolling land gave way to the rise of green hills.

Annabel leaned against the rail, taking it all in, trying to remember. Was this her home? Had she been happy here?

Luis came to stand beside her. "You fell in love with the island the first time you saw it."

"How long ago was that?"

"Eight years ago."

Eight years? She'd spent eight years of her life here. Why didn't she remember?

"We'd just been married," he said. "You were twenty-one."

"Then I'm twenty-nine."

He nodded. "You'll be thirty on the fourth of October."

"How old are you?"

"I'm thirty-eight."

He would have been thirty when they married, nine years older. But she was too young. Twenty-one was too young to marry. Had he swept her off her feet? Had she been so in love she hadn't wanted to wait? What had it been like, living with him on this island? Had she ever felt lonely? Had she longed for the companionship of friends, or had it been enough to be here with him? Loving him.

Now that they were on the island, here in his home, their home, perhaps she would remember.

She turned to him, nervous, uncertain. "Are there other people on the island?" she asked. "I mean, do other people live here? Are there other houses? Other families?"

"Only the men and women who work for me. They're from the small village on the other side of the island. But no one else lives here. No strangers."

That gave her pause. There would be no neighbors, no schmoozing in the mall, no running to the supermarket for a loaf of bread. It made her wonder, and she asked, "Where do you get your supplies?"

"They come in by boat from Nassau every couple of weeks. Samuel—you saw him at the harbor in Nassau—will be arriving with supplies any day now."

He tacked into the wind and she saw to her left a high cliff and below a rocky shore where the surf rolled in, pounding hard against the rocks, slamming with a terrible force into the huge boulders, sending water and foam high into the air.

"Hard currents and strong undertows there," Luis said. "But the swimming on the other side of the island, nearer to the house, is fine."

He headed the boat that way, and now it seemed to her that indeed this was an island paradise. But so remote, so far from anything or anyone.

When they drew near to the dock, two men appeared. They ran out onto the dock, waving their arms, broad smiles on their faces. Rob stood on the deck and barked at them.

Luis tossed one of the men a line. The man, barefoot, clad only in denim shorts and a tattered straw hat, grabbed it. "We been worried 'bout you," he said. "Heard 'bout the storm that be blowing in across Cuba and figured maybe you was right in the path. You be all right?"

"We're fine, Moses. But it's good to be home. Everything all right here?"

"It be just fine, boss man."

The other man, older than Moses, with frizzed gray hair and a beatific smile, looked at Annabel and bobbed his head. "How you be, Mrs. Alarcon?"

"I'm fine, thank you..."

"David," Luis said.

"Thank you, David."

"It sure be nice to have you back."

Rob jumped down off the deck, tail awag, barking. David bent down and grabbed Rob's ears, giving him a shake. "What's the matter with you, dog? You glad to be on dry land? Is that it?"

Rob woofed and the two men laughed.

"Ambrosia got your room all fixed up," Moses said. He was a tall man, stick skinny, with knobby shoulders and bony knees. His smile was wide, his teeth were white, and his skin was the color of dark chocolate.

"She be so excited you back she can't hardly stand it. Been cookin' and fussin' for two—three days." He reached out a hand to help Annabel, and to Luis said, "Me 'n' David take care of the boat, Mr. Luis. You and Mrs. Alarcon go on up to the house."

Mrs. Alarcon. As though in a daze, Annabel let Luis take her hand and lead her off the dock onto a path that led up and away from the beach, past sea grape and blooming hibiscus, through a lushness of fern, leafy banana trees and oleander.

The large white house with the red roof stood perhaps a hundred yards from the beach. Sheltering palms graced the stone walk and a small waterfall bubbled over a rock garden. There were roses and birds of paradise and beautifully terraced green lawns. The back of the house was bordered by junglelike trees.

"La Casa Bonita." Luis looked down at her as though waiting for a sign of recognition. But there was none.

"Perhaps when you're inside the house you'll remember," he said, sensing her disappointment.

"Perhaps." But there was a hopelessness in her voice, and with a sinking heart she followed him into the house.

Her first impression was one of coolness and light, of stone and soothing shades of gold and ivory. Servants in white pants and white cotton jackets bowed them in. A large woman with dark skin and snapping black eyes stepped forward. Hands on her hips she said, "'Bout time you be gettin' here, Mr. Alarcon, sir. You had us worried half to death, thinkin' 'bout the storm and poor little missus out on the boat, bouncin' up and down them waves. Coulda swallowed you up, boat 'n' all, just like Jonah and that whale. How come you didn't be flyin'?"

"I thought the sea air would be good for Mrs. Alarcon." He tried not to smile as he urged Annabel forward. "This is Ambrosia, dear," he said. And to the older woman, he added, "Because of Mrs. Alarcon's accident, she's having trouble remembering things. I'm sure once she's back in familiar surroundings her memory will come back. After you've shown her to our—" he hesitated "—to her room, and after she's rested, I'd like you to take her around the house, help her get reacquainted with things."

"Yes, sir. I'll do that." She patted Annabel's shoulder. "You come 'long with me, missus. Soon's you have yourself a nice rest you be feeling better."

"We'll eat at seven but we'll have a drink out by the pool at six. You'll probably want to change before dinner. Your clothes are in your closet. Ambrosia will show you." Luis brought Annabel's hand to his lips. "I'll see you then," he said.

"All right," she replied, and turned away to follow the woman she did not think she had ever seen before.

The room she was taken to was very light and very large. Part of it was a sitting room with a sofa, two chairs and a bookcase filled with a variety of books. She glanced at a few of the titles; they weren't familiar.

The bedroom itself was quite beautiful. The queen-size bed was covered with lace-trimmed white damask. There were bedside tables, a peach-colored chaise, a small, beautifully carved table near the French doors and a dressing table as well as a double dresser.

The part of the floor that wasn't covered with a white rug was of clean and polished tile. A ceiling fan moved slowly overhead.

Because Ambrosia stood watching, waiting for a reaction, Annabel said, "It's a lovely room."

"Your clothes be in this closet. Mr. Alarcon's things be in the closet over there." Ambrosia slid back mirrored doors. "Here be your things," she said.

There were clothes in the closet, long skirts and short skirts, blouses and dresses and pants. Shoes were neatly arranged in shoe racks on the floor, sweaters and scarves, swimsuits and nightgowns on shelves. The clothes were pretty. But were they hers?

She felt lost, bewildered, and perhaps the hopelessness showed in her eyes, because Ambrosia said, "Why don't you rest, missus? All that rockin' on the boat be enough to weigh a body down."

"Yes, I think I will rest for a little while, Ambrosia."

"The bathroom be through that door. You want anything at all, you pick up that phone over there and ask for me." She smiled. "It's real nice havin' you back, Miss Annabel. Real nice."

Back? Annabel thought when she was alone. But was I ever here? Nothing was familiar, not the house, not Ambrosia, not this room. She opened the French doors and went out on the flower-filled balcony that overlooked the sea. Certainly San Sebastián Island was a beautiful spot, a romantic place in the middle of the turquoise sea. Had she been happy here with Luis? Lord, how she wished she could remember. Had she shared this room with him? Had they lain together on that damask-covered bed?

So far, except for the two times he had kissed her, he had not acted as if he expected anything from her. But they were here on his island now. Would things be different? Would he expect her to act like a wife?

A chill that was somewhere between fear and excitement zinged down her spine. Then, because she didn't want to think about it, she took her shoes off and, curling up on the peach-colored chaise, went almost immediately to sleep.

Luis was waiting on the pool terrace when Annabel came out. She stood for a moment, bewitched by the scene, this perfect merging of sea and sky. She was surrounded by water, only water as far as she could see.

"This is my favorite time of day." Luis stood and motioned her to one of the chairs at the side of the pool. She was wearing white silk pants with a white silk off-the-shoulder blouse. With her newly acquired tan and her blond hair loose about her shoulders, she looked very pretty, very feminine.

When she was seated he handed her a tall glass. "Your favorite," he said.

"Vodka and tonic?"

"*Gin* and tonic. Don't you remember?"

She took a sip and frowned. "Apparently not. I'm afraid I prefer vodka."

"Of course." He picked up a small silver bell, and when a servant Annabel had not seen before came out onto the terrace, Luis said, "Would you bring a vodka and tonic for my wife. And some caviar, please." He turned to Annabel. "You *do* remember caviar, don't you?"

"I think I remember a song about a virgin sturgeon." She smiled. "Is it a song?"

"If it isn't, it ought to be." He took a sip of his drink. "Do you feel all right? No headaches?"

"No, I'm fine. I haven't had a headache since I left the hospital."

He knew he'd taken a chance by insisting she leave Nassau with him. He'd checked with the doctor, of course, and Hunnicut had assured him that Annabel was well enough to travel. Hunnicut had even given him a few pamphlets on amnesia, which he'd read before he and Annabel left the island.

"As far as her physical condition," the doctor had said, "she has recovered well enough from her ordeal at sea. She'll need to rest, though, and she can do that on the trip back to your island. As far as her memory is concerned, only time will tell. Very little is known about amnesia. Most people regain their memory within a few months, but I've read of cases where it's taken years, even a few where the memory has never come back. You're going to have to be patient with your wife, Mr. Alarcon. Don't try to rush her."

Patience. He had to remember that.

His servant brought her drink, along with a tray with little dishes of caviar, onions, salted nuts, cheese and several kinds of crackers.

She put a bit of caviar on a rye cracker and sprinkled some chopped onion on it. "Delicious," she said when she tasted it. "I love *botanas*. I could make a meal out of them."

"You said *botanas*. That's a Spanish word."

"Is it?"

"You speak Spanish fairly well."

"I do?" She looked surprised. "I don't remember."

"Well, *poco a poco*."

"Little by little?"

"That's right." He felt a surge of elation because he knew now he'd been right to bring her here. This was a breakthrough, he was sure of it. And though he told himself he didn't want to press her, he said, "Do you remember anything, Annabel? Anything about the accident?"

She stared down at her drink. "No," she said. "My first recollection is of waking up in the hospital in Nassau with you and the doctor standing over me."

"And nothing at all about the boat you'd been on, the people you'd been with?"

"No, nothing."

"The coast guard thought you'd been adrift for three days when they picked you up. You were only semiconscious, dehydrated and sunburned. You had a concussion, some cuts and bruises." He waited, and when she didn't say anything, he went on. "You were the lone survivor. All that was found of the boat you'd been on were bits and pieces of debris. And an all-weather jacket that belonged to a man by the name of Zachary Flynn. Do you remember him?"

She shook her head.

"Any of the other people?"

"No."

"Do you have any idea where you were going?"

"No!" Distressed, on the verge of tears, she faced him. "I've told you, I don't remember."

"All right. I'm sorry. I shouldn't have brought it up. It's just that I thought once you were back here you would start to remember."

"I don't."

He put a little Brie on a cracker and handed it to her. "I'm sorry," he said again.

For a little while they didn't speak. The sun sank down into the sea. Luis switched on the underwater lights of the pool, as well as the lights of the palm trees on either side of the terrace. They finished their drinks, and when the servant came to see if they wanted another drink, Luis said, "No, we'll have dinner now.

"You don't mind eating outside, do you?" he asked Annabel. "We can go in if you'd rather."

"No, it's lovely out here."

It was a perfect evening, with only the most gentle of breezes drifting in from the sea. A man with a white jacket and white gloves brought a lighted table candle, then a silver bucket with chilled white wine before he served a shrimp and crabmeat cocktail. That was followed by a green salad and broiled pompano amandine, and finally by a mango sorbet.

In spite of the fact that she had no memory of ever having been here before, Annabel found herself enjoying the evening. The food was good, the setting perfect. A Mozart concerto... how did she know it was Mozart?... drifted out from somewhere inside the house.

Whether or not she was Luis's wife, whether or not she had been here before, this was a pretty nice way to live. Sooner or later, if he had brought her here under false pretenses, she would find out. Until she did, she might as well enjoy herself and think of this as an island vacation.

But what if he really is your husband? a small voice inside her head whispered. In the half darkness she studied his face as though trying to see beyond the facade of gentlemanly manners to the man inside. The man who said he was her husband.

David, the older man at the dock, seemed to know her and so did Ambrosia. When Luis had told her to go along with Ambrosia, he'd started to say, "Our room."

Their room.

And again came the question in her mind: Now that they were here, would he expect to share that room with her? And if he did . . . ?

"I think I'll go in," she said, pushing back her chair. "I'm a little tired."

"Of course." He rose at once and came around the table. "Is there anything you need?"

"No, thank you." She looked out over the water. "It's a beautiful night, isn't it?"

"Yes." He took her hand and led her to the edge of the pool. "Sometimes we swim here at night," he said. "After the servants have left and we're alone."

She looked down at the still blue water.

"We swim naked." He tightened his hand on hers. "And afterward we make love."

"Luis..." She tried to free her hand but he wouldn't let her go.

"In the pool or here on one of the chaises." He turned her toward him and she could see the passion in his eyes. "Sometimes I carry you into the house, into our room." His voice was low, husky. "Our bodies are still wet, but it doesn't matter because we can't wait, we have to have each other. We have to..."

Before she could move away, he put his arms around her and drew her close. "I want you," he said against the fall of her hair. "Don't you know how much I want you?"

"Luis... please."

"It's been too long. I need you. I..." With a groan he covered her mouth with his. It was not a tentative kiss, it was possessive, demanding. He ground his mouth against hers, and when she tried to push him away, he held her closer.

"Kiss me," he commanded. "Just this once, Anna, kiss me as though you remember. Kiss me..."

She was trembling, trying to fight him, trying... But, oh, the arms that held her were strong and solid and good. And the mouth that covered hers was warm, so warm. She didn't want to; she told herself she wouldn't. But still, her mouth softened under his and the hands that had tried to push him away crept up around his neck to hold him closer.

"Amor," he whispered. *"Amor de mi vida."*

The words thrilled her. Remembered words? Or was it simply the warmth of the way he said them, the soft sound of Spanish? *Mi vida.* My life.

He kissed her eyelids, the curve of her ears, the hollow of her throat. He cupped her breast through the silky fabric of her blouse, and when she moaned, he kissed her mouth, taking her moan, her whisper of pleasure.

"You do remember," he said. "You do."

"No!" She pulled back. What was she doing? She didn't know him. She didn't... She stepped out of his arms, her breath coming in painful gasps, her body on fire with longing.

"It's too soon," she said. "I can't."

For a moment he didn't speak, but at last he said, his voice constrained, "I shouldn't have tried to rush you. It's just that having you here..." He turned away from her. "It won't happen again, Annabel, not if you don't want it to." His mouth curved in the semblance of a smile. "Each time I kiss you I tell you that, don't I? I mean it when I say it. I tell myself I won't kiss you again, but when I see you as you were that day in the water, or after the storm, or tonight when the air is soft and you're so beautiful..." He held his hands out to her in an appealing gesture. "Forgive me," he said. "I really will try to behave myself."

He touched her face very gently. "It's late," he said. "You'd better go in."

"Yes." But still she stood, as though hesitant to leave him, until with a murmured "Good night," she went into the house.

She found her way back to her bedroom, their bedroom. The sheet had been turned back and there was a bowl of strawberries on one of the bedside tables. She sank down on the bed, trembling with reaction because she hadn't wanted to leave Luis, because she'd wanted him to make love to her. With her. Because when he had asked her forgiveness, she'd longed to put her arms around him.

"We made love in the pool," he had said. "Or on one of the chaises. Sometimes I carried you to our room...." Our room.

She made herself get up and undress. She put on one of the nightgowns, and when she hung up the pants and blouse, she began to look through the closet.

The clothes were pretty, most of them pastel shades of blue, pale green, turquoise and ivory. One dress in particular was lovely. She took it out, admiring the silky material and the way it was cut. Perhaps she'd wear it tomorrow night at dinner. It was... She stopped, shocked. Frozen.

There was a tag on the dress. Size eight. Two hundred and fifty dollars.

She stared at the tag. The dress was new.

With shaking hands she put it back. She looked at the other clothes. There were no more tags, but they all looked new, as though they'd never been worn.

She went through the sweaters then, and on a sky blue cashmere she found another tag. She refolded the sweater and put it back.

Luis had lied. He wasn't her husband. Then why— dear God, why—had he brought her here? What did he mean to do with her?

Chapter 6

Too often now Luis found himself thinking of what it would be like to make love to Annabel, make love until this terrible craving that kept him awake at night was satisfied.

He took a sip of the brandy he'd poured for himself after she left him, and because he knew sleep would be a long time coming, he went into the library. There he searched the shelves for something to read, and when he could find nothing to hold his interest, he went to stand before the portrait that hung above the fireplace.

Alejandro de Alarcon, his great-great—too many "greats" to count—grandfather. Alejandro, captain of the *Cantamar*, which had gone down somewhere here in the Bahamas in the year 1714 with a cargo of Mexican silver, emeralds from Colombia, gold plates and spoons, necklaces, pearls and a fortune in gold doubloons.

Next to the portrait of Alejandro was the portrait of his wife, the beautiful Maria de Castilla. He had taken her with him on what proved to be his last voyage.

What had it been like that fateful October day when the hurricane winds had come raging across the sea? Did the captain have any warning of the storm to come? Had he tried to reach land before it struck?

In his mind's eye it seemed to Luis that he could almost see Alejandro at the wheel, trying—as he, Luis, had tried during the storm he and Annabel had been in—to keep the *Cantamar* on course. But the storm that hit Alejandro had been ten times more fierce. It would have caught him unawares because there had been no charting of hurricanes then, no weather bureau to warn of a killer storm.

How strong had the wind been that fateful day? A hundred and fifty miles an hour? A hundred and sixty? How high were the waves that swamped the ship and carried it into the depths of the sea?

In those last terrible moments when Alejandro knew there was no hope, did he clasp Maria in his arms? Did he cry out when he saw the wave that would carry them down?

And Maria? Did she think of the two sons she had left behind? When the water closed over her head, was there a moment of fear? Or did she feel a sense of peace because she was with Alejandro, holding him as he held her while they faced that final moment together?

They were gone, lost forever in the deep waters of the Bahamas. But the *Cantamar* was still there, waiting to be found. By him. Because by the right of his heritage she belonged to him.

He'd been searching for her for almost ten years. There had been other ships, a Portuguese galleon and an English ship. He'd made a small fortune salvaging them, but it was the *Cantamar* he wanted. *Cantamar,* Song of the Sea, calling to him like a Lorelei.

He would risk anything to find her, not just for the worth of her, but because of Alejandro, because somehow he knew that's what Alejandro would have wanted. It would be like coming full circle when he found the *Cantamar,* laying to rest the memory of the captain and his beautiful Maria.

And yes, when he found the ship, what he and his crew salvaged would be worth millions in silver, emeralds and gold doubloons. Gold doubloons like the one Annabel had in her pocket when the coast guard picked her up.

She was the key to the mystery of the lost ship. She and Zachary Flynn. Flynn the bastard. Flynn, the man he had hired four years ago to help him find the *Cantamar.*

On that last day, just the two of them alone on his boat, without his salvage crew, diving at almost two hundred feet, they'd found bottles of brandy that had broken loose from the lost ship. Another few days and he knew they would have found her. They would have if it hadn't been for Andrew, the hurricane that came raging across the sea with winds up to a hundred and sixty miles an hour, sending waves crashing over his boat, shifting the ocean bottom, hiding the *Cantamar* once more in the bowels of the sea.

His leg had been broken, his chest and shoulder crushed, and he'd been unconscious from a blow on the head. He came to in the dinghy. His boat was gone and so was Flynn, along with the charts that showed the location of the lost *Cantamar*.

He didn't know how long he'd drifted there on that empty sea without water, without food. He'd slipped in and out of consciousness, knowing that the chances of his being picked up were slim. All that kept him alive those last two days when his skin had burned and his tongue had swollen with thirst had been the thought of what he would do to Zachary Flynn if he lived through this. That and the thought of Annabel.

He had whispered her name through lips that were cracked and bleeding. He'd relived every moment he'd ever spent with her and conjured up visions of how she had looked the first time he saw her, the first time he kissed her, the first time they made love. In his mind he had asked her forgiveness for whatever wrong he had done. She'd been so young when they married and, God forgive him, he'd wanted to mold her into his idea of what a perfect woman should be.

Again and again in those terrible days adrift in that lonely sea he had prayed for another chance. In that state of half consciousness he told her again and again how much he loved her. "Love you," he whispered. "Love you."

He hadn't even seen the fishing boat that found him and took him to Eleuthera. From there he'd been flown to a hospital in Miami. He'd been in the hospital for almost two months, and when finally he was released, he went back to San Sebastián. It had taken his body a long time to heal, and by the time it did, he fought with himself about whether or not he should try to find Annabel. If she had made a life of her own, a life without him, would it be fair to her if he walked back into her life? And so he had waited.

Instead he had gone looking for Flynn, through boat brokers, boat people, dock masters and yacht clubs from Maine to Florida. But there'd been no trace of him, not until his windbreaker jacket had been picked up by the coast guard.

Flynn had died in the explosion on the boat that had gone down near Eleuthera. Annabel had been the lone survivor; she had known Zachary Flynn.

If she and Flynn, and whoever else had been with them, had been searching for the *Cantamar,* then she knew the location of the galleon. And if she did...

Luis looked up at the portrait. "I'm going to find your ship," he said. "No matter what it takes, Alejandro, I swear to you that I will find the *Cantamar.*"

He raised his glass. *"Esta es mi promesa para ti.* This is my promise to you."

He downed the brandy, then, drawing his arm back, threw the glass into the fireplace, where it shattered.

It was well after midnight before Annabel fell asleep that night. When she awoke a little after eight the next morning, she bathed, and because she felt a reluctance to dress in clothes that were not her own, she put on a pair of shorts and a shirt that had been purchased for her in Nassau.

And because she did not want to face Luis this morning, she picked up the phone and asked if breakfast could be brought to her room.

Ambrosia, bearing a breakfast tray, knocked at her door some twenty minutes later.

"Good morning," she said with a smile. "Don't you look fresh and pretty. Did you sleep well? Where you be wanting to have your breakfast? Here by the windows or out on the balcony? The sun be shining bright as a pumpkin. Better on the balcony, yes?''

"I prefer to eat in my room," Annabel said coolly. "Leave the tray on the table by the windows."

"But the sun be warm and the day be beautiful."

"Just leave the tray."

Ambrosia looked hurt. For a moment she stood where she was, uncertain, holding the tray.

Annabel turned away. She felt betrayed by this woman who had greeted her so warmly the day before. "It's real nice having you back," Ambrosia had said.

Back? But she'd never been here. Ambrosia had lied, just as Luis had lied. But why? Why?

And because the woman still stood looking at her so uncertainly, Annabel said, "That's all. I'll call if there's anything else." She waited until she heard the door close before she crossed the room to the table.

The glass of orange juice and fruit plate looked appetizing, as did the mushroom omelet. But she wasn't hungry. She ate a little of the papaya and took two bites of the omelet. The food stuck in her throat. Because she'd been unkind to Ambrosia. Because she was afraid.

She went to the closet and took the white bikini from the shelf. When she put it on, with one of the looser-fitting shirts over it, she left her room by way of her balcony and found the path that led to the beach. As she started down it she heard Rob bark, and when she turned, she saw him racing toward her.

"Hey," she said. "What are you doing here?"

He jumped up, all tail-wagging eager. She laughed and pushed him down. "Come on," she said, feeling her spirits rise. She started running toward the water. "Last one in is a sissy."

He came after her, yapping, darting in front of her then off to the side and back again. When she reached the beach she took off the shirt and ran into the water. Rob plunged in, too, but only until it reached his belly. Then he stopped and barked.

"Okay," Annabel said. "I'm going to swim. Go find yourself a fish to play with." And with that she headed out beyond the waves to where the water was calm.

She swam for a long time, stroking easily, feeling the release of tension, trying to think what she was going to do now. She was trapped here on Luis's island, with no way out except by boat, his boat. He had said that she was his wife, but he had lied. She wasn't his wife, she was his prisoner.

Puffs of white cloud drifted overhead in the clear blue sky. The water was warm and crystal clear. Back on the shore palm trees swayed in the breeze and tropical flowers grew in a beautiful blending of colors: scarlet and pink, bright yellow and orange, lavender and deep purple. If this was her prison, then surely it was the most beautiful prison on earth.

She decided that perhaps it would be best not to let Luis know how she felt, not to say anything about the clothes that were supposed to be hers but weren't. She would go along with whatever game he was playing, and when he had been lulled into believing he had fooled her, she would be able to find out the real reason she was here.

Finally, feeling more cheerful and certainly refreshed, Annabel headed for shore. Rob came partway out to meet her, and when she stood in water to her knees, she said, "Okay, boy, catch me if you can," and started running toward shore. Suddenly she screamed.

Had something bitten her? Had she stepped on a shell? The shock of pain sickened her. She had to get out of the water. Had to... She hopped on one foot and tried to let the waves carry her in. When she reached shallow water, she managed to pull herself up onto the beach.

Once there, she sank down on the sand, moaning in pain. Rob circled her, nervous, whining. She grasped her foot. Two jet black, ugly sea animals, with spines like black needles, were stuck to her.

Without thinking, only wanting the pain to go away, she grasped one of them and screamed again, for now it was embedded in her hand.

Rob ran back and forth, barking.

She had to get to the house. The only problem was that she couldn't walk on the foot with the spiny animal still stuck to it. Moaning in pain, she managed to get onto her knees and her one good hand and started to crawl across the beach toward the path. Before she'd gone more than a yard or two, she saw Luis running toward her.

"What is it?" he called out. "I heard Rob barking. Are you hurt?"

Then he saw the spines in her hand, the black sea creature stuck to her foot.

"Ay Dios!" he cried, and scooping her up in his arms, he ran with her toward the house.

She tried to hold back her cries of anguish. It hurt, oh God, it hurt.

He carried her into the kitchen, and Rob followed them in. Ambrosia was there with a woman Annabel hadn't seen before. Both women looked up when Luis rushed in.

"Mr. Luis!" Ambrosia cried. "Wha' happen?" She saw the sea urchin in Annabel's foot. "Oh, Lord," she cried. "Oh, Lord."

"Pliers," Luis said. "Get me the pliers. And canvas gloves. Hurry!"

The other woman dashed to one of the drawers and fumbled through whatever utensils were there. When she found the pliers she brought them to Luis. Ambrosia handed him the canvas gloves, and after he had set Annabel in one of the chairs, he put them on.

"I have to pull this out of your foot," he said. "It will hurt."

She looked at the ugly blackness. "Do it," she said, gripping the side of the chair. "Just do it."

He grasped the sea urchin. Annabel moaned. He took the pliers, fastened them around one of the spikes and carefully pulled it out. Then the other. The sea urchin fell to the kitchen floor.

Annabel was pale, her face beaded with sweat.

"Now your hand," Luis said.

She held it out, trying to fight the nausea that rose in her throat. Ambrosia came to stand behind her. She put her hands on Annabel's shoulders. "It be over soon," she murmured. "Be easy, be easy."

Annabel took a deep breath. Luis pulled the sea urchin out of her hand. Two of the spikes broke off, one in her palm, the other in the fatty part of her thumb.

"Get me hot water and soap, Meadowlark," he said to the other woman. "And antiseptic." He tightened his hand around Annabel's wrist. His face was al-

most as white as hers, and sweat glistened on his forehead. He picked up the pliers; Annabel closed her
eyes. With the pliers he grasped the spine embedded in
her palm. He pulled and she gasped in pain. Please,
she wanted to say. No more, please.

"One more." He pulled at the other black, spiny
prong. It didn't come out. The other woman, Meadowlark...what a strange and pretty name, Annabel
thought...began to cry.

Luis tried again. This time he wiggled the spine to
loosen it. Her hand was on fire; jabs of pain ran up her
arm to her shoulder. "Wait," she pleaded. "Wait."

He stopped. "Water," he said to Ambrosia. "Bring
her some water." And when the woman brought it, he
held the glass to Annabel's lips. "It's almost over," he
said. "Another few seconds and it will be out."

She took a sip and handed the glass back to him. He
gave it to Ambrosia. And to Annabel he said, "Hold
on." Then he grasped the black needle with the pliers
and pulled.

It was like being burned with a red-hot poker. Pain
ran up her arm. She gasped and slumped forward.
Luis eased her up against his shoulder.

"It's over," he said.

She leaned against him, weak with relief and pain,
shaking with reaction.

He held her there, and when he let her go he bathed
first her foot, then her hand with hot, soapy water and
applied antiseptic to the wounds. Meadowlark
brought bandages. He wrapped Annabel's foot and
hand and when he finished said, "I'm going to put
you to bed."

He picked her up and started out of the kitchen.
Rob trotted after him. "No!" Luis said. "Stay!"

"Let him come," Annabel said. "Please."

"All right, if you want him to."

He'd have given her anything she wanted right now. If she'd told him to let a parade of elephants into the house, he would have. He'd have done anything he had to, given anything he had to ease her pain.

He carried her into her room and gently laid her on the bed. Rob leaned his head on the bed beside her and she patted him with her good hand. "I'm all right, boy," she assured him.

Luis left her there while he went to get aspirin and an all-purpose antibiotic he kept on hand for emergencies like this. He helped her to sit up and held water to her lips. When she lay back down he said, "The aspirin will help."

"Thank you. I . . . I'll be all right now. What were they? Those ugly black things. What were they?"

"Sea urchins." He smoothed the sweaty hair back from her face. "I know how much it hurt when I pulled out the spines, Annabel . . . how much you're hurting now."

She looked up at him. His eyes, more silver than gray, were concerned. His face was pale. It was almost as if her pain had become his pain. As if he really cared about her. Did he? Did he care?

"I'm sorry you were hurt," he said. "Sorry I had to hurt you." He lifted her injured hand and brushed a kiss across her wrist. "Rest now," he said. "I'll sit with you until you sleep."

"You don't have to."

"I want to." He placed her hand on the coverlet. "Close your eyes, Annabel. Sleep if you can."

And in a little while, watched over by him and guarded by the dog at her side, she slept.

* * *

In the late afternoon when she awoke, her hand hurt
and her foot felt as though the spiny needles were still
in it. She moaned in pain, and Luis, who had been
sitting beside her bed, asked, "What is it, Annabel?
Are you all right?"

Without thinking, she leaned on her hand to shift
her position and yelped with pain.

"Easy," he soothed. "I'll get you something for the
pain." Something stronger than aspirin, something to
help her sleep. He should have gotten her out of her
bathing suit before, but she'd been in such pain he
hadn't wanted to cause her any more discomfort.

But now he said, "We'd better get you out of your
suit."

"No. I . . . I'm all right."

"No, you're not," he said patiently. "You'll feel
better once you've rinsed off and put a nightgown on.
I'll help you."

"No!" she cried. "I can do it."

"Do you want me to call Ambrosia to help you?"

She shook her head. "I can manage."

He frowned, and getting up, he went to her closet
and took a pale blue gown from the shelf and put it at
the foot of the bed. And though she said, "Wait a
minute! What are you doing?" he lifted her off the
coverlet, placed her in a chair and went to turn back
the sheet on the bed. Then he picked her up and carried her back to the bed.

"You've got to get out of your bathing suit," he
said, and before she could object he unfastened the top
of her suit and pulled it off.

"Wait! Stop that. Don't—"

"Lie down."

She did, glaring at him, and pulled the sheet up to her chin. He reached under it and eased the bottom of the suit down over her legs, being careful of her foot.

She was still sputtering with indignation when he crossed the room and called "Come" to the dog. Rob, with one last appealing look at her, scooted out.

Luis went into the bathroom. When he came back with a porcelain bowl filled with hot water, he put it on the bedside stand.

Annabel clutched the sheet even more tightly. "Don't be silly," he said, and pulling the sheet back to the rise of her breasts, he began to bathe her arms and shoulders.

She'd been sandy and saltwater sticky, and though she was loath to admit it, the warm, soapy water felt good on her skin.

He lowered the sheet, and though she cried, "No! Don't!" he bathed her breasts, her back and her belly. He tried to be objective, tried to act like a doctor with a patient. Tried not to let his gaze linger on the small, soft mounds of her breasts or the pink-tinged nipples.

She didn't look at him but held herself stiffly and let him minister to her.

When he finished, he pulled the sheet up to cover her, then raised it from the bottom and washed her legs.

His hands were cool on her skin and seemed somehow to soothe away the pain. She didn't understand him, she didn't trust him, but for now it felt good to lie here like this and let him bathe her.

When he finished he put the basin aside and handed her the nightgown. "Do you need any help?" he asked.

"No." She knew she was blushing now. "No, thank you. I can manage."

He nodded and went back into the bathroom. By the time he returned she'd put the gown on. He gave her another antibiotic capsule and two pills that he said would help the pain and also help her to sleep.

"I have to go to the bathroom."

"I'll help you." He pulled the sheet back and lifted her into his arms.

"Listen," she said. "I can do this."

"You can't walk."

"But I can hop."

He carried her to the bathroom door and put her down, helped her in, then closed the door behind her. When she opened the door a few minutes later, he picked her up again and carried her to the bed.

"How do you feel?" he asked. "Does your foot still hurt? Your hand?"

"Not as much as before." She yawned. "I think the pills you gave me are taking effect."

"Good."

"I'm all right now. You don't have to stay."

He nodded but he didn't leave.

She turned on her side, facing him. "Thank you for taking care of me."

He took her injured hand and brought it to his lips. "Anytime," he said.

Her eyes drifted closed. He smoothed the hair back from her forehead. She smiled, murmured something he didn't understand and scrunched down into the bed. In a little while her breathing evened and he knew she slept.

When evening came and he was hungry, he went out to the kitchen. Meadowlark fixed him a sandwich, which he ate at the kitchen table.

When he went back to check on Annabel, she was restless, moving from side to side. Was it a bad dream or was she in pain?

He rested a hand on her forehead. It was warm. He didn't think she had a fever, but she was restless. He wanted to help her but he wasn't sure how. She whimpered again. "Annabel?" he said, but she didn't answer.

A look of indecision crossed his face, then, before he could change his mind, he took off his trousers and his shirt and, wearing only his briefs, turned back the sheet and lay down beside her.

"What are you . . . ?" Her eyelids fluttered and she tried to move away.

"Sh," he said, gathering her in his arms. "It's all right. Go to sleep, Annabel. I'm here."

She stiffened, but as he talked, whispering to her, stroking her shoulders and her back, she began to relax against him.

"That's it," he soothed. "Sleep now. Sleep."

And at last, still murmuring a protest, she relaxed. And cradled in his arms, she slept.

Chapter 7

Curtains moved in the ocean breeze, bringing in the scent of the sea. The overhead fan turned slowly and patterns of morning sun streaked the floor. Annabel stretched, opened her eyes and came face-to-face with a broad expanse of chest and a thatch of curly chest hair. Chest hair? Startled, she looked up. Silver gray eyes met hers.

"Good morning," he said.

She was frozen, unable to move. She knew a moment of panic as she wondered, If his chest is bare, is he like that all over?

"How do you feel?"

"All right. Well...my hand hurts, but otherwise I'm okay."

Polite conversation for the morning you wake up with a man in you bed? "What...uh, what are you doing here?"

"You were restless, hurting. I didn't know how to help you so I got into bed with you."

And held you like this all night. Heard your sighs and your whispers. Felt your softness. Breathed in your scent. Content just to hold you.

She shifted a little away from him. The brush of her body against his aroused him, and he knew that if he didn't get out of bed quickly, he wouldn't at all. But still he lingered.

Her face was flushed from sleep, her hair in tousled disarray. The sheet had fallen to her waist and one strap of the blue gown had slipped over her shoulder. Her creamy smooth shoulder. Small nipples pushed ever so slightly against the silken material. If he didn't get up...

He eased the other strap down. Instantly alarmed she said, "What...what are you doing?"

He stroked her shoulder. Her skin was soft. So soft.

"Annabel?" he said. And though he had told himself he would not do this, he kissed her.

For a moment Annabel didn't move. As he put his arms around her, she murmured some plea. But when he gathered her closer, it felt so good to be held this way, to smell the warm man smell of his skin and feel the length of his body against hers.

He kissed her gently, not forcing her, and her lips softened under his with a familiarity, a shadowed memory that she had been like this before. Had he held her like this before? Had she lain with him like this?

He kissed the corners of her mouth, her eyelids and the tip of her nose. He leaned his cheek against hers and whispered, "Annabel. My Annabel."

When he began to stroke her breasts, a warm sweetness flooded her body. Though she told herself she would not, she moved closer into his arms. She would be like this for only a moment more. But, oh, how nice the moment. How gentle the hand on her breasts, stroking, stroking.

"You have to stop," she whispered.

"I will. I will." Even as his lips closed around the peak of her breast.

She smothered a moan. "No, you shouldn't... shouldn't..." Her voice faded and she gasped with pleasure when he took a tip between his teeth to tease.

"Shouldn't do this?" he whispered against her skin. "Or shouldn't stop."

"I... I can't think when you touch me that way."

"Nor can I."

His mouth was soft and moist against her breast. He scraped the tip with his teeth and held it there while his tongue circled round and round.

Heat surged through her body. She had to stop him, knew she had to stop him. Herself. If she didn't now, right this minute, she wouldn't be able to.

"I don't want..." she struggled to say. "It's too soon. I can't." She backed away. In a voice that trembled with all she was feeling, she said, "I can't do this, Luis. Not now. Not yet."

He hesitated before he took a deep breath to steady himself and pulled the straps back over her shoulders. With one final quick kiss he threw back the sheet and swung his legs over the bed.

"Breakfast?" he asked in a matter-of-fact voice.

Annabel tried to keep her voice steady. She didn't look at him when she said, "Uh, yes, please."

He picked up the phone. "Meadowlark? Would you ask Ambrosia to come and help Mrs. Alarcon? And would you send our breakfast in about half an hour?"

He put the phone down. "I'll leave the door open for Ambrosia," he said. "And if it's all right with you, I'll be back to have breakfast with you."

"Of course." She still didn't quite meet his eyes.

"Don't try to get up alone. Let Ambrosia help you."

"All right."

"Well then . . ." Still he hesitated, not wanting to leave her. He rested a hand on her thigh, squeezed, and then with a sigh he picked up the shirt and trousers he'd discarded so rapidly last night and left the room.

Annabel lay where she was, trying to get her breathing back to normal, knowing she should have stopped him sooner. But heaven help her, she had liked his kissing her, liked his touching her that way.

She was twenty-nine. She knew she must have had some sexual experience. With him? Had the familiarity she felt in his arms only been the familiarity of a remembered love affair with someone else. Or had Luis been the man in whose arms she had lain, whose lips she had kissed?

"'What lips my lips have kissed, and where, and why . . .'"

Lines of a half-forgotten poem came back to her. Edna Millay? Strange that she could remember that when she couldn't even remember her own name.

Was Luis Miguel Alarcon really her husband, or was this all a great game of pretense, a web of fabrication being woven around her, drawing her in? And if it was, what was the why of it? If Luis had lied about the clothes, what else had he lied about? How could she trust him?

Luis was an attractive man, an intensely masculine man with a sexuality that seemed barely held in check. His kiss had excited her, his touch had inflamed her. Would she be able to resist him the next time?

Tortured by all kinds of conflicting thoughts and emotions, she barely heard Ambrosia call out, "It be all right if I come in?" And when Annabel said yes, she came in and helped her to the bathroom.

Sitting on the low porcelain seat in the tub, Annabel showered and washed her hair. She dried it with the dryer in the bathroom, then brushed her hair back into a ponytail, touched a bit of mascara to her eyelashes and lip gloss to her lips.

When she finished, Ambrosia helped her dress in a summer sundress she knew she had never seen before.

When Luis knocked at the bedroom door she told him to come in.

"We'd better have a look at your hand and your foot," he said, and carried her to the chaise, where he took the wet bandage off her foot.

"It looks better," he said, touching it carefully. "But we'll bandage it again just to keep it clean for another day. Now let's see your hand."

It still hurt. The two places where the spinelike needles had broken off were red and sore. He put more antiseptic cream on them, then rebandaged her hand and gave her the antibiotic. And although she insisted she could walk, he picked her up and carried her onto the balcony.

Meadowlark had decorated the table with bright red hibiscus and set it with fine English china.

"How pretty," Annabel said with a smile.

Meadowlark smiled back. She was an exceptionally lovely young woman, Annabel thought, with skin the color of coffee and cream. Her eyes were slightly tilted and her eyelashes were impossibly long. She wore her curly hair short, and colorfully bright earrings dangled from her ears.

Now, before Luis could, she pulled out Annabel's chair and said, "If there be anything else you want, you just holler out."

"Everything looks wonderful," Annabel said. "Thank you, Meadowlark." Then, because she was too curious to restrain herself, she added, "I love your name. Where does it come from?"

"My mama." Meadowlark grinned. "She say right at the moment when my daddy plant his seed she heard a meadowlark singing. She say she knew right then she was going to be pregnant, and that if I be a girl, she name me after the bird."

Luis raised a skeptical eyebrow, but before he could make a comment, Annabel said, "That's wonderful, Meadowlark. Thank you for telling me."

"Yes, ma'am." She patted Annabel's shoulder. "You want anything, anything at all, you let me know."

There was fresh orange juice, a platter of fruit, ham and eggs and buttered croissants, mango jam and a silver carafe of coffee.

Annabel had eaten very little yesterday but she made up for it now. The fruit was delicious, the ham succulent and the eggs just right. When she buttered her second croissant and added a dollop of mango jam, she looked up to see Luis grinning at her.

"I have a hunch you're going to live," he said. "Nobody with an appetite like yours is sick."

"I guess I was hungry." When she took a bite of the croissant, a smudge of the mango jam pebbled her lower lip and she put her tongue out to lick it off. "Everything is delicious, Luis. You really do live very well here."

"*We* live very well here," he said, barely restraining the impulse to leap across the table and nibble on the lip that she had licked.

She took a last sip of coffee. "I've never been here before."

"Of course you have."

Annabel shook her head. "You're all pretending that I have, but I don't believe it. Or you. Any of you, Ambrosia, the two men at the dock..." She lifted a bit of the material of her skirt. "I've never worn this dress before, not this or any of the clothes in the closet."

"Of course you have. They're your clothes."

"They're *new* clothes. I found the price tag on one of the dresses and on a sweater."

A muscle jumped in his cheek. He looked startled, angry. "We...we went to Puerto Rico last month. You shopped there."

"And threw out everything I'd owned before?" She shoved her chair back from the table. "That doesn't make sense. I wouldn't have done that."

"Not everything in your closet is new. Ambrosia takes good care of your clothes. They just look new."

She didn't believe him. He saw in her eyes that she didn't. He wanted her to, not just because she would be easier to handle if she did, but because it would be easier for her, too. Whatever might have happened, whatever conspiracy she might have been involved in, above all else he wanted to protect her.

Last night she had felt very small and defenseless in his arms and he had experienced feelings he hadn't known for a long time, feelings he did not entirely welcome. He reminded himself now that he had brought her here for a reason. No matter how appealing she might be, he had to keep his mind focused on his real objective. And so he steeled himself to say, "You're being ridiculous, Annabel. The clothes in the closet are yours. Don't start imagining things."

With that, he pushed his chair back from the table and stalked off. Leaving her alone and wondering if, after all, she had only been imagining things.

The dreams came again that night. She was on the boat. The day was hot, muggy. The sea was a flat gray and there were storm clouds overhead. A man put his arm around her. "What a perfect day," he said. "If this was the last day of my life, I'd die a happy man."

Someone laughed.

"Die..." The words echoed in her mind. "Die a happy man."

"You get your wish, pal."

A woman screamed.

Mouths opened in horror, screaming a silent scream.

Bullets sprayed—*thunk, thunk, thunk*—and a man, a man who seemed to be looking at her through a pane of rain-spattered glass, smiled a terrifying smile. Another man, eyes wide with terror, windmilled his arms and tried to run. Two bullets tore into his back and he fell, as though in slow motion, facedown on the deck.

A gun, black steel, was aimed at her chest. She was going to die. God in heaven. Going to die. "No!" she screamed. Screamed and couldn't stop screaming....

"Annabel!"

"Oh my God! Oh my God, he's going to kill me!"

"It's only a dream, a nightmare. Wake up. You're all right. You're safe."

"He killed them," she cried, her eyes wide, unseeing. "He killed them all."

"Who?" Luis asked. "Who killed them?"

"He . . . he killed him and then her and . . . and another man, and then he . . . he was going to kill me."

"What did he look like? The man in your dream. Can you tell me, Annabel? Can you tell me what he looked like?"

She was trying to focus, fighting to get things in perspective. But she was terrified, so terrified her teeth were chattering.

Luis gripped her shoulders. "Think, Annabel. Try to think."

She closed her eyes. "Dark . . . dark eyes. A narrow face and a scar, a scar on his chin. He was wearing a jacket." She opened her eyes and looked at Luis. "It was hot but he was wearing a jacket."

The grip on her shoulders tightened. "Can you remember his name?"

She shook her head.

"Flynn," he said. "Zachary Flynn. Does that mean anything?"

"I . . . I don't know." She covered her eyes and tried to stop shaking. "I don't remember."

"All right," he said. "No more questions. Try to sleep."

The hands that had come up to cover her eyes lowered and she shook her head. "I'm afraid to sleep," she whispered. "Afraid of the dream."

"I'll stay with you."

She tried to see his face through the darkness, the face of this man who said he was her husband. He had lied to her, she knew, but she didn't want to be alone, and when he eased her back into the bed and carefully covered her with the sheet, she was reluctant to have him leave.

Still... "You don't have to stay." She yawned. "I'll put the light on and read for a—" She yawned again. "For a while."

He stroked the hair back from her face.

"I'm all right now. Really. I..." But while she was trying to think about what she wanted to say, she fell asleep.

When she did, Luis lay down beside her, on top of the sheet, his head propped on a doubled-up pillow. He thought about her dream and the way she had described Zachary Flynn, which meant of course that she was beginning to remember, if not in her conscious mind, then surely in her subconscious.

She'd said in her dream that he had killed the others. But it was the explosion that killed them. Yes, the coast guard had found Flynn's jacket floating in the water with other debris, so it was pretty obvious he had been aboard. But presumably he'd died in the explosion, too.

Why had Annabel dreamed about people being shot? Dreams weren't true to life, of course, they were only dreams. And Flynn was dead, just as the others were.

Was Annabel starting to remember? Could some of what she'd dreamed have been a horrible reality?

Was she as innocent as she looked, or had she been a part of some devious plan?

So many thoughts, and all the while so aware of her here in the bed beside him. In the shadowed light he could make out the shape of her body, the length of her legs, the mound of her hip, the tangled spread of her hair on the pillow next to him. He eased his own pillow down, and finally, telling himself he wouldn't, he, too, slept.

The rain started sometime toward dawn, changing the temperature, chilling the air. Luis shivered and without waking crawled under the sheet. He awoke an hour later to find Annabel snuggled up against him, her face against his shoulder, one arm thrown over his waist.

He lay where he was, realizing he must have moved under the sheet with her, and that if she woke, she wouldn't like it. If he could ease out of bed without waking her... But when he began to slide away from her, she mumbled in protest and tightened her hold on his waist. Her gown had hiked up. He felt the line of her bare leg against his, the softness of thigh, the roundness of hip. And the sudden insistent strength of his arousal.

He was afraid to move, afraid to have *her* move. But just then, as though reading his mind, she snuggled closer. Her breast brushed against his chest and he groaned.

"Whazzat?" The mumbled word was accompanied by a sinuous cat stretch and a sleepy purr.

"Annabel?"

She nuzzled against his chest.

"I...uh, I have to get up."

The arm around his waist tightened. She put one leg over his.

"Por Dios, Annabel!"

Her eyes flew open. She stared at him, started to say, "What are you...?" when he kissed her. Kissed her with all of the pent-up passion he'd held in check for the past few days. Kissed her and couldn't stop kissing her.

She said, "Wait!" and began to struggle against him. When she pushed against his chest, the straps on her gown slipped down, exposing her breasts.

"Love," he said against her lips. "Oh, love, it's been so long."

"Let me go!"

"Annabel, I... I've waited so long." He kissed her again and said, "Kiss me back. Part your lips for me."

"No," she whispered. "No, I..." But when his kiss deepened, when he moved his mouth so fiercely against hers, her lips softened, parted.

"Yes," he said. "Yes, *mi querida. Amor de mi vida. Corazón. Corazón.*"

He touched her breasts and began to stroke them, softly, lightly, coming ever closer to the poised and hardened peak. She moaned into his mouth and he said, "So soft. So soft." And leaned to kiss her breasts.

And, oh, the feel of his mouth on her that way, the flick of his tongue against the hard peak of her nipple. He slid his hands under her back to raise her higher and rested his head between the mounds of her breasts, rubbing his face back and forth, whispering words in Spanish she didn't understand.

He held her there, gently caressing, gently suckling her, drawing out her passion, her heat. And when he reached to stroke between her legs, he said, "You're waiting for me, wanting me as I want you." And before she could reply, he kissed her mouth again and, grasping her hips, thrust himself into her.

"No!" she whispered, even as she lifted her body to his. "Oh, no!" she cried, even as her legs came up to hold him closer, even as her mouth sought his mouth.

She was caught in a whirlwind of remembered passion she couldn't control, clinging to him as he clung to her, lifting her body to his, whispering his name in a litany of need. "Luis, Luis, Luis." With each thrust, "Luis."

He left her mouth to capture a breast. His teeth closed over one tender peak, and when he flicked hard with his tongue, she cried out.

There was no holding back now. Her body was on fire, yearning, yearning, oh, sweet heaven, wanting him, wanting to be closer, to be a part of him, to merge her body with his. She climbed higher and yet higher in the grip of sensation after sensation, dizzied, frantic.

"Yes!" he said. "Yes!" He thrust hard against her, again and again while she clung to him, close to fainting, lost in an immensity of feeling, carried higher and higher on the crest of passion.

"Oh, please," she said. And then, "Oh, yes. Oh, yes!"

She cried aloud, shattered and broken and his.

"Oh, love," he said. "Love."

And when he collapsed over her, she held him close and whispered, "Luis. Luis."

Afterward, heart thudding against heart, he buried his face in that space between her throat and shoulder, his lips against her skin.

There were no words now as they clung to the fading heat, and knew a sense of loss, of sadness.

He held her close, stroking her back, the curve of a hip. Had he been wrong to be with her like this? he asked himself. But how could it be wrong when it felt so good?

He kissed her again, and though she made as if to move out of his arms, he held her there. For now at least there was no past, only the here and now with Annabel, his beloved Annabel, back in his arms where she belonged.

Chapter 8

The brown pelican perched on one of the dock posts, looking, Annabel thought, like a wise old country judge.

He blinked at her, as though in disapproval, and she laughed, which helped ease some of the tension she was feeling this morning. So did sitting here at the end of one of the docks, dangling her legs in the water. Actually she felt pretty good, better than she had in a long time. At least for as long a time as she could remember.

The air was clean and fresh, the sky a cloudless blue. Wind rustled through the palms, waves slapped gently against the shore, and from the other dock, the bigger one where *Straight On till Morning* was moored, came the voices of the men unloading the supply boat that had arrived earlier.

Rob was there with them, tail wagging, sniffing at the boxes, getting in the way. Luis, wearing only khaki shorts, worked alongside his men. Even from here she could see the sweat glistening on his body, the splay of the muscles of his bronzed shoulders.

And again she wondered, as she had this morning when she awakened alone, what manner of man he was.

They had made love in the early light of dawn. She wasn't sure now how she felt about that. It was something she hadn't intended to let happen, but when Luis kissed her it had somehow seemed natural to turn into his arms. Making love with him had been... She couldn't put words to it. More than nice. More than pleasurable. Wonderful. Yes, wonderful beyond words.

Lying there alone in her bed after he had left her this morning, with the sheet thrown back and the sea breeze caressing her naked body, she had asked herself if there had been a familiarity about making love with Luis. If she was his wife, they would have made love hundreds of times in the eight years they had been married. But it hadn't felt like eight years of lovemaking last night; it had felt like the very first time. Was that because she didn't remember, or because in reality it had been the first time?

When she went into the bathroom she looked at herself in the mirror. She didn't think she looked different, yet in a way she couldn't explain, she felt different. She touched the lips that he had kissed. And wondered about so many things.

He had been out on the terrace just finishing his breakfast when she'd left her room. He stood when he saw her and said, "Good morning." He held a chair out for her, and when she was seated he rested his hands on her shoulders.

"Annabel," he had started to say, just as Ambrosia appeared with a fresh pot of coffee and a plate of fruit.

She and Ambrosia exchanged greetings. Ambrosia asked if Annabel was feeling better. "Yes," she said, "I feel fine. Wonderful. Better than I have in a long time." And blushed because it was Luis who had made her feel that way.

The hint of a smile curved his mouth. "The supply boat arrived this morning," he told her. "The men are busy unloading. I'd better get down and see how things are going."

"Of course." She looked at him, then quickly away. She wasn't sure what she had expected, but something, surely something to acknowledge what had passed between them. Their bodies had joined in the intimate act of love. What had that meant to him? Had it been only a physical release without meaning or emotion? Had the words he'd spoken in the height of mutual passion meant nothing? And when, after the loving, he had cradled her in his arms and held her until she slept, hadn't he known the same sense of belonging she felt?

Last night she had experienced a bonding with Luis, a merging of her body and all that she was with him. Was it because this wasn't the first time she'd ever made love to him? Had there been, without her having been aware of it, the memory of other times? Was that why she had responded with such feeling?

She looked up now and saw him hefting a crate onto the dock. Rob darted forward and she heard Luis raise his voice and try to push the dog out of the way. *"Larguese!"* he said. "Get the hell out of here, Rob."

She stood then and called out, "Rob, come!"

The dog pricked up his ears and bounded out to the dock where she was.

"What're you doing?" she said when he reached her, laughing and trying to fend him off when he jumped up and tried to lick her face. "Okay, okay, take it easy."

He did until he spotted the pelican. With a "Woof!" he made straight for the bird, who, with a flap of its wings, sailed out over the water. Rob ran down the dock, barking frantically, but when Annabel called out to him, he came back to her.

She and the dog sat side by side, watching the pelican circle out over the sea, and two great white herons swoop low over the water for fish.

Luis, watching them, felt a sudden and inexplicable sadness, a longing for things to be not what they were but what he wished they could be.

This early morning he had left her bed without a word, slipping away as though ashamed by what had passed between them. It had been a mistake, but was he ashamed? Or sorry? Of course not. For how could he be sorry when making love to Annabel had been... He stopped, because it hadn't been quite that way. He hadn't been making love *to* her, he'd been making love *with* her. There was a difference. For the first time in his life he realized there really was a difference.

Had he been too controlling, too demanding during those first few years of their marriage? Too concerned with his pleasure and not enough with hers? He'd been so crazy about her, so much in love that he could hardly keep his hands off her. But had he taken the time to please her?

He wished he had kissed her sleeping mouth before he left this morning, wished he had told her what being with her like this meant to him. But he hadn't; he'd simply left her bed. And this morning when she looked so shy and ill at ease, he should have said something. He'd intended to, but then Ambrosia had appeared and he hadn't. He'd left Annabel alone with her doubts and her shyness. Left her as though nothing of importance had passed between them.

And it had been something of importance. It had been a coming home, a rebirth of all the love he had felt in those early years of their marriage. And an awakening of tenderness he had not even known he possessed.

Later that afternoon when the supply boat left and all of the supplies had been stowed, Luis showered and shaved. Dressed in white shorts and a T-shirt, he went looking for Annabel.

He found her in the library, standing in front of the portraits of the sea captain and his wife.

"Alejandro de Alarcon and his wife, Maria de Castilla," he said.

"He's very handsome, isn't he? His face is so strong, so masculine."

"Yes, I suppose he is."

"He looks like you. I . . . I mean you have some of his features." Embarrassed, she stepped closer so that she could read the small brass nameplate at the bottom of the portrait. "Alejandro de Alarcon," she read, "1712."

"The portrait was done two years before his death."

"How did he die?"

"He and Maria were lost in a hurricane somewhere here in the Bahamas."

"She was with him when the ship went down?" she asked, surprised.

Luis nodded. "It was the first trip she ever made, the first time he'd ever taken her with him."

Annabel looked up at the woman in the portrait. Maria, who must have been in her early twenties when the portrait had been done, was quite luminously beautiful. Her hair, a warm chestnut brown, curled softly about her face. She smiled a smile that didn't quite reach her eyes, for in their warm brown depths there seemed to be an expression of sadness. Sadness because her sea captain husband was away, or because somehow she knew how very short their life together would be?

The bodice of her pale pink dress revealed only the suggestion of the rise of her breasts. Her skin was porcelain smooth. She wore a gold necklace set with rubies at her throat, a ruby ring on her finger.

"He shouldn't have taken her with him." Luis, as he had done this morning, rested his hands on Annabel's shoulders. "He should have insisted she stay at home in Cádiz with her two young sons."

Warmed by his touch, Annabel took a steadying breath. "No, I don't think so, Luis. I think it was the way it was supposed to be. She was meant to be with him when his ship—what was it called?—went down."

"The *Cantamar*."

"Song of the Sea. What a lovely name."

"You're remembering your Spanish," he said.

"Yes, I suppose so."

"The last time we were in Madrid we stayed for almost six months. You took classes."

Madrid? How could she have been to a city like Madrid and not remember?

"You liked it there." And when she shook her head, bewildered and uncertain, he said, "I took your picture by the Fuente de la Cibeles. The Cibeles Fountain."

A picture? Then there was proof—he had proof that they were married. She stepped away from him. "Where . . . where is it?" She tried very hard to keep her voice steady. "May I see it?"

He hesitated before he said, "It's somewhere here in the desk, I think."

She watched him move to the desk. The fact that there were no pictures of either her or Luis in the house was something she hadn't thought about until now. There should have been wedding pictures. And a wedding ring. If she was married, where was her wedding ring?

He opened one of the bottom drawers, shuffled through it and took out a five-by-seven framed photograph. He handed it to her.

There she was, a younger version of herself, smiling at the camera. "It must have been taken a few years ago," she said.

"Yes, it was."

She handed the photograph back to him. He hesitated for a moment, then, instead of putting it back in the drawer, he placed it on the desk.

Why hadn't it been there before? Why had he hidden it away? Why weren't there pictures of the two of them together?

"Did we have any pictures together?"

"Yes."

"I'd like to see them."

He avoided her eyes. "They must be around somewhere."

"What about wedding pictures?"

"There weren't any. We didn't have a formal wedding, Annabel. We were married by a judge in Miami."

"I see." She hesitated. "What about our honeymoon? Where did we spend it? In Miami?"

"There was no time for a honeymoon. We spent the night in Miami Beach and the next day we sailed for San Sebastián."

"From Miami?"

"Yes."

Newly married, they would have spent a week at sea aboard the *Straight On till Morning*. That had been a honeymoon, hadn't it? What had it been like? He'd told her they had been married when she was twenty-one. Had she been inexperienced? A virgin? Had he been a tender and patient lover? So many things she wanted to ask but was afraid to.

"Did I have a wedding ring?"

"Of course."

She held up the ringless fingers of her left hand. "But I wasn't wearing a ring when I woke up in the hospital in Nassau."

"You..." He didn't quite meet her eyes. "You must have lost it in the accident."

"Yes, I...I suppose so." Suddenly confused, once again unsure, she looked up at the portraits. "I wonder how long they were married," she said.

"Almost fifteen years. I have a packet of their letters to each other. You can read them sometime if you'd like to."

"I'd like to, very much."

Luis looked at his watch. "It's almost time for dinner. There's something I need to check in my office.

Why don't you ask Ambrosia to fix us a couple of drinks. I'll meet you on the terrace in, say, half an hour." He started out of the room, hesitated as though to say something, then with a shake of his head left the room.

Annabel looked up at the portraits of Alejandro and Maria. What must it be like to have a love like theirs? she wondered. For though they had died together, they'd also loved together.

She moved closer to study the portrait of the beautiful Maria, dressed in her pink gown, a pale hand touching the gold-and-ruby necklace at her throat, a necklace her husband had given her.

And Annabel knew, somewhere in her heart she knew, that when the waters of the sea closed over their heads and Alejandro clasped Maria in his arms for the last time, Maria did not weep or cry out in anguish, for she was with her love, now and for all eternity.

Annabel wore an ankle-length flowered cotton dress for dinner. Her hair had been pulled back from her face into a french braid in which she had woven a bright yellow ribbon. And because she was more beautiful than Luis had even imagined her to be, he said in a voice made gruff by all that he was feeling, "Here you are at last. I've been waiting for you."

"Sorry." She took the drink he offered, sipped it and said, "It's very good."

"Are you hungry?"

"A little."

"I asked Meadowlark to prepare Spanish food tonight." And when Annabel didn't respond, he added, "You like that kind of food."

Do I? she wanted to ask. But didn't.

"How's your hand?"

"Much better. It doesn't hurt."

"Let me see." She'd taken the bandage off. Her hand still looked a little red but it wasn't swollen. "It looks all right, but you'd better put some more salve on it tonight before you go to bed."

"I will."

He kept her hand in his. "About last night." He hesitated. "I didn't intend for it to happen. I had hoped it would, of course, sooner or later, but I had planned to wait until you were more sure of yourself. Of me."

He touched her hair and with a half smile said, "It was your fault, you know. You were close to me when I awoke, all warm and soft." He touched a wisp of hair and gently tucked it behind her ear. "Making love with you meant a great deal to me, so much more than I can ever tell you." He drew her into his arms. "I wanted to tell you this morning. I wanted to wake you and love you again." He smiled. "Again and again."

Why didn't you? she wanted to ask. Then, confused and afraid he could read her thoughts, she turned away and went to stand by the railing looking out at the sea.

That's where she was when Rob padded out to the terrace. He looked from Luis to Annabel and went to stand at her side.

Luis forced a chuckle. "Man's best friend. He obeys me but I've got a hunch he's your dog."

She bent down and scratched Rob behind his ears. "I've never had a dog before," she said.

"Oh? How do you know that?"

"Well, I mean I don't think I ever had one. Did we have a dog?"

We. That gave him a sense of satisfaction, but he tried not to show it when he said, "No, we didn't. We were traveling a lot, that's why."

"Where did we go?"

"To Spain of course. And once to Paris. I bought you a nightgown in Paris."

If he had, it wasn't with the new nightgowns on the shelf in her closet.

She finished her drink, but when he asked if she wanted another, she said no.

She wasn't aware of it of course, but in the last rays of the sun he could see every line of her body outlined through the cotton material of her dress. He thought of how it had been last night when he had stroked all the lovely curves and planes, the intriguing hollows of her body. And because he felt his own body tighten, he turned away from her and called out, "Ambrosia! We'd like dinner to be served."

The table had been set with flowers, fine china and crystal glasses. White wine was served with the cold gazpacho, a red Rioja with the *Moros y Cristianos,* black beans and rice, and the paella, a wonderful mixture of saffron-flavored rice with seafood, chicken and vegetables. Dessert was a fresh pineapple sorbet.

Luis poured the wine and served the after-dinner coffee. There was very little conversation. When he finished his coffee he said, "I'm sorry, Annabel. I hope you'll excuse me because I need to check on some things in my office."

"Of course."

He stood and went around to her chair. Lifting the braid from the back of her neck, he kissed the tender skin there. "You smell of jasmine," he said.

She felt his breath on her skin and a weakness came over her. But before she could say anything, he motioned to the dog. Rob lifted his head from his paws but made no move to get up. Luis snapped his fingers, and with something like a sigh the dog got to its feet and followed him.

"Well then . . ." He hesitated a moment more, then he said "Come" to the dog and left her alone on the terrace.

For a few moments in the library today she'd almost believed that she really had been Luis's wife. And now, with that single caress, she had felt the same return of passion that she had felt this morning.

But the doubts were still there, for if she was his wife, would he have walked away from her like this just now?

Tears stung her eyes when she pushed back her chair, and with something close to a sob, she ran back into the house.

Luis worked at his desk until midnight. Rob snoozed close by and did little more than open one eye when Luis got up to study the sea charts spread on the big table in the center of the room.

It was hard to concentrate. He tried to focus his eyes on Matecumbe Key and Steamboat Channel. Then down to the Great Bahama Bank, the Crooked Island Passage. His vision blurred, his mind wandered, and it seemed to him that he could see Annabel swimming up out of the depths of the blue-water markings of the charts spread out before him. Annabel, with water glistening on her breasts, braided hair with the yellow ribbon trailing in back of her. And her face, so young, so beautiful.

He gave a hoarse cry and slammed his fist down on the chart table. He wanted her, he needed her so.

"Annabel." He whispered her name there in the silence of the room. "Annabel."

Rob opened both eyes and went to stand by Luis.

Luis scratched the dog's ears. "Come on, mutt," he said. "What we need is a walk on the beach." Anywhere to get the thought of Annabel out of his mind.

She was asleep when she felt the weight on the bed. "On the floor, Rob," she mumbled without opening her eyes. "Not on the bed."

Luis put his arms around her. "It's not Rob," he said. "And I don't want to sleep on the floor."

She opened her eyes. "I . . . I'm not sure we should do this."

"Annabel. Annabel, please . . ."

Please. Had he ever said that before? Had he ever really asked for anything, or had he simply taken what he wanted, what had been offered and willingly given?

This was different. Annabel was different. He wanted her with a need that was more than physical, though Lord knows it was that. But this feeling was something he had never experienced before, this need to hold her and love her went soul-deep.

He tightened his arms around her. Her body was warm from sleep, and soft, *por Dios,* so unbelievably soft. He wanted to lose himself in her, get lost in her arms, be drugged by her scent.

He buried his face in the fall of her hair and closed his eyes, content for the moment to hold her this way. He whispered her name, "Annabel," and felt her body quiver in response.

He kissed her, and Annabel felt her body warm to his. But still, as though not sure she should do this, she brought her hands up against his chest to push him away. She curled her fingers in the thick thatch of chest hair and tried to push him, told herself she tried.

But, oh, his mouth was warm, his lips so full and firm. Her hands flattened and smoothed the chest hair, stroked the nipples.

He groaned. She felt his body tighten, and when his mouth covered hers again, her lips parted and she kissed him as he was kissing her.

"Annabel." A smothered moan. "Oh, Annabel."

She was lost, lost in the mouth that consumed her mouth, in the hands that stroked her breasts. Flame curled in her body, down, down to that most intimate of places.

He kissed her throat, he breathed her name against her ear and gently nipped a lobe, then healed it with his lips and with his tongue. He slipped the straps of her gown over her shoulders, down to her waist, and turning her onto her side, he began to kiss her breasts.

She tunneled her fingers through his hair and held him there, loving his touch, his kiss. And when, with his hot tongue, he flicked hard against her nipple, she cried aloud because the flame had become a fire and she was burning, burning.

She took his face between her hands and brought him up to kiss her mouth again. "Luis," she whispered. "Luis, please."

"Please what, *mi amor?*"

"You know."

"Oh yes, I know." The kiss deepened. She felt his hardness against her thigh, and half in fear, half in passion, she grasped his waist and lifted her body to his.

He was over her then, in her, moving against her, fast and fierce and wonderfully hard. She was wild now, uninhibited and out of control, calling out to him, telling him how good this was.

He plunged into her, then withdrew to plunge again and again.

She followed where he led, giving as he gave, lifting her body to his in total abandon, loving it. Loving him.

He kissed her mouth. He leaned to lave her breast, to take one tortured nipple between his teeth to tease and to pull.

A smothered scream and she was on the edge, climbing higher and yet higher toward an immensity of passion she had never known. As though from a distance she heard him call her name. Then his mouth covered hers. "Yes," he said against her lips. "Now, yes." And his body was like thunder over hers.

She opened her eyes and in the faint light that filtered in through the curtains saw him above her, watching her, and his face filled with the agony and the ecstasy of all that he was feeling.

"Oh, love!" he cried. And it happened. Like fire and lightning running through her body, it happened and went on happening as his body exploded over hers, as he took her mouth and took her breath and held her when she wept with all that she was feeling.

Luis couldn't move, he could barely breathe. He felt her tears against his throat and felt his own eyes smart. For this was Annabel, here at last where she belonged.

Chapter 9

Morning came softly. Luis's body was curled around her back, his face nuzzled against her neck. In a half-waking, dreamy state, Annabel thought how good it felt to awaken like this, how warm and snuggly. She murmured, "Mmm," and when he tightened his arm around her waist, she remembered how it had been last night, how mind-boggling, bone-melting good. And more. So much more.

Luis was a passionate and a tender lover who brought her to a height of ecstasy she hadn't even known existed. And afterward, when she lay quietly in his arms, he had held her and stroked her until her eyes drifted shut and she slept. Even then, on the edge of sleep, she had been aware of his touch, of his hand on her skin, stroking, stroking.

She felt him sigh, and sensing that she was awake, he kissed the back of her neck and said, "You smell good."

She smiled and, reaching back, rested a hand on his thigh. "Did you sleep well?"

"With you in my arms?" He trailed a line of kisses across her shoulders. "I haven't slept like that for a long time. Not since... Well, not for a long time." He ran the tips of his fingers across her breasts, and when she shivered he said, in a pleasantly conversational tone, "If your foot is better we could swim this morning before breakfast." He pinched one tender nipple. "If you'd like to."

"I..." Her breath started coming fast. "Yes, I... yes, that would be..." His touch inflamed her. "Mmm, oh, nice," she managed to say.

"Then that's what we'll do." He rubbed his hand across her rib cage, down over her belly, between her legs. "Later," he said. "A little later."

"Luis...?"

"Yes, *querida?*" All the while touching her, stroking her. "What is it, Annabel?"

"Maybe we should get up."

He turned her so that she faced him. "Not yet, *querida.* Not quite yet."

He kissed her mouth and all the while he touched her, touched her until every inch of her was aquiver with the tension of waiting for what she knew was to come.

When it did, when he rolled her beneath him and joined his body to hers, she cried out, clasping his shoulders, seeking his mouth, lost in him and in this feeling that was so new to her she barely understood it. Had it been like this in her forgotten past? Had her body lifted to his like this? Had she whispered his name and said, "Oh yes, oh, darling, yes"?

He moved so slowly, so exquisitely against her. She touched his face and held him close, loving this…the pleasure. Oh yes, the fine pleasure.

He pressed his hands under her bottom to lift her closer. His movements quickened and she clung to him, riding with him, holding him as he held her. He kissed her breast and she cried aloud, wanting to weep because she knew she was close to that glorious moment of release. And when it came, when her body surged against his, she kissed his mouth and took his cry to mingle with her own.

For a long time they held each other, but at last he said, "How about that swim?"

"Swim?" she murmured. "I'm lucky if I can stay afloat after this!"

It was the first time she'd heard him really laugh, a laugh that came from the belly, that sounded rich and free from tension. When the laughter died, he looked at her and said, as though surprised, "You have a sense of humor."

"Yes, I guess I do." And wondered why, if they had been married for eight years, that surprised him.

He went to his room to put on swim trunks. They met on the terrace and with Rob beside them went down to the beach and waded into the surf. The water, like clear, clean glass, was just cool enough to be refreshing. They swam out a hundred yards or so, then came back in to swim parallel to the beach.

When they were tired they treaded water, and when a wave brought them closer and their bodies touched, Luis put his arms around her and, as they had when they swam together off the boat, they sank beneath the waves.

In the cool, clear water Annabel opened her eyes and saw that his eyes, too, were open. He kissed her there beneath the water, a salty, wet kiss, and she thought suddenly that this was the way it had been with Alejandro and Maria. When that last and terrible wave closed over their heads, they, too, had opened their eyes and looked at each other the way she and Luis were looking at each other now.

And strangely, when he kicked to bring them to the surface, she felt a sense of loss.

He brought a newspaper to breakfast with him, a copy of the *Miami Herald* that had come on the supply boat the day before. But he didn't say anything about it until they finished eating and the table had been cleared.

Only when they started on their second cup of coffee did he say, "There's a follow-up story about the boating accident in yesterday's paper. They've identified the boat and the people who were on it. They already had your name, of course."

She set her cup down so abruptly coffee spilled over the edge of it.

"Would you like me to read it to you or shall I just tell you the gist of it?"

"Tell me."

He picked the paper up and she saw the headline on the front page: Prominent Miami Family Aboard Mystery Boat.

"Their name was Croyden," Luis said, watching her. "Louise and Albert Croyden and their son, Mark. They owned a small marina and sales office in Miami Beach. The boat, the *Distant Drum*, belonged to them. It was a cabin cruiser, a real luxury model." He looked across the table at her. "They must have been friends of yours. Do you remember them at all?"

"Croyden." Annabel closed her eyes and tried to remember. "No," she said at last. "I don't. But if they were friends of mine, wouldn't you have known them?"

"Probably not." He avoided her eyes. "You took a lot of trips to Florida by yourself. You'd lived there before, you still have friends there and you like to visit them."

"But—"

"Zachary Flynn was on board, too," he said before she could go on. "It was his jacket the coast guard found. I told you about him."

Luis waited, hoping for a reaction. When there was none, he went on. "No one can ascertain for sure the cause of the explosion, but it's assumed it was caused by gasoline vapor in the engine compartment." He handed the newspaper to her. "The pictures of the Croydens are on the front page."

She reached for the paper; her hands were shaking. Louise Croyden, age fifty-five. Thin, suntanned face. Short, very blond hair. Her husband, Albert, fifty-eight. Looking affable in a sailing cap, grinning into the camera.

Below them was a photo of their son, Mark, thirty. The picture had been taken on one of the sailboats in the marina. He stood holding on to the mast, handsome and dark-haired, wearing white shorts. Windblown and happy.

Mark? she thought. Mark?

"He liked jazz," she said slowly. "He was crazy about the old-timers like Jimmy Rushing, Bessie Smith and Louis Armstrong. He'd play an Armstrong record over and over again. 'Listen to that riff,' he'd say. 'Nobody does it like Louis.' ''

Luis held his breath. ''You remember him.''

''I . . . I remember about the music. 'I Get Ideas.' ''

''What?''

''That was one of the songs Louis Armstrong sang. 'I Get Ideas.' Mark played it over and over again.''

He could see the pain in her eyes, the desperation that trying to remember caused. Because Mark Croyden had been someone she had cared about. Someone she had loved? Her lover?

His jaw tightened, but he managed to keep his voice under control. ''Flynn's picture is on the inside, on page five,'' he said.

Annabel took a deep breath, then, as though with an effort, she turned to page five and looked at the photograph of Zachary Flynn. Short but solid body, muscled arms. Gray hair cut military short. He wore tight swim trunks; a diving tank was strapped to his back.

''Anything?'' Luis asked. ''Does he look like the man in your dream?''

''I . . . I don't know. How long ago did he work for you?''

''Four years ago. I've been trying to find him ever since. After he quit he headed for Mexico. I almost caught up with him in Cancún, but by the time I knew where he was he'd disappeared again. Somebody told me he was in Peru, somebody else said he was in Panama.'' His voice hardened. ''I'm sorry the sharks got to him before I did.''

Annabel stared at him, her eyes wide with horror. ''Sharks?'' She thought of the photographs she'd just seen of the Croydens, Louise and Albert. And Mark.

"Oh, no," she moaned. "Oh, no." And with a sob she covered her face with her hands.

He knew it had been a stupid thing to say. Whether she remembered them or not, the people who died in the explosion had been her friends. Mark Croyden had probably been her lover.

"I'm sorry," he said stiffly. "That was a thoughtless thing to say. I know that the Croydens must have been friends of yours, even though you don't remember them."

"I want to remember!" Tears stung her eyes. "I'm trying so hard to remember."

"I know you are. The doctor said your memory would come back—"

"When?" She looked at him then, knuckling the tears away. "When? God, Luis, you don't know what it's like not to remember anything. Anybody." She fought for control. "Does the paper say anything about me?"

"They repeated most of what was said when you were found. It's there," he said, pointing. "Next to the story about the Croydens."

She began to read.

"Annabel Alarcon, wife of entrepreneur Luis Alarcon, was the only survivor. Picked up near Eleuthera by the coast guard after what was believed to have been three days after the explosion, she was taken to the hospital in Nassau and is now recuperating at her husband's home on San Sebastián.

"Mr. Alarcon is well-known as an adventurer and treasure hunter. In 1991 he found the English galleon *Sir Francis Drake* and salvaged a fortune in silver and jewels from the ship that had gone down off the coast of Andros Island in the early 1700s.

"Attempts have been made to question Mrs. Alarcon about the events that happened aboard the *Distant Drum,* but because of poor health she has not been available for comment."

"*Has* anyone tried to reach me?" Annabel raised her eyes from the paper.

"There have been calls on the shortwave from newspapers and magazines and a couple of television talk shows. I knew you weren't up to it so I put them off."

She hadn't known anyone had called. Shouldn't Luis have told her? Shouldn't he have let her make the decision about whether or not she wanted to talk to anybody?

She read the article again. "It says that you're an adventurer, a treasure hunter."

Luis pushed his chair back from the table and went to stand at the edge of the terrace. "A treasure hunter? Yes, I guess I am." He pointed out toward the sea. "Beneath those waters are the remains of ships that went down centuries ago. Spanish ships like the *Cantamar,* English and Portuguese and Dutch ships sailed by sea captains like Alejandro. Pirates and privateers, too. English buccaneers, slave traders and rumrunners. They all plied these waters, Annabel. And when their ships went down, whether in battle or in storms, they took with them fortunes in gold and silver and precious jewels."

She raised a disapproving eyebrow. "And you go after that gold and silver, the treasures beneath the sea."

A slight smile softened his mouth. "The treasures beneath the sea," he mused. "That's what dreams are made of, Annabel. At least for me. Especially when it comes to the *Cantamar*. She's mine. She calls to me like a sea siren."

He turned away from the railing and faced her. "Perhaps you don't remember...," He paused, waiting for a reaction, and when there was none, said, "We searched for her together. We sailed in the Bahamas, around Abaco, Eleuthera and Nassau, down through the Windward Passage between Hispaniola and Cuba, all the way to the Lesser Antilles and back up to the Bahamas again. We almost found the *Cantamar*. You helped me make the charts."

"*I* helped you?" There was an expression of disbelief on her face.

"We charted the course together right around Eleuthera before we came back to San Sebastián. After we returned it took me a few months to arrange a salvage crew. While everything was being pulled together, you and I took two months off and went to Spain. When we returned I sailed back to the place you and I had charted."

"I...I didn't go with you?"

He looked at her, his silver eyes watchful, penetrating. "No, you didn't." His expression was unreadable. "I almost found her then," he said. "I would have if Andrew hadn't come along."

"Andrew? I don't understand."

"Andrew was a killer hurricane with winds up to a hundred and sixty miles an hour. It forced us to leave—it probably shifted the *Cantamar*'s location."

He debated about whether or not to tell her the truth, watch her reaction, see if she remembered having been a part of the betrayal. "I had a crew," he said, trying to keep his voice even. "It was headed by Zachary Flynn."

"Zachary...?" Her eyes widened. "The man whose jacket was found floating in the water?"

Luis nodded. "He stole the charts I'd made—the charts *you* helped me make—that show the approximate place where the *Cantamar* went down." He waited, bracing himself for whatever reaction she might have. But she didn't say anything. She only gripped the back of her chair so hard her knuckles went white.

"The place where they found the wreckage of the *Distant Drum* was only a few sea miles from where I'd been searching for the *Cantamar*."

He went closer, and when he stood face-to-face with her, he said, "What were you doing with Flynn, Annabel? Why were you with him that day? Was he looking for the *Cantamar?* Were you helping him?"

"What...what do you mean?" She backed away from him as though afraid, her face suddenly white. "What are you saying? That I know where the *Cantamar* is? That I was on the *Distant Drum* with those people because of the *Cantamar?*"

"I'm only asking..."

He said something else, something she didn't quite hear, because suddenly all kinds of thoughts were tumbling around inside her brain. Thoughts...and voices...voices clamoring to be heard over his voice.

"Let's take the *Drum* over to Bimini," Mark said. "Or down to the Keys. Just the two of us. Maybe to the Dry Tortugas."

The *Drum*. He called it the *Drum*. She looked out at the sea, looked into the setting sun until she was blinded by the brightness. And all the while the word, like the name, pounded in her head. *Distant Drum*. The *Drum*. The *Drum*.

She closed her eyes, and as though in a dream, she saw herself in the bow of the boat next to Mark. They were laughing at something his father said. His father was drinking beer from a can. From below deck she could hear music, jazz, Fats Waller playing "Muskrat Ramble." The woman with the short blond hair said something funny and they were laughing again.

They were all laughing when it happened. The popping sounds. Like firecrackers or a car backfiring. Crack! Crack! Crack! And then they screamed.

Bright spots wavered in front of Annabel's eyes, turning black, turning everything black. The darkness closed in on her and she felt herself falling into nothingness.

Somebody called out to her. Was it Mark? Mark with his funny, boyish grin, Mark who held her hand and made her laugh.

"Annabel!"

"Mark?" she said. Her eyes fluttered open. "Oh, Mark. Is it you?"

"It's Luis." His voice was harsh, angry. "Luis."

She tried to focus. "Luis? What...what happened?"

He helped her sit up. A wave of dizziness made everything around her spin. She closed her eyes and waited for it to pass. "What happened?" she asked again when she opened her eyes.

"You fainted. I think you remembered what happened. Can you tell me, Annabel? About the boat?" The hands that had helped her to sit up tightened on her arms. "About Mark Croyden?"

"Mark?" She shook her head as though not understanding.

"Mark and his parents were with you the day of the accident. You saw his picture in the paper."

"Yes, I remember his picture, but..."

Rob, whining and looking anxious, ducked under Luis's arm and licked her face. She put her arms around him and hid her face against his furry neck so that she wouldn't have to look at Luis, to see the suspicion in his eyes.

When she let go of Rob she said, "I'm feeling a little shaky. I think I'd like to rest for a while."

"You've got to try, Annabel. Try to remember."

Tears filled her eyes. "I can't," she said. "Don't you understand? I can't!"

He helped her up. "I'll take you to your room."

"No. I...I'm all right." She had to get away from him. "I can manage."

"Shall I send Ambrosia to help you?"

"No, I don't want anyone." She paused. "No, thank you."

Get away. Be alone. That's all she could think about. Get to her room and close the door.

Rob went with her. He stood at the door of the bathroom while she splashed cold water on her face. And when she lay down, he stretched out on the floor beside the bed.

"Yes," she said, reaching down to pat his head. "Stay with me, Rob. Stay."

She closed her eyes and put an arm over her face to try to block out the image of Luis's face, the suspicion in his eyes when he asked her if she had been helping the man named Flynn find the *Cantamar*.

She had no remembrance of things past, but there was one thing she was sure of—she would never have betrayed a trust. How could Luis believe that of her after what they had shared? It hurt, oh God, it hurt so much to know that he did.

Annabel spent the remainder of the day in her room. When, in the evening, Ambrosia came to tell her that dinner was ready, she said, "Tell Mr. Alarcon that I'm resting and that I'd like to have my dinner here in my room."

"Be you sick?"

Annabel shook her head. "I'm a bit tired, that's all."

"I'll bring your dinner in."

"That would be nice."

The woman gestured to Rob. "You come on outta here. Better you don't be bothering Missus Annabel."

"He's no bother."

"Mr. Alarcon told me to be bringing him out, ma'am. Said he might be disturbing you."

"But he's not. I really..." But before she could finish, Ambrosia took hold of Rob's collar and started toward the door with him.

He hunkered down, nails skidding on the tile floor, whining and trying to get away. But Ambrosia wouldn't let him go.

"You gotta come 'long with me, dog," she said, and pulled him out of the room.

Annabel didn't like it, but neither did she want to make an issue of it. She had little to say when Ambrosia returned with her dinner, only "Thank you," and that, no, she did not want her dinner served on her balcony, she preferred to eat here in her room.

An hour later Ambrosia came to freshen her bed and take the dinner tray away. "Mr. Alarcon tell me to ask if he could see you for a few minutes."

"Please tell him I'm tired and that I'm going to bed now. I'll speak to him in the morning."

"But he say—"

"Good night, Ambrosia."

The woman stood, hands on her hips, frowning and uncertain. Then with a shrug she went out and closed the door behind her.

Annabel had half a mind to lock the door between her room and Luis's, but even as she started toward it she hesitated. If Luis wanted to come in, a locked door wouldn't stop him. She could only hope that he was gentleman enough to stay away from her tonight.

She read for a while, and when at last she felt herself growing sleepy, she put the book down and turned off the light. The night was warm. Even with the overhead fan and the door to her balcony open a few inches, it was too hot in the room. She got up and opened the door wider and stood for a moment looking out toward the sea.

Out there, somewhere beneath the water, the *Cantamar* waited to be found. By Luis? In spite of the heat she shivered. She had been along on the *Distant Drum* with Zachary Flynn. Had Flynn been looking for the

Cantamar? Had she known where the ship had gone down?

But surely she wouldn't have betrayed Luis. He was her husband. How could she have betrayed him?

And at last, exhausted by all the thoughts running round and round in her head, she went to bed and almost immediately to sleep.

She dreamed of the sea. Not a frightening dream, at least not at first. She was swimming far from land. The sea was warm and clear. She looked beneath the surface into the turquoise green depths and watched the schools of tiny multicolored fish. Perhaps they were called schools of fish because they were like children, she thought, darting back and forth, first this way, then that way.

She laughed, and because she wanted to see them better, she dived beneath the water, down, down to where the fish played. Like a mermaid she swam with them, laughing when they came closer, enjoying the feeling of lightness the water gave to her body.

Suddenly, though, it became hard to breathe, and she knew she had to get to the surface. Now. Quickly. Couldn't breathe. Frantic. She kicked her legs but they barely moved. She had no air left in her lungs. Had to breathe! Had to but couldn't! She struggled, thrashing about with her arms, trying to kick with her legs. Smothering.

She struck out and heard a sound, felt a strange softness over her face. Soft, but pressing down... pressing. Breath was going. Brain screaming. Help me. Oh God, help me!

With the last of her strength she twisted her body to the side, gasped for air and screamed.

As though from a distance she heard the sound of barking. She screamed again and heard footsteps running across the tile floor of her room.

"Missus!" Her door flew open. Rob ran toward the bed, Ambrosia close behind him. "Missus, what is it?"

"Someone..." Hand to her throat, trying to breathe. "Someone was here."

Luis hurried into the room. "Annabel! What happened? Are you all right? I heard you scream. What is it?"

Rob, growling low in his throat, ran to the door. He barked, then ran out into the night.

"Pillow..." she tried to say. "Someone... someone held a pillow over my head."

Luis switched the light on. He picked the pillow up off the floor. "You had a bad dream," he told her.

Annabel shook her head. "No." She was trembling with reaction now. "Someone...someone tried to kill me." She looked up at Ambrosia. Ambrosia had come in first, not Luis. Yet Luis had the room next to hers.

He'd been angry earlier, angry because she couldn't remember, angry because of Mark, because he thought she had betrayed him. But was he angry enough to—

No! Oh, please God, no.

He went to the door that led out to her balcony. "Had you left it open?" he asked.

"Yes. I...I like the fresh air."

He closed it. "Just in case," he said. And to Ambrosia, "You can go now. I'll stay with Mrs. Alarcon."

She didn't want Ambrosia to go. She didn't want to be alone with him.

Ambrosia left. He locked the door. "Don't be afraid," he said to Annabel. "I'm here now."

And that's exactly what she was afraid of.

Chapter 10

The morning following what Luis was sure had only been Annabel's nightmare, he checked her balcony and the part of the beach leading away from it. He did so not because he thought there really had been someone in her room, but simply to appease her. However, a light rain had fallen that early morning, and if there had been any footprints, which he certainly doubted, they had been washed away.

He questioned the men who worked for him, asking if they had seen or heard anything the night before. Moses and David, as well as Samuel, who had returned on the supply boat from Nassau, were men he trusted with his life. Like the others, they had grown up on San Sebastián and had been with him for years. He knew the other islanders, too. Some of them had sailed with him; most of them had worked for him. He couldn't imagine any one of them sneaking into Annabel's room in the dead of night to try to kill her.

Unlike the other islanders, who lived on the opposite side of San Sebastián, Moses and David had small houses back from the beach and closer to the main house. Though he didn't think it necessary, Luis asked Moses to move up to the house and had Ambrosia, who shared a room with Meadowlark, fix a room off the kitchen. If there was even the remotest possibility that someone on the island meant Annabel harm, it wouldn't hurt to have Moses handy.

She had been very quiet since the incident. She had breakfast in her room, and though she said she didn't want any lunch, Luis insisted she eat on the terrace with him. He almost wished he hadn't, because they had so little to say to each other.

When pressed, she told him of her dream of swimming beneath the sea among the schools of fish and that suddenly she couldn't breathe.

"It sounds like a panic attack," he said. "You were upset by the article in the *Miami Herald*. I'm sure that even though you didn't recognize them, seeing the pictures of the Croydens upset you. Especially the picture of Mark. It's obvious that the photographs and the story upset you yesterday, Annabel. Upset you so badly you fainted."

He waited a moment, and when she didn't say anything, he steeled himself to observe, "It's possible that you and Mark Croyden were lovers."

"Lovers?" Annabel stared at him. "But you're my husband. I wouldn't have—"

"Wives have been known to cheat on their husbands before," he said with an ironic smile.

"But I wouldn't have done that," she insisted. "Not to you, not to anyone."

He let it go, but because he'd said it, the gulf between them widened even more.

She took long walks on the beach with Rob. At night the dog slept on the floor beside her bed. And Luis knew that if anyone came into Annabel's room without her invitation, Rob would attack. That amused as well as angered him.

For the next few days they had little to say to each other. Annabel still had breakfast in her room and spent as much of the day there as she could. One morning, three days after what she knew to have been an attack on her life, she asked Ambrosia to bring her the copy of the *Miami Herald* with the story of the accident at sea.

First she reread the story about the Croydens and Zachary Flynn, then the recap about herself and the fact that there had been an explosion aboard the *Distant Drum,* probably caused by gasoline vapor in the engine compartment. But why, if the boat had blown up, did she, in her dreams, hear shots being fired? How did she know, somewhere in her subconscious mind, that the shots had come first, then the explosion?

She studied the photograph of Louise Croyden. Louise . . . and suddenly she knew, but did not know how she knew, that Louise Croyden had been a dynamite lady, full of fun and laughter and the joyful absurdity of life.

And that Louise had a thirst for Scotch. That she could drink ten strong men under the table while carrying on a lively and completely coherent discussion on world trade or the history of the ancient Mayas. Louise, who had been her friend.

Tears stung Annabel's eyes. She let herself weep then, weep for Louise and for Albert, overweight, lovable Albert, who delighted in telling off-color jokes. Albert, who thought Louise was the most beautiful, the most wonderful woman in the world. Both of them gone. Lost in the explosion.

And Mark? She studied his picture. Had they been lovers? She couldn't remember her life before she'd come to this island, nor did she have any recollection of the woman she had been. But if it was true that Luis was her husband, she did not think she had been an unfaithful wife, that she would have risked destroying their marriage with infidelity.

But she remembered Mark, remembered how much he'd loved jazz. And Louis Armstrong. "Louis," he always said. Not Louie.

She wished there was someone she could talk to, Dr. Hunnicut or pretty Rebecca with her cocoa brown skin and sparkling eyes. She felt so isolated, so cut off from everything and everyone here on this island of San Sebastián.

This copy of the *Miami Herald* was the first newspaper she'd seen since she'd been here. Luis had said there'd been calls on the shortwave radio from newspapers and magazines and television talk shows, but at the time he hadn't told her. Why? Why was he keeping her hidden away like this, so far away, so out of touch with the world outside?

Someone had tried to kill her, and nothing Luis said would convince her that what she had experienced had only been a dream. There was no one else on the island except for the two of them, the people who

worked for Luis and their families. Yet someone had
tried to kill her. But who?

She watched him watching her, and each day the
suspicion grew that it had been Luis who'd held the
pillow over her head. But why? Why would he want to
kill her? Because he suspected her of having had an
affair with Mark Croyden? Or because he thought
she'd been along on the *Distant Drum* to help Zachary Flynn find the *Cantamar?*

The *Cantamar.* That was what she dreamed of now,
of the ship, of Alejandro and Maria, and one day at
lunch she said to Luis, "You told me you had letters
that Alejandro and Maria had written to each other.
Could I see them?"

He looked at her, a little surprised, but said, "Yes,
of course." And that afternoon he brought her a small
packet of letters tied with blue ribbon.

"The writing is hard to decipher," he told her.
"And faded with time, of course. But I think you can
make out my translation from the original Spanish.
Alejandro's letters are on top."

She took them with her out to her balcony to read,
and there in the sunshine she opened the first letter. It
was dated April 6, 1714.

Beloved Wife,
I write these words from Hispaniola and will send
the letter by clipper ship that is to embark from
here on tomorrow's tide, bound for the port of
Lisboa and from there to Cádiz.

I trust these lines will find you well. I pray, too,
that both Alfonso and Luis Miguel are in good
health. I miss them, and you, good wife, more
than these simple words can convey.

Since first I saw your lovely face at Sunday mass there has been no other save you in my heart. You are my love, my life and, yes, my lust. I long for you as a man too long without light longs for the sun. Each time we part it is as though I lose a part of myself, for you, Maria, are truly a part of me.

I remain, as always, your devoted husband

All of his letters were in the same vein, speaking of his love and how much he missed her and their two sons.

With a sigh Annabel put his letters aside and began to read Maria's letters to him.

Like her husband's, the young wife's letters also spoke of the love they shared. In her last letter she had written:

Dear Husband,

I count the days until you return. If all goes as planned you will be with me soon, and only then will I be whole, for without you at my side I am incomplete.

Our boys are well. Luis Miguel, who each day tells me he cannot wait until he is old enough to sail with you, excels in mathematics and reads Greek almost as well as his professor. Alfonso, too, does well in both Greek and Latin, but I fear not so well in mathematics. However, he excels in drawing and I encourage him in that.

Luis Miguel will be ten next month and Alfonso will soon be eleven. They are growing fast and I have been thinking, dear husband, that I would like to accompany you on your next voyage. I have spoken to my mother and to sister

Consuelo about this and they have agreed, with your permission of course, to care for the boys in my absence.

Please give this idea your consideration, husband. I want to be with you, I need to be with you. Let us then, on your next trip, set sail together on the *Cantamar*. If you should hesitate and say it is not my place, think then of the biblical words, "Whither thou goest, I will go." And know, dear husband, that I, like Ruth, would go with you.

I remain, dear Alejandro, your faithful wife,

Maria

Annabel looked out at the sea. Had Maria somehow sensed this would be her husband's last voyage? Was that why she had chosen to go with him?

What must it be like to love someone so much that you would follow him anywhere, even unto death? And what of the sons they left behind? Alfonso, who liked to draw. Luis Miguel, who longed to go to sea just like his father? Which young son had been the forebear of the Luis Miguel who said he was her husband?

At dinner that night she handed the pack of letters back to him. "Thank you for letting me read them, Luis. They loved each other very much, didn't they?"

"Very much." He filled her glass with wine. "But of course he shouldn't have allowed her to sail with him. He should have insisted she stay behind with their children."

"But that wasn't what she wanted." Annabel looked away from him, out toward the water, and with a catch in her voice that told him she was close to tears, she said, "I think Maria knew it would be his last voyage. That's why she wanted to be with him."

He wanted to laugh, to tell her she was fantasizing, making up a story to suit her romantic notions. But something in her expression stopped him, a look of sadness in her eyes, of loss, as she gazed out across the water.

He realized then, perhaps for the first time, how sensitive she was to matters of the heart, how easily hurt by an unkind word. And felt the shame of remorse at ever having hurt her.

It had always been hard for him to show his feelings, to say the words he wanted to say. Only when they made love could he tell her with his kisses and the urgencies of his body how much he cared.

He went to her and, pulling her to her feet, said, "Perhaps you're right. Perhaps Maria did somehow sense that it would be the captain's last voyage." He rested a hand on her head. "But it happened a long time ago, Annabel. Don't be sad, don't cry for them."

I'm not crying for them, she wanted to say. I'm crying for myself, for us, and for what might have been but isn't. And perhaps for what never was.

He tightened his hands on her shoulders. His voice softened. "My dear, let me . . ."

"No." She stepped away from him. "You tell me I'm your wife and yet you accuse me of adultery. And worse. You think I plotted against you, that I would try to steal something that you feel by birthright is yours. The *Cantamar* is your heritage, Luis. Finding it means everything to you. How could you think that

I would betray you, that I would have helped someone to take what was yours?''

''Annabel—''

''Maybe I did.'' She looked up at him, her eyes bright with tears. ''What if I really did have an affair with Mark Croyden? What if I tried to help Zachary Flynn find the *Cantamar?*''

She looked at him, tears streaking her face. ''What if it's true? What if that's who I am? Who I was?''

Her body shook with sobs she couldn't control, sobs that came from her very soul. He tried to hold her but she bent forward, hands across her stomach, as though trying to hold in her grief. He picked her up, carried her to the chaise and sat next to her there. And though she tried to pull away from him, he gathered her in his arms.

''You're not any of those things,'' he said. ''You couldn't be.''

''How do you know? How do you know?'' She was racked with self-doubt, with the belief that perhaps . . . perhaps she was all the things he had accused her of being.

She tried to move away from him but he wouldn't let her go. He held her there, and when at last the crying stopped, he smoothed her hair back from her face and said, ''Better?''

Small catches of breath, a smothered sob. ''Yes,'' she managed to say. ''I'm all right.''

When he let her go she lay back against the cushions, and when she could speak of it, she said, ''But what if it's true, Luis? I have no memory before the hospital in Nassau. Well, not . . . not really.''

''Not really? What does that mean?''

"I remember Louise Croyden. I know she was a friend of mine, both she and Albert. I remember she drank Scotch..." A slight smile curved her mouth. "A lot of Scotch. And that it never seemed to bother her."

"And Mark?" Luis held his breath. "What do you remember about Mark?"

"Only that he liked jazz." She shook her head. "Only that. Nothing else."

They stayed like that for a little while, but finally Annabel stretched. "I'm tired," she said. "I think I'll go in."

He rose and helped her up. He didn't say anything, he only waited. And because she could not say the words she knew he wanted to hear, she said, "Good night, Luis." And turning away, hurried in from the terrace.

When she was gone he went to stand by the rail and looked out into the night. The moon came out from behind a cloud, and not too far from shore he saw something. Was it a sail shining white in the moonlight or only the reflection of the moon? But then the moon disappeared behind the clouds and he could not be sure what he had seen.

Besides, his mind was on Annabel. He wanted to go to her. To hold her and tell her it didn't matter if she'd had an affair with Mark Croyden. All that mattered was that she was here with him now. He wanted to lie with her again, to love with her again. He gasped with the pain of his need. And told himself he was a fool.

She couldn't sleep. Rob, too, was restless. Time and again he got up from his place beside her bed to go to stand at the door that led out to her patio. Finally

Annabel got up and, opening the door said, "Okay, fella, go on."

He looked up at her, head cocked. The patches of brown over his eyes that made it look as though he had eyebrows rose in question.

"It's all right," she said. "Go chase moonbeams or whatever else you think is out there." She laughed when, with a woof, he bounded out into the night.

She closed the door behind him and wished she, too, could disappear into the night. Actually, she'd like nothing better than a swim in the sea.

She turned her bedside light on. One-fifteen. No, it wouldn't be a good idea to swim at night, especially alone. But in the pool? She was too restless to sleep. A dip in the pool might relax her.

Quickly then, she took off her nightgown and put on one of the swimsuits from the closet shelf.

The house was very quiet when she went through the dining room out to the terrace. The moon was half-obscured by clouds, but the night was soft, with only the most gentle of breezes to stir the air.

The moon slid behind the clouds; it was very dark.

She sat on the edge of the pool and dangled her legs in the water before she slowly lowered herself into it.

The water felt like satin against her skin. She began to swim in long, lazy strokes from one end of the pool to the other. Then she quickened her pace, doing laps, touching one end, flipping over and stroking hard to the other end. Again and again, seven laps, eight. Let's go for fifteen, she told herself.

She was gasping a little now, out of shape but determined to make it. Twelve laps, thirteen. Slowing down. Come on, come on. Only two more. No breath left. Okay, let's settle for fourteen. Enough breath left

for one more lap? Almost to the end of the pool. She
touched the side, gasping.

Suddenly, from out of nowhere, hands grasped her
head, then her shoulders. They pushed her down, held
her down, held her there beneath the water.

She fought. Tried to fight. Had to get air. Had to
breathe... And screamed a silent scream. *Alejandro!
Alejandro!*

The hands on her shoulders tightened, pushing,
pushing her down into the darkness of the pool.

Luis didn't know what woke him, why suddenly he
was sitting straight up in bed, sweat on his body, his
heart pounding hard against his ribs.

"Annabel?" he said. Then he was out of bed, and
without waiting to grab a robe, he ran across the floor,
through the connecting door and into her room.

Her empty room.

The door leading to the balcony was closed. He
opened it with a jerk and peered outside. She wasn't
there. Where in the hell was she? He saw her nightgown on the bed then, and the closet half-open. Had
she gone for a swim? What in the hell had she been
thinking of? Surely she wouldn't have gone swimming in the sea alone. The pool? Yes, probably.

That made him smile. He'd told her not too long
ago that they used to swim naked at night. He wondered if she was naked and that if she was... The smile
died. Something was wrong. He'd known it when he
awakened so abruptly.

"Annabel!" he said aloud, and then he was running through the house toward the pool. He reached
the doorway, stood looking out at the pool, trying to

see her. He saw a figure leaning over the far end and called out, "Annabel?"

The figure rose, turned swiftly and ran toward the beach.

What the hell? What was he doing at the side of the pool? Who...? Oh my God!

Luis ran naked out into the night, calling her name. "Annabel! Annabel!"

He didn't see her. Where was she? He snapped the pool lights on. They shone overhead and beneath the water. He saw her there, under the water, drifting down, down.

He ran to the edge of the pool and dived in. She was almost at the bottom. He grabbed her hair and pulled her up, got his arm under her shoulders and kicked, kicked hard, heart pounding against his ribs, one thought screaming in his brain, Don't let it be too late. Don't let it be too late.

He reached the surface, got her to the edge and hoisted her up and over the side. Then he hefted himself out. He bent over her, turned her over and lifted her from the waist. Water gurgled from her mouth. He felt for the pulse in her throat but could hardly discern a beat. Rolling her onto her stomach, he lifted, pressed, lifted, pressed. More water came out. She coughed. He slapped her back. She murmured, "Wait...wait."

He called out, "Ambrosia! Moses!" He eased Annabel onto her side. She coughed, gagged and vomited water.

"That's it," he said. "Get it up."

"Somebody...somebody pushed me. Held me under. He—"

Ambrosia ran out onto the terrace, Moses a few steps behind her. "What be happenin'?" Moses said before he saw Annabel. Then, "Oh, Lord! Oh, Lord! It be the missus."

"Somebody tried to drown her." He motioned Ambrosia forward. "Take Annabel to her room. Stay with her. Take care of her." And to Moses, "He's out there somewhere. Get the men. I want every inch of the island searched. Come on!"

"You naked, boss."

"To hell with it!"

"You might need a gun."

Moses was right. He picked Annabel up and ran with her back into the house, Ambrosia only a step behind him. He hurried into the bedroom and put Annabel on the chaise.

Her face was bone white. She was shaking, and her teeth were chattering.

"Get a blanket," he told Ambrosia, and quickly stripped Annabel out of her suit. Her skin was cold, ice-cold.

Ambrosia came back with the blanket and he wrapped it around Annabel. "Stay with her," he said to Ambrosia. And to Annabel, "You're safe now." He put his arms around her and held her close. He knew he had to leave, had to find the man who had done this to her, but God, how he hated to leave her.

"I'll be back," he said. "Ambrosia will be with you. I'll be back."

Then, before he could change his mind, he stood and ran into his room. He grabbed a pair of shorts off a chair, the gun from his bureau drawer. Somebody had tried to kill Annabel. He had to find the bastard, kill him.

Kill! The word burned in his brain and he knew that he would, just as soon as he got his hands on whoever it was who had done this to Annabel.

Luis and his men searched until way past daylight but they found no trace of the man who had tried to drown Annabel.

It was Samuel who found Rob.

"Over here, boss man," he called out from the dock. And when Luis ran over he saw the dog, unconscious and bleeding but still alive, at the end of the dock.

"I'll take care of him," Moses said.

But Luis shook his head. "He's Annabel's dog. I'll take him up to the house. You keep looking."

He picked Rob up in his arms and for the first time since this nightmare had started felt the sting of tears behind his eyelids.

"You're going to be all right," he told the dog. "You've got to be. For Annabel's sake."

Chapter 11

Because he didn't want Annabel to see Rob hurt and bleeding, Luis carried the dog into a room off the kitchen. Meadowlark, wearing an old chenille robe, her hair tied up in a blue bandanna, stood at the kitchen sink.

"I be making tea for the missus," she said nervously. "Ambrosia be telling me what happen' and..." She saw Rob and gasped. Blood matted the dog's hair, and his head lolled on Luis's arm. "Oh, sweet Lord," she whispered. "Be he dead?"

"No, but he's badly hurt. See what you can do for him. I'll take the tea in to Mrs. Alarcon."

"I know some things to do, sir. Island things and doctor things, too, because my brother worked for two years for a veterinary in Miami. I be taking good care of the dog, you take care of Mrs. Alarcon." She poured water into a teapot and put the pot on a tray alongside a cup and saucer.

When she put some towels on the floor, Luis laid the dog down on them. With his hand on the back of Rob's neck, he said, "Rob? Rob?" And though the dog didn't open its eyes, Luis received an answering whine. "I'll be back, boy," he said. "You hang in there, Rob. For Annabel."

He took a bottle of brandy out of the cupboard then and hurried toward Annabel's bedroom. The thought that someone, an outsider, was here on his island and had tried to kill Annabel had him clenching his teeth and swearing under his breath.

He realized now that the same person who'd tried to kill Annabel tonight had held a pillow over her face a few days ago to try to smother her. What he had insisted had been a nightmare had been a reality. She hadn't imagined it.

Whoever that someone was, he had come close to succeeding tonight. He would have, too, if Luis hadn't awakened and rushed out to the pool, compelled by some force he didn't understand.

He had a sudden terrible vision of awaking this morning, of strolling out to the terrace and finding Annabel there at the bottom of the pool. Blood rushed to his head and he sagged against the wall, weakened by the thought of what had almost happened. He made himself take a couple of deep breaths and hoped he looked reasonably calm when he opened the door of Annabel's room.

She was huddled on the chaise, shivering as though with a terrible chill. He poured tea into the cup, added a generous splash of brandy and handed it to her. "This will warm you up," he said, and knelt beside her.

She took the cup and brought it to her lips. It clicked against her teeth but she managed to drink a sip or two.

"Run a hot tub," he told Ambrosia.

"I already run it, Mr. Alarcon."

"All right, thank you. I'll take care of Mrs. Alarcon now."

"You need anything, you call me." Ambrosia headed for the door. "Anything, sir."

Luis nodded. Annabel's face was still bone white. Her eyes were frightened and too big for her face. "Drink your tea, Annabel," he said, and when he saw that her hands were shaking, he took the cup from her and held it to her lips. When she drank from it, he put it down and took her hands in his. They were ice-cold.

"We've got to get you warm," he said.

"I'm . . . I'm all right."

"No, you're not. You're freezing cold."

He picked her up and carried her into the bathroom. There he took the blanket off and helped her into the steaming, swirling water of the big tub.

He took his shorts off then, and though she looked startled, he didn't give her time to object. He got into the tub and eased himself behind her.

"Lean against me," he said. "Let me warm you."

The water was hot, but still she shivered. "It's all right," he told her. "You're all right now, Annabel. You're here with me. I'm not going to let anything harm you."

He kept talking, soothing and comforting her, and in a little while her body warmed and she stopped trembling. He didn't try to question her, he only held her close. And thanked God he had gotten to her in time.

For as long as he lived he would never forget the way she had looked when he turned the pool lights on. Arms out to her sides, blond hair floating free, she had drifted slowly, slowly toward the bottom of the pool. If she had drowned he would never have forgiven himself. Nor would he have been able to go on without her.

He had no idea who would want her dead. He trusted the island men and couldn't believe that any of them had tried to kill Annabel. But somebody had; somebody wanted her dead.

For a long time they stayed as they were, but at last he said, "We'd better get you out and into bed."

She seemed almost in a daze when he helped her out of the tub. He spoke to her softly, gently, and she stood meekly still while he dried her body with a soft white towel and wrapped her in a terry-cloth robe.

Back in the bedroom he gave her one of the pills Dr. Hunnicut had given him to help her relax. She took it without speaking and he helped her into bed.

"You'll sleep now," he said. "Ambrosia will stay here in the room with you and I'll be close by if you need anything."

Annabel looked up at him from the bed. "Where's Rob?" she asked. "Let Rob come in."

Luis hesitated, but he knew that sooner or later she had to know. "Rob's been hurt, Annabel. Meadowlark's taking care of him."

"Rob? Rob's been hurt?" She pushed herself up on her elbows. "What happened?"

"Someone struck him, probably the man who tried to drown you."

"But who?" The color that had come back to her face faded. "Why...why would anybody hurt Rob? Why would anybody want to kill me?"

He sat beside her on the bed and took her hand. "I don't know. Do you?"

She stared at him. "No!" she cried, and tried to stifle the sobs that rose in her throat. "I don't remember, Luis. I don't even remember who I am."

He saw the fear and the desperation in her eyes, and though he longed to comfort her, he knew that he couldn't, not yet. Whoever had tried to kill Annabel was still out there somewhere. He had to find him, because until he did, Annabel's life was in danger.

He picked up the phone and asked for Ambrosia. When she answered he said, "Please come to Mrs. Alarcon's room. I'll wait until you get here."

She came almost immediately. "I want you to stay with Annabel," he said. "No matter what happens, I don't want you to leave the room."

"I won't, Mr. Alarcon."

And to Annabel he said, "Rest now, Annabel. Ambrosia will be here with you and I'll be back later."

"Take care of Rob," she whispered.

"I will." He kissed her forehead. "It's going to be all right. We're going to find out who it is and stop him. I promise you."

He didn't want to leave. She looked so pale, so small. So frightened. But he had to, he had to find the man who had done this to his Annabel.

Ambrosia sat in one of the chairs by the doors leading out to the balcony. "You sleep now, missus," she said. "I be here."

Annabel closed her eyes. She could feel the pill beginning to take hold and tried very hard to give in to it. But every time she did, every time she reached that fine edge of sleep, she remembered the hands on her shoulders, the water closing over her head, and jerked awake with a cry.

And she remembered, too, that in the final moment when she knew she was going to die, she had called out to Alejandro. Alejandro had been dead for almost three hundred years, drowned as she was drowning. Yet she had called out to him. But why? Dear Lord, she had lost her memory; was she losing her mind, too?

When Ambrosia saw that she could not sleep, she moved her chair closer to the bed and began to sing a lullaby in a soft-as-velvet voice. Soothing words. Quieting words. Annabel reached for Ambrosia's hand. And slept at last.

Luis took three of his men with him and directed the others to search the rest of the island. Though San Sebastián was small in area, ten miles long and five miles wide, there were many places to look—jungle-like greenery, fertile lowlands, rugged, heavily wooded areas, sea caves and inlets.

And there wasn't only his island to worry about. Less than half a mile beyond San Sebastián lay three small, uninhabited islands. What if somebody was on one of them? Whoever it was could have come here in the dark of the night and slipped in to shore without notice. But who? In the name of God, who could it have been?

He posted four of the men along this exposed section of the beach and gave orders that they were to patrol it night and day. The men who had searched the other side of the island reported to him that they had seen no sign of anyone. He hadn't expected that they would, because that was the rocky part of San Sebastián. With its high cliff and the rocks below, he doubted anyone would have attempted an approach from there.

He decided not to post guards on the cliff because he could better use them in other parts of the island. It was far more likely that someone would approach by way of the beach, hide in the heavy foliage or in one of the underwater caves at low tide.

While his men continued searching, he went back to the house to check on Annabel. Ambrosia reported that she had had difficulty falling asleep, but that once she did, the pill had taken over and she had been sleeping most of the afternoon.

He went to see Rob. The dog was awake, his wounds had been bound, and Meadowlark reported that he'd eaten half a dish of his food.

By the time Luis returned to his men they had completed searching the whole island.

"There be no trace of nobody, boss," Samuel reported.

"I want men posted all around the house," Luis said. "Moses, I want you and Samuel inside the house. You take the day shift, Samuel will cover at night. I want everyone armed. Tell the men who don't have weapons to come up to the house. I'll issue guns and ammo."

"This be serious, boss?" Moses asked with a worried look.

"Yes, Moses, it's serious. Twice now somebody has tried to kill Mrs. Alarcon. I want the bastard caught."

Moses and Samuel and the men standing nearby nodded. "We catch him," one man said.

"When we do, he goin' to be shark bait," another one said.

Luis shook his head. "I want him alive. I want to know what he's after, why he tried to kill my wife."

His wife. The words, though they should not have, sounded strange to his ears. Annabel de Alarcon, a mystery woman. His woman.

She was up, sitting at the table near the open doors of her bedroom, when he went in.

"How's Rob?" she asked quickly. "Is he—"

"He's going to be all right," Luis said.

"Thank God."

"I'll bring him in later if you like."

"I like." A faint smile curved her lips, but faded when she asked, "It was the same man, wasn't it? I mean, whoever tried to drown me hurt Rob."

"Yes, probably."

"But you know everybody on the island. Why would any of them want to kill me?"

"It wasn't my island people, Annabel. It was somebody else." She started to say something then, but before she could, he turned to Ambrosia and said, "I'll be here with Mrs. Alarcon now, Ambrosia. Thank you for staying with her, Ambrosia."

"No need to thank me, Mr. Alarcon." She patted Annabel's hand. "You want anything, you be calling me. Yes?"

"Yes, Ambrosia. And thank you."

When they were alone Luis took the chair across from Annabel. "I know how difficult this is for you," he said. "I know how frightened you are. But you're safe now. I've posted guards on the beach and around the house and I have men inside. Believe me, Annabel, nobody is going to get close to you again.''

"But, why..." She shook her head. "I don't understand it, Luis. Why would somebody want to kill me?"

"I don't know, Annabel." He took her hand. "But maybe you do."

"Me, but I—"

"Somewhere back in your memory you know. Something terrible happened to you on the boat, something so terrible you don't want to remember."

"But I do want to remember," she insisted. "The boat exploded. There was gasoline vapor in the engine and it blew up. I had a concussion... that's why I can't remember."

Luis shook his head. "I think it's something else. I think the memory of whatever it was that happened on the boat that day traumatized you so badly you've blocked it out." He tightened his hand around hers. "But it's there and you've got to find it. You've got to try to remember."

"I want to," she said. "I'm trying to. But I can't. I can't."

She pulled her hand away and, standing, went out the open doors onto her balcony. Luis followed her. He knew she was upset, that she didn't want to talk about it, but she had to. Her life might depend on it.

"You read the story in the *Herald,*" he said. "You know what the authorities think happened that day." He stood behind her and rested his hands on her shoulders. "Was there something else, Annabel? Something you dreamed that was different from the story in the paper?"

"Yes, but... but that was only a dream."

"Tell me."

"Shots," she whispered. "There were shots."

"What?" He turned her so that she faced him. "What did you say?"

"In my dreams there were shots. Popping noises. Like firecrackers or a car backfiring."

"Go on. What else?"

"I...I don't know."

He tightened his grip on her shoulders. "Think!" he ordered. "What else?"

She swayed, but he held her. "What else?" he insisted.

"I remembered...when I saw their pictures, it was as though I could see them...Louise and Albert. And Mark. We were sitting in the bow of the boat. There was music from down below in the cabin. Fats Waller playing 'Muskrat Ramble.' We were laughing and then it...it..."

She shook her head as though unable to go on; tears were streaming down her face.

"Tell me," Luis insisted. "Tell me, Annabel."

"It happened. The shots. Crack! Crack! Crack! And then—and then they screamed. They all screamed...."

She sagged in his arms. He picked her up and carried her back into the bedroom, where he laid her on the chaise. She was as pale as death, trembling uncontrollably. He knew he'd been a brute to question her this way, but he'd had to. If what Annabel remembered was real, then somebody on the boat had killed the Croydens and Zachary Flynn. Only Annabel had somehow managed to escape.

"Louise and Albert and Mark were sitting in the bow," he said in a low voice. "Were you with them?"

"Yes. I . . . I think I was sitting between Louise and Mark. Albert was standing, telling a joke. He . . ."

"Go on," he said gently. "Where was Zachary Flynn?"

She looked puzzled. "I . . . I suppose he was handling the boat."

"You don't remember seeing him?"

She shook her head. "It's strange, but no. I remember someone, a man, but I don't remember who it was."

"There wasn't anybody else on board? Flynn didn't have somebody helping him?"

"I . . . I don't think so."

"Do you have any recollection of how you got off the boat and into the rubber raft?"

"No. I . . . I'm sorry."

"It's all right. You've done very well remembering."

"Remembering?" Annabel shook her head. "What if it's not a memory, Luis? What if, after all, everything is only a dream?"

"I don't think it is. I think your subconscious is trying to tell you what happened." He let go of her hand. "We'll work it out, Annabel. I'll help you remember."

He stood and, changing the subject, said, "Do you want to have dinner on your balcony or on the terrace?" He smiled. "Either way we'll eat together."

"Here," she said. "On the balcony."

"In half an hour? I'd like to clean up first." He started toward the door, then stopped. "From now on there'll be no separate bedrooms. I'm going to sleep in here with you because I want to be able to reach out my hand and know that you're safe."

"And I don't have anything to say about it?" she asked, getting angry.

He was glad for the anger, glad that two bright spots had appeared in her cheeks.

"No," he said. "You really don't. But as far as our making love, yes, you have everything to say about that. Whether we do or not will be your decision. That's my promise and I'll keep it." He grinned. "I'll even wear my robe."

She frowned at the closed door when he left. Robe indeed. What she needed was a wall of Jericho kind of separation like the one Clark Gable and Claudette Colbert used in *It Happened One Night.*

It Happened One Night. How strange that she could remember a movie that had been made more than fifty years ago but she couldn't remember her own name.

"Loco," she said aloud, wondering how she knew that meant crazy. Wondering if she was.

They had dinner together on the balcony of her room and afterward, while Luis sipped a brandy and she had another cup of tea, they watched the moon come up over the water.

"Ambrosia sang to me today," Annabel said. "A song about palm trees blowing in the breeze and the moon shining overhead."

He smiled. "Ambrosia has been crazy about you since the first day I brought you to the island almost eight years ago. She lost a daughter who would have been about your age when you first came here and I think she transferred all of her maternal feelings to you."

He took a sip of his drink and looked out at the fading night. "You were so young, Annabel, so dif-

ferent from other young women your age, more like
the young Spanish women I'd known when I was
growing up in Spain. There, a young woman of a good
family is carefully guarded until the day of her wedding. Today in America it isn't like that. I don't know
if that's good or bad, but I knew that when I married
I did not want my wife to have experienced other lovers."

"But you had, of course," she said with a lift of her
eyebrow.

"Of course. But it's different with a man."

She gave what sounded like an unladylike snort, but
before she could say anything he went on. "There was
an innocence about you that enchanted me, Annabel.
I knew from the first moment I saw you that I would
make you mine."

"Where?" she asked. "I mean, where did we
meet?"

"I told you. We met at a Mardi Gras ball in New
Orleans. You were wearing a long, pale blue dress.
Someone introduced us and I asked you to dance. We
danced until your date cut in. I let him have you for a
minute, then I cut in again." He laughed. "I cut in on
every man who asked you to dance that night, and
there were a lot of them.

"I called you the next day," he went on. "Actually, I called you every day for two weeks before you
said you'd go out with me. And when you went back
to Miami I followed you there. We were married two
months from the night we met."

"That was awfully fast."

"Yes, it was. But I knew, I knew right away that
you were the girl for me."

"Woman," she said. "I was a woman."

"A very young one."

That disquieted her, but she wasn't sure why. She wasn't even sure if the things he said about their meeting and marriage were true.

"You said before that we were married in Miami. Was that where I was living?"

"Yes."

"But what was I doing in New Orleans?"

"You were there to visit friends."

"Did you meet them?"

"It was eight years ago, Annabel. I really don't remember."

There were so many questions, questions without answers. But she was tired, still suffering from the terror and reaction of this early morning. For a little while she'd been able to forget, but now that it was bedtime, everything came rushing back. And after all, she was glad Luis had insisted on staying with her.

She went in to change into a nightgown, a *long* nightgown, while he went to the room he'd been using. She was in bed by the time he returned and got into bed with her. "Are you ready to sleep or would you like to read for a little while?"

"I'm ready to sleep."

"Well then." He snapped the light off. "Good night, Annabel. Sleep well."

"You, too." She lay on her back and watched the shadowed motion of the overhead fan turn slowly around. She didn't move when Luis reached to take her hand because it was comforting to have him close by. But if he tried to make love to her...

He didn't try. But when at last she turned onto her side, away from him, he curled his body around hers.

"Sleep," he said. "Go to sleep, Annabel. I'm here, *querida*. Nothing will harm you now."

She sighed, and in a little while her breathing evened and she slept. But it was a long time that night before Luis did.

Her bottom snugged tight against him, and though at first he felt a quick surge of desire, he managed to quell it. Annabel needed him, that's what was important now. It made him feel protective, filled with a tenderness and caring stronger than any other emotion. She made a small sound, her muscles quivered and he knew she was dreaming.

"Sh," he whispered. "It's all right, *mi niña*, my girl. I'm here. I'm here."

He patted her bottom as though she were a child, and when at last she grew quiet, he kissed the back of her neck. And held her all through the darkness of the night.

Chapter 12

The next few days were relatively peaceful. Rob recovered, and the next morning when he was able to get along on his own, he scratched on Annabel's door. He was admitted by a sleepy and disgruntled Luis and an overjoyed Annabel, who—"Just this once," she said—allowed Rob up on the bed.

She seemed to have recovered from the latest attempt on her life, but when, two days later, Luis suggested a swim, she looked so alarmed that he didn't press it. She'd had two close calls with water and, for the moment at least, she wanted no part of it.

She took long walks every day, usually with Luis, but if he was busy, Samuel or Moses went with her. And Rob, of course. The dog rarely let her out of his sight, except at night, when Luis put his foot down. Rob could sleep outside Annabel's door, but Luis was damned if he was going to share her bed with the black Lab.

The four men who patrolled the beach reported they hadn't seen anything, nor had they noticed any activity from the islands that faced San Sebastián. But Luis knew that whoever had made the second attempt on Annabel's life was out there on one of those islands or hiding somewhere right here on San Sebastián. Until they caught him, Luis had no intention of letting down his guard.

He continued to share Annabel's bed, but though it cost him, he made no attempt to make love to her.

As for Annabel, she told him she was quite all right now and perfectly able to sleep alone, but in fact she had become accustomed to his sleeping with her. It was very comforting to know he was there and that she had only to reach out her hand to touch him. Sometimes, when he turned away from her in his sleep, she leaned her face against his back because she liked the feel of his skin against her cheek, liked to breathe in the good male smell of him.

There were times when she awoke in the morning with her head in that wonderful hollow between his shoulder and his chest. And though she always moved quickly away, she sometimes felt an urgent longing to be closer.

And finally, one early morning when the first faint light of dawn crept into the room, when the air smelled sweet with the scent of gardenia and island jasmine, she did snuggle closer. Sure that he was still asleep, she could not resist the impulse to feather kisses over his shoulder and make little cat licks against his skin.

"*Madre de Dios,*" he whispered. "How much do you think I can stand?"

"I didn't know you were awake."

Awake and ready. My God, so ready. He tried not to move, tried to think about something, anything except the terrible urgency of his body. Soccer. Think about soccer. The next World Cup. It didn't help. He was rigid as a goalpost, panting like a puppy.

She touched him, felt a thrill of excitement, a sudden heating of her body, and said, "Oh my."

Which Luis felt was pretty close to being the understatement of the year. "Listen," he said, his voice made hoarse by all that he was trying to control, "if you don't want to wind up flat on your back in thirty seconds, you'd better stop that."

"What?" She began to stroke him. "This?"

"Annabel..." He groaned. "*Por Dios,* Annabel, you've got to stop."

Half-ashamed because she liked touching him like this, she whispered, "Don't you like it?"

"Like it!" He closed his hand over hers. "You know what you're doing, don't you?"

"Oh, yes," she said, "I know."

He kissed her then, kissed her with all the longing and the passion he'd kept in check these last few nights. She answered his kiss and their mouths clung, searching, exploring, and all the while she stroked him, stroked him until he knew he could no longer bear it.

He rolled her beneath him then, and with his mouth still on hers, he entered her. And moaned with sheer joy when her softness closed around him. And when she said, "Oh, yes. Like that, yes," he thought he would die with the pleasure of it.

She lifted her body to his in total abandon, giving all that she had to give. She held his face between her hands and kissed his mouth. She tasted his lips, licked the skin of his shoulder, and whispered her pleasure into his ear.

She held him with her arms and with her legs, and when he cupped her bottom to bring her closer, when his strokes deepened and his movements quickened, she went a little wild, reaching, reaching for that final incredible moment. And when it happened for her, when she cried her cry against his lips, he, too, went a little wild.

He crushed her to him, holding her close, frantic because he didn't want it to end. He wanted her to keep him close like this, to feel the clench of her muscles holding him, the small quivers that shook her body and told him what this was doing to her.

He kissed her mouth and told her in Spanish what he could not tell her in English. And when with a great cry it ended for him, he raised himself over her and cried, *"Anna! Mi querida amorcita, mi preciosa. No voy a permitirte que salgas de mi lado nuevamente."*

She barely heard the words, didn't think she understood them. Nor did she understand why she wept. She only knew that it was heaven to be close to him like this. And that she loved him.

When at last he made as though to draw away, she said, "No, Luis, don't leave me. Not yet."

She kissed the side of his face. He felt her tears and licked them away, then held her close with arms made strong with love.

They drowsed awhile, and though he said, "I'm too heavy for you," she would not let him go.

In a little while he felt himself grow again, and when he began to move against her, she said, "Oh, yes. That's nice, Luis. So nice."

In that half state between waking and sleeping they clung to each other while he moved slowly, deeply inside her. He kissed her mouth and the side of her face. And thought of all the things he wanted to say, but could not. And in the moment of release it was he who felt hot tears sting his eyes.

Later, when he left her to go to his room to shower and shave, he faced the realization that he had to tell her the truth about who she was and why he had brought her here. For if he did not, if she regained her memory before he told her, he would lose her forever. He couldn't bear that. Not again.

Ambrosia filled the tub with hot, scented water. Annabel selected a tape of Spanish music and stepped into the water to the music of "Malagueña."

With a murmured "Mmm," she lay back and closed her eyes. And knew she had never felt quite so content, quite so fulfilled. Her body felt light, her mind dreamlike, floating.

That's what it had been like when they made love the second time, when, half-asleep, their bodies still joined, they had moved together to that final moment. She hadn't known making love could be that way.

The music of "Granada" filled the misty room. *Granada, tiera sonada por me,* land of dreams...

Had she been there with Luis? Had they made love under the Spanish moon and listened to the music of Spanish guitars? Had she loved him very much?

A smile curved Annabel's lips. Perhaps, after all, there was something to be said for losing your memory. Now everything she saw, everything she did, was new to her. Like making love to Luis. The first time they did it had been like the very first time for her.

Even now there was joy in discovery as their bodies became accustomed to each other. Love was a mystery that was only now beginning to unravel. How exciting it was, starting life all over again.

From now on, everything she saw and everything she did would be new to her, for she was being given a second chance at life. There would be new things to see and to experience. She and Luis would go to Spain and she would be seeing it as though for the first time.

She sank down to her chin in the water and blew soap bubbles off her fingers. And smiled, smiled because she had been given a second chance to fall in love with Luis all over again.

She remembered the words he had spoken in Spanish, words he whispered in the throes of his passion. "My little love, my precious one. *No voy a permitirte que salgas de mi lado... neuvamente.* Again. I will not let you leave me again."

Again?

Her eyes went wide with shock. Had she misunderstood the Spanish words? She didn't think so. Somewhere in the back of her mind, in that part of her brain that remembered, she knew Spanish well enough to have understood.

He'd said "again." Had he meant he didn't want her to make any more trips without him? Like the trip she'd made to Miami to visit friends? Or had he meant something else? She didn't understand.

The music of "Ojos Verdes" filled the room. Green Eyes. "Serenos"...serene eyes. But Luis's eyes weren't serene. Never serene, but always filled with questions, with shadowed mystery.

Puzzled and oddly disturbed, Annabel left the tub. She dressed in a pair of white shorts, an off-the-shoulder yellow blouse and white sandals, then brushed her hair back off her face and braided it.

She was ready by the time Luis knocked and said, "Ready for breakfast, *querida?*"

She didn't say anything, didn't question him until they finished breakfast. Then she said, "This morning when we . . ." Color crept into her cheeks.

"When we what?" he teased.

"You know."

He reached across the table and took her hand. "When we made love?" He kissed her fingertips. "Such wonderful love, my Annabel."

She looked into his eyes, caught for a moment by something she had not seen there before. Unable to look away, she forced herself to take a deep breath and say, "Yes, Luis, when we made love. You said . . . you murmured something in Spanish. You said you would not let me go again." She drew her hand away. "You said 'again,' Luis. What did you mean?"

Tell her! a voice inside his head screamed. Tell her now! But he couldn't. Not yet. Instead, not quite meeting her eyes, he said, "You liked to go to Miami. To shop and visit friends. I meant I didn't want you to leave me like that again."

And because he wasn't sure she believed him, he said, "Wherever we go now, Annabel, we'll go together. Back to Spain, to places there you've never been, to Segovia, Granada."

"Tiera sonada por mi," she murmured.

He looked at her, startled. If she remembered Spanish she would remember other things. He had to tell her. And he would. Soon. Another day, another night.

He forced himself to smile and, rising, took her hand and brought her up beside him. "We'll go many places together," he said. "When we find the *Cantamar* and when we salvage her we'll go back to Spain. And Morocco. You'll love Morocco, Annabel. There are wonderful things to do there, colorful, exotic sights to see.

"There are places that haven't changed in hundreds of years. The souks, the bazaars where you can find everything you've ever dreamed of buying."

He touched her cheek. "I'll buy you a robe and a gossamer veil. I'll pretend you're a slave girl I bought at auction for a king's ransom. I'll make you dance for me, and when the dance has ended, I'll take away the robe and the veil. I'll perfume your body with scented oils from the East and rub henna on your breasts."

His eyes grew dark with passion, and in a voice made rough with the fire that burned in his belly, he said, "I'll fasten golden earrings in your ears and a slave bracelet around your ankle."

He went on, telling her all the things he would do to her, for her. She was mesmerized, caught up in his erotic dream, trapped by the intensity of his gaze, the throaty, impassioned tone of his voice. She was trembling, heated. Weak with sudden desire.

"I'll make love to you in a thousand and one ways," he whispered. "I'll fill my nostrils with your scent, my mouth with your taste. And when it's over, you will be my Anna again."

Again. A shiver ran through her, but before she could speak, he swept her up into his arms and pressed his lips to hers. He kissed her with passion and with need. She felt the frantic beating of his heart and gasped when he started across the terrace with her.

"Luis. Wait. "What are you...?" She caught a glimpse of Meadowlark's startled face, heard a smothered chuckle, and then she was swept away, her senses reeling. His captive.

Across the terrace into the dining room, up the stairs, down the hall, past her room to his. Inside he kicked the door shut, and then she was on the bed and he was over her, pulling down her shorts, his shorts.

"Luis," she tried to say. "Luis..."

He took her words, he took her breath. He was over her, in her before she had a chance to protest. If she had wanted to protest.

The loving was hot and wild and so fierce it frightened her. He held her so tightly she couldn't have gotten away if she had wanted to. But she didn't want to. She clung to him, gasping with pleasure, a little afraid of him and of what was happening to her. But loving it. Oh yes, loving it.

Almost as quickly as it started it ended, ended like a million skyrockets going off, red and yellow and blue and purple and green, all merging into a rainbow of light that dazzled and weakened.

He cried out, cried her name, "Annabel!" and collapsed over her, his body shaking with all that he experienced.

She felt the frantic beat of his heart against her breast and was suddenly overwhelmed with tenderness that a man so strong could become so quickly vulnerable. For now, in this moment, with her arms around him, Luis became hers. Her man. To have and to hold and, yes, to love.

They stayed in his room all that day. They made love in the shower and in the Jacuzzi on his private, screened-off balcony. On the floor of the bathroom and in his bed.

He kissed all the secret places of her body and brought her to a release she hadn't thought possible.

Once he urged her up over him and, giving her full rein, let her set the pace while he caressed her breasts. He looked at her with eyes hooded with passion, and when, on the edge of desire, she closed her eyes, he said, "No, open your eyes, Annabel. Look at me when it happens for you."

And when it did, he said, "Oh, love. Oh, love."

He was insatiable, unable to get enough of her. Or her of him. They loved and rested and loved again, and when at twilight they ventured out onto his balcony and stood looking out at the sea, he said, "This is a small madness, isn't it?"

Annabel smiled and touched his face. "Perhaps, Luis. But a good madness, one I hope we'll always have."

He kissed her, tenderly and without passion, and because he did not want her to know all that he was feeling, he smiled and said, "But you'll be walking funny when you're ninety. I wonder what our grandchildren will have to say about that."

"They'll be green with envy." She laughed, but when the laughter died, the thought struck her that though she and Luis had been married for eight years, they hadn't had children. She wondered about that. Hadn't he wanted children? Hadn't she?

"Luis," she started to say, "why didn't we—"

"I'm starved," he broke in. "On the verge of collapse. A man can't do what I've done all day without sustenance." He rested his hands on her shoulders and gave her a gentle shake. "You keep doing what you're doing, woman, and you're going to make an old man out of me."

"Too bad." She nipped his earlobe. "Because I plan to keep right on doing what I'm doing."

His grip on her shoulders tightened and his eyes took on a smoldering look that she knew was a presage of rising passion. With a laugh she stepped away from him. "Food," she said. "You need food."

He laughed, too, and arm in arm they went out to the terrace.

They ate a prodigious amount of food, big bowls of conch chowder, broiled crawfish, peas and rice and steak, blood-rare for him, medium for her. For dessert, though Annabel said she couldn't possibly eat another bite, there was guava pie served with rum sauce.

"I can't move," she said when she finished. And, stifling a yawn, added, "I feel as if I could sleep for a week."

"With me?"

"Of course," she said softly. "Always with you."

It got to him. Somehow those three words hit him right in the solar plexus. Annabel had decided to trust him and he knew, deep in his soul he knew, he wasn't worthy of that trust.

Perhaps all that he was feeling showed on his face, because she said, "What is it, Luis?"

"Nothing." He made himself smile. "How about a walk?"

"On the beach," she said. "We'll walk barefoot in the sand and hold hands in the moonlight."

"All right. We'll…" No, he thought, they couldn't walk on the beach because someone, whoever it was who had tried to drown Annabel, might still be out there, hiding, waiting.

Every inch of the island had been searched. Now he wondered if indeed it had been an intruder, if perhaps one of the island people, someone he thought he knew and trusted, had been behind the two attempts on Annabel's life.

One of the women, he couldn't remember if it was Ambrosia or Meadowlark or one of the women who occasionally helped out, had a brother who'd caused trouble on the island before. Something to do with a woman. Had the man assaulted a woman? He couldn't remember, but tomorrow he'd find out.

In a way it made more sense that it would be somebody like that rather than an outsider. He had no enemies that he knew of, nor could he conceive of Annabel having enemies. It didn't make sense, but until the culprit had been caught, he would be careful.

"We won't go far," he told her. Then, just to be sure that nothing happened, he told her that he would be right back and went into his room to take his gun from his dresser drawer.

It wasn't there. He frowned, told himself that maybe he'd put it in another drawer by mistake. He searched all his drawers, he looked on all the closet shelves. The gun wasn't there. What in the hell had happened to it? How could anybody have gotten in here without his knowing it? Could it have been one of the servants?

He didn't want to alarm Annabel, and if he mentioned the missing gun she would be alarmed. So when he went back to her, he said, "Let's put that walk off until tomorrow. I guess I'm a little beat." And with a forced grin he added, "You wore me out today, lady. How about a brandy in the library while we watch a video?"

"Fine with me. What have you got?"

"*Dr. Zhivago?*"

"It always makes me cry."

"*Casablanca?*"

"That makes me cry, too, but I like it. Maybe this time Bergman will decide to stay with Bogart."

They sat on the leather sofa in front of the television set and sipped their brandy. Sure enough, Annabel cried when Bogie said, "Here's lookin' at you, kid," and sent Ingrid flying off into the wild blue yonder with Paul Henreid.

He put *Tootsie* on, but halfway through it Annabel fell asleep. He turned the TV off and picked her up and carried her to her room. Rob was waiting outside her door. Luis said, "Sorry, fella, not tonight."

He put Annabel on the bed and undressed her. "Sleepy," she murmured.

"I know you are, sweetheart." He got into bed beside her and took her in his arms.

She turned her face into his shoulder. "But if you want to, we could...could..." She began a purrlike snore.

He chuckled and tightened his arms around her. "In the morning," he said.

Then he, too, went to sleep. And thought of how it would be in the morning.

The next few days were the happiest Annabel ever remembered. Her memory might be short, but surely nothing she had experienced before could possibly have made her as happy as she was now.

In the early days, when Luis first brought her by boat from Nassau to San Sebastián, he had seemed different, sometimes distant, often cold. But he wasn't cold now. He was everything she might have dreamed a man could be, tender and loving and thoughtful. And not just in bed. By every gesture, every word, he showed how much he cared. And though he had not said the words "I love you," she was sure that he did.

Just as she was sure she loved him. And she would tell him. Soon she would tell him.

He questioned Moses and Samuel about the islander before he approached Ambrosia and Meadowlark.

"That be Ambrosia's cousin, Henry John," Samuel said. "He be an innocent. Not..." He made a circular motion on the side of his head. "Not like a crazy person, Mr. Alarcon. More like a child. Never hear tell of him doin' anything bad."

Maybe not, Luis thought, but he had to make sure, so he approached Ambrosia and asked her about Henry John.

"He be dead goin' on three months," she said. "Barracuda got him when he was net fishin'. Liked to have bit his leg in half. My sister did all she could, but he got an infection and died real quick."

"I'm sorry," Luis said, and meant it.

Because if it wasn't poor Henry John, then whoever it was who wanted Annabel dead was still here on his island.

That scared the hell out of him.

Chapter 13

Luis doubled the guards on the beach and ordered that every inch of San Sebastián be searched again. Armed with an automatic pistol, he scouted out all the places where a man or men might hide. The only place he didn't search was the sea caves below the cliff that were flooded because of the high tide.

"Nobody be hiding in there," said Samuel, who was with him. "But if they were, they be drowned and washed out to sea by now."

"You're probably right." Still, Luis hesitated. It was true that when the tide was in, the sea caves were impossible. But when the tides were out? Yes, then, at least for a few hours, the caves would be the perfect place to hide. He couldn't search now, but he would come back at low tide and have a look.

"Let's climb up and check the area around the cliff next," he told Samuel. "There are a lot of trees up there, dense undergrowth, places where a man might hide."

But they found nothing, only a few cigarette butts left behind by his men who had searched here.

He went to stand at the edge of the cliff and looked down at the beach and out beyond to the sea. There were no ships on the horizon, no sailboats or cruisers. Only the endless sea, as deep and clear a blue as the sky. Yet someone had come here to his island. Where was he? Who was he?

He looked toward the three small islands and decided that tomorrow he would search there. Meantime he would double the guard both inside and outside the house. He had to find the man who wanted Annabel dead. He had to.

That evening when the sun was low over the water, when the sky turned the color of flamingo feathers and the sea was streaked with gold, Annabel and Luis sat together on the terrace sipping champagne from crystal tulip glasses.

She had taken special care of her appearance this evening. Instead of her usual braid she had washed her hair, dried it in the sun on her balcony, then brushed it so that it lay softly about her shoulders. She'd put on a long cotton dress in shades of pale turquoise and blue, perfumed her skin, and added just enough makeup to make her eyes look, she hoped, exotic and mysterious. She wanted tonight to be special.

Luis stood when she came out onto the terrace. For a moment he didn't say anything, but when he came toward her, he took her hands and drew her closer.

"You look very beautiful," he said. "It's as if you're a part of all this, of the sea and the sky and the sunset.'' He brought her hands to his lips and kissed them, and led her to the chair next to his so they could watch the sunset together.

They sipped their champagne, not speaking, until in a burst of glory the sun slipped into the sea.

It was then Annabel said, ''I have something to tell you.''

Luis put his glass down, suddenly apprehensive. He hoped his voice was calm when he asked, ''What is it?''

''It's about us, Luis. About my not remembering.''

''Someday you will.''

''I hope so.'' She took a sip of the champagne, then set the glass down. ''I know that because I'm your wife and that we've been married for almost eight years, I must have loved you.'' She touched his hand. ''But I have no memory of that love, Luis.''

''I know.'' He held his breath, afraid to move, afraid to breathe, caught by the intensity of her gaze, the open honesty in her eyes.

''It's very hard,'' she went on. ''Not remembering my life before I awoke in the hospital in Nassau is very hard. But the hardest part is not remembering you. I want so much to remember everything—the day we met, our first dance, the first time we kissed. But I don't, Luis. I don't remember anything at all about our life together and that makes me sad.''

''We're together now.'' His voice choked with all he was feeling. ''That's all that matters, Annabel.''

''Is it?'' A look of loss and of sadness crossed her face, then she smiled and the look faded. ''But that's not what I want to tell you. I want to tell you that even though I don't remember—our marriage or our love— I ... I've fallen in love with you all over again.''

"Annabel. *Querida...*" He wanted to say more, tried to say more, but he was too filled with emotion to utter a word.

"Isn't it strange," she went on, "falling in love with one's own husband, I mean. It's like starting all over again with everything new and fresh and wonderful." She looked at him with eyes that were filled with love. "And it is wonderful," she said softly. "Loving you, Luis. Making love with you. I hope and pray I'll get my memory back someday, but if I don't, I think now that I'll be able to live with the new todays we have, with all of the days yet to come."

She touched his face. "I love you, Luis. I know now that I must have always loved you."

The last rays of reflected sun touched her face like the soft strokes of color on canvas; her eyes were luminous and filled with love.

He stood and brought her up into his arms. Unable to speak, he held her, his face against the cloud of her hair, and thought of all the things he should tell her now, that he had to tell her. And he would, he told himself, but not yet. And so he only said, "I loved you from the first moment I saw you. I loved you then, I love you now."

Darkness crept in over the sea while they stood there, holding each other, loving each other. And still he did not tell her the dark secret that lay buried in his heart.

There followed then a time of bliss, a time for loving and a time of peace. She was aware of the guards both in the house and out-of-doors, but she was no longer afraid. Luis was her husband. He loved her, he would take care of her.

But a few days later, perhaps because she had let down her guard, the nightmares returned. She would awaken weak with fear, too frightened to go back to sleep. And though Luis was with her to calm her fears and gentle her back to sleep, the nightmares left her hollow-eyed and nervous.

When at last they began to fade, they were replaced by dreams that were in their own way more disturbing than the nightmares because they were of Luis. Were they only dreams, she asked herself each morning when she awoke, or was she beginning to remember?

Though she had told Luis about her nightmares, she did not tell him of her dreams. Instead she said, "I'm not sleeping well, Luis. Do you think it would be all right if I took one of Dr. Hunnicut's sleeping pills?"

He shook his head and with a smile said, "Let's try one of Dr. Alarcon's injections first."

"An injection? I don't..." She grinned. "Oh," she said. "Yes, perhaps that would help."

They made love then, and afterward, exhausted and sure that tonight she would not dream, she fell asleep in his arms.

But the dreams came, in disjointed flashes, like the previews of coming attractions.

"Wear the black dress."

"But—"

"The blue is too revealing. It makes you look cheap."

"Cheap? But I—"

"The black. Don't argue. I know what's best for you. Put it on."

"Red wine with boeuf bourguignonne.*"*

"I—I really prefer white wine."

"Red," he said to the waiter. *"A Bordeaux, I think."*

"Did you read the Gabriel García Márquez?"
"No, I— It . . . it's in Spanish and my . . . my Spanish isn't that good."
"It would be if you applied yourself."

Books. Stacks of books, so many books, piling up all around her, closing her in, surrounding her. And music, deafened by the soaring sounds of a hundred violins, by the blast of horns and the clash of cymbals, sopranos and tenors singing in a language she didn't understand. Flamenco guitars and French horns. "Listen," he said. *"Listen and try to learn."*

Wearing party gowns she didn't like to parties she didn't want to go to. "Try the oysters," he said.
"I don't like oysters."

A painful sigh. He put one on his fork and handed it to her. It was slippery and wet. She took it and made a face.

"Dios," he said. *"Will you ever learn?"*

Tears and recriminations.
Finally, "I'm going to leave you."
"I'll never let you go."
"I will! I will!"
"You're behaving like a child."

A child . . .
She was crying when she awoke, and she told herself it was only a dream, not a memory. For how could it have been a memory? Luis wasn't like that. He was thoughtful and loving, he'd never tell her how to dress or how to behave. It was only a dream.

There were other dream-memories. Her wedding day. She wore a simple white dress and a wreath of daisies in her hair.

"Do you, Luis . . . ?"

"Do you, Annabel . . . ?"

"I now pronounce you . . ."

A proper kiss. The murmured words, "You're mine now."

Her wedding night. A nightgown with a high neck and long sleeves. Shyness. Fear of the unknown. His impatience.

Dreams. Only dreams?

One morning she asked, "What kind of a dress did I wear for our wedding?"

"White, I think." He put down the copy of the *Miami Herald* that had come in that morning on the supply boat and with a smile added, "And you had daisies in your hair. You looked like a wood sprite and far too young to be married."

Daisies in her hair.

"I was twenty-one."

"A young twenty-one. Some women are mature at eighteen. You weren't."

"No," she said. "I was very frightened, very unsure of myself."

He looked at her, startled, and she said, "I . . . I've been having these dreams, Luis. About before, when we were first married."

He held his breath and in a careful voice said, "Perhaps you're starting to remember."

"Perhaps."

"Well . . ." He cleared his throat. "That's good, isn't it?"

"Yes, of course."

And again that voice inside his head said, Tell her! Tell her now! For if she's starting to remember, if it all comes back to her before you tell her, she will never forgive you. And God help him, she had so much to forgive.

This was a second chance for him. Because of the accident, as terrible as it had been, Annabel had no recollection of the past. He had a God-given opportunity to make up for all the mistakes he had made in the past. And he would.

Annabel wasn't the girl she had been when they married. She was a woman with opinions, likes and dislikes of her own, and he would respect that, respect her enough to allow her to be her own woman.

In every way there was he would show how much he cared, how much he loved her. It was not often a man was given the opportunity to start over. It had been given to him, and this time, as God was his witness, he would be different.

He would be the man she deserved; the man he should have been eight years ago.

She dreamed again that night, and awoke in the morning restless and disturbed.

Luis left early. "I want to have a look at the sea caves before the tide comes in," he said.

She longed for a walk, needed fresh air to clear the cobwebs out of her mind. There were guards patrolling the area; surely it would be all right.

Almost two weeks had passed since whoever it was had tried to drown her. There'd been no other attempts on her life. She was tired of being cooped up in the house. She wanted to walk, climb a hill, maybe lie in the grass, look up at the clouds and try to remember. She didn't want Samuel or Moses along. Rob would be a silent companion as well as a guard.

She had breakfast on the balcony of her room, and a little after ten, when she knew that both Ambrosia and Meadowlark would be busy in the kitchen, she called Rob and together she and the black Lab slipped out a side door.

Instead of taking the path that went down to the beach, she headed for the trees that surrounded the back of the house and led up to the cliff. It would be a good walk, and when she reached the cliff she'd see a part of the island she hadn't seen before.

With Rob at her side, Annabel cut through the trees and the overgrowth of brush. It was wild and beautiful here. Poinciana trees bloomed in dense clusters of color, cacao pods hung from small evergreen bushes and passionflowers bloomed. There were banana trees and wild orchids, shrimp plants and orange trumpet vines.

Rob raced on ahead, chasing an errant butterfly, a squirrel or a bird, as happy to be roaming free as she was. She saw no guards and supposed they were down at the beach with Luis. That meant she'd have the whole morning to herself. Maybe in the quiet she'd be able to sort out all of the things that were bothering her.

The trees grew thicker when she started to climb. The brush and tangled vines made walking difficult. The air was hot and humid here in the shadows, with only patches of sun shining through the trees. She had an uneasy feeling that she shouldn't have ventured out alone, that perhaps, after all, she should have told

Ambrosia she was going to climb up to the cliff. It wouldn't have hurt to have had Moses with her.

No, she told herself, she was being foolish. She was perfectly all right, and besides, she wanted to be alone. Didn't she? Soon she would be out of the shadow of the trees, up where she could see the sea and there would be a cooling breeze.

Rob trotted along beside her, but suddenly he stopped, ears pricked up, tail pointing. She stopped, too. "What is it?" she whispered nervously. "What do you hear?"

There was a rustle of sound in the bushes ahead of them. She stepped closer to Rob just as a rabbit ran out of the bushes. It stopped as though startled, then darted back into the vegetation. Rob barked, and though Annabel called out, "Rob!" he ran into the bushes after the rabbit. She doubted that he would catch the small animal and had a hunch that, if he did, he'd simply chase it round and round until he tired of the game and came back to her.

But she wished he hadn't left her.

She continued climbing, and now that she was close to the top she could smell the sea, and that made her hurry her steps. She stopped once, thinking she heard something, then went on because it was probably just another animal. That's what she told herself, an animal, not a snake.

At last she stepped out of the tangle of vines and bushes into a clearing. The air was cooler here and she went forward, out to the very end of the land, onto the cliff overlooking the sea.

It was higher here than she had thought it would be. The waves below came thundering against the rocks in great, crashing blows, then swirled in a foam of whirlpool currents.

It was as beautiful as it was terrifying, and suddenly, for a reason she could not explain, she felt uneasy. She did not think she was afraid of heights, but in spite of the beauty of this place she wished she hadn't come.

She backed away from the edge of the cliff. Was there a rustling noise? A footfall? She said, "Rob?" and turned just as a man stepped out of the undergrowth of tangled vines and bushes.

"Well, well, Annabel. Here you are at last."

She stared at him. "You! But... but you're dead. You died in the explosion."

"Dead?" He smiled and shook his head. "Oh no, my dear. I'm quite alive."

He took a step toward her and she saw the gun in his hand.

Like the other gun, that other day. And suddenly she knew that this was Zachary Flynn and that he had killed her friends.

Mark first, because he was the strongest. Then the others.

As though it were being played in fast forward on a movie screen, she saw it all.

They were sitting in the bow. It had started to rain and Mark said, "We'd better get inside before it gets worse. Or maybe you're game for a swim, Annabel." And then he sang, in a bad imitation of Gene Kelly, "Swimming in the rain, just swimming in the rain... This is the happiest day of my life," he said. "If I died right now I'd die a happy man."

He saw Flynn and looked up. "Hi, Captain," he said. "What's up?"

"You get your wish," Flynn said.

"Is that a gun?" Mark looked startled. "What're you doing with a gun? Going to start shooting the fish instead of using a rod and reel?"

Flynn aimed the gun at Mark.

"What . . . ?" Mark began. "What . . . ?"

She saw a dart of flame, heard the crack, the whomp when the bullet hit Mark in the chest. He had a strange look on his face, like a little boy who'd been playing cowboys and Indians and had suddenly discovered the bullets were real.

He rose, arms outstretched, fists clenched, and staggered toward Flynn. "Run!" he croaked, turning slightly. "Ann—run . . ." The other bullet hit him and he fell facedown on the deck.

The rain came harder. There were puddles on the deck. Blood and water turning the puddles pink.

He shot Albert next. Then Louise. She didn't die right away. She lay screaming on the deck, blood matting her too blond hair. Flynn picked up the club he used to kill the big fish with and hit her until she stopped screaming.

"Now you, Miss Annabel," he said. "I've had my eye on you from the day I walked into Croyden's office at the marina. Thought you'd do me some good, in more ways than one, maybe. But you didn't. Didn't know or wouldn't tell. But we're close enough. With the charts and what we've found this trip, I'll be able to find her."

Find who? What was he talking about? Had he gone mad?

The rain came harder, blinding sheets of rain.

"Wish I had the time to take you below for a little while, but I don't. The fuses are set and the *Drum*'s about ready to blow." He looked at his watch.

She turned, got one foot up on the rail and jumped. She dived down at a crazy, twisted angle, and when she came up, a bullet pinged the water an inch from her head. She went under again. Down, down into the turquoise sea, trying to get away from the bullets that splattered the water, bullets that pinged close when she surfaced.

She dived down again and again, and when she came up, half-blinded by the rain, she saw that she was fifteen or twenty yards from the boat.

Suddenly, like a bomb going off, it blew, with a flash of fire, a great fireball and a terrible booming noise that reverberated across the water. Pieces of it shot up into the sky, wood and steel and bodies. . . .

It hadn't been a dream. It had happened. She remembered. God help her, she remembered it all.

"It would be better if you jumped," Zachary Flynn said.

She looked at him, still caught in the picture unfolding in her mind.

"You jumped before," he said. "From the boat that day. I thought you were dead. I thought I'd killed you, too. But then I saw in the paper that you'd been picked up by the coast guard and taken to Nassau. And that Luis had rushed to your side. How did that happen, Annabel? Why didn't you drown?"

"I . . . I don't know."

He moved closer and she edged back toward the cliff. Back toward the edge.

"You were in the dinghy when they found you, the dinghy I'd put over the side to make my escape in. It must have come loose and somehow you managed to find it. I had to take the smaller one." He smiled. "Much like the one I have hidden back in one of the sea caves. That's how I'll get out of here tonight, after I'm finished with you."

He took another step toward her.

Fear knotted her throat. "You'll never get away with this," she whispered.

"Won't I? I got away with killing the Croydens, didn't I? You were my only loose thread and now I'm going to take care of you. Tonight I'll slip away into the darkness and no one will ever know that I'm alive."

Another step. Closer. Closer.

She looked behind her, down, down to the terrible rush of water, down to the rocks.

"It's all over," he said.

"Oh, please," she whispered.

"Goodbye," he said.

Chapter 14

Luis stood ankle-deep in the water of the sea cave and shone his light up on the rock ledge above his head. He saw something shining up there and with a muttered "What in the hell . . ." he looked closer. And saw the dive tank. Dive tank!

He handed the light to Samuel, found a foothold in the rocks and heaved himself up for a better look. Alongside the tank there were a mask, flippers, a buoyancy vest, weight belt and compressor. He pulled the tank out and handed it down to Samuel. It was in good shape, not rusted. The flippers and other equipment looked almost new.

"Lord, Lord." Samuel rolled his eyes. "Somebody be in here, boss. Keepin' their stuff here. Hidin' when the tide be high, maybe even stayin' way back and breathin' with the tank."

Luis flashed the light around the walls of the cave.

There was another ledge. He climbed up. It held a de-flated rubber raft, candles, canned food, beef jerky, granola bars. A coil of rope. A box of bullets. *Por Dios!* Bullets!

This was where the man who had already made two attempts on Annabel's life had been hiding. He was here on the island. *His* island. With a growl of fury and a premonition of fear unlike anything he had ever experienced before, Luis jumped down and hurried out of the cave, where two of his men waited.

"Spread out," he cried. "The bastard we're after has been holing up here in the cave. I want two men on guard but out of sight. When he comes back, grab him. If you can't grab him, kill him."

To Samuel he said, "Get the men from the village. I want everybody—"

"Boss." Samuel's voice was low, barely above a whisper. He was looking up, his eyes round, scared. "Boss," he said. "Up there."

Luis looked up. And froze. He couldn't move, couldn't breathe. Annabel... Oh my God, Annabel was up there on the edge of the cliff. And a man, advancing on her, a man with a gun in his hand.

Dios! Ay Dios! He felt as if his heart were being torn from him, helpless because he was here and she was up there with a madman. He reached for his gun, aimed, ready to fire, and hesitated. What if he missed? God help him, what if he hit Annabel?

"*Dios. Dios, ayúdame.* God, oh God...help me."

He cried aloud, a cry that seemed to come from his very soul. "Annabel! Annabel!"

She turned and looked down, wavering on the edge.

It was too late, he couldn't save her. Annabel, his life, his love.

Luis! Too late. Too late. Nothing would save her now. Not Luis, not anyone. She whispered his name, she whispered a prayer. "Now I lay me... The Lord is my shepherd ... If I should die before I wake..."

This wasn't real. It couldn't be happening. She watched Flynn's finger tighten on the trigger and closed her eyes.

Suddenly there was a low growl, a rush of air. She opened her eyes and saw Rob, fangs bared, a dark and vengeful figure hurling straight for Zachary Flynn's throat.

Flynn, eyes wide with terror, mouth agape, backed to the edge of the cliff, hands up to try to fight off the big black dog.

Rob sprang. Sharp teeth fastened on the man's throat and hung on. Hung on as man and dog went over the edge. Flynn's arms windmilled out, flailing the air. And he screamed. Oh God, how he screamed.

Sickness rose in Annabel's throat. The ground tilted. She sank to her knees. No one could survive a fall like that to the rocks below. Not Zachary Flynn. Not Rob.

Shaking with reaction, sobs racking her body, she lay there on the stony ground at the edge of the cliff, sobbing as if her heart would break. As indeed it had.

Luis found her there. She had stopped crying and lay quite still. He knelt beside her and pulled her into his arms. "It's over," he said. "You're safe now."

She looked at him without answering.

"Annabel," he said. "*Querida,* it's over. The man who was after you is dead."

"Zachary Flynn."

"Yes, but how—"

"Rob?" she said. "Is Rob...?"

"He was a brave and wonderful dog, Annabel. He saved your life." He brushed the hair back from her face. "His back was broken. I had to put him down. I'm sorry."

He tightened his arms around her then and she said, in a voice as cold as ice, "Let me go."

Shock, he told himself. She's in shock.

She started to get up, and when he reached to help her, she said, "No," and pulled away from him.

"Annabel, what is it? What—"

Moses ran into the clearing, crying, "Little missus be all right?"

"Yes," Luis said, but he was looking at Annabel. "Yes," he called out, "she's all right."

Moses hurried forward. "That man be dead, missus. He don't be botherin' you no more. Imagine he be hiding down there in one of those caves. Mr. Luis found everything—a dive tank, food, even a rubber raft. Imagine that!"

"I'm glad it's over," she said. "I...I'd like to get back to the house now."

"Me 'n' Mr. Luis, we get you there. You rest some, you be feeling better in no time. I be mighty sorry about Rob. That dog be some kind of hero."

"Yes, I know. If it hadn't been for him..." And because she knew if she thought about Rob right now she wouldn't be able to stand it, Annabel turned away from the cliff and, with Moses on one side and Luis on the other, walked back to the clearing.

When they reached the house, Luis helped her into her bedroom. She lay on the chaise, silent and pale. He went into the bathroom and came out with a wash-cloth and a towel. He wiped her face and her hands and, when he finished, said, "Would you like some tea? A drink?"

"No, thank you." She looked at him. "I know," she said. "I remember."

"What . . . what do you mean?"

"I'm not your wife. We're not married."

"Annabel—"

"We haven't been for almost six years."

"I wanted to tell you. I was going to tell you."

"When? Before or after you made me love you again?"

"Annabel . . ." He gripped her arms. "Listen to me. You've got to listen to me."

"It was because of the *Cantamar,* wasn't it? You thought because I was on the *Distant Drum* with Zachary Flynn that maybe I knew where the *Cantamar* was. That's why you brought me back to San Sebastián."

He looked at her, and remembered the day six weeks ago when the news came over the shortwave that a pleasure craft had exploded in the Bahamas and that a man by the name of Zachary Flynn had been aboard. The only survivor, according to the report, had been a young woman who, because of a bad concussion, had no memory of who she was. They'd described her: approximate age, twenty-eight or -nine; height, five foot four; weight, about one-fifteen; blond hair, blue eyes. And he'd known, somehow he'd known it was Annabel.

He'd chartered a plane and flown to Nassau. He still remembered walking into her room at the hospital, standing over her bed, and the terrible effort to hold back his tears. Her head had been bandaged. There were bruises on her face and cuts on her arm. He'd felt, oh God, a love unlike anything he had ever known. In that moment he would willingly have given his life for her. He wanted to gather her in his arms, to tell her how much he loved her, and that always and forever he would take care of her.

Yes, later, the thought, the suspicion had come that if she had been on the boat with Zachary Flynn, she might know the location of the *Cantamar*. But in the days that followed, in the days when he fell in love with Annabel all over again, the suspicion faded. Annabel was here with him, and that's all that mattered.

He had to tell her that, tell her that all that mattered to him now was their love. But before he could, she said, "Finding the *Cantamar* means that much to you, doesn't it? So much that you'd pretend I was still your wife. You made love to me..." Her voice broke, and she couldn't go on.

"It wasn't that way," he said, desperate to have her believe him. "All right, maybe...maybe when I first heard about the *Drum* blowing up and that Flynn had been on board, yes, maybe I thought then that you might have been working with him. But when I saw you in the hospital, all that mattered was that you had been hurt. And that I loved you.

"I love you, Annabel," he said, his voice husky. "I never stopped loving you."

She turned her face away. "Please," she said, "Just . . . just leave me alone."

And he knew he had lost her.

Annabel stayed alone in her room the rest of that day. That night she locked the door connecting her room with Luis's. When he knocked and said, "We have to talk," she answered, "Not now."

He had lied to her—all this time, lying together in bed, making love. He'd lied when he brought her here to San Sebastián as his wife. But she wasn't his wife; she hadn't been for a long time.

Later that night, when the house became quiet and she heard no sound from the adjoining room, she went out onto her balcony and sat looking out at the sea. There, alone with the night, she let herself remember everything. She brought it all back, every bit of her life.

She remembered her parents, Emily and Richard Brandford, and the big white house on Oaklawn Street in Winston, Oregon, where she had grown up. She remembered the mulberry tree in the backyard, bird songs in springtime and the sound of the lawn mower under her bedroom window.

She remembered her first-grade teacher, Mrs. Vercamen. And friends: Shirley Lee Tacey, Meggie Dillon, Paula Detmer. She remembered high school and that in her sophomore year she had dated red-haired Eddie Loringer. She even remembered the first time they kissed, how nervous she'd been, how worried about noses and keeping her lips pressed tight together, because Dorothy Berlinger, her best friend who lived just down the block, had told her that all the boys wanted to put their tongue in your mouth, and that as far as Dorothy was concerned, that was really yucky.

She remembered her senior prom. George Berlinger, Dorothy's older brother, asked her to the prom before Eddie had had a chance to, so she'd had to go with him. She hadn't liked George all that much, and after the prom she'd had to hit him over the head with her purse to get away from him.

After high school she'd gone to Gonzaga University in Spokane on a partial scholarship. At the end of her first year there, her parents said they'd drive to Washington so she could take back all of her things. But they didn't make it to Gonzaga; they were killed in a three-car pileup coming into Spokane.

She remembered the first time she had gone into the big white house alone, and how she had wandered from room to room, as though searching for her parents. In their bedroom she stood for a long time looking at their wedding picture. They were smiling at each other, just the way they'd smiled at each other all through their marriage.

She sold the house in Winston, and when Dorothy, who was living in Miami and going to the U of M, suggested Annabel come to Florida, she packed her bags and headed south.

She and Dorothy moved into an apartment in the Art Deco part of South Beach—even if it was too far from the university—and traveled back and forth in the car Annabel had bought with part of the money from the sale of her parents' home.

The following year Dorothy met David Goldman, a New Orleans attorney, and when Mardi Gras came around, David invited both young women to come to New Orleans for a dance some of the city's elite put on every year.

That's where she met Luis.

He'd cut in on the man she'd been dancing with and swept her into his arms. He was nine years older than she was, smart, well traveled and sophisticated. She'd been impressed out of her twenty-one-year-old mind.

His name was Luis Miguel Alarcon, he told her. He had been born in Spain, educated at the University of Salamanca, and though he loved Spain, he preferred living in the Bahamas. He lived on an island, San Sebastián, and he was in New Orleans on business.

He insisted she sit beside him at dinner. He poured her wine and buttered her roll. When a crumb stuck to her lower lip he stroked it away with his thumb. And holding her with his eyes, he said, "As soon as you grow up, I'm going to marry you, Miss Annabel Brandford."

"I...I'm twenty-one," she'd stammered. Then blushed because that sounded as if she could hardly wait.

He took her back to David's parents' house that night. He walked her to the door and he kissed her.

Strange, she thought now, how strange that she would still remember that kiss. A man's kiss, not a boy's, and the arms that held her had been a man's arms. It thrilled her, it frightened her. As he did. Because he was older and foreign and experienced.

He asked if he could see her the following day. She'd said no, she had plans, because she was just a little bit afraid of him. He'd called anyway, called every day she was in New Orleans. Finally, the night before she left, she agreed to have dinner with him.

He took her to Antoine's, a restaurant more elegant than any she'd ever seen. He ordered in French— *les escargots à la Bordelaise.* She didn't know until after they were married that she'd eaten snails. *Fonds d'artichauts* and *chateaubriand pour deux.* Pink champagne before dinner, white wine with the escargots, red with the chateaubriand. And finally *café brûlot,* which, Luis had told her, was a New Orleans tradition and every bit as delicious as the less criminal forms of sin.

She was overwhelmed, out of her league, scared to death and giddy from the wine.

After dinner they listened to jazz at Preservation Hall. When they left, she thought he would take her back to the Goldman house, but instead he drove out to Lake Pontchartrain. They parked along the seawall and he said, "I want to see you again."

"But I'm going back to Miami tomorrow."

"Then I'll see you there." He put his arm around her shoulders to bring her closer, and when he kissed her, she didn't try to move away. She was filled with wine and warmth and feelings she had never experienced before.

He said, "Part your lips for me," and when she did, he touched his tongue to hers. It wasn't at all yucky, as Dorothy had told her it would be. It thrilled her, excited her.

He touched her breasts, but when she closed her hand over his wrist and said, "Don't," he stopped.

"I told you the first night we met that I was going to marry you, Annabel." He tilted her chin so that she looked into his eyes. "Make no mistake about it, I will." Then he'd kissed her again. And this time when he touched her breasts, she let him.

He came to Miami a few days after she went back. They dated every night for three weeks, and every one of those nights he asked her to marry him.

He bought her a wedding ring, a circlet of diamonds as bright as teardrops in the sun, and on a hot summer's day they were married in front of a judge at city hall.

They spent their wedding night at the Fontainebleu Hotel. It wasn't a happy experience. She was too nervous, he too impatient. She had expected skyrockets to go off, but not the pain. He had expected and had gotten a virgin, yet seemed disappointed that she was so inept.

The next day he took her to some of the finest shops in Miami Beach, but instead of letting her choose the clothes she liked, he selected everything for her.

"You look like a child half the time," he said. "You're a woman now, you need to look a bit more sophisticated."

Though she felt strange in some of the dresses she was sure were too old for her, she really didn't mind. She'd been on her own for the two years since her parents had died, and she liked being taken care of this way.

And she was in love, hopelessly, wonderfully in love. She wanted to please him, to be everything he wanted her to be. She told herself that if he seemed a little controlling it was because he loved her. He was Spanish, he had been brought up in a different society than she had, a society where women, especially young women, were looked after this way by their husbands. It amused her that he wouldn't let her wear a low-cut sundress or a bathing suit that he said was too revealing.

There were good times. Loving times. He became more patient, he taught her about making love, and in a little while skyrockets really did go off. But perhaps that, she realized now, was in its own way a form of control, for then, when she rebelled, when she said, "I hate that dress," or, "I can't stand opera," he would stop her words with a kiss, tease and love her until, weak with desire, she acquiesced to whatever it was he wanted her to do.

They sailed back to San Sebastián on his boat, *Straight On till Morning*. "This is the way we will be," he said that first night at sea. "Together, Annabel, straight on till morning."

At night when he anchored in the lee of a cove, they made love out on the deck under the stars. And she had loved him. Oh, she had loved him.

It took them almost six days to get to San Sebastián, and this, for her, had been the real honeymoon. Now that they were alone he let her wear a bikini, off-the-shoulder blouses and shorts. "But for me," he said. "Only for me."

Once they reached San Sebastián he introduced her to the servants. Meadowlark hadn't been there then, but Ambrosia had. Ambrosia, who'd said when Annabel had arrived a little over a month ago, "It's real nice having you back, Mrs. Alarcon." She hadn't known then that Ambrosia had meant, "after such a long time."

They stayed on San Sebastián for almost six months, and in that time she grew to love the island and the people. And every day, though at times he was difficult, she fell more and more in love with Luis.

A man came to the island one day and Luis introduced her to him—Zachary Flynn, a deep-sea diver. Luis had told her about the *Cantamar*. "I've been searching for her for a long time," he'd said. "Flynn's had experience as a diver. He's found other galleons, he'll help me find the *Cantamar*."

The three of them, together with Samuel, had set sail on *Straight On till Morning*. She remembered now that she had wished at the time that she and Luis could have been alone, for while she liked Samuel, she didn't like Zachary Flynn.

They cruised the Bahamian waters, and when they drew close to the island of Eleuthera, Luis said, "The ship is here. Somewhere. I know it is, I can feel it. The *Cantamar* is here in these waters."

They went into Eleuthera to replenish their food and water supply, sometimes to spend the night. But most of the time was spent diving. Luis and Flynn made charts at night and dived during the day.

Hurricane season came, and Luis, looking worried, said, "We can't stay out much longer. We've got to head back to San Sebastián."

They took Flynn back to Nassau. "We'll search again when we know the weather is clear," Luis said.

The winter came and went, as did both spring and summer, and though they searched, they were no closer to finding the *Cantamar* than when they'd started.

The following fall Luis took her to Spain. By now they had been married more than two years. She celebrated her twenty-fourth birthday at a party in Madrid, where Luis introduced her to his aunts and uncles, what seemed like a great number of cousins and lots of small nieces and nephews. They were all warm and wonderful people, who treated her as though she belonged. She began to feel part of a family, and to long for a family of her own.

She had brought up the subject of having a child several times during their two and a half years of marriage. Each time she did, Luis said, "A baby? Good Lord, Annabel, you're only a baby yourself. We have plenty of time before we start thinking about having a family."

At his insistence, though she hadn't wanted to, she continued taking the Pill.

She stopped taking it in Spain the night one of the small nieces, an adorable three-year-old whose name was Silvia, said, "I want Tía Anna to put me to bed."

She'd gone upstairs with the child, helped her undress, and when she tucked her in, Silvia said, "Sing, Tía Anna." She sang the only song she could think of, "Oh, Susanna!" in a slightly off-key voice that almost instantly put little Silvia to sleep.

As she sat there smiling down at the little girl, smoothing the hair back from her face, she decided that she wanted a baby now. And that no matter what Luis said, she was going to get pregnant.

And she did. Two and a half months later they took a trip to Sevilla, then to Toledo. It was in Toledo, excited but nervous, clenching her hands together behind her back, that she confessed she had stopped taking the Pill and that she was pregnant.

Luis was furious. She had betrayed him, he said. She'd known how he felt about having a child and yet she had deliberately gone against his wishes.

At first she had been defensive, chagrined. But when she thought of the tiny life growing inside her, she said, "I'm not a child. I'm a woman and I want a baby."

"You should have told me."

"I tried to tell you how much I wanted one but you wouldn't listen. You never listen."

He stormed out of the room. When he returned later that night he didn't speak to her. Nor did he speak to her the next day.

They had agreed to meet a distant cousin for lunch. Luis spoke to her then because he had no choice. And when after lunch the cousin suggested they visit the Museum of the Santa Cruz to see the paintings and the wonderfully graceful marble stairway, they had little choice except to let him take them there.

"Go, go," the cousin said before he hurried away to his office. "Enjoy."

The staircase was indeed beautiful. They climbed to the top and then, touched by the beauty and wanting to make it up with Luis, she said, "I'm sorry, Luis. I know I should have discussed my not wanting to take the Pill with you." She rested her hand on his arm. "Please, darling, try to understand how much I want this baby."

"I don't understand." He shrugged her hand away and, turning his back on her, started down the stairs.

"I'm not in the mood for a museum," he said. "Stay if you want to. I'm going back to the hotel."

"Luis. Luis, wait." She took a step down without looking and somehow missed the step. And fell, fell all the way down that long marble stairway.

When she awoke in the hospital Luis was with her. She put her hands over her stomach and knew there would be no baby.

She was in the hospital for three days, and when she was well enough, they returned to Madrid. He tried to talk to her, but now she was the one who was silent and withdrawn.

The day after their return to Madrid she went to an airline office and made a reservation to fly back to Miami. When Luis saw the ticket on the dresser, he said, "What's this? What are you doing?"

"I'm going back to Miami," she told him. "I'm leaving you."

She remembered now how white his face had gone, how strained his voice had been when he said, "You . . . you can't do that."

"Yes, I can," she said, facing him. "It's over, Luis. I'm going to file for a divorce."

He gripped the edge of a chair. "I won't let you."

"Let?" She shook her head. "I'm sorry. I can't live with you anymore."

He took her to the plane. When he tried to kiss her, she turned away from him.

Once in Miami she did as she had told him she would—she saw a lawyer and filed for divorce. She did not see Luis again, only his attorney. Though she had not asked for any kind of a settlement, his attorney informed her that Luis had deposited half a million dollars into a Miami bank in her name. She said she didn't want it. "It's yours," the lawyer said. "Do with it whatever you want to."

She bought a condo in North Beach. She gave away the clothes Luis had always selected for her and bought the kind of clothes she liked. And as soon as the divorce was final she looked for a job.

Because of Luis she knew a bit about boats and so she went to apply to companies that made or sold boats. Albert Croyden hired her to work in the sales office of his company at the marina. She had been happy there, and soon both Albert and his wife, Louise, had become friends.

She and Mark had started dating a year ago. She liked him, and when he asked her to marry him, she almost said yes. But she didn't. In spite of everything that had happened between them, she still loved Luis. Though they were divorced, in her mind he was still her husband. And, God help her, he always would be.

Almost five years had passed since she'd seen Luis. He had come to the hospital in Nassau, and because she had no memory, he had claimed her as his wife.

She knew now that she could have forgiven the deception if he had done it because, after all this time, he still loved her. But that's not why he'd gone to Nassau. He'd gone because he thought she might know something about the *Cantamar*. Because she'd had a gold doubloon in her pocket when the coast guard found her.

And the lovemaking? The words whispered in passion in the darkness of the night? Had they been said in the hope that someday she would remember what had happened on the *Drum?* Because she might have learned where the *Cantamar* had gone down?

She looked out at the quiet night and wept for the friends who had died. And for a love she had only thought she had found again.

Chapter 15

He lay alone in the bed he and Annabel had shared.
From the open balcony door came the sound of the
sea, from above the slight whoosh of the fan turning
slowly overhead. He had almost lost Annabel today,
and now, every time he closed his eyes, he saw it all
again. Annabel, backed to the edge of the cliff, sea
foam swirling against the deadly rocks below, Zachary Flynn, with a gun in his hand, advancing on her.
Then Flynn's terrible cry as man and dog hurled over
the cliff to the rocks below.

A terrible sickness rose in Luis's stomach, because
if it hadn't been for Rob, it would have been Annabel's body that lay broken and dead at the bottom of
the cliff instead of Flynn's. If that had happened he
would never have forgiven himself.

He had brought her back to San Sebastián against
her will. He had lied to her, deceived her. And tried to

make her love him again. If she had died... "Oh, God," he whispered. "God, help me." He covered his mouth with his fist to stifle the sound of his anguish.

He had never loved anyone the way he loved Annabel, he never would. If she had died, a part of him, the best part of him, would have died with her.

Rob had saved her, big, wonderful Rob, who had adored Annabel from the day they'd found him on that deserted island.

Flynn had been killed instantly, but Rob was still alive when Luis reached him. He'd been thrown a few feet from where Flynn lay, and when Luis approached, the dog had looked up at him and whined. His back had been broken.

"He be suffering somethin' terrible," Samuel said.

"I know."

"He gotta be put out of his misery. I'll take care of it. You go on after Miss Annabel."

Luis knelt by the dog. "No, I'll do it." He scratched Rob behind his ears and gently stroked his head. "I know you're hurting, fella," he said. "I'm going to take care of that for you in a minute. You saved her life, Rob. You're a brave and wonderful dog and I'm going to miss you."

Rob whined again. But tremors shook his body and Luis knew what he had to do. He had the gun. He rested a hand on the dog's side. "Go to sleep, Rob," he said. "Go to sleep, boy."

Even now, as he lay alone in the darkness of the night, it seemed to Luis that he could hear the blast of his gun and feel Rob's last quiver of life.

He would buy Annabel another dog. They'd go to Miami for a few weeks and he'd buy her any kind of dog she wanted. They'd stay at the Fontainebleu just as they had on their brief honeymoon eight years ago.

Their honeymoon. He'd been thirty years old, experienced and worldly when it came to women because he'd had his first sexual experience when he was fourteen. Twenty-three-year-old Rosalinda, a maid in his parents' home in Madrid, had introduced him to the ways of lovemaking. By the time his father found out what was going on, he'd acquired an enormous appetite for sex and had become fairly adept with women.

He'd been in and out of love a dozen times before he met Annabel. Once, when he was twenty-two, he'd even been engaged to someone his father said would make him a suitable wife. Pilar Villareal came from a wealthy Andalusian family. Her father and his father had gone to the University of Salamanca together.

"It will be a match made in heaven," his father told him. "Her family is rich and she is pretty enough."

Yes, pretty enough. But she giggled. My God, how she giggled.

He couldn't imagine Annabel ever giggling.

He fell in love with Annabel the first time he saw her. She was beautiful of course, incredibly feminine, with rosebud breasts and a waist he could span with his two hands. There had been a charming, unsure-of-herself awkwardness about her, an endearing innocence that instantly captivated him. The first time he put his arms around her when they danced that night in New Orleans, he knew he wanted her. Once he made up his mind to have her, she didn't stand a chance.

He'd known almost immediately that Annabel was different from the other women he'd met and made love to. But she was a woman, and with time and patience he could have seduced her. That wasn't what he wanted; he had fallen in love with Annabel, and he wanted her for his wife.

He held himself in check during their courtship, but each day his desire for her grew. And when finally, legally, she came to him as his bride, he could no longer wait.

He knew now that he had been too impatient. Annabel had been innocent to the physical side of love, and instead of leading her gently along he had demanded a response, a passion she had not yet learned. Even as he reveled in the fact that Annabel was a virgin, he had been annoyed by her inexperience.

He'd been an insensitive fool, but she had loved him. In spite of everything, Annabel had loved him.

Later, when he learned to be more tender, more patient, he had reveled in teaching her the many ways of love. How quick she'd been to learn what pleased him, how sweet her trembling words each time he took her to the brink of passion.

Their best times were spent at sea on the *Straight On till Morning*. She'd been seasick her first time out, but she soon got her sea legs and they'd had a happy time of it. They sailed the Bahamas together, following the charts he'd made, getting ever closer, he was sure, to the place where the *Cantamar* had gone down.

It was the trip to Spain that finished them off. He still remembered, though he had tried for five long years to forget, his harsh words when she told him she was pregnant. How could he have been so insensitive to her feelings? Why couldn't he have rejoiced with her that together they would soon bring a new life into the world?

The memory of that day, that terrible day in the museum in Toledo, would never leave him. Even now when he closed his eyes he could see her falling, falling down those hard marble stairs. He had knelt beside her there at the bottom of the stairs. "Forgive me, forgive me," he said over and over. But she had been unconscious, unable to hear.

The two days he sat beside her bed in the Madrid hospital were the longest two days of his life. When finally the doctor told him she would live, he turned his face to the wall and wept. For her and for the child that would never be born.

She left him then, and when she did she took a part of him with her. The best part.

He thought of the child they might have had. Their son or their daughter would have been five now. Would have been. Would have been.

Why had he acted the way he had when Annabel told him she was pregnant? Why couldn't he have been happy with her, proud that together they were creating a new life? Because you wanted her all to yourself, a voice in his head whispered. You didn't want anyone, not even your own child, to come between you.

What a selfish bastard he'd been. No wonder she left him.

There had been no one else in the five years they had been apart, for in his mind and in his heart Annabel was still his wife, she would always be his wife. He would always love her, for she was his beautiful Annabel, his Annabel Lee.

He thought then of the lines of Poe's poem and knew that for him they rang true—that the moon never beams without bringing him dreams of his beautiful Annabel Lee. His darling...his darling...his life and his bride.

Forever and always Annabel would be his wife. No legal paper could change that.

In the early hours before dawn Luis fell into a troubled sleep, and awoke before seven feeling haggard and drawn. He wanted to talk to Annabel, but because it was too early, he pulled on a pair of trunks and went down to the beach for a swim.

A storm was brewing and the sky was as gray and leaden as he felt. There was a chop to the waves and he waded out, waited for a roller and dived through it. When he surfaced he swam straight out, waves breaking over his head, the current tugging at his legs, and when he knew he'd gone too far, he started back in. He was breathing hard by the time his feet touched sand, but his head was clear.

He went back to the house to shower and shave and dress in a clean pair of white shorts and a pullover shirt. Then, bracing himself because it had to be done, he went into the room where he kept the shortwave radio and contacted the Miami police.

He told them about Zachary Flynn, that Flynn had not drowned on the *Distant Drum* as had been reported by the coast guard. He had been very much alive, hiding here in San Sebastián. He told them, too, that Flynn, in an attempt to kill his—Luis's—wife, had fallen from a high cliff to the rocks below.

Yes, he said in answer to their questions, he would come to Miami soon and sign whatever papers were necessary.

That done, he went to Annabel's door. When he knocked, she said, "Yes?"

"May I come in?"

There was a moment of hesitation before she said, "If you want to."

He opened the door. She was wearing a short white skirt with a blue ruffled top. There were dark circles under her eyes and he knew she hadn't slept any better than he had.

"I haven't had breakfast yet," he said. "Have you?"

"I'll eat later."

He shook his head. "Don't do this, Annabel. Don't shut me out this way." And before she could say anything, he held her bedroom door open and said, "We'll have breakfast and we'll talk."

She nodded, but she didn't say anything.

They ate out on the terrace overlooking the sea. Neither of them ate very much, nor did they say very much. Meadowlark served them, and when she saw how silent they were, she, too, was silent.

But because he thought it should be spoken of, Luis said to Annabel, "When Rob was hurt—before, I mean, when you almost drowned—it was Meadowlark who took care of him and nursed him back to health."

Annabel looked up then. "That was kind of you, Meadowlark."

"Rob was a real nice dog, Mrs. Alarcon. I'm sorry he's gone. If you want, I be askin' over in the village if there be a dog you might like. Some dog always be having puppies. Rob visited over there a time or two, and I wouldn't be surprised if one of them puppies look like him. I could bring one on over to you.''

''I don't think so. I'm not going to be here much longer. I'm going back to Miami.''

Something twisted inside him, a visceral pain that had him sucking in his breath. Annabel was leaving him. Again. She was going away. Again.

He didn't say anything until Meadowlark left. Then, trying to keep his voice level, he said, ''Perhaps some time away from the island would do both of us some good.''

''Both of us?'' She shook her head. ''I'm going alone, Luis. As soon as you can arrange it.''

''You left me once. I won't let you leave me again.''

''You won't let me?'' A bitter smile curved her lips. ''I'm not the girl you married eight years ago, Luis. I've changed, I grew up.''

''I know that.'' He reached for her hand. ''I love you, Annabel. I've never stopped loving you. There's been no other woman in my life since the day you went away. There never will be. I know I made mistakes in the past, terrible mistakes, but I want to make it up to you. I *will* make it up to you.'' He tightened his hand on hers. ''I love you,'' he said again.

''Do you?'' Annabel shook her head. ''You've lied to me from the beginning, Luis. Since that first day you stood beside my bed in Nassau you've done nothing but lie to me. You said I was your wife and you made love to me....'' Her voice broke, and because that made her angry, because she wouldn't cry in front of him, she said, ''It was because of the *Can-*

tamar, wasn't it? When you heard about the accident at sea and knew it was close to where we had searched for the *Cantamar,* you thought I might have been aboard. A woman with no memory had been found and you took a chance that it was me."

"It wasn't that way."

Her eyes challenged him, dared him to look away. "It was because of the gold doubloon they found in my pocket, wasn't it? You thought we'd found the *Cantamar* and because I was the only survivor that I could tell you where it was." She looked at him with scorn. "But I couldn't remember, not about the *Cantamar,* or you, or that we had been married.

"It was the perfect opportunity, wasn't it, Luis? You could pick my brain, hoping I'd remember, and meantime, until I did, until I knew that though we'd once been married but were divorced, you'd enjoy the sex."

"It wasn't like that." He felt himself tighten with anger, an anger he tried to control before he said, "There's a difference between sex and love. Sex is easy to get, Annabel. I could have had it anytime I wanted it, here on the island, on any of the trips I made to the States or to Spain. I could have brought a woman back with me. But I didn't because I loved you, because you were the only woman I wanted to make love to."

He leaned closer, his dark eyes burning with all he was feeling. "And that's the difference, Annabel, making love to someone you love is different."

She looked away from the intensity, the passion in his dark eyes. She didn't want to hear him, couldn't bear to hear him speak of love.

In a voice as gray as the threatening sky, she said, "You didn't come to Nassau because you loved me, Luis. You came because you thought I might know how to find the *Cantamar*."

He lowered his eyes, afraid to meet hers because a part of what she said was true. He'd wanted to see her, to make sure it really was Annabel and that she was alive, and yes, God help him, because he thought she might know where the *Cantamar* had gone down.

"I'll tell you how it was," she said, "about the Croydens, about Mark—"

"Was he your lover?" He hated himself for asking and wished he could have bitten the words back.

"No," she said coldly. "He wasn't. There's been no one since you." Then, without giving him a chance to say anything, she went on. "When I went to Miami, and after the divorce was final, I wanted to work. I knew a little about boats because of you, and I got a job working for Albert and Louise in their sales office at the marina.

"Albert was fascinated with the history of the ships that had gone down in the Bahamas and the Caribbean in the sixteenth and seventeenth centuries. He went to Key West to see Mel Fisher. He pored over all of the things Fisher had brought up from the *Atocha*. There were pieces of eight, emeralds—a fortune in emeralds—gold spoons, gold plates, all the things that Fisher had salvaged. It was all Albert talked about, how one day that's what he would do.

"He'd heard about the *Cantamar* and he'd heard of you. Maybe that's why, in the beginning, because I still used the name Alarcon, he hired me. He questioned me about the *Cantamar* and about you, but I didn't want to talk about it and he finally stopped asking.

"Everybody around the marina, and probably in Key West, knew about Albert's interest in the *Cantamar*. One day Zachary Flynn came into the office. He told Albert he'd worked for you and that he was pretty sure he knew the location of the *Cantamar*. He said he had charts—"

"The charts he stole from me," Luis said.

"I didn't know that." She waited, and when Luis didn't say anything, she went on. "He told Albert he would provide the expertise if Albert would finance a search. First they would go out on the *Drum* on a scouting trip, then they would arrange for the salvage boat. Albert deposited a million dollars in a special account in his bank in both his and Flynn's name."

"Insanity," Luis said. "Pure insanity."

"That's what Louise told him. Mark tried to talk to him, too, but Albert was so positive Flynn could lead him to the *Cantamar* that he wouldn't listen."

"Why did you go along with them?"

"Flynn suggested it. He knew I'd been married to you and he thought I could help them find the galleon."

"And did they?"

"I think so. Flynn and Albert had brought a . . . I don't know what you call it. It's a type of hose you put way down in the sand and it sucks up sand and shells. Albert said that was how Mel Fisher brought up all the emeralds."

Luis nodded. "Go on."

"We were out for almost two weeks, near Eleuthera, where you and I had searched. Mark and Flynn did most of the diving. I didn't like Flynn. He tried to question me about where you and I had searched, and he tried . . ." She hesitated, then with a shrug said, "It doesn't matter now."

"He tried to move in on you?"

"Yes."

Luis swore under his breath.

"Mark saw him. Flynn had backed me into a corner. I was trying to get away from him. He had his hands on me. Mark hit him and after that they barely spoke. I didn't like Mark diving with him. I was afraid of Flynn, afraid he might do something to Mark." She turned away. "And he did. He killed him first."

Luis wanted to touch her, to tell her to stop, tell her she didn't need to go on with this. "It's all right, Annabel," he said. "You don't have to do this."

"Yes I do." Her eyes were bright with unshed tears. "Two days before it happened—the murders, I mean—Zachary Flynn and Mark found the gold doubloons. They were encrusted with sand and shells, but Flynn cleaned and polished them. They were perfect and he knew . . . he knew they'd found the *Cantamar*."

"And that's why he killed them, killed everybody on the *Drum* and pretended he was dead, too," Luis said. "He would have assumed a new identity, maybe had some plastic surgery, and in six months or a year he would have hired a crew and gone back to salvage the *Cantamar*."

"What about the money in the bank? How could he get to it if he was supposed to be dead?"

"He'd probably siphoned most of it off before you and the Croydens left Miami on the *Drum*. He had it all figured out. There was only one flaw in his plan."

"Me."

Luis nodded. "You were alive. You knew what had really happened aboard the *Drum*. He didn't know you'd lost your memory. He only knew he had to get rid of you."

"He almost did," Annabel whispered. "If it hadn't been for Rob..." She stopped, unable for a moment to go on.

Luis poured more coffee for both of them before he said, "Why did you go up to the cliff yesterday, Annabel? You knew it might be dangerous. Why did you go?"

"I needed to be alone. I had started remembering, just fragments of memory of... of how we met, the first time we danced..." She turned away. "And Spain. My pregnancy."

He gripped her hands. She tried to pull them away but he wouldn't let her. "There is no way I can ever tell you how sorry I am about what happened that day. If there was any way I could relive those days I would. I'd do anything to make them up to you."

His grip on her hands tightened. "It's not too late, Annabel. We could make it right. We could have a child, as many children as you want. We could—"

"No!" She pulled her hands away and stood. "No, I won't go through that again." She faced him, hands behind her back so that he wouldn't touch her. "Don't you see, Luis, it wasn't just the baby, it was the marriage. You wanted me to be something I wasn't, a perfect Spanish wife. You told me how to dress, what wine to drink, what books to read and what music to listen to. And I let you."

"Annabel, please—"

"Maybe some of it was my fault. I know I was young, and naive... God, I was so naive. But I should have stood up for myself. I should have said, 'This is who I am, this is the woman you fell in love with. Take me this way or let me go.'" She shook her head. "But I didn't because I was so in love with you. So much in love..." She waited, and when she could speak again said, "I would have done anything for you, anything to please you."

He felt as if he'd received a mortal blow, as if his insides were being ripped apart. Somewhere in the distance he heard the rumble of thunder. The sky darkened and he felt the first hard drops of rain.

"I love you, Annabel," he said. "I've never stopped loving you." His dark eyes filled with anguish. "Don't leave me again," he pleaded. "Marry me, Annabel. Let me make it up to you. We'll have a child. We'll—"

"There is no we," she said. "Not anymore."

The rain came harder, but neither of them moved or made an attempt to go inside. He put his hands on her arms and brought her closer. In a voice that broke with all that he was feeling, he said, "I can't lose you."

He held her there and kissed her, unmindful of the rain beating down, desperate to have her respond. She didn't fight him, she simply stood there, her lips cool and unresponsive.

He knew then that he had lost her. He let her go and stepped back.

The rain came harder. Thunder rolled and a sudden wind picked up one of the chairs and sailed it across the deck.

''You'd better go in,'' he said.

But she stood there for a moment looking at him, her face set and solemn. Then she swiped her wet hair back and, with a barely perceptible nod, turned and left him there.

Alone on the terrace. Alone in the rain.

Chapter 16

It rained all that night, and though it stopped for a while the following morning, by noon it started again, harder than ever, and the wind picked up. It was too late in the fall for a hurricane, but Luis was worried, and that afternoon he checked the weather station on the shortwave radio.

"There's a severe tropical storm that's affecting most of the Bahamas all the way from the Turks to Grand Bahama Island," the forecaster said. "Batten your hatches and pour a tot of rum. This blow is going to last for three or four days."

That's what Luis did, at least the batten the hatches part. He and Samuel and some of his other men made sure the *Straight On till Morning* was securely moored. Equipment had to be moved from the sheds to the house in case of heavy tides, and the windows facing the sea had to be boarded up.

On the second day of the storm they lost the generator. That night he and Annabel had dinner by candlelight.

"How long do you think the storm will last?" she asked.

"Another day at least."

She looked out at the turbulent water. "I'd hate to be out on a boat in this weather."

"Boats would have been warned and hopefully had time enough to put in to a port. But this storm came up suddenly. If someone was far from land, finding a safe harbor might be tough going." He poured more wine into her glass. White wine. And looking at her, he almost wished the generator would never work again because in the candlelight she looked so extraordinarily beautiful. And because as long as the storm raged she could not leave him.

She'd had little to say to him these past two days. He'd been busy working outside much of the time so he'd only seen her in the dining room when they had dinner. He had a hunch she didn't want to see him then but that she hadn't wanted to make it obvious to the servants.

She was polite but withdrawn and spoke when spoken to. Tonight she seemed unusually quiet. And nervous. But finally, when Meadowlark had cleared the dishes and served their coffee, she cleared her throat and said, "I'd like to leave San Sebastián as soon as the storm is over."

He looked down, steeling himself, waiting a moment before he answered, "I'm afraid that won't be possible."

She stared across the table at him, her face set, angry. "What do you mean?"

"There'll be a lot of cleanup work to do after the storm. I won't be able to leave for at least another two weeks. Even then I'll have to make sure the boat's all right, make whatever repairs have to be made...." He was stalling. It didn't matter. He'd do anything to keep her here. Drive a hole in the *Straight On* if he had to.

"I want to fly back to Miami," she said.

"There aren't always planes available." He reached across the table for her hand. It lay pale and cool in his. "I don't want you to go," he said again. "I know I was wrong in not telling you the truth when we were in Nassau. But if I had, you wouldn't have come with me."

She tried to pull her hand away, but he wouldn't let her go.

"I thought if you were here with me we could begin again, that I could make you love me again." He tightened his hand around hers. "I've never stopped," he said. "All those years we were separated I never stopped loving you."

"Luis, please—"

"When I saw you again in the hospital in Nassau..." He had to stop for a moment to control his voice. "Your head was bandaged, you were scratched and bruised and pale. Oh God, so pale. But it was you, and you were alive, and I knew I'd never stopped loving you, that I would love you till the day I die.

"Everything came back to me, the times we'd spent at sea together, the nights we'd slept up on deck and made love under the stars. I knew then that I'd do anything to have you back with me, even if it meant lying to you."

He looked at her through the candlelight, his face so serious, his eyes so filled with love. "I told you we were still married and I brought you back to San Sebastián because it was an opportunity to try to make you love me again, to wipe out the past and begin anew."

She wanted to believe him. She almost wished her memory hadn't come back, that there had been no past. She wished that her love for Luis had begun in the moment when she opened her eyes and saw him standing by her hospital bed.

But it was too late. She couldn't block out the past, or Spain, or the baby he hadn't wanted. There was a coldness in her heart that only time, pray God, would soften.

She rose from the table. "I'm tired," she said. "I want to go to my room."

"The corridors are dark. I'll go with you."

"No, it's all right. Finish your dinner."

But he got up and, taking the candelabra from the table, motioned for Annabel to precede him.

The flickering candles cast a ghostly light against the pale walls when they left the dining room and went through the hall that led to the living room. In the reflected candlelight she could see their two shadows, phantom figures, surreal and strange. He saw them, too, hesitated, then held the candelabra higher. Their figures became elongated, one taller than the other, but a pair. Still a pair.

Rain slashed hard against the roof and thunder rumbled overhead, and still they stood there, looking at their shadowed forms.

He said, "Annabel," in a voice she could barely hear above the clash of thunder. She looked at him, caught for a moment in the intensity of his gaze, then at the shadow looming over her shadow.

"No," she said. And turned away.

They went out into the corridor without speaking. When they stopped at the door of her room, he said, "Let me come in and light the candles for you."

The room, except for the candelabra, was in darkness. Rain slashed against the windowpanes and beat hard against the glass doors. He lighted the candles she had on the dresser and the one on her bedside table.

"Will you be all right?" He set the candelabra down. "The storm seems to be getting worse. You won't be frightened?"

"No," she said. "I won't be frightened."

"Well then..." But still he hesitated. "Let me stay with you tonight, Annabel."

"No." Her voice was cold, unrelenting. "No."

"I won't touch you if you don't want me to. I just want to be with you. To..." A blast of wind hit the house, and with a terrible bang and a swoosh of air, the balcony doors flew open. The candles flickered and went out, rain swept into the room.

He grabbed the doors and, fighting the terrible blast of the wind, managed to close them. "Give me something to tie them with," he said. "A scarf, anything."

She ran to the dresser, tried in the dark to find a scarf and, when she couldn't, fumbled for a pair of panty hose and hurried across the room to hand them to him.

"Lean against the door," he said, and when she did, he bound the door handles together. "That should hold." He stepped away. "But you'd better spend the night in my room."

"No, I'll . . . I'll be all right here now that you've fixed the doors." She turned away too quickly and because of the darkness stumbled over the end of the chaise and fell.

"What happened?" He reached down to help her up. "Are you hurt?"

"No, I just . . . I forgot the chaise was there."

"I'll light the candles." But still he stood, holding her, not wanting to let her go.

The only sound was the slash of rain against the house, the crash of thunder, the only light a flash of orange lightning. And in that light he saw her face, the eyes wide and a little frightened, lips parted as if about to speak.

He said, "Annabel," and then he kissed her. Kissed her with all the longing of days past, of sorrow and of need.

And though she stiffened in his arms, though she whispered, "Let me go," he could not.

"Stay with me," he said. "Not just for tonight, Annabel, but for always. Be my wife again, love me again."

"I won't! I can't! Let me—"

He smothered her words with his mouth. He tightened his arms around her and held her so close he could feel the frantic beating of her heart. He pressed one hand against the small of her back to bring her closer, and knew she felt the heat of his desire.

"Please," she whispered. "No, Luis. Let me..." But her mouth softened under his, her lips trembled against his.

"Oh, love," he said. "Oh, love."

She couldn't do this. She told herself she wouldn't do this. She felt the edge of the chaise against the back of her legs. He eased her back until she fell against the chaise. And when she did, he came over her and held her there. He kissed her again, kissed her until she couldn't think.

"I love you," he whispered against her lips. "Always and forever. That hasn't changed. It will never change. I'll give you a baby, as many babies as you want—"

"No!" She thrust him away from her. "No," she said, her voice breaking. "Just...just leave me alone."

He fell back against the chaise, breathing hard, willing his passion to ebb.

Annabel stood and felt her way to the dresser. He heard her fumble for matches, heard a scratch and saw the flickering flame as she lighted one of the candles.

He stood. "I'm sorry," he said. "I apologize for forcing myself on you. It won't happen again." He took one of the candles and crossed the room to the connecting door. He paused there and, turning back, said, "As soon as the storm passes I'll try to arrange for a plane. If one isn't available I'll let Samuel take you to Nassau on the boat."

Annabel didn't answer. She stood by the dresser until he went out and closed the door. For a long time she didn't move from where she was, but finally, with a smothered sob, she went back to the bed, to lie face-down and cry for a love that had been and was no more.

The storm grew worse. Wind blew against the house, rain beat against the windows and rattled the doors Luis had tied with her panty hose.

She blew out the bedside candle and tried to sleep, to block everything from her mind except the need for rest. And finally, burying her face into the soft down pillow, she did.

To dream. A strangely vivid dream of a storm at sea. And a boat, no, not a boat, a sailing ship. A sailing ship battling its way through thirty-foot waves, plunging up on a high crest, then down again, all but swallowed up by the turbulent water, until like a broken toy boat it struggled up again. Only to plunge down. Down . . .

"Get back to the cabin," he cried.

"I want to be with you."

"It is too dangerous. You must go below."

"Will the ship survive?" she screamed above the roar of wind. *"Will we?"* And when he did not answer she fought her way to him, staggering from stanchion to stanchion, almost hurled into the sea with the slanting of the deck and the terrible force of the wind, until at last she stood at his side.

He pulled her closer. "Will you not do what I say?"

"I will not leave you."

He put her against the wheel in front of him and held her there, trying to shelter her with his body. "You should not have come with me."

"This is where I want to be, at your side in this moment of danger." She saw the wave then, bigger than the other waves, surely as high as the great church of Cádiz. And knew this was the end.

He clasped her in his arms. *"Oh, my love!"* he cried.

The boat tilted beneath their feet. They slid across the deck, holding on to each other. Water closed over their heads and they went down, down into the dark depths of the sea.

"Alejandro! Alejandro! Alejan—"

His arms were around her, holding her. His mouth pressed to her mouth. She couldn't breathe. Couldn't . . .

Breathe.

Annabel came awake with a start. She was clutching the pillow over her face, uncertain for a moment where she was or who she was.

She thrust the pillow away and lay there, her heart beating hard against her breast, the words, "Alejandro! Alejandro!" screaming in her brain.

The rain still beat hard against the windows. She threw back the sheet and reached for the matches and the candle beside her bed. Her hands were steady when she lighted the candle. She got up, and as though she were a sleepwalker, not bothering with a robe or slippers, wearing only her long white nightgown, opened the door of her room and went out and down the long dark corridor to the library.

Thunder rumbled and lightning snaked in from a window that hadn't been boarded up. But she wasn't afraid, not of the thunder or the lightning, not of the wind.

She went into the library. It was very dark with only the candle to light her way. She felt her way past the black leather sofa, the two easy chairs and the desk. Her picture was still there, the picture Luis had taken of her at the Cibeles Fountain in Madrid.

She raised the candle and looked up at Alejandro de Alarcon. He looked down at her, looked at her with Luis's eyes and solemn mien.

She turned to the portrait of his wife, his darling Maria de Castilla, so delicately beautiful in her pink dress with the soft flowing lines, one hand touching her necklace. From Maria's letters she knew that Alejandro had given her the gold necklace set with rubies on their tenth wedding anniversary.

Love is a rare and precious gift.

She trembled. Were the words spoken or imagined? Why did they echo in her mind?

Love is eternal... eternal.

Tears filled Annabel's eyes, tears for their lost love, and for her own. Alejandro and Maria had been gone these many years, but she and Luis were alive. And if they loved... Oh yes, she thought, we love. Then how could she turn and walk away from him? How could she let the past stop them from having a future?

She had grown and changed and so had Luis. They had been given a second chance. Could she walk away from him?

"Annabel?"

She turned, frightened for a moment by the reality of the voice. Luis's voice.

"What are you doing here?"

"I...I don't know. I had a dream. About them. About when the ship went down."

She shivered and he said, "Where is your robe?"

She shook her head as though not understanding. "I had to see them," she said.

He took the candle from her and put it next to his on the desk. "You're cold. Let me warm you."

She looked at him, then up at the portrait of Maria. "Yes," she said. "Warm me."

He put his arms around her. He kissed the top of her head and held her as together they looked up at the portraits of the captain and his wife.

"He loved her so," Annabel whispered.

"As she loved him." Luis put a finger under her chin so that she would look at him instead of Alejandro. "As I love you," he said. "As I loved you from the first moment I saw you, I love you now."

He kissed her. She did not respond, nor did she try to move out of his embrace.

"I'm sorry I deceived you when I brought you here again. But I had to. You didn't remember the unhappy years, or me, or the marriage. Fate had given me a second chance and I couldn't let it go. You were here on our island. I thought I could teach you to love me again."

Annabel looked up at him. "I never really stopped loving you, Luis. I tried to, but the memory of you wouldn't go away." She touched his face. "I won't leave you," she said. "I'll never leave you now."

She did not know why it was so, she only knew that it was. She loved Luis, she would never leave him.

He kissed her, and when her lips parted under his, he carried her to the black leather sofa and gently laid her down. "Let me warm you," he said.

They lay in each other's arms. He took off the white gown, and in the flickering light of the candles her body was like pale ivory. He kissed her mouth, her throat, and feathered soft kisses across her breasts.

She held him there, caressing his bare shoulders, lacing her fingers through the thickness of his hair. Her love, her life, her lust. Luis. Forever, Luis.

He buried his head between her breasts. "Never leave me," he whispered.

"I never will," she said.

He moved up over her then and joined his body to hers in the act of love.

"Yes," she said. "Oh, yes." And felt him move deep inside her, so deep inside it seemed he touched her very soul. For this was a joining of love. She knew that now as she lifted her body to his and held him as he held her.

"Oh, love," he said. *"Mi querida, mi Anna para siempre."*

"Yes," she said, *"para siempre."*

He moved with exquisite slowness, melding his body to hers, making them one. He kissed her lips, he kissed her breasts, and when she whispered her pleasure, he felt tears sting his eyes because she loved this, and him. His Annabel Lee, his darling, his darling, his wife and his bride.

He moved more quickly now, lost in an ecstasy of feeling. She took his face between her hands and looked up at him with love-filled eyes.

"Yes, my darling," she whispered. "Yes, now." She kissed him then, she gave him her cry then, and held him while his big body thundered over hers and he answered her cry with his own.

They held each other close and whispered how good this was, how incredibly right. He smoothed the tumbled hair back from her face, she stroked his back. When the air grew chilled, he covered them both with her gown.

They did not leave, but stayed as they were. And when it began again they loved again, and finally, at peace, went to sleep in each other's arms.

They awoke to silence. "The storm has passed," he said.

She sat up, yawning, rubbing her eyes, and found herself looking up at the portraits of Alejandro and the beautiful Maria de Castilla.

It seemed to her as she gazed up at them that there was in their expressions something she had not seen before. It was as though . . . She tilted her head, puzzled. It was as though they, too, were at peace. As though, in a way she could not define, everything had come full circle. She knew then that love, enduring and everlasting love, does not die. It continues on, generation after generation, seed of seed. Forever.

Luis took her hand to help her up. "I love you," she said.

He drew her close and together they looked up at the portraits. "We'll find his ship," he said. "Someday we'll find it."

"Yes," she said. And kissed him.

* * *

Two months later they left San Sebastián. *Straight On till Morning,* repaired and freshly painted, had been outfitted with enough fuel, food supplies and water to last until they reached Eleuthera.

Samuel cast off the mooring ropes, the sails were up and the wind was good. Annabel stood at the wheel next to Luis. A young black dog who looked suspiciously like Rob staggered across the deck trying to get his sea legs. He barked at a pelican and Annabel laughed.

They headed for the breakers and then they were past them, out on the open sea with the wind billowing the sails and the tangy smell of salt in the air.

It was good to be at sea again, to have Annabel beside him looking so tanned and beautiful, so happy.

"I called Eleuthera this morning before we left." Luis gestured for her to come closer, and when she did he put an arm around her. "I talked to the minister there. He'll marry us as soon as we arrive."

She held up her left hand. "I need a ring," she said.

"I'll find you one."

"*Find* me one? What's the matter with *buying* one?"

"I will, a plain gold band for the wedding ring. But for an engagement ring..." He smiled. "I'll bring one up from the sea for you."

"When we find the *Cantamar.*"

"Yes." He pulled her to him and kissed her so hard she let out an involuntary cry. When she did, Young Rob bounded across the deck straight at Luis, barking and showing his teeth.

"Damn," Luis said with a grin. "This one's your dog, too."

Annabel laughed, then she kissed Luis and said to the dog, "It's all right, fella. He's going to make an honest woman of me."

They stood there together, facing into the wind, the man at the wheel and the woman beside him. Just as long ago another woman had stood beside her man.

There would be no storm on this trip. The winds were fair, the skies were clear. And they were together, straight on till morning.

Epilogue

Madrid, Spain
Two years later

They stood at the top of the red-carpeted stairway. She wore the blue sequined gown she had bought in Paris the week before. Her blond hair had been pulled back from her face into a fashionable chignon.

"Señor and Señora Alarcon." The maître d' hurried over. "Your table is ready. Please come this way."

Luis took her arm as they started down the stairway. "You look absolutely radiant tonight," he said.

She smiled. "Because I have a secret."

"Oh?" He raised an eyebrow. "Care to tell me?"

"Later," she said, and smiled again.

People around them turned to stare when they passed by the tables. The orchestra began to play

Agustín Lara's "Madrid," and when they were seated, a white-jacketed waiter appeared to take their order.

"Champagne," Luis said.

"And mineral water," Annabel added.

"Would you like to dance?" he asked when they were alone.

"Later perhaps."

The waiter brought the champagne in a silver bucket. The cork popped when he opened the bottle. "I'll pour," Luis said.

But when he started to fill Annabel's glass, she said, "I'll just have the mineral water, thank you."

"Is anything wrong? Aren't you feeling well?"

"I feel fine." She touched the necklace at her throat. It felt warm against her skin, almost as if it held a life of its own. Candlelight glittered on the rubies set in the old gold.

"Her necklace looks lovely on you," Luis said.

"Yes." She touched it again, then reached for Luis's hand. "We've been in Europe for almost five months," she said. "It's time to go home."

"I thought we'd stay for the April fair in Sevilla."

Annabel shook her head. "I want to go home," she said.

"Then we will. I'll make the reservations tomorrow." He hesitated. "Are you sure you're all right?"

"I'm perfectly fine," she assured him. "It's just a touch of pregnancy."

"Oh, good. I'm glad it's not anything..." He froze, his eyes wide, startled. "Pregnancy? You're pregnant?"

"Two months." She took a sip of her mineral water. "I hope you're pleased."

He stared at her, eyes wide with shock. And turned away.

She went cold. Oh, no, she thought. Oh, no. She touched his arm. "What is it?" she whispered. "Aren't you pleased?"

He looked at her then and she saw the tears in his eyes. Before she could speak, he stood and went around to her side of the table. He knelt there and put his arms around her.

"Annabel," he said. "Oh, Annabel."

He kissed her then, and when at last he rose, he saw that the people at the tables around them had grown silent. He reached for his glass and, raising it, said, "We're going to have a baby."

For a moment there was only startled silence. Then a woman smiled and a man said, *"Felicidades!"* Others joined in. Glasses were raised, a few bravos called out.

Luis took Annabel's hand. "Come and dance with me now," he said. "I want to hold you."

He took her hand and led her to where the orchestra played. They danced to the music of a Spanish waltz and held each other close.

"If it's a boy..." he started to say.

"We'll name him Alejandro," she finished.

"And if it's a girl she'll be Maria. Maria Annabel."

He kissed her cheek and she thought of how it would be when their baby came. And how, after all, life really had come full circle.

*   *   *   *   *

Take 4 bestselling love stories FREE

Plus get a FREE surprise gift!

Special Limited-time Offer

Mail to Silhouette Reader Service™

3010 Walden Avenue
P.O. Box 1867
Buffalo, N.Y. 14240-1867

YES! Please send me 4 free Silhouette Intimate Moments® novels and my free surprise gift. Then send me 6 brand-new novels every month, which I will receive months before they appear in bookstores. Bill me at the low price of $3.34 each plus 25¢ delivery and applicable sales tax, if any.* That's the complete price and a savings of over 10% off the cover prices—quite a bargain! I understand that accepting the books and gift places me under no obligation ever to buy any books. I can always return a shipment and cancel at any time. Even if I never buy another book from Silhouette, the 4 free books and the surprise gift are mine to keep forever.

245 BPA A3UW

Name	(PLEASE PRINT)	
Address		Apt. No.
City	State	Zip

This offer is limited to one order per household and not valid to present Silhouette Intimate Moments® subscribers. *Terms and prices are subject to change without notice. Sales tax applicable in N.Y.

UMOM-898

©1990 Harlequin Enterprises Limited

FORTUNE'S Children™

Bestselling Author
LISA JACKSON

Continues the twelve-book series—FORTUNE'S CHILDREN
in August 1996 with Book Two

THE MILLIONAIRE AND THE COWGIRL

When playboy millionaire Kyle Fortune inherited a Wyoming
ranch from his grandmother, he never expected to come
face-to-face with Samantha Rawlings, the willful woman
he'd never forgotten...and the daughter he'd never known.
Although Kyle enjoyed his jet-setting life-style, Samantha and
Caitlyn made him yearn for hearth and home.

MEET THE FORTUNES—a family whose legacy is greater than
riches. Because where there's a will...there's a *wedding!*

*A CASTING CALL TO
ALL FORTUNE'S CHILDREN FANS!*
If you are truly one of the fortunate
few, you may win a trip to
Los Angeles to audition for
Wheel of Fortune®. Look for
details in all retail Fortune's Children titles!

Look us up on-line at: http://www.romance.net

FC-2-C-R